Also by Mary Sheppard
from Indigo Sea Press

*The Hills of Pride*

*The Valley of Pride*

indigoseapress.com

# Shenandoah Pride

## By

## Mary Sheppard

Sepia Books
Published by Indigo Sea Press
Winston-Salem

Sepia Books
Indigo Sea Press
PO Box 26701
Winston-Salem, NC 27114

For information regarding bulk purchases of this book,
digital purchase and special discounts, please contact the publisher at
indigoseapress@gmail.com

Cover design by Pan Morelli
Manufactured in the United States of America
ISBN 978-1630663537

Shenandoah Pride is dedicated to the memory of those valiant people of Winchester who did live and suffer just as my fictitious Jamie and her friends did.

—Mary Sheppard

# Acknowledgements

I would like to thank three people without whom this book could never have made it to publication. First is my treasured friend, Judy Slater, whose encouragement and determination that I would not let advancing years or retreating eyesight deter me in the completion of this last book in the story of Jamie and the real life happenings in Winchester and the Shenandoah Valley during and after the War Between the States. Then, upon completions of it, her proofing and suggestions were invaluable.

Second is Sarah Sands. She is another cherished friend with a careful eye and she used it willingly to help correct my innumerable errors. Her help meant so much to me and to this book.

And third is my son, Randy, who in spite of his belief that his mother is probably the worst typist in the land, took Judy's and Sarah's innumerable corrections and incorporated them with his own into the finished product. I could never have done what he did so I am eternally grateful to him, as well as to Judy and Sarah.

My thanks, too, go to the publisher of Indigo Sea Press, Mike Simpson and to his staff. I am proud to say that he has other previously written books of mine that will be published now that I have completed the "Pride" series.

—Mary Sheppard

# 1

June 9, 1865
Winchester, Va.

The War Between the States had been over for two months when Jamelle Montgomery reluctantly opened her eyes to what she expected to be just another deceptively-bright June morning. She wasn't sure why she hadn't bounced out of bed as she usually did, knowing she had to get started on her many tasks. Instead, she lay there a few moments, thinking drowsily that she had something unusual to do, but being too groggy to put her finger on what it was. She gave a little inward shrug and thought she must have been dreaming. This was bound to be just another day of nothing but work. Just more back-breaking labor trying to bring some semblance of order to her life and to her beloved— but now bedraggled—Fairdale, if indeed such a thing as order might even exist anymore.

She almost let herself drift off again, but her half-open eyes caught a glimpse of the jagged edge to what had been the high post of her once-nice bed. The memory of how proud she had been when Pa had bought it for her kept her eyes from closing. Poor, dear Pa. And poor her and her bed. Two of the posts had been broken off; the rose-colored ruffles that had once reached from one high post to another all around the bed had been snatched down and trashed. And to think that, after all the destruction they had caused, the Yankees actually insisted on calling the last four years "The Civil War." How ridiculous! If there had been anything even approaching *civility* about this war, she and the other Winchester folks sure had missed it.

Of course, her still not-fully-awakened mind went on to think, she had never wanted the dratted war in the first place. Certainly not when she had known that a war would be bound to ruin the first good life she and her pa had ever had. It had cost him his life

1

and almost destroyed her and her home. By the time the Yankees had rung all of Winchester's church bells to announce their victory, it had also killed everything inside her that mattered. All she had left was a determination to rebuild Fairdale in memory of her pa.

She had sent Curt, the Yankee who she knew had truly loved her, away forever, thereby hurting him terribly. That would have pained her too if she had not blocked him from her devastated mind. If she had let herself remember him and his parting vow that this was not the end, that she was his and would be forever, she could not have coped with what she had had to do. She knew now that the strong, life-sustaining emotion she had felt for him during her desperate days had really come from need and appreciation, certainly not from real love. But, no matter what it had been, she had known that she could not go with him to his Philadelphia or allow him to stay with her. After all that had happened, she had known that not then or ever again could she bear the thought of a Yankee…any Yankee…ever touching her or her Fairdale again.

She turned restlessly on the rickety bed, knowing that she simply must get up. There was so much to do. But still she did not move. For some reason, she just couldn't make herself do it. The peas were plentiful enough for her to be canning, but how could she can anything when all her jars had been smashed to smithereens? Mr. Rea would surely get some in. Maybe he already had them somewhere, but the Confederate dollars Pa had left her were so worthless that they might as well be consigned for use in the "garden house," if she still had one. That name, she remembered idly, was what Mammy Rose had learned at Jamie's own grandparents' plantation and had always insisted that she use for what most people referred to as outhouses or privies. Hadn't the Yankees known how much pain and embarrassment they would cause by destroying such an unwarlike thing as an outhouse? A *garden house,* she reminded herself with an inward smile, snuggling down under the worn sheet again for just a few more moments of sleep. She deserved it after the way she had been working for so long.

Before sleep completely claimed her again, she gave another tired sigh, wondering as she had so many times what they could possibly have done to justify what they had been forced to endure for four long years. Surely the South's desire to have its own country couldn't have been really wrong. Certainly not, when Dr. Graham and the other preachers in Winchester had declared regularly from their pulpits that God would see them through because He was always on the side of right and justice. Then, as she hated to do but couldn't help doing, she remembered the quiet moonlit night when she had sat on her porch steps with the Yankee and told him that she knew the South would win because of that. He had responded by saying, if that should be true, there sure would be a lot of surprised people in the churches up in the North. The voices of their preachers were reverberating all through their sacred halls and assuring their congregations of the exact opposite. They said, and definitely believed, that God was on the North's side.

Curt's words had disturbed her then so much that she had stormed into the house. Now she couldn't even force herself out of the bed, much less storm anywhere. Nevertheless, what he had said had worried her then and still did. *Why had God let their own preachers be so wrong in what they truly believed? Why hadn't He seen to it that the South won? Or had God not really cared who won? Could He have been so annoyed with both sides that He just said to heck with the whole thing and He'd let them fight it out among themselves? But did God do things like that?* she wondered. She'd have to ask Reverend Graham about that the next time she…

The last thought hit her like a sledgehammer to her head and brought her out of bed almost as though she had been shot out by a cannon. *What's wrong with me?* she was screaming to herself as she tore off her night dress and tossed it wherever it landed. Thank the good Lord that the Reverend's name had given her back at least a smattering of sense. But how could she possibly…either awake or asleep…have forgotten for even a moment that this was her wedding day? Of course, she'd see Reverend Graham when he married her and Clay this afternoon at four o'clock.

She was finally going to become a Haynesworth, she thought exultantly, as she almost tore her chemise yanking it over her head. Hadn't that been the reason she had let Clay talk her into this hurried wedding? That, she quickly added, plus the fact that she had loved him from the time her eyes had first fallen on the elegant young man who had been Clay in those long-ago days. She'd been too worried then about what kind of a house Pa could possibly have won in a craps game and too conscious of the fine new clothes she had not yet gotten used to wearing that she had hardly known anything, but she had still known that. Of course, she had! Clay had been too handsome, too impressive, too close to the perfect type of man she had seen in her dreams for her to possibly miss.

As she was frantically pulling on her pantaloons, she was wondering wildly how any girl could possibly forget her own wedding day. How could she conceivably have forgotten that this day she would actually become a Haynesworth! The name that would free her forever from the fear of being known as a "woods colt." She might always be what she had been born, but nobody would ever point a finger of disdain or scorn at a Haynesworth. The life she had longed for was finally here. If only Pa and Mammy Rose could know! Please God, surely they did!

She was frantically pulling the old gingham dress over her head, then attacking her hair with her almost worthless brush before dashing from the room on bare feet. Down the steps to the main floor she ran, then dashed on across the hall to the door that opened onto the flight on down to the basement kitchen.

"Mammy Rose!" she called excitedly, then as memory rushed over her, she stopped and fell against the stairway wall. Mammy Rose, her dearly-loved Mammy Rose, was gone. Couldn't she ever get that through her thick head? Dead for many months and now lying out there under the big oak tree near the little stream on the left side of Fairdale's wide and deep front yard. That was why she had chosen to be married out there instead of at her own Kent Street Presbyterian Church or even, as Clay had wanted, at Christ Episcopal. Their Episcopal church had survived the destruction of the war far better than her own because it had been the one the Yankees had used for their own services. That fact alone had been sufficient to make her refuse. Besides, she had wanted Mammy Rose somewhere near when she finally became what that dear old soul had wanted for her so much—to become a Haynesworth! She went on down the stairs at a slower pace.

Rhody, the rather tall, gawky-looking woman standing at the kitchen stove turned as Jamie came into the room. "So you is finally up. I was thinkin' somebody'd have to pull you out if'n you didn't show yo'self pretty soon. It ain't ever' day you is gittin' married, and you ort not to be missin' a minute of it."

Jamie sank gratefully into the chair by the beaten-up wooden table. "Well, that's for sure. I'm fully expecting this to be the only such one that I'll ever have. You reckon you could spare one of those eggs you've been saving? I'm as jittery as a scalded cat, but I'm still feeling powerfully hungry."

"Yes, ma'am, I sho' can. Soon as I git this stove wood in de fire. I been sort of lettin' it burn down so's not to be too hot in here. But you sho' can git a egg in a minute or two. I ain't never seen de likes of what folks been bringin' out here. I ain't knowin' what all is under dem white raggedy cloths what's coverin' de stuff. Folks sho' must be plannin' fer a real party."

"They are?" Jamie cried. "Oh, how wonderful! And I was so afraid that practically no one would come." Then she let her words drain away. She had to remember that she was not talking to Mammy Rose. Mammy Rose had known everything about her from the day she had been born, but this rough-edged but good-hearted wife of Pa's man, Steven, knew very little. That was the way Jamie intended to keep it. She was more grateful than she could ever express that Rhody had come walking in a few days after the war had finally gasped its last torturous breath. Her coming had given Jamie the other female presence in the house that she had known she had to get somehow. Also, the woman's always-willing hands were most welcome.

Jamie looked around the kitchen and saw nothing unusual. "If folks have brought food, where is it?" she asked. "I don't see anything."

"I been puttin' ever'thin' up in de dinin' room and shuttin' de door. Ain't no other place, is there?"

Jamie gave a happy laugh and relaxed. "Of course, you're right. Oh, Rhody, what would I have done if you hadn't come back from Lexington?"

"Why, course I'd come," the woman said almost indignantly. "Ain't Steven been my husband since de days when we wuz both young and wid Marse Frank McKay? Ain't Miss Sally done tol' me dat a wife stays wid her husband? That's why when Marse Frank stopped farmin' and didn't need Steven much no more, he wouldn't sell him off to nobody but somebody close to hand."

"I guess you're right," Jamie said. "I know Mr. McKay practically gave him to my pa so he would be here right up the pike a piece from them and from you too. He also told Pa that you had been their cook, and they sure didn't want to lose you."

"Cook?" snorted the woman. "I warn't just a cook. Before de war, I done most ever'thin' what was done in dat house. Miss Sally was into church work, ladies' meetin's and ever'thin' else in town and Miss Linda, she warn't never worth nothin' 'cept to make a mess. I reckon since Marse Frank done passed, Miss Sally thought she and de other sister they was living wid could clean up Miss Lina's messes now widout me. Now dat I wus free, dey tol' me dey wouldn't mind if I moseyed on back down here. So dat's what I done."

"And are we really going to have enough food for a wedding party this afternoon?" Jamie asked eagerly. "Oh, I remember the wonderful supper and dance the Haynesworths had when Miss Priscilla married Mrs. McLaurine's son. Well, I suppose I don't recollect that evening too much, for that was the night I got the typhoid and nearly died. But to think that Mr. Clay and I might also have a real big party is a wonderful feeling!"

"Ain't you already been knowin' dat?" the woman asked as

she opened the door on the cook stove to stir up the coals and add some of the wood. "Now I'm gonna heat you one of dem biscuits somebody brung. I'm thinkin' they even got ham in 'em." She turned around and looked at Jamie. "Where you reckon anybody got ham?"

"Ham?" the girl cried. She jumped up from her chair and looked around eagerly for it. "Do you mean that Mr. Rea has actually got ham in what remains of his store?"

"Ain't knowin' what Mr. Rea has got, but you got ham biscuits fer yo' weddin'. Dey's awful little but dat sliver of stuff sho' looks like ham to me. I ain't ate one, of course, but I slipped one out and brung it down here fer your breakfast." She turned back to the stove, picked up the coffee pot and grinned at Jamie, "And look what Mr. Clay brung by a while ago."

"Coffee?" Jamie said wonderingly. "I thought I smelled it as I came down the steps, but I thought I was dreaming."

"No, ma'am, you ain't. Mr. Clay said his bride ort to have real coffee on her weddin' day so he brung by what looks like a whole pound."

"Oh, that's wonderful! Please pour me a cup, Rhody. And isn't Mr. Clay the most wonderful person you ever saw?" she ended softly as she sank back down in her chair.

The woman gave her another snaggle-toothed grin. "Reckon so, long as he's got real coffee. I done had a cup myself. I'm hopin' you ain't mindin'."

"Of course, I don't mind. I hope you gave Steven a cup too."

"I ain't done dat, but I sho' would like to."

"Then do it as soon as he comes in." She picked up her cup in both hands and savored the aroma before she took a taste. She sipped it with great satisfaction. "Just think, Rhody, I'm going to be one of those Haynesworths too. A *real* Haynesworth. Just as much a member of that family as Miss Caroline or any of the others. Isn't that wonderful?"

Rhody stood with her hands on her big-boned hips and looked at the girl as though she had said something really strange. Then she said, "Yes, ma'am, I reckon it is. Wonder what me and Steven be now? We ain't never had no name 'cept Steven and Rhody. Reckon we is gonna be called Haynesworth too?"

Jamie didn't know whether to laugh or cry at the question. She sure didn't know how to answer it either, so she put her chipped cup down and thought for a moment. *How would it be to have never had a real last name?* Was she making too much of the change in hers? But, she argued with herself, her case was different. Besides, it wasn't just the name she wanted. Surely she wasn't that shallow. It wasn't even everything that went with that impressive name, most of which the war had probably killed off anyway. The Haynesworth's beautiful Crestview was now nothing but a windblown pile of ashes, and the overbearing, pompous Mr. and Mrs. Haynesworth would soon be heading for her family in England. Except for Clay and Pris, there wasn't even a Haynesworth left in this part of the state, and Pris was a McLaurine now anyway. She hadn't seemed to mind giving up the name that Jamie had so coveted. But then Pris had never been a...

"Oh, pshaw," she finally told Rhody. "Who knows how anything will be in the future? I sure don't. But no matter what my name is, you and Steven will always have a home with Mr. Clay and me. We've still got to rebuild Fairdale just like we were planning before he came back."

"Yes, ma'am," Rhody said enthusiastically with a grateful smile and turned back to the stove.

So, though she was happy to finally have a name that had never carried even a hint of shame, that was still not the real reason she was marrying Clay. She was delirious with joy because she loved him and he loved her. That love had brought her out of the deep depression that all the tragedies of the war had caused. She had actually thought she was dead to such feelings as romantic love, but Clay's kiss had touched what she had thought was dead and brought it, and the rest of her, back to life. He had saved her just as surely as Curt had saved her during…. No, that memory was blocked from her mind, and it was going to stay that way forever.

"Isn't that stove hot enough for the egg yet?" she asked Rhody.

"Yes'm, it sho' is." The woman soon put the chipped plate holding the scrambled egg and a tiny ham biscuit before her.

"Oh, Rhody! What a wonderful breakfast on a wonderful day."

"Yes'm, it sho' is." She turned and looked at Jamie for a long moment. "You ain't nuthin' like you was when I got back from up de Valley. You looked then like a fly settling on yo' shoulder would be enough to knock you right off yo' feet."

Jamie picked up the cup again and sipped before answering. "I was feeling awful poorly. And why shouldn't I have been? I had nothing to look forward to but work." Then she made such a wide gesture of enthusiasm that she spilled some of her coffee on the table. "Oh, shucks! Just look what I've done!" she exclaimed, setting down the cup and grabbing up the bottom of her dress to wipe up the spill. "Spilling precious coffee and messing myself up as well."

"Ain't no never mind," the woman assured her. "We got plenty o' hot water fer washin'. Steven's been heatin' it for you since dawn. He knowed you'd be wantin' a bath in that big old tub. Warn't it lucky he buried it befo' de Yankees come so dey couldn't lay hands on it? He's done scrubbed it wif sand till it shines like it was new."

Jamie settled herself back down and ate gratefully. She had been eating practically nothing except unseasoned vegetables and had had very little of those until the gardens had begun coming in again, but seasonings were still rare. Having a ham biscuit that even tasted a little bit like ham seemed almost too good to be true.

"Yes, I sure am grateful to Steven for saving my tub. Those Yankees would have drilled holes in it or maybe taken it if they had found it. They tried to destroy everything I had."

"Dey sho' did. Steven done tol' me 'bout it. He says you and Miss Priscilla was moughty brave not to be skeered out of yo' wits when de Yankees came to burn you out."

"*Brave?*" Jamie cried. "Oh, Rhody, if you only knew! We

9

were literally scared nearly to death. And especially when they were going to burn the house with Mammy Rose still in it." Her voice broke and she shuddered visibly. The other woman noticed and walked to the kitchen door to look outside. Neither of them said anything until Jamie got herself back into control and managed to speak in a fairly normal-sounding voice, "But those aren't the memories I want to be having on my wedding day. I just want you and Steven to know that I'm glad you decided to stay and help me rebuild Fairdale. Mr. Clay and I haven't talked about it much, but I'm sure he feels the same way."

The woman now turned back around and looked at Jamie. The muscles around her chin seemed to be twitching. "What you talkin' 'bout, Miss Jamie? Ain't you knowin' we ain't got no place else to go? We's happy to be here and to do fer you, fer it makes us feel dat we still got a home too."

Determined not to shed tears on this happy day, Jamie gulped out a grateful, "And you're right. It's a favor to me too, for if he hadn't been willing to stay here and if you hadn't come back to join him, I don't know what I'd have done. The Yanks would have really killed me."

"And came pretty close to doing it anyway," Jamie heard a different voice say.

She looked around and saw her best friend and soon-to-be sister-in-law coming in the kitchen door from the outside.

"I figured you'd be down here," Pris said, struggling as she carried in a heavy-looking tray covered with a white cloth and put it carefully onto the table where Jamie sat. "Whew! That thing is heavy," she said, and started rubbing her arms vigorously.

"What is it?" Jamie asked, jumping up and reaching for the cloth as Rhody crowded in close to see too.

"Oh, no, you don't," Pris cried, leaning over the table and covering the gift with both her arms. "Mother Mac said for me to be sure you don't see it till we have the cake-cutting."

"Cake-cutting?" Jamie asked excitedly. "Do you mean it's a cake? A real wedding cake?"

"Of course, it is, you goose. Didn't you know that Mother

Mac would see that you had one? She had trouble getting what she needed to make it, but Mr. Rea helped her. It's got icing and all that good stuff. But you might as well quit trying to burrow a hole into that old tablecloth, Jamie. You aren't going to see it yet."

"That's mean," Jamie said, but she didn't mean it. She was actually so thrilled and excited by what Pris' mother-in-law had done that she could hardly contain herself. Still, she wasn't really surprised. Mrs. McLaurine was now, as she had been all through the terrible years of war, a pillar of strength to most of the others still in town. Having her actually seeing to it that there was a real, tiered wedding cake made tears start in Jamie's eyes, but then she remembered that Clay was the brother of Mrs. McLaurine's daughter-in-law and the best friend of her son, Brad. Of course she knew that dear, thoughtful woman would have wanted to do all she could for Clay.

As though reading the other girl's mind, Pris said, "She told me that this was just for you. The bride's family usually has the cake-cutting or whatever is done when a girl is married, and she wanted you to know that, to her, you are family. The cake-cutting part of the wedding is her gift to you."

Now the tears did come, but Jamie wiped them away hurriedly and said a husky, "Thank her for me." She turned to Rhody, saying, "If that's what Mrs. McLaurine says, that's what we'll do. Would you please carry this upstairs and put it with the other things that have come?"

"Other things?" Pris asked. "Has a lot already come?"

"You'll have to ask Rhody. I haven't checked."

"Yes, ma'am," the woman said. "Things been comin' since right after sun-up. Dere's cookies and deviled eggs and I ain't knowin' what else 'cept some biscuits dat looks like dey got ham in 'em."

Pris turned a surprised look to Jamie. "Ham? Where on earth did that come from?"

Jamie shook her head. "I have no idea. As far as I know, there hasn't been a pig or a hog around here in a long, long time. If

Rhody knows, she isn't telling."

'I ain't knowin'," said Rhody, picking up the tray and heading for the stairs up to the dining room. She disappeared from sight, carrying the cake as carefully as if it were a newborn baby.

Pris turned to Jamie as she rubbed one of her arms and then the other. "That thing felt like it weighed a ton," she complained. "My arms hurt like the dickens."

"Surely you didn't tote it all the way from town," Jamie asked. "I don't see how you could do it."

"I couldn't. Brad toted it most of the way, and even he had to stop and rest his arms several times. Then he gave it to me when we got here. Just bringing it around the house was more than enough for me, but he needed to get back to town for some best-man sort of things for Clay." She quit rubbing her arms and looked at the cup Jamie held. "That some of that coffee Clay got you?"

"It is. And forgive me for not asking if you'd have some…that is, if there's any left." Jamie put hers down and went to the cook stove, checked the coffee pot and looked back at Pris. "Yes, there is some more so get a cup from the shelf and I'll pour it for you."

When she had the cup and was pouring, she said, "I hate for Clay to see that I only have three of these chipped or cracked old cups. They're in hot water on the stove most of the time, but, as you well know, I can't help it."

"I do think," Pris said as she took the cup, "that Clay has noticed there's been a war on and that your house was ransacked. I'll see if Mother Mac can scare up another one somewhere so you'll have enough for Brad and me when we're out here. Oh," she interrupted herself to say as she sipped, "this is so good! I really shouldn't be drinking yours, for Clay brought us a pound too. He got it in Richmond as he was coming back from Rose Hill. He just happened to be passing by where somebody had some coffee to sell. He didn't know or care how the man got it."

Both girls sat back down, with Pris in the unsteady chair. It teetered on its shaky legs, but she managed to straighten them without spilling a drop of the coffee. "The guests may look like a motley crew," she told Jamie, "but it seems that everybody who can possibly make it will be here. Mother Mac has spread the word that all those who can scrape up anything to eat on or to drink out of should bring it with them. It won't be the most elegant wedding party ever planned, but she says that most everybody is looking forward to it."

"They are? Oh, Pris, I'm more grateful than I could ever say. I was afraid folks would remember the talk about me and refuse to come."

"Horseradish!" her friend snapped. "Everybody is so pleased to have a happy time to get together that they'd probably come if you were marrying the devil himself."

Jamie made kind of a face. "That doesn't exactly thrill me. You reckon anybody mentioned it to Rebecca Wright?"

"Rebecca Wright?" Pris scoffed. "I should hope not. Folks are hardly speaking to her after what she did to help those Yankees. Mother Mac says we should remember that she's a Quaker and that she was a really good school teacher. She also said we shouldn't be grudge holders, but I saw her cross the street the other day when she saw Rebecca coming so she wouldn't have to speak to her."

Jamie joined in the little laugh, knowing that she would have done the same as Mrs. Mac, but she said nothing.

"Oh…" Pris went on, changing the subject, "I've just been thinking how my mother would have loved to be having this wedding for Clay if only she still had Crestview. He's always been her favorite child, you know."

"No, I didn't know," Jamie replied. And, she thought to herself, nobody else would have known that either, had he or she been present when Mr. and Mrs. Haynesworth had come with their feigned kindness to tell her why she could never be their son's wife. Clay's wishes and his love for her hadn't affected his parents in their determination that a woods colt could never be a Haynesworth. Jamie gave Pris a sad look. "Are you so sure of that when you remember who he's marrying? Your folks had their chance at that a long time ago, and they sure refused it."

"Oh, horseradish again!" Pris exclaimed. "All that stuff is over and done with. Clay went down to Rose Hill to tell them that he was going to marry you if you'd have him after all that had happened. They gave him some of those precious Yankee dollars, and they were bound to have known for what and on whom he'd be spending them. But, anyway, they'll be sailing for England in a week or so. Surely by the time they get back, they'll have lost some of their pigheadedness and their overdone pride."

Jamie shook her head. "You think being over there with your English grandparents will make them more open-minded? I don't think England is exactly the place to become less concerned about family pride or class."

"Huh!" Pris snorted. "With all that 'other side of the blanket' stuff that goes on even in the royal family and of which my Cooke grandparents over there are fully aware, I don't think any of them are in any position to look down on somebody like you. But enough of that. Clay has finally gotten some iron in his system, and everything is going to be all right with you two whether my folks ever change or not. And," she added, reaching for her friend's hand, "I am so glad to finally have you as my sister. I've wanted that from the first."

"So have I," Jamie said, squeezing Pris' hand.

Pris gave a little laugh. "And to think that I wasted all that time worrying that you'd be running off some day with that Yankee of yours." There was still a question in the look she gave Jamie.

"You knew better than that," Jamie said, trying to reassure her. "Besides, I've already told you all there is to know about him. You might not think so; but, Yankee or not, he is a really fine person. But regardless of that, I could never marry a Yankee; and, equally as much, I could never leave Fairdale and all the fine people that I love so much here in Winchester. I'm a Southern girl, Pris, and I'll stay that way till I die."

"That's great," Pris said enthusiastically and jumped up. "Now I've got to get back into town and see what I can do to help Mother Mac. She's got a lot still to do to see that we can somehow scrounge up enough stuff for a wedding party."

"That is so amazingly wonderful of her," Jamie said with real feeling, as she got up with her friend. "I still know that she's really doing all that because it's your brother who is getting married, but that doesn't diminish my gratitude the least bit."

"You realize nothing of the sort. So most folks do know you accepted help from a Yankee. So what? If some Yankee had done what he could do to help anybody in town, especially when things were as bad as they were for you, do you think they'd have been dumb enough to turn it down? If they'd had the gumption of a grasshopper, they would not! We're going to forget all of that anyway. The men who can are trying to get their Rebel uniforms cleaned up enough to wear this afternoon. That's all that most of them still have anyway, so Confederate uniform, homespun and whatever, they're coming to wish you and Clay the happiness you deserve."

Jamie threw her arms around her friend. "I know we Southern women don't go around hugging each other, but it's all right to hug a sister, isn't it? Pris, I love you as much as I ever could love a real sister."

"Me too," Pris whispered back and then took one of her hands away to wipe a tear. "We were close from the first, but I think we became welded to each other under fire the day the Yankees burned our Crestview and then tried to burn yours."

"We did indeed," Jamie said, swallowing her own sad tears of remembrance. "You stood by me when there was no one else to do it, and I'll never forget it."

Pris pulled away and, heading for the outside kitchen door, said, "My arms are finally getting the feeling back in them after carrying that heavy cake so I'm going back home. See you as close to three o'clock as I can make it. We've got to do something to make you look like you're not just a stack of bones in that yellow dress of yours."

Jamie groaned at the thought and waved goodbye.

# 2

Rhody was coming back down the stairs as Jamie started up. "Now don't you be doin' no peepin'," the bony woman warned Jamie as they met. It was so much like what Mammy Rose would have said that Jamie felt the tears start again. She blinked them away and pressed herself to the side wall to let the woman by on the stairway.

"I'll be ready to wash my hair and have my bath anytime that Steven can bring the tub and water up. No," she interrupted herself to say, "I'll wash my hair in the back yard if you will come pour the water over it for me. That way I won't mess up my bath."

"Yes, ma'am. I'll have de hot water outside de kitchen door anytime yo' is ready," Rhody assured her. "Steven's been keepin' the wash pot full and hot too, so there should be plenty for yo' hair and yo' baf."

When Jamie finished with her hair, she dried it on one of the towels that had been saved from the Yankees' trash pile and went back upstairs for the bath that was waiting.

As she lay in the tub of hot water, she thought back to the bath she had had in the Taylor Hotel over four years ago. Mammy Rose had been there to set the screen to block off the windows from the porch that went across the three floors of the elegant hotel. There had been a roaring fire in her room, and as she had lain in that tub, she had felt that nothing could ever be more wonderful. She had dressed in the yellow silk that she had loved so much and had gone downstairs on Pa's arm to one of the finest meals she had ever had in her whole life.

She and her pa had thought that their lives had finally become good enough to make up for the terrible years they had suffered before that desperately-sad Mr. Chase had appeared in their lives. He had deliberately lost his home place to Pa before throwing himself over the side of the riverboat to join his beloved family in Heaven. His wife and every one of his children had died in the terrible typhoid epidemic, and he could no longer face life alone. He had come down the river searching for a needy but deserving person to whom he could leave what he had to before dying. Thank God that he had found her pa to be just the type of person he had wanted to be living in his treasured Fairdale. It still made her sad to think about that poor man, but she had known that she would be forever grateful for what she felt sure was God's hand in bringing them to Winchester.

Then in less than three months came the beginning of the end. Why couldn't those miserable Yankees have left them alone? She and her pa had had it all, and it had all disappeared in the wave of Yankee hatred.

Then came the thought from which she could never get away. Even without the war, she would still have been what she was and the Haynesworths would never have accepted into their blue-blooded aristocracy a...a...a *bastard*. She forced herself to say the word that she despised more than any other in the world, for it had been that word even more than the war that had denied her what she wanted so much. But still it was the war...the war that she had hated so passionately...that had finally made it possible for her to marry the man who she had desired from the first day she had met him.

She climbed out of the tub, wishing so much that she still had her dear Mammy Rose to help her, but still grateful that Rhody was here.

Jamie had put out her underclothes before washing her hair. She looked at them in distaste, remembering all the pretty things that Mammy Rose had so painstakingly made over the years for her trousseau. After the Yankees had ransacked Fairdale and had left what they did not want in a messy heap, not one of her pretty underclothes had been found. She had known that instead of being here for her on her wedding night as Mammy Rose had planned, those pretty garments were now gracing the bodies of those fancy women who had followed the Yankees every time they had come to town.

Well, there was nothing to be done. If the finest undergarment store in the country had been just across the pike, neither she nor any of her friends could have gone in and bought a thing, for their Confederate money was as useless as was melted snow in the making of a snowman. She drew the washed-out things that were the best she could find onto her thin body, took as good a look as she could manage in the piece of broken mirror that Steven had found and retrieved for her, then sank down on her bed in despair. How could Clay or anybody else ever want her the way she looked now?

"Miss Jamie," came Rhody's voice outside her door, "ain't you done finished wid dat baf? Me and Steven is waitin' to git all dat stuff out of yo' way. And I done tried to git every spot out'n dat yellow dress dat I can."

Jamie opened the door and said to the woman, "Yes, Rhody, I'm ready for the dress. I know you've done the best you could, so however it is, it will have to do. I've got the hoops here that Mrs. McLaurine found for me. So if Steven can come get the bathtub out of the way, we'll see what we can do. I'll sit on the porch in the sun to dry my hair while he does that. Mammy Rose used to do a beautiful job of fixing these curls of mine. Did you ever help Mrs. McKay or Miss Malinda with their hair?"

"No, ma'am, I sho' ain't. Dey just pulled deirs back and did it in a ball at the back of deir head. Ain't dat good enough?"

Jamie smiled sadly. "No, Rhody, it isn't good enough for all this hair of mine. I've watched Mammy Rose do it, though, so maybe I can do it myself. Anyway, I can try. But I've got to get it nearly-dry first. Will you call Steven?"

"Ain't you wanting to git in yo' dress 'fore I calls him?"

Jamie gave an embarrassed little laugh. "Oh, of course, I am. I'm getting so excited about everything that I'm afraid you two will have to help me."

"Yes'm. We'll sho' do dat. Why don't you put on sumpin' and go dry your hair whilst we gits dis cleaned up? Den you can fix yo' hair and I'll help you git into de dress. I'm a-thinkin' you're gonna have a passel of paddin' in some places to make it look like it ort to, but we'll see about dat when yo' hair is dry."

Jamie thanked her, pulled on an old cotton dress and ran down to the side porch. She sat on the steps there and spread her hair in the sunlight. She kept fluffing it and fluffing it until she felt it was dry enough and then rushed back up the stairs.

Her room was tidy again, and the yellow silk that had served her so well in the past lay on the bed. Rhody had done everything she could to get out the spots left by Yankee boots, and Jamie hoped that the folds in the full skirt would hide most of the others. She lowered it over her head and was buttoning the many tiny buttons down the bodice when Rhody tapped on the door.

"Come in," Jamie called, more thankful to have help than she would have wanted to admit. It wouldn't be like having Mammy Rose, but it sure would be better than trying to get ready by herself.

"I brung some towels and most everythin' cloth I could find," the woman explained, dumping an armload of cloths on the bed. "You ain't gonna fill dat dress out like it ort to be, so when we git it buttoned and dem things in, we'll see what we can do."

"I can set the hoops right," Jamie told her, "but this dress is just hanging on me at the top like an empty bag over a fence post."

"Ain't doin' no good 'round yo' hips neither. Here, let's slip some of dese here towels in de top of yo' pant'loons and we'll see what we can do 'bout dem hips. Den we've got to have more to stuff in your stay cover to make you have some tiddies."

Jamie had never liked that word, but at least she did know what Rhody meant and knew she was painfully right. "We'll never make it look right," Jamie wailed. "I can't go out like this."

"We ain't done," Rhody said unperturbedly.

They stuffed and re-stuffed till Rhody announced that it looked all right to her. A glance in the broken mirror showed Jamie enough to know that Rhody's statement might be true. She pulled on the only full petticoats she had and adjusted the hoops under the skirt. When she finally stood off before Rhody for the final decision, the woman nodded her head.

"I'd say you was all right. Folks is bound to know that ain't all you, but it ain't too clear what it is. I ain't thinkin' we can do no mo'. Maybe when Miss Pris gits here, she'll know a heap sight more about sech things than I does."

"You've been a wonderful helper," Jamie told her and meant it sincerely. She knew she could never had gotten all that stuffing done and shaped by herself. "Now I'm going to see what I can do about my hair. Mammy Rose would roll it in curls over my head and leave some hanging down in the back. I've had no reason to try to do it myself so I'll just have to do the best I can."

"Yes'm, you sho' is. But you's lookin' pretty good. I ain't thinkin' Mister Clay is gonna be a bit disappointed when he sees you." Then the woman covered her mouth and laughed. "At least he ain't till you git all dem towels out."

Jamie felt herself flush, but said nothing. She just grabbed up her brush and started to roll her hair around her finger. She tried to make the curls stay in place till she could do the next one. "If only I had some pins," she moaned.

"I picked up a few dat I found on de floor," Rhody volunteered. "I could git dem if you wants me to."

Jamie whirled around. "You do? You actually do?" she cried. "Oh, please, Rhody, will you get them for me?"

"Yes'm, I sho' will. I found dem right after I got here, and I stuck dem in a drawer downstairs. I thought you mought want 'em some day."

"I'll never want them more than I do right now. Please get them in a hurry."

The woman stalked out and was back in a few moments. "Ain't but five. Will they help?"

"They sure will. I'll make them do and I sure thank you. I'm so nervous right now, it's a wonder I haven't pulled my hair out by the roots."

"Let a little bit hang around yo' face," Rhody suggested. "Ain't I seen girls doing something like dat?"

"Yes, you have." She gave a great sigh and sank down in the little rocker by the window. She looked out and gasped. People

20

were already gathering on her lawn. Good gracious, Pris had been right. Whatever the reason, the townsfolk were coming to see her get married. That put a lump in her throat that felt too big to swallow around and made her know that, curls or no curls, she'd have to hurry down to greet them. "Is it awful?" she asked Rhody a little desperately.

"Ain't bad," the woman said after looking her over. "Fact is, you're lookin' moughty purty to me. Maybe Miss Pris will be here soon, and she can see if I ain't right."

A tap sounded on the door. Jamie just stood and looked helplessly at Rhody.

"I'll see who it be," the woman said. She went and opened it. "Why, Steven," Jamie heard her say, "what you doin' up here now? Miss Jamie ain't got no time to be talkin' to you."

"That's a…well, I reckon…"

"Is that Steven?" Jamie called.

"Yes, ma'am, it sho' is," Rhody said, "but he ain't talkin' no sense."

Jamie ran to the door as fast as she could with her hooped skirt. "What's wrong, Steven? Are you all right?"

"Yes'm. I's fine. But he done come back."

"Who's come back from where? What do you mean?" Jamie asked nervously, patting her curls back in place.

"It de Major," he blurted out. "He done come back."

At first, Jamie just stood there. "You… can't mean Major Darby?"

"I reckon I does, but somehow he ain't lookin' right."

Those words scared Jamie so much that she could hardly breathe. What had she done to Curt? Even now, she could remember his anguished parting cry, *"This is not the end. You're mine and you always will be."*

"But he…he is all right?*"* she managed to get out.

Steven stood on one foot and then on the other. "I ain't sayin' 'cause I ain't knowin'. He just ain't quite like hisself."

Oh, no! Not kind, loving, big-hearted Curt! He didn't deserve whatever she had done to him. She had not meant to hurt him as she had, but there was nothing she could have done differently because he *was* a Yankee. Then other words he had said blasted through her mind like arrows shot by a mighty bow. "I'll kill that puny Haynesworth boy before I'll ever let him have you," Curt had sworn more than once. Now he had somehow found that she was actually marrying Clay, and he had come to do as he had said. Oh, dear God, what could she....

Jamie didn't finish the fearful thought for she had slumped to the floor, as completely out as a candle that had just been snuffed.

# 3

When Jamie regained consciousness, she was lying flat on her bed. The first thing she saw was that her skirt was standing high over the lower part of her body because of the hoops. She made an involuntary move to try to cover herself.

"Don't bother about that," Pris said quickly. Her words came out so loud and sharp that Jamie's head jerked around to look up at her. "There's nobody here to see but Rhody and me," Pris went on. "What on earth happened to you? Did you trip on something?"

Jamie just stared at her blankly. "I… I don't know. Why am I here?"

"That's what I want to know," Pris said, holding her chest and still breathing hard. "When I got up the stairs, you were lying there in the doorway with Rhody trying to wake you up. It was a hard job, but the two of us just got you up on this high bed and haven't had time to do anything else. I was just before running down to see if Dr. McGuire or Dr. Miller had arrived when you began to come to. Should I go ahead and get one of them anyway, if I can?"

"No. Please, no doctor," Jamie moaned.

"Well, why not?" Pris demanded, beginning to get her breath under control. "If not one for you, then maybe for me. The sight of you out like that nearly did me in." She took another deep, shuddering breath. "You may be as skinny as a fence post, but it still wasn't easy getting you and all that padding up on this bed." Then she leaned close to the other girl and asked urgently, "But what on earth happened to you? Rhody won't tell me a thing except that you fainted. I could see that for myself."

Jamie looked from one side of her bed to the other to stare vacantly at each of them. As her memory returned, she gave a cry and covered her face with both her hands. "No," she moaned, twisting onto her side and trying to draw her knees to her chest, which wasn't easy with all she had on. "Not now. Not today."

"Miss Jamie," Rhody entreated. "Don't you be messin' yo'self up. We ain't got no mo' stuffin'."

Jamie snatched her hands away and straightened herself on the bed. Then with scared eyes, she looked up at Pris. "Is...is Clay all right?" she asked in a strangled-sounding voice. "He...he hasn't been hurt or anything yet, has he?"

*"Clay hurt?"* his sister repeated incredulously, straightening up and staring down at Jamie. "What *are* you talking about? Of course, he hasn't been hurt or anything else. Not unless he cut himself shaving. That's what he was doing when I left to come on out here to help you. But it's you I'm worried about, not Clay. Did somebody hurt you?"

Rhody was shaking her head almost violently at that, but neither of the girls was looking at her. "Rhody must have been here, but she wouldn't tell me a thing. For Pete's sake, tell me what happened. Did you slip and hit your head?"

Neither Jamie nor Rhody spoke, so Pris started for the door. "I'm going to go get somebody to help. We've got to get you up and down those stairs in a very few minutes, and there's no way I can do that by myself. Somewhere in that passel of folks down there, there's bound to be somebody to help."

Before she could get away, Jamie reached out and tried to stop her by grabbing her arm. She got her sleeve instead. She didn't even hear the tearing sound of the faded pink voile dress, but Pris did. She stopped and quickly investigated the torn ruffle that had fallen from her elbow down to her wrist. "Oh, shucks! Look at that. Well, I'll see about it later." She started on.

"No! Wait," Jamie begged. "Help me up. I've...I've got to go down and somehow stop him."

Pris sprang back, still trying to get her ruffle in some kind of shape. "Maybe I should tear off the one on the other sleeve too, so the two sides will at least match. The matron of honor shouldn't look like she's been in a fight. I'll..." she began, but Rhody broke in.

"Miss Jamie's got a few pins in the bureau. I'll get dem and pin dat purty ruffle back on," she volunteered eagerly. "Ain't nobody goin' to know nothin'.'"

"I guess you're right," Pris agreed a bit dubiously. "It's not torn off completely anyway."

As the woman rushed to rummage through Jamie's bureau drawer, Pris turned and stared back at Jamie. The girl was struggling to get her feet over the side of the bed and her borrowed hoops down where they should be. "What was that you said, Jamie? Stop who from doing what?" she demanded, finally grasping what Jamie had said. "I don't know what you're talking about. And I'm beginning to wonder if you do."

Jamie didn't answer. Instead, she still struggled to get herself standing steadily. When she managed that, she grabbed onto the colored woman who was now trying to pin the torn ruffle back on. Her trembling body showed that the weakness had not yet passed. "Where's Steven?" she asked Rhody.

"I ain't knowin'," the woman answered without stopping her work but twisting around as much as she could so Jamie could hold onto her. "When you fell, he was out of here like one of dem bullets. I'm thinking he went downstairs to git rid of dat man."

"Thanks, Rhody," Pris said, holding her arm out to try to see how the repair job looked. "And I think you're right. The way you've pinned it, nobody will notice." She gave the ruffle a fluff and then turned to Jamie. "What man?" she asked, now standing indecisively halfway between the bed and the door, and almost shrieking the words. "Have both of you completely lost your wits? I didn't see or hear Steven or any man when I came through the hall downstairs."

"I 'spects Steven done got rid of him," Rhody said in a voice that was hardly more than a frightened whisper.

Jamie, remembering how Steven had gotten rid of another man who had threatened her, nearly collapsed again. Instead, she released her hold on the woman and took a shaky step toward the door. "Oh, dear God, please help me," she moaned as she went. "I've got to stop both of them."

Pris grabbed her tightly by the arm and yanked her back. "You're not going anywhere till you've regained your senses and can stand by yourself. Also, not till I know what the Sam Hill is going on. What man is Rhody talking about and who are you thinking you've got to stop?"

Jamie grabbed back onto Rhody and tried again to head for the door. "It's Curt Darby," she said in a voice that was more an explosion of breath than real words.

"It's de Yankee major. He done come back," Rhody supplied.

Pris had not grasped Jamie's words, but, when added to Rhody's, she knew. "*Your Yankee?*" she asked in a voice not much louder than those of the other two.

"He is not *my* anything except my friend." Jamie tried to snap out her answer, but the words were weak and scared-sounding.

Pris just stood there with her mouth hanging almost open. "Why on earth?" she started, but changed it to a crisp, "How does he know about today? Did you write him?"

"*Write him?*" Jamie tried to shriek the words. "Of course, I didn't. I didn't want him to ever know. I was afraid…" Her words drained off.

"Know what?" Pris demanded. "That you're marrying Clay?" Her face had drained of color until she was almost as white as Jamie. "You think he's come to…to try to keep you from marrying my brother?" she finally got out.

Jamie had backed up and was now leaning against the bed and wringing her hands. "I don't know. I just don't know," she moaned distractedly. "I haven't seen or heard a thing from him since…since that terrible day I sent him away. At first, I was afraid he would come back, but when he didn't, I just wiped him from my mind as though he had never been." She released her tight hold on Rhody, grabbed for Pris' hand and held it tightly as she said in words so garbled that the other girl hardly understood, "He…he…he said more than once that he'd kill Clay before he'd let him have me."

The two of them stared at each other, Pris breathing hard and Jamie hardly seeming to breathe at all. Finally, Pris said, "He couldn't have meant it. Men just say things like that when they're under duress."

"I know," Jamie whispered back, "but the war made killing easier. I remember a night when…" Then her words dwindled away again. She had never told anybody but Curt about the night that her attacker had been killed to save her, and she wasn't going to tell it now. "I'm awful worried about… about what Steven will do too. He promised Pa he'd protect me and… and…" She stopped and looked around as though expecting help to come from somewhere. None did, so she went on.

"Well, he's sure proved he meant it. I know he'll do whatever he has to." She hesitated, then ended, "He'll go to any length to do that. He even threatened Curt with a knife the morning he left. I know he'll use it if he thinks Curt is causing real trouble for me. And I'm afraid that's what I'm…" Again her voice drained away until she finally got out the words, "so afraid that's what Curt has come to do."

"Miss Jamie," came the colored woman's voice, urgent now and sounding almost stern, "you ain't got no time fer dis. We's got to redo some of dat paddin' if you ain't wantin' one tiddy to look bigger dan de other. I 'spects we ort to be doin' it right this minute. Steven done told me he'd take care of de man what's come and fer me to git you down dem steps on time. Don't you be fergittin' you is gittin' married."

Both of the girls looked at her, surprised at her tone, but her words filled Jamie with even more fright. "But no, oh, please, not that way. Not by Steven harming Curt. He'll do it…I know he will…if he feels he has to."

"You're worrying about that Yankee who's come to kill the man you're marrying?" Pris cried incredulously. "Oh, Jamie, what are…"

"I'm worried about them all," Jamie got out desperately. "I love Clay but I owe Curt so much."

But Pris was not there to hear her words. Like a flash, she and her floating pink dress were gone from the room. "Nobody's going to kill *my* brother!" she screamed as she raced for the stairs.

Jamie and Rhody stood staring at each other. Then Jamie said in a stronger voice, "I've got to go downstairs and…and stop everything. Help me, Rhody."

"You ain't stoppin' yo' weddin'?" the woman asked with consternation.

"Certainly not. Not unless I have to. Come on." She grabbed Rhody by the arm as they headed for the stairs.

When they reached the landing, indistinct voices were coming from the parlor. Steven was standing near the door that led down to the kitchen, looking as though he was primed to start off in some direction but not knowing which. He looked up at her with the whites of his eyes showing starkly in the worried darkness of his face. "Miss Jamie," he said apologetically, "I done my best, but he wouldn't go. I couldn't do nothin' wid all them folkses here. Miss Pris, she found him where I'd shut him up in de parlor. She's in dere wid him now."

Jamie felt that she could hardly stand, but she was remembering another day when she had stood on this landing and confronted Curt Darby. So much had happened since that day, but that memory still gave her strength. "Never mind, Steven. You and Rhody go in the dining room or on into the kitchen. I'll see him."

As she and Rhody reached the hallway, she heard Pris saying in a shrill voice, "If you aren't, then who in tarnation are you?"

A mixture of relief and amazement flooded Jamie so much that she grabbed for the banister for extra support. Once she had a firm grip, she felt that her fingers became glued to the wood and she would never be able to loosen them. She raised her eyes heavenward, murmured a desperate prayer and pried them loose. One thought was swamping her shaky mind. *Could it actually not be Curt? But, if not, who could it be? Steven had thought it was Curt, and he had known him well enough to know.* But, she remembered, he had said, "The major warn't quite hisself." That must have been what he meant. *But, if not Curt, who could it possibly be?*

# 4

Rhody still held onto her till they reached the parlor door. Then Jamie shook off the supporting hand and motioned for the woman to go on and join her husband. After Rhody had done as asked, Jamie stood alone. She took several deep, trembling breaths as she tried to find the courage she knew was not there. But, as she had had to do so many terrifying times in these last years and especially the last months, she had to face whoever and whatever waited behind the parlor door—and do it alone. She leaned against the facing for another weak, shaky moment, then opened the door partway.

She could see the back of a tall man in boots, nice-fitting but wrinkled trousers and over his long-sleeved white shirt was a shirtwaist that must be unbuttoned, for it hung loosely on his narrow hips. She had never seen Curt in clothes like this, but above his shoulders was a head of thick yellowish-blonde hair that she had seen so many times and knew so well. Most of her remaining strength left her as she slumped against the facing and gasped out, "Curt?" in a trembling voice.

The young man whirled around and stared at her. "Jamie? You're Curt's Jamie?" he said in a voice filled with great relief and pleasure. He rushed toward her with outstretched hands. "Oh, Jamie, I'm so glad I got here in time. Curt would never forgive me if I missed his wedding. But why in the world didn't he let us know about the delay? Has he been sick or was he injured somehow?"

Pris had rushed over with him. "I keep telling this ignoramus," she said in an exasperated voice, "that you are marrying *my* brother, not his, and you're doing it in a few moments. He won't believe it."

Jamie ignored Pris. Still feeling almost out, as indeed she was, she said nothing. Relief and wonder filled her. It was not Curt!

But who? Who could this man be who spoke like Curt, looked a lot like Curt but definitely wasn't Curt.

Suddenly, the truth hit her. Dave! Curt's brother. It wasn't Curt. Just Dave, the brother Curt had told her that people said looked like him. *Oh, dear God, thank You!* But still, she was having trouble grasping everything. What was he doing here? Why was he here *now*? Had Curt sent him to, to…

When the young man reached her, she turned loose of the facing and stretched out her hand to him. The hands that grabbed hers so eagerly and held it so tightly in both of his were smooth and well-cared-for. No calluses from having held a weapon so long. No indication of this ever being a fighting man's hand. Definitely not Curt Darby's. Still, the knowledge that his brother was here was almost as upsetting as if it were Curt himself. "Why," she quivered, "are you here?"

Pris was there beside him, looking at Jamie in something like distress. "I can't get it through his head that you are marrying my brother in a few moments. You tell him." She gave a sort of frustrated sound and turned away to lean her shoulder against the wall not far from them.

"Please, Pris. Let me handle this. I think I know who this is." Then in a voice that was still not steady, she asked, "You are Dave, aren't you? Curt's brother? He…he told me that you two were said to look a lot alike."

"Well, of course I am," Dave said with a relieved laugh. "And we do look something alike, only he's about two inches taller than I am; and, if those girls who've chased him for years are any judge, he's better-looking all around. The similarity is mostly this corn-colored hair that we got from our grandma." Then he turned very serious. "Oh, Jamie, Jamie! Am I glad to finally find you. I never thought that you'd still be here. I thought Curt had gotten you and that you two must have had trouble somewhere along the way home. What happened? And where is Curt? Is he already out there with that crowd I saw in the yard? And why have you put off the wedding for so long?"

"See what I mean?" muttered Pris.

"Couldn't we please sit?" Jamie said, feeling that if she didn't get off her feet, she'd soon be flat on the floor again. "I'm not feeling so well at the moment."

"Oh, I'm so sorry," Dave said apologetically. "Your friend said you had just fainted, but I thought she was just trying to get rid of me."

"I was," Pris said from her place against the wall. Neither of them paid her any attention.

"But you are all right, aren't you?" Dave went on. "Shall we sit on that divan over there?" He led her toward it, sat her down as carefully as his brother would have done and then sat beside her.

Pris moved over and stood before them in a belligerent stance. "So, you're not your brother, but that doesn't alter a thing. There is a wedding taking place in a very few minutes, and it does not involve you *or* your brother. Jamie does not have time for this."

Curt's brother ignored the obviously irate girl. He just looked at Jamie and said in a voice as soft and caring as Curt's had been so many times, "I don't understand all this, but I know you can't be marrying anyone but my brother. He even wrote me once of how much he loves you and that he was so thankful that you felt the same way about him."

She couldn't meet those bright blue eyes that were so much like Curt's. She looked at Pris in entreaty, but there was no help from there—or from anywhere else.

Dave's voice went on, becoming more strained as he talked, "It would be the same as killing him if you were doing what your friend says; but, from what he has told us about you, I know that can't be true. But where is he? I know he was coming by here to get you, but why in the world didn't you come on home as expected or let us know that you weren't?" He looked at her with eyes that seemed to drill right into her.

Jamie just sat, trying not to look at him and not saying a word.

"Please, Jamie," he begged, his voice sounding desperate now, "you have to tell me what happened. When you didn't come as expected, Papa started wiring every place he could think of that Curt might have taken you, but he couldn't find out a thing. Then he sent me out to scour the countryside looking for you. I've been in every hotel and town, big or small, in the two states. I've been all over Washington City and Baltimore. I've been looking for over four weeks, but I just can't go home and admit defeat. That would kill Mama. But now I'm worn out and so are my clothes." He looked down at his rumpled clothes in distaste.

Jamie's mind was whirling like a top that couldn't stop. She was feeling pure terror at all she was hearing but couldn't seem to open her mouth to say a word.

Dave rushed on, "When I could find no one who knew a thing about a couple in trouble, I thought I'd better come to the starting point and begin again. It hadn't even occurred to me before that you hadn't even left here, but I'm so glad it finally did. Help me, Jamie. Please help me."

When Jamie didn't answer, he went on in a voice that was beginning to sound almost harsh, "I know what you meant to him, Jamie. He didn't write too often during the war, but when he did, his letters were full of nothing but his wonderful Jamie. I think his love for you might even have helped save his life, for he was determined that nothing happen to him that would keep him from marrying you."

The words were tumbling from him so fast she could hardly understand them. "Oh, Jamie, this must be even harder for you than for us. You thought he had been killed, didn't you, and you couldn't face life alone?" He stopped a moment and then asked, "Is that why you might have even turned to someone else as that girl says you have? Oh, Jamie, you must have been hurt terribly if you're doing that. But don't do something hasty. I'll find him for you. I know I will. And my family and I will take care of you in the meantime. Curt would never forgive us if we didn't do that. And he wasn't killed in the last fighting. We'd have been notified. He's somewhere hurt or something, and I'll find him for you if it's the last thing I ever do."

Jamie tried to swallow a deep agonized moan as she heard those words, but she couldn't say a word.

Dave went on, "When we knew you were coming, Mama gathered all the family and had about half of Philadelphia on tap, waiting eagerly to meet you. Every storage place for food was filled to the brim with things for the big welcome party that our family and friends were waiting to give you two. Then…nothing. Why, Jamie, why? And please, *please* tell me where my brother is."

Jamie still didn't answer. She felt that she couldn't get a word out, so appalled was she at what she was hearing. Could Curt possibly have been so uncaring of the hurt and worry he was bound to have known he was causing his family? No, the Curt she knew would never do that willingly. Something had happened to him. But what? Had his disappointment in her caused him to do something unbelievably foolish? No, she told herself. It had not, for he hadn't given up. She could still hear the words that meant he had not given up hope. *"This is not the end!"* he had shouted. But where could he have gone and where was he now? Feeling that she could not face the worry and the horrible accusation she knew she would soon be seeing on that clean-cut young face of his brother, she gave a deep, trembling breath and let her still unsteady head fall onto the back of the divan. The boy started to reach out for her but drew back and waited. Jamie could feel his intense worry and impatience. Finally, she raised her head and looked at him. "Oh, Dave," she moaned, "what can I say?"

He leaned toward her eagerly and grabbed up the hand that lay on the seat between them. "Just tell me what happened. And, most of all, tell me where my brother is. He adores you so we knew he would never have willingly left you here. I know too that you aren't feeling well so I don't want to push you too much, but please, *please* help me. When he didn't bring you home as we expected, we remembered that he had said he might give you a wedding trip before coming. That comforted Mama for a while, but when you were over a week late, the whole family was concerned. Cynthia Ann and her husband had to go back to New York, and everybody was just waiting. That was when Papa started wiring everywhere he could to see if Curt and his beautiful bride..." He broke off and looked into her face for a long moment, then ended softly, "And he was sure right about that. You are beautiful."

Jamie forced herself to sit up and knew her face had turned a deep red in embarrassment that was mixed with guilt. "I...I feel and look like an over-stuffed rag bag. I'm down to nothing but skin and bones, but I might not even be that if it hadn't been for your brother. He's... a wonderful man."

"I've always known that, but why didn't he bring you home?" He was holding onto her hand as though it were some kind of lifeline to his brother. "And where has he been for all these weeks?  We haven't heard a word from him since he wrote that he'd be bringing you as soon as he could, unless you stopped somewhere for a few days. Surely you can see that that's nearly worried the daylights out of us."

"I...I had no idea that had happened."

"You didn't?" he demanded immediately in obvious surprise and dropped her hand as though it had suddenly lost its power to help him. "Why didn't you? His letter said he was coming for you as soon as he could get everything straightened up around the camp." Dave's voice was getting even more agitated, as was the expression on his face.

Pris, now at the partially-open door, hissed a desperate sounding, "*Jamie!*" The other girl didn't even hear her.

What had been running around in her brain but that she had not been able to grasp or to accept suddenly sounded as loud as a drum. She had to speak. She had to admit what she had done and why she had had to do it. She sat up straighter and forced her big eyes up to meet those of the fast-becoming frantic young man by her. "Are you saying that you and the rest of the family haven't heard from him since that last letter? Is that what you've been trying to say?"

"Yes!" He almost shouted the word. "Where have you been? Of course, that's what I've been trying to tell you. We haven't heard a word since right after the war ended and he wrote that he'd be bringing his wife home as soon as he could."

"Then where is he?" Jamie asked, knowing she sounded stupid but feeling that she couldn't help it.

Dave grabbed his head with both hands, looked away, then shook his yellow head as though he were the one who didn't know what was going on. He turned back to her and looked at her intently for a moment before he asked, "Are you all right? Haven't you understood what I've been asking you? Do you mean you don't know where Curt is?"

She shook her head.

"Did you quarrel?" he asked in desperation. "I can't believe he'd let anything upset him so much that he'd leave you behind. Or has something happened to you? But that wouldn't have deterred him. *He loves you, Jamie!* Don't you understand? If that girl over there is right and you are actually marrying someone else, something catastrophic must have happened. Jamie," he ended in a voice that came out with difficulty, "is my brother... dead?"

It suddenly became more than she could take. "No!" she screamed, jumping up and glaring down into his face. "No. But I don't know anything about him. I just don't know. I haven't seen or heard from him since the day I sent him away."

"Shh," hissed Pris. She rushed to the window to see if anybody seemed to have heard. Neither of the other two paid her the least bit of attention.

Dave's face became frozen as he jumped up beside her. "*You sent him away?*" he said between clenched teeth. "You threw him and his great love for you away as though it were nothing?"

'I...I...had to," she stammered, trying to turn away from him.

He grabbed her back by one arm and held her. "*You had to?*" he said in the most accusing voice she had ever heard.

"You don't understand," she tried to say, but he cut in.

"You're sure right about that! You let my brother love you, risk his life for you over and over again, but *you had to send him away when you were finally safe?*"

"It wasn't like that," she said miserably, giving up on trying to get away from him. "You can't understand how it was. When the war finally ended, it had been months since I had last seen him. Terrible things had happened to me during those months. You can't imagine how it was. The world as I had known it had died around me, and I truly felt that I had died too. And I had…inside. All the tragedies had literally killed me. When he came for me, I was like a dead person. I could feel nothing—nothing for him or for anyone else. I could feel only one thing, and that was that I had to rebuild my home in memory of my dead pa. And when I thought of how the Yankees had destroyed everything they had touched, I somehow also knew that I couldn't bear the sight of a Yankee…not even Curt."

"You do not have time for this," Pris said in a sing-song voice that neither of the other two heard.

"Too dead to feel any love for the person who had done everything possible for you for years, but not too dead to be marrying someone else less than a few weeks later? Oh, Jamie, Jamie! Where has the girl my brother loved so much gone? Or was there ever such a person in the first place?"

Jamie felt like screaming and almost did, but forced herself to say. "I did love him. I do love him…"

Pris gave a gasp, and this time Jamie heard her. "I loved Curt in my way as much as he loved me in his, but they weren't the same way. I loved him as my friend, my…"

Dave broke in with a scornful, *"Friend!"* He turned her loose, grabbed his head in his hands again and hunched over with his back to her.

"And," Jamie went on determinedly, "I'll always love him that way."

Dave straightened and turned back to her with hard, cold eyes. "Did you kill my brother?" he grated out.

"Kill him?" she almost screamed the words and fell back onto the divan, trying to stand again even as she did so but not making it. "No! Of course, I didn't. I had been waiting for him to come for so long that…"

"Yeah!" he said, cutting her off. "Go marry that chap that

you've probably been holding on the side all the time. If one got killed in the war, the other one would do. Unfortunately, neither of them were killed so you had to get rid of one of them. Thank the Lord that you didn't end up with my brother. I don't know where he is now, but I do know that he'd have spent his life in Hell if he had married you."

"Oh, Dave," she begged, still trying to struggle up to reach him, "please try to understand. I did love him and I didn't mean to deceive him. You just don't know what the Yankees did to us. They destroyed the only decent life Pa and I had ever had. Curt was wonderful to me. I would have loved him for that if for nothing else but in the end..." she ended sadly, "he was a Yankee."

Dave gave her another unbelievably long, hard look and, without another word, dashed from the room.

Jamie fell back again onto the divan with both hands over her face, weeping bitterly.

# 5

Pris was by her side instantly. "I'd like to have kicked him in the shins," she said. "But you don't have time for tears now. Don't say a word to anybody about that fellow's being here, and I won't either. He, nor anybody else, is going to spoil this wedding for my brother. Or for you," she added hurriedly.

When Pris practically pulled her out into the hallway, Rhody rushed up to straighten some of her top padding as Steven said, "He's gone, Miss Jamie. I heared his horse go gallopin' off 'cross de back."

Jamie hardly knew what was being said to her. When Rhody had finished with her, she let Pris head her out the front door. There was the sound of music coming from at least one French harp, but she didn't really hear it. She barely saw all the people standing around her front yard or sitting on whatever they had brought to protect their tired bodies or the clothes that had long ago passed any benefit they would receive from such care. Others lounged on the grass and weeds that Steven had laboriously cut over the last two days with a borrowed scythe to give a reasonably-nice green look to the yard.

"That's supposed to be the 'Wedding March,' I think," Pris told her. "They've played it two or three times already so you get yourself down there. Hold onto the rail as you go down the steps. Don't fall. Clay is to meet you there as soon as he sees you come out. Brad and I will go down ahead of you. He'll stand to the right and I'll be on the left of the altar." She gave a nervous giggle at what she called the leafy branches the men had placed into the ground near the creek and had stuck wild flowers all through the leaves.

"Dr. Graham is waiting and Betsy Gains is going to sing 'Oh, Promise Me.'" Expecting a complaint from Jamie on that, she whispered, "I know, but she insisted. And she does have a fairly good voice."

Jamie scarcely took in a word she was saying. She just stood on the porch clutching the banister as Brad came up to get the matron of honor. He gave Jamie a big smile that she didn't even see. Then with Pris on his arm, he moved slowly on down through the people on the left of Jamie's lawn.

Clay didn't wait till she got down the front steps but bounded up to get her before she could start. "You all right?" he asked. "Pris said you had a fall a while ago. It didn't hurt you, did it?"

She gave a shake of her head and wished she hadn't. "No," she said back to him. "I'm still kind of woozy, but I'm fine otherwise."

"Then hold onto me and here we go." With her arm tucked securely in his, they followed the matron of honor and the best man down to the improvised altar. If he noticed her red eyes, he said nothing, and she offered a silent word of thanks for that.

*No more tears, please,* she told herself desperately as they went. She simply could not, *would not,* let herself be practically out on her feet or in tears on the most important day of her life. Nor could she let any of her problems cause unhappiness to the man she was finally marrying. So she kept a tremulous smile on her face and hoped if anyone noticed the tears standing in her eyes, they would think they were tears of happiness. But it wasn't easy, for she couldn't get over the look on Curt's brother's face or the last harsh words he had thrown at her as he had stormed from the room.

"I've lived for this day for so long, my darling," Clay whispered softly. "My wife to love forever."

"Yes, forever," she whispered back, still hardly knowing what was being said.

A few moments later, when Dr. Graham was leading them through their wedding vows, her "I do" was so soft that very few noticed the tremble in it, but Clay's was so loud and firm that no one in the yard could fail to hear him. Above the rustle of amusement over Clay's enthusiastic reply, the minister pronounced them husband and wife.

As the ceremony ended, Betsy was singing "I Love You

Truly," and the townspeople came clustering around them to offer their congratulations and best wishes.

Jamie looked over at the slight mound under the big old oak that stood nearby. *I hope you know and are happy, Mammy Rose*, was the thought that suddenly drove Dave Darby from her mind. *I am what you always wanted for me to be. I am finally and truly a Haynesworth.*

Jamie felt in a daze as she continued trying to be the happy bride she was expected to be. She *was* happy, she told herself over and over as the Winchester friends swarmed around her and Clay. She didn't remember ever having seen some of the people, but Clay seemed to know them all and introduced her proudly. Several of the women whispered to her that they'd be expecting to see her at the next meeting of the Ladies Memorial Association. She wondered what that was but knew that, if a Haynesworth woman were expected to be in it, she certainly wanted to be.

Her new sister-in-law waited till the crowd around them had thinned before she edged over to Jamie and whispered, "Are you all right?"

"Yes," Jamie answered softly, "but my legs feel as weak as a newborn kitten's. I want to sit down awfully bad."

"Hold onto Clay till you can, then find a grassy spot and you both can sit. But don't you dare tell him a word about what happened up there in your house. I guarantee you'll ruin everything if you do. I'm doing the best I can to accept all I heard because I have to, but I hate to think what it would do to Clay if he knew."

At that, Jamie felt a miserable pang that reached all the way down through her trembling legs. "I guess you're right, but it will be hard."

"Of course, it will, but that's what you get for fooling around with Yankees." Seeing the hurt look on Jamie's face, she softened her words a little, "Oh, I guess I can understand in a way, but then I'm not your husband."

Pris turned to Mrs. McCord, who was waiting to speak to

Jamie and raised her voice. "Oh, hello, Mrs. McCord. I didn't mean to be monopolizing the bride, but I am so delighted to have her as my new sister."

"That's fine, Priscilla," the older woman said graciously. "Take your time. I'm in no hurry, but I did want to speak to Clay and his wife."

"I've got to go anyway," Pris told her. "I need to go up to the house. Mother Mac wants to relieve Jamie from any responsibility for the refreshments, such as they are, and I'm supposed to help her. I'll see you both later." And, holding her faded pink dress carefully to protect its hooped skirt from the dirt, she hurried off.

"She's such a dear," Mrs. McCord said, watching Pris rush away. "So like her mother when it comes to doing good deeds. Caroline Haynesworth and I go back to the days when we were both young brides and that's a long, long time. It's a shame she's not here to help Mary Williams and Eleanor Boyd with the LMA, but I expect you'll soon be taking her place."

"Well, I'll certainly try, but don't expect me to really fill Mrs. Haynesworth's place. I'm afraid I could never do that," she said, hoping it was the right thing to say. She had no idea what she was agreeing to do. Obviously, she should have known about that organization before, but she had been thinking of so many other things…or trying *not* to think of anything…that she couldn't remember if she had heard about it or not.

Mrs. McCord was shaking her head sadly. "Don't you know it was a terrible shock to the man who found that first one. If it ever happened to me, I think I'd die right there on the spot. But surely it won't, since I don't do any digging except close around my house."

Jamie had no idea what the woman was talking about, but when she murmured, "I do hope not," thinking that surely was safe, the woman looked at her as though in fear. "You think some could even be there in town where I live? Oh, my goodness! I thought surely they would just be on the farmlands."

"Yes, ma'am. You're bound to be right."

The woman, whom Jamie didn't really know, but who seemed to be very nice, patted her on the cheek and said, "Of course, I am. But a wedding is no time to be thinking about such as that. I'm just so happy that you and Clay have finally gotten together. He's a fine young man and from such a great family."

"Yes, ma'am. I'm proud to be a member of it."

"Of course, you are. Caroline was never one to boast, but from things I've heard over the years, it's been clear that she's from a wealthy, well-established family over there in England. Well, my dear, I'd best be moving along. Much happiness to you and your new husband."

Jamie heaved a sigh of relief at the woman's departure, for she had had no idea what they had been talking about so much of the time. But how could she know anything that was happening when she hadn't been into town since the first time the bells had rung or after things had gotten so bad and very seldom even before that. She had hardly seen Pris until she and Brad had come to check on her after Curt had come and gone. Then Clay had come, and they had had the wedding to talk about. But she'd find out sooner or later, she thought, and turned to greet the next guest.

"I know he's terribly disappointed that his folks can't be here for his wedding, but I feel sure that will be his only disappointment. I'd say that he's getting a nice, sweet girl as a wife."

Jamie beamed in pleasure and relief. "Thank you for saying that," she told the middle-aged couple before her. She knew she'd met them, but right now she could hardly remember her own name and certainly not theirs. "I'll sure try to make him happy," she assured them.

"I know you will. Now come along, Homer," the woman told her husband. "This poor girl can't stand here talking to us all day. She must be worn-out by now."

Just then Clay turned back to her and said, "Honey, this esteemed merchant just said that you're looking mighty pretty today. I didn't think you'd want to miss hearing that."

"Indeed I wouldn't," she said, and, as she gave the man

standing there a smile, her big eyes were gleaming. "Indeed, I wouldn't. Thank you so much, Mr. Rea."

"You're welcome, and I can assure you that I was speaking the truth. Your new husband had me try to get enough lemons to have lemonade today, but I couldn't do it."

Clay and Jamie both laughed. "I like lemonade," he said defensively. "Nothing wrong with that. Of course, I would have preferred champagne, but I knew better than to even bring that up."

"You were sure right on that. I doubt there's been a drop of champagne in the town since the war got underway," the merchant said.

Jamie had been trying hard to forget the guilt that Dave Darby had dumped over her, but it reappeared with a vengeance as the memory of Curt risking his life to bring her food intended for his Yankee general, including a bottle of that very same wine, flashed into her mind. Suddenly, renewed guilt flowed over her like escaping waters of a dam that had just burst. She tried desperately to push it away, but it wouldn't go. She could do nothing but hold onto Clay tighter in an effort to keep herself upright.

"You all right?" he asked, looking at her worriedly.

"Sure," she said, trying to smile at both of the men, but she was afraid it was more of a grimace than anything else. "It seems that I'm not too steady on my legs today."

Clay was still looking at her as the other man asked him, "Why don't you run get her a drink of water? She does look like she could use it. I'll keep her company till you get back."

"I'll do that," he said, relinquishing Jamie's arm and dashing off.

She almost grabbed onto Mr. Rea to replace the needed support but thought better of it. She just steadied herself as best she could and said, "I do hope that your store will soon be rebuilt and have all those wonderful things like it did back when my father and I first came to Winchester. These last years have been bad for you, haven't they?"

Some man that Jamie didn't know was standing by waiting to speak to her, and he joined in the conversation. "Been bad for everybody and still is. But changes are bound to come; and since things around here couldn't get worse, any change will make things better. Don't you agree, sir?"

"I certainly do," the merchant told Jamie as he reached for the man's arm to pull him closer. "Let me introduce you to Mr. Jones, Jamie. He was involved in real estate before the war so I feel sure he'll be keeping up with everything that has to do with our property." He looked at the other man with a smile. "And I know we'll all be happy to know that some Yankee appraisers have been here."

Mr. Jones, a small man with a nearly-bald head, gave Jamie a big smile. "Yes, Mrs. Haynesworth. It is good for the Federal government to know how completely they destroyed our town."

Jamie smiled back at him, "I'm sure you're right about that, but I'll probably remember you forever for another reason."

Both men looked at her in surprise.

"You see," she went on, "you're the first person to ever call me by my new name. I think I'll remember that."

Mr. Jones chuckled. "Not exactly a monumental feat, but it's good to be remembered for something."

"Indeed it is," the other man agreed with a smile.

Mr. Jones returned to the subject that seemed to be on his mind. "If those rascals hadn't made our money worthless, I might someday forgive them for some things.... No," he interrupted himself, "how can any of us forget them? The South will probably still be hating the North when the centennial for this so-called peace comes along. And to think that they even chased our president and his family down like he was a common criminal and threw him in jail. That just burns me to a crisp."

Jamie stared at the man. That just couldn't be. "Is that actually true?" she asked before she could stop herself. She could have kicked herself as soon as she said the words. Why advertise that she had let herself become an idiot? But surely that hadn't happened to the Confederate president and she hadn't known a thing about it. Oh, how she did wish Pa could still be here. Pa would have known and told her before she ended up looking as dumb as she must have appeared.

She actually felt so dizzy at the thought that she reached out to grab one of the men to keep from falling out but pulled her hand back. She couldn't be grabbing onto men! Neither could she let these men know that she had been so withdrawn from the world that she had no idea what had been happening. "That is distressing," she managed to get out. "Can he get out soon?"

The men, apparently noticing her upset, looked at each other before Mr. Jones said, "Well, probably not right away. Mrs. Davis and the children got out almost immediately, and they aren't calling for anything really dire for Jeff Davis himself. They just want to try him for treason."

"Treason?" she repeated. "How can he be any guiltier of that than all the rest of the South?"

Mr. Jones actually chuckled. "Kind of hard to put the whole South in prison, although those rascally Republicans sure would like to do it."

"Come on," the other man said. "We're scaring this girl with all that talk. I see her husband coming, and I don't want him thinking that we've been giving her a hard time."

Mr. Jones smiled and said, "Oh, sorry. I do get carried away. The president will probably come out all right."

"I do hope so," she said. "Thanks for everything, Mr. Rea, and it's been nice to meet you, Mr. Jones."

The grocer waved off her thanks, assured Clay that they had taken good care of his wife and then moved on with Mr. Jones.

"Nice and fresh from the spring. You all right?" he asked as he handed her the cup.

She held tightly onto his arm again and sipped the water as Mrs. McLaurine and her recruits started passing the trays of food around. Strange indeed for a wedding party, but still very welcome to all these people who still treasured any bite of food they could get. Sliced cucumbers, radishes, little carrots and green onions undoubtedly had all come from early gardens. The ham biscuits apparently were already gone so Jamie was thankful for the one she had eaten for breakfast. There were even a few bite-sized sandwiches and cookies. Jamie knew those cookies surely must have come from Mrs. Bell by way of the Baltimore friend who had done what she could for the hunger problem here. How long had it been since there had been a cookie baked in their own town?

"Are you feeling all right? I sure don't want you to be knocking yourself out again."

She smiled as reassuringly as she could. "I'm fine as long as I have something to hold onto. Let's find a spot on the grass and sit down."

"Good idea. We've spoken to the people closest to us already. The others can wait or come to where we sit." He looked around and saw a nice green spot that was either grass or trimmed weeds near the creek. "You sit down over there, and I'll see if I can scrounge us a little bit of food before it's all gone too. It's amazing what the folks came up with, isn't it?"

"It sure is," she agreed. He helped her get seated with her skirt spread around her and then rushed off. She looked at the stones in the stream and wished they could sit on that big one as they had the first day he had brought her here. But then she looked at the hoop skirt and knew that was a foolish thought.

Clay was back immediately, holding some bite-sized sandwiches in his hand. "I hit it lucky," he said with a big grin and popped one of the tiny sandwiches into his mouth. "Got almost the last ones on the plate, but Mrs. Mac insisted, since it's our day."

"They're sure little, but they do look good," Jamie said, starting to reach her hand for one, but drawing it back as the next one went into his mouth too. Her heart sank, but she decided to ignore it and went on as enthusiastically, "Oh, Clay, isn't this a great party? I just heard something really disturbing that I want to talk to you about later, but for now I just want to think about this. I still can't get over how many people came. Even though we had it announced in both our churches last Sunday, I still didn't expect people like this. I sure wish my pa could see it. He'd be so proud."

"Yeah, I wish my folks could be here too," he said as he ate another of the little sandwiches. "Hmmm, some kind of meat, I'd say. Canned, I feel sure. But as far as the crowd is concerned, I knew a Haynesworth wedding would bring out everybody who could make it. Folks wouldn't want to miss my wedding."

*It's my wedding too,* she wanted to say, *and I want one of those tiny sandwiches.* But, of course, she didn't say that, for she knew perfectly well that he was right. People did hold his Haynesworth name in far higher regard than they did her Montgomery one. And suddenly she was again the little girl who had just found out what being a wood's colt meant.

# 6

The hated tears almost started, but she told herself again that she would *not* cry at her wedding party, not even if it were more for the man she had married than for herself. Still, the glow she had been determined to feel had dimmed. Then, almost immediately, came the happy thought that she too now shared that illustrious name. She was just as much a Haynesworth now as was the proud Caroline who now was her mother-in-law and who had once declared that she, Jamie, would never be allowed to mix the taint she had carried since birth with their own one-hundred-proof pure blueblood.

That thought restored her feeling of elation, and she glowed again. Clay might still be a bit self-centered (and hadn't she always known he was and hadn't really cared because she felt he deserved it), but he had married her in spite of his parents' objections. He was hers and she loved him with her whole body and soul, sandwich or no sandwich. Then he reached out his hand and said, "Here, my love. The last three are yours." She took them and almost laughed but restrained herself, for she knew he would wonder what was funny.

She watched some of the women who were helping Mrs. McLaurine serve. They were now bringing out deviled or sliced eggs on chipped plates and passing them along to those who were milling around or sitting on the lawn. She knew that there were people here who would love to grab them all, but she knew too that they were so used to their hunger that they could control such urges.

Jamie noticed Rhody in one of Mammy Rose's big, starched white aprons and a neatly-tied turban, bringing fresh water from the spring to keep the water buckets filled. The dippers hanging on the sides of the buckets were being freely used. Steven and his old mouth harp were under the old oak, playing one happy tune after another. Two of his friends who had always been some of the many free ones who lived there had the same kind of French harp, and they sat up in the sturdy old tree above Steven and played along with him. The music, especially their many renditions of Dixie, added greatly to the festivity.

Suddenly, a rather loud voice from a group of four older men near them made them turn. Seeing how thin and decrepit they looked, Jamie wondered how they had made it out here and did hope they had gotten rides in one of the few wagons. Like almost every man there, they were wearing suspenders under their open waistcoats. Jamie felt sure those suspenders would be necessary to keep their pants up over their skinny frames when they stood. Their expressions belied their attire, though, and Jamie felt sure they had once been successful men who had stayed in town and borne the hunger and deprivation that the other Winchester people had faced. Jamie did not recognize any of them, but they had a look on their faces—one bearded, two with handle-bar mustaches and the other clean-shaven—that did not fit with their probably once-nice but now worn-looking clothes. One was complaining loudly, "It's those confounded Republicans in Congress who are determined to make the South crawl on its belly, begging to be taken back in their dratted Union. It's enough to make us grab our guns and start fighting again."

*Oh, no*, Jamie thought in sudden alarm. *Crawl if you have to. Do anything those miserable Yankees demand. But please, please no more war.* The sudden panic that hit her was as brief as a flash of summer lightning. No matter how influential these men had once been and no matter how much they still wanted to beat the North, the South had nothing left with which to make war. There was no possibility of more fighting. A strange blessing, but she was still grateful to the Lord above for at least that.

"Did you hear what that man said?" she whispered to Clay.

"About the Yankees having caught President Davis?"

"Well, that too. I hadn't even heard that."

Clay grinned. "We've had other things on our minds. It never occurred to me to tell you."

"That's all right, but that man said that the Republicans in Congress won't let the Southern states back into the Union unless they come crawling. Is that right?"

"That's what they're saying up at the courthouse," he replied softly. "Two of the men in that group are lawyers who my father came up against several times. I'd say they know what they're talking about."

"Well, why on earth are those Congressmen doing that?" she asked. "I thought they fought to keep us in."

"Punishment. They want to punish the South for starting the war which, of course, is total hogwash. My father explained it to me when the trouble started. Abe Lincoln started the war by handing out his proclamations before he'd hardly found the way to his White House office or knew what to do when he got there.

"He never tried to work things out in a way that might someday have worked for all. Thomas Jefferson had already freed his people, and it didn't ruin him. My grandfather is a great admirer of Mr. Jefferson, and Father said that old fellow's action had even made Grandfather think. But to be hit over the head with an order to do it now or else was nothing more than a declaration for war, and Abe Lincoln is bound to have known it.

"The slavery issue was not the real reason for the war, anyway. The South was getting too prosperous, becoming too successful in trading with foreign countries with our cotton and tobacco. They were also holding onto their belief in states' rights. Lincoln and his cohorts were determined to gain and keep economic superiority and keep the Federal government in charge of everything rather than letting the states have what the Constitution gave them. That's what my father explained right at the beginning of the war, and I know he was right."

"Shhh," Jamie cautioned. "Not too loud."

Clay went right on, but he did keep his voice low. "Those old fellows probably think Father should have stayed here and helped us rebuild, but I know he felt he was doing the right thing by taking Mother, Mary Lilly and Cooke off to our English grandparents for a while. They deserve a decent life, but I sure do miss him and his guidance."

Jamie wanted to clasp her hands over her ears before she heard another word of that. She had been so sure that Clay had become his own man during those four hard years of war, and she didn't want to see or hear the slightest indication that he still didn't want to stand on his own feet. He had come back determined to marry her in spite of his parents' objections… and he had. That had been proof enough for her, and she had reveled in his strength. She wanted that overly-controlling hand of his father completely off of Clay and hopefully forgotten.

"But," Clay said now, "politics and religion are two things that should not enter the conversation at wedding parties. Don't you agree?"

"Yes, I do. But let's listen to them. They may say something more that's interesting."

He raised his eyes upward and whispered, "Heaven help me. My wife wants to meddle in politics." But, he did hush and try to listen to the next thing being said by one of the men.

"You're right as rain about everything you've been saying," Jamie heard but wasn't sure who was speaking. She did know he spoke with the sound of authority. "We fought those rascals for four years to get away, and now they're refusing to let us back in unless we kiss…" He let his voice fall. "I say, let's stay out, if that's the way they want it. We'll have trouble forever, otherwise. They insist that all the freed darkies get full citizenship… voting rights and everything else. That's idiotic and could ruin the country."

"You know we can't stay out, sir," said Clive McCord, whom she did know. He was passing by and had apparently heard the remark. "But I sure wish we could. I hear that those numbskulls in Washington City have a whole list of things our commonwealth has to do before we can again be what we didn't want to be anyway."

"That's a heck of a note," Josh Pritchard called over from where he was sitting with his wife. "That idiot who shot Abe Lincoln sure did the South no favor. Abe was in favor of being easy and getting everybody back together."

Jamie raised questioning eyes at Clay. He nodded. "That's what I've heard. Now that Andrew Johnson's president, he was going to follow the same path, but those Republicans in Congress won't allow it. Or, at least, that's what folks are saying."

"Well," one of the older men who Jamie thought she had finally recognized as Mr. Miller said bitterly, "let those Republicans keep that up if they want to turn every last one of us Republicans into Democrats. If they want a solid Democratic South for years to come, let them keep on with their vindictive shenanigans."

"I think he's right about that," Clay told Jamie quietly. "Father was always a Republican so I've followed his lead. But, if that's what they want to do, I'll change my registration to Democrat and stay with it forever. The thought of our having to grovel to get back in sure grabs me where I don't want to be grabbed."

"If women could vote, I'd sure join you," Jamie said loyally.

He gave her a quick kiss on the cheek. "Well, of course, you would. You're my wife and also a woman. But the day will never come when women like you can vote. What do women know about politics?"

Mr. Miller had heard that and called over, "It's a good thing that women are non-political for, otherwise, they couldn't do what they're doing. You'll want to get involved in that movement, Mrs. Haynesworth, if you aren't already. It's fantastic what our ladies are up to, and the Federal government can't do a thing about it. But hello here!" he broke in on himself to say. "I see Mrs. McLaurine waving to us from the front porch. I think that means it's about time to cut that cake that my wife says Mrs. Mac spent all day yesterday making. Somebody give me a hand up, and we'll go see how good it is."

Clay jumped up and went to help the elderly gentlemen to their feet. Then he turned back to his wife. Jamie took his proffered hand and stood with him. "They're right. Everybody seems to be getting up and ambling toward the house. We'd better get ourselves up there in a hurry, for we're supposed to cut the first slice, aren't we?"

"We are that," he agreed. "Brad said his mama was going to have the cake-cutting on the side porch since folks will have to hold it in their hands. No point in getting crumbs all over the house. Oh, I do wish my parents could be here for this," he added. "You remember, don't you, the fantastic cake Mother had Clenzy make for Pris' wedding party?"

Jamie shook her head as they walked along with other folks obviously heading for the same place they were. "You may have forgotten what happened that night, Clay, but I sure haven't. That was when I came down with the typhoid."

He pulled her to a sudden stop and grabbed her in a tight hug, causing the couple behind to bump into them and then to kid them a bit. "No," he said softly into her ear, "I haven't forgotten that, and I never will. I thought you were going to die, and I knew that, if you did, I'd surely die too."

She gave a little shiver and wiggled herself free of his arms. "Later," she whispered. Then as they started walking on, she said, "Yes, I did nearly die. I would have been frantic about any of you catching it if I hadn't been out of my head most of the time. Wonder why nobody else did. I know that sometimes it becomes a real epidemic. It must have here with the people who owned Fairdale before Pa."

"The Chases," Clay said as they hurried along. "The youngest little girl got it first and then the others. Mrs. Chase nearly killed herself looking after them. And then she got it too. They all died. Mother wouldn't let us out of the house for weeks, afraid we'd get it."

"Yes, I know they all died. That's why Mr. Chase was determined to get rid of Fairdale and why he let Pa have it like he did. That poor man couldn't bear to even see the place after his family had all died."

"He was a broken man alright, but it never occurred to anybody that he'd run off, sell Fairdale and then kill himself."

"I don't think," Jamie said sadly, "that he considered it as suicide. Pa thought he was a fine person who just wanted to join his family in Heaven."

Clay gave her a skeptical look and said, "Whatever. As I've told you, I knew them all well. I felt awfully sorry for him, but I'm sure glad Mr. Montgomery got Fairdale. If he hadn't, you and I would never have met. I'll always be grateful for that meeting."

"Me too," she said, remembering how scared she had been that a house her pa had won in a craps game might be nothing but a shack. She had never told anybody, even Pris, exactly how Pa had gotten Fairdale, and that was one more thing that she would never tell anybody.

That brought to mind the other things that she could not share with her husband. The memory of Curt and his brother slammed back with such force that it almost seemed to be audible. She gave a scared glance at Clay but he, of course, had heard nothing. Still, she simply couldn't be going to cut her wedding cake with one man and worrying herself sick about another. She felt it was a wonder that she wasn't struck dead by the wrongness of it. But how could she possibly bear never knowing what had happened to the man who had loved her so dearly? The answer was something she didn't know, but neither did she know how she could bear having to remember that her wedding day had been marred by her worry about another man.

*Oh, dear God, help me*, she breathed.

But if God were listening, He did not give her a reply she could recognize. She just had to keep her mind from going there. At least, not now. Not today.

"Anything wrong?" Clay asked solicitously as they neared the steps. "You suddenly looked like you'd lost your dearest friend. That, honey, is not the proper look for a bride," he ended, obviously trying to tease her into a smile.

She gave him the brightest one she could manage, and her smoky black eyes gleamed brightly with unshed tears as she said, "How could I possibly look sad on the day that I have finally married you?"

He smiled at her in return and held her arm firmly to help her up the front steps and through the hall to the side porch. As she looked down those steps, the night when she had sat on them in bright moonlight and heard a Yankee voice that had turned soft and caring…

*Stop it! Stop it!* she told herself so firmly that she looked at Clay again to be sure she had not spoken aloud. He obviously had heard nothing.

"Come on," he whispered. "We'll never get rid of all these folks if we don't give them at least a taste of that cake. Then," he said with a tight squeeze of her hand, "we can finally get onto what a wedding is all about."

She knew her face flushed, but as she stepped onto the porch with him and saw Mrs. McLaurine there behind a table she didn't recognize, she beamed with pleasure and surprise. There was also a white lacy table cover which she had never seen either. "Oh, Mrs. McLaurine," she cried softly, "that's the most beautiful cake I've ever seen. Thank you so very much."

The woman reached out and touched Jamie's cheek. "You're more than welcome, dear. I remember the cake when Priscilla and Brad got married. I wanted you, my almost-adopted daughter, to have one as nearly like it as I could manage. Of course, it fell far short, for I didn't have the butter I needed or nearly enough sugar. Well, actually I was short on everything, but it is kind of pretty, isn't it?"

"Oh, yes." At the words "adopted daughter," tears came rushing into Jamie's big black eyes. She tried frantically to blink them away, but, in spite of her efforts, they overflowed down her cheeks. Clay dug a handkerchief out of his pockets and said teasingly again, "Honey, don't cry. The cake might be better than it looks." Laughing and still wiping tears, she fell into his arms and hid her face in his refurbished gray-clad shoulder.

Most of the guests had come to surround the porch and watch the proceedings. They made a strange sight with the men in everything from frock coats to moth-eaten suits that had never been worn except to church, grubby work clothes or uniforms the wives had done their best to make as presentable as possible. Many of the women were in washed-out everyday clothes, but there were quite a few in dresses that had once been lovely with their full skirts and hoops. Looking at them, Jamie felt an urge to cry again at what had once been, but she was determined that her face would remain dry for the rest of the party.

They cut the first slice, and the crowd clapped as though they had accomplished a great feat; then Clay turned the knife over to Pris. By the time the last tiny slice had been served, Jamie was so tired that all she wanted to do was find the nearest chair, fall into it and never get up again. When the sun had disappeared behind the Alleghenies, the last grateful "thank you" said and the final "goodbye" called as the three McLaurines disappeared up the avenue, Jamie looked at her new husband and said, "I'm so tired I could drop."

"Don't you dare do it. Our wedding celebration is not over yet. Come on. You just need some food." He grabbed her hand and led her into the house.

# 7

"Come on in, my darling wife," Clay said softly as they entered the hallway. "I have something special for you."

She tried to be interested. This was her wedding night, for goodness sake. She was tired, but how long had it been since she hadn't been? And hungry? She did wish she could have something to eat, but she knew the cupboards were practically bare. But, she told herself, she'd been hungry before too. And, as far as that terrible news that Dave Darby had brought, she sure wasn't going to let the thought of *any* Yankee ruin her wedding night with the man she had fallen for the first day she had laid eyes on him. Not if she could make it up those stairs. But she was far from sure that she could.

Rhody was waiting at the door into the dining room as they came in. "It's as ready as I could get it, Mister Clay," she said and moved away from the door.

"I'm sure it's fine," he said and took Jamie into a candlelit room. There were wildflowers and greenery down the center of the table.

Jamie at first saw nothing but all the white candles. "Where did you find all those candles? I thought we'd been out for months and years. Oh, Clay, this is beautiful. Thank you so much."

"The evening is just beginning," he told her proudly. "Bring it on, Rhody."

"Yes'suh," the woman said and hurried down the basement stairs. In a moment she was back, carrying a small bottle of wine and two wine glasses.

Again, Jamie stared. "I thought all my glasses had been dashed to smithereens. Where did you find these?"

Clay grinned happily. "Mrs. Mac had tucked a few things away so far back under the eaves in her attic that no Yankee ever found

57

them. I decided there was no better way to spend the Federal money Father gave me than on our wedding dinner. Mrs. Mac said no way were we going to toast our life together with chipped or cracked cups. Actually, she brought out four glasses. I think she might have had Pris and Brad in mind, but I didn't think a wedding supper should be a foursome."

Jamie giggled as Clay put her in a chair and sat beside her. "No, I don't think so," she said, almost forgetting the terrible fatigue that had swamped her a few minutes before. "And what is that wonderful smell? I was feeling so weak from hunger that I thought I must be dreaming it."

"Beef tenderloin," he said proudly. "I wanted us to have the wine first, but I guess it will be just as good with the meal. Tell Steven to bring it on," he told Rhody.

The woman raced for the stairs, and in moments Steven brought in a chipped platter with the beautifully-browned meat in the center. Green onions, little potatoes and carrots were around it. "And don't forget the bread, Rhody," Clay reminded her. "It should be done by now, shouldn't it?"

"Yes'suh, it sho' is."

"Rhody tells me," he explained to Jamie, "that she knows how to make really good yeast bread. It's going to be coming out of the oven in just a minute, so we can see if hers can match what our Clenzy used to make."

Jamie didn't want to say anything that would take away from the pride that both Clay and Rhody were obviously feeling. The woman was nodding as she went to the sideboard and brought out two plates. She put one before each of them.

"You will notice," Clay said, "that there's not a chip or a crack on either of these."

"Where did you get them?" Jamie asked, feeling more and more amazed at what her new husband had managed to do. "More from Mrs. Mac's attic?" she asked.

"More treasures probably from somebody's," Clay said, "but these came from a different one. I don't really know whose, but there's a little shop that's sprung up on the way to Harper's Ferry.

58

I saw them and couldn't resist. They cost only a very little bit of Federal money. Bone china. Mrs. Mac says it's really a fine make and once was very expensive. A lot more than what they cost me," he ended proudly.

Jamie almost laughed at the thought of a Haynesworth actually being proud of getting someone's once-treasured plates for such a pittance, but it was too sad to laugh about. It was actually disheartening that people were so hard up that they had to sell their fine things for practically nothing to get money for a little food.

Clay was right, though. No sadness on one's wedding day, and she willed her depression away. Gone too was the tiredness that made her feel that she could not go on. The sight of that beautiful roast would surely have been enough to revive her if she had been stone cold dead. "Let's eat," she said urgently. "I'm starved."

"Still hungry," he asked as though greatly surprised, "after those cucumber sandwiches I brought you and those two little bits of wedding cake?"

"Yes, I definitely am. I know I also had a better-than-usual breakfast, but it's been a long time since then. Please, Clay."

"All right, honey," he said, giving her a kiss as he got up to pull the tray in front of him and serve. "Actually, I'm so hungry myself that even those scrawny little vegetables look mighty tempting. Steven almost mourned about having to take them up before they got bigger, but I insisted. Cooked with the meat, they're bound to be good. Hey, Rhody, you did bring a knife, didn't you?"

"Yes'suh. It right dere beside de meat."

"Oh, yes. I see it. Now, Rhody, if you'll run down and bring up the hot bread and that cake of butter, we're going to have ourselves a pretty good dinner."

"Pretty good?" Jamie questioned. "Oh, Clay, Clay, how did you ever do it?"

He dropped the flippant tone he had been using and said seriously, "Actually, by spending more of that fifty dollars in

Federal money that Father gave me than I probably should have. But I don't regret a penny of what I spent. I'm never going to get married again. I have the only girl I'll ever want, but I will have more money someday. I promise you that. And with everybody's gardens coming in, nobody's going to be starving again."

"Oh, Clay," she cried softly and fell into his arms for the ardent kiss she knew was coming. "Clay, I love you so much."

Jamie drank sparingly of the delicious grape wine, for she remembered the night she had not been careful and had gotten so sick. She knew she didn't want another night or another memory like that. Not on her wedding night, of all times.

"I forgot about dessert," Clay confessed as the meal was winding down. "Can't imagine why I did that unless I was expecting some wedding cake to be left. Foolish thought."

"It sure was," she agreed.

"Well," he said, "maybe another slice of that still-warm bread with some butter and jelly…if we had any jelly…would do the trick."

She laughed. "If we had the best dessert ever made, I couldn't eat it tonight. For the first time in I can't remember how long—" actually, she could but she absolutely was not going to allow herself to do it "—I'm full to the brim."

"Me too," Clay said, obviously pleased with himself. "It was a pretty good wedding dinner, wasn't it?"

"The best I've ever had," she said and giggled again. "Well, actually, as you well know, it's the only wedding dinner I've ever had. I'll never forget it."

Suddenly, Clay snapped his fingers. "Well, dadblame it! We've got to go back out again." He jumped up and went to the door to the kitchen stairs. "Hey, Rhody!" he called. "You can clear the table now. You and Steven can have some of everything, but leave us enough for dinner tomorrow. And put these candles somewhere we can use them again. I'm taking one upstairs with us."

He came back to the table, picked up Jamie's wine glass and drank the half that she had not. Then he grabbed her hand and pulled her with him down the hall and onto the porch. "I forgot to carry you over the threshold," he explained, "and that won't do. Bad luck or something."

He scooped her up in his arms and carried her back in to the stairway leading up. "I didn't want to miss a thing from the night I had been planning for since the day I met you. I have always meant for it to be like a wonderful wedding gift for both of us. I love you, my darling wife, and I will forever. I want this night to be perfect."

The worries she had been feeling so guilty about seemed to disappear, and the rest of the evening became exactly how she had always dreamed her wedding night would be.

# 8

"No!" Jamie screamed as she tore herself from Clay's arms and sprang up in bed, still trying to clutch the worn sheet tightly to her. "No! Please, no! I didn't! I didn't! Oh, please help me!" she cried. "Won't somebody help me?"

Clay sprang up beside her, trying to pull her back to him. "What is it, Jamie? What's wrong?"

She looked at him, wild-eyed with fear. "Clay!" she cried and cringed away from him. "What are you doing here? I've told you and told you…"

Clay shook her gently. "Jamie! Jamie, wake up! I'm supposed to be here. Don't you remember? We're married. Where else should I be?"

She pulled away and yanked the sheet even tighter to her. "No! You saw them! You were there when they accused me, and you didn't say a word. You let them!"

He reached for her again, trying to pull her close, but she scrambled so close to the edge of the bed that she almost fell off. She caught herself with one hand and held up the other to ward him off. "No! Get out of here. I want my pa or Mammy Rose. Oh, please, please won't they or somebody help me?"

"Jamie, stop it!" Clay said urgently. "You're scaring the living daylights out of me. Is that what you want to do? I'll help you. That's what I'm trying to do. You just had a nightmare and you're still not half-awake. But, please, honey, believe me. You are all right. Everything is fine so please wake up and realize that."

She stared at him as though she'd never seen him before. "Get out of my bed! I don't remember any…" And then she did, but what she remembered was being in the courthouse. She was handcuffed and about to be taken away. "I didn't do it," she said, the words mixed in with a sudden burst of tears. "I didn't do it. I would never kill anyone. You should know that, but you didn't try to help me. I saw you there on the front row, and you didn't say a word in my defense. You were there and you let him accuse me of murder, and you didn't even…"

He inched closer and reached a tentative hand out to her again. "No, honey. You're wrong. I've been right here in bed, just like you have. You've just had a bad dream. That's all it was. You're all right."

"But you were there," she began again. 'You heard them convict me of murder. I didn't…I couldn't murder anybody. Oh, Clay, don't you know I could never do that?"

By now, he had gotten close enough to put his arms around her and say soothingly, "Oh, my dearest girl. I do know that, and I would never let anybody do that to you. Nobody! No one's ever going to accuse you of anything again. I won't let them. Don't you know that? Don't you know you're safe with me?"

"But I saw you. You were there, not saying a word in my defense. Pris too. She just glared at me and mouthed the word 'murderer.'"

Clay tried a little chuckle. "Then I'll give her the dickens for that the next time I see her," he went on soothingly. "But doesn't that prove to you that you've just been dreaming? Pris would be fighting for you to the last ditch if you were ever in trouble. But you aren't. You're safe and where you should be…in your husband's arms. Are you all right now?"

She stared at him. *Husband? Was that really true?* Then the memory of the past day rushed over her, and she felt a confused wave of embarrassment. Of course, he was. What on earth was wrong with her? Had she finally lost her mind?

She gave a shuddering sigh. "Maybe. But I don't know for sure. It was so real, and everybody in the courthouse was blaming me."

Clay managed a relieved chuckle. "No wonder they're blaming you if you were there in nothing but that thin sheet. Maybe instead of murder being the charge, you were convicted of indecent exposure. As your husband, I'm the one who should be complaining about that."

She looked at him as if he were speaking a foreign language. "I'm sorry," he said quickly. "I shouldn't have been trying to tease you, but I was just trying to make you see that your fear is foolish. You're here with me, and I won't let anybody or anything hurt you. You can count on me. We're married, Jamie. Wipe that nightmare from your mind and remember yesterday and last night. You haven't hurt anybody. We're safe and you always will be with me."

She tried to relax and let him pull her close. She knew he was speaking the truth, but somehow that other image wouldn't quite disappear. Guilty. That was the way she still felt, even after hearing Clay's reassuring words. But she now knew where she was and that she had to get herself under control. They had gotten married. She hadn't murdered anybody, but then the image of Dave Darby's accusation flashed into her mind, and she almost screamed again. She raised her head from Clay's chest where she had let it fall and looked at him. "I didn't do it," she told him. "I couldn't ever." The realization of what she was saying swept through her, and she hushed. Couldn't she ever keep her mouth shut?

"Of course, you wouldn't," Clay said assuredly. "I don't know who accused you of such a thing, but tell me who he is and I'll go beat him up tomorrow. Somehow, I'm not much for getting in a fight on my wedding night."

"It was Dave," she blurted out before she could catch herself. She knew she was talking too much and tried to shake the horror of the nightmare as she added, "He seemed to be a stranger to all, but they wanted to convict me and they did."

"Dave?" Clay was saying. "I don't think I've ever known a Dave here in town, so let's forget him. I'd be willing to bet that it had something to do with what you were unfairly made to feel in the past. I don't want you to ever think about any of that again, and right now I want you to lie back down and get some rest. You've pushed yourself almost beyond the limit, but that's another thing that's not going to happen again since I'm here.

Now, let's call a recess in court, lie back down and get a little more shut-eye before it's time to get up."

With an almost overwhelming relief, she did as he said. She let him get her stretched out again, the sheet over both of them and her head on his shoulder and his arms holding her. "I'm sorry I woke you," she whispered into the darkness. "You were tired too."

"Not the slightest problem," he assured her, "but I would like to know one thing. Do you have nightmares like that often? If so, I want to prepare myself for a heart attack."

By now, she had recovered enough to give a weak chuckle. "No, thank goodness. I do have dreams that I wish I didn't have, but, as far as something like this is concerned, I've never had one before. It was just that..." She caught herself in time and ended with, "This hasn't been exactly a run-of-the-mill sort of day."

"You can say that again," he said, chuckling once more. He tightened his arms around her. "No, you go back to sleep. Nothing is going to hurt you tonight or ever again. I simply will not allow it."

With a feeling of great relief, she curled into his side and murmured, "I really do love you, Clay."

"You say that as if there's been some question of that," he shot back.

Again, she felt a dart of alarm. "Of course not." she assured him and closed her eyes, hoping with all her heart she would never have to go through something like this night again.

# 9

The next time Jamie woke she could tell that the sun was unbelievably high in the heavens, but she lay in bed as she had the day before, feeling wondrously relaxed and peaceful. She must have dropped off again sometime after she had seen the sun edging over the Blue Ridge.

Gone were all the feelings that she had when she woke after the nightmare. She had felt they should get up and get to work. It was still odd to feel someone in bed beside her, but she liked it. She had not slept with anyone since she was a little child and had to sleep with Mammy Rose because her pa could only afford two rooms. Now she reveled in the feel of Clay's arms around her and felt something like real bliss at the thought that finally she was his wife. After all they had been through, he was finally forever hers and she was his. She was now and would be forevermore a Haynesworth. What a blessed thought!

Clay's decision that they were going to have an at-home honeymoon was wonderful. Though she had argued about it at first, it was good to finally realize that she really didn't have to be the deciding factor on everything anymore. She had been in that position so long—actually ever since Pa had joined the army—but Clay had shown her that it was a habit she would have to break.

A tiny worry did creep in that he might have too much of his father still in him, but she told herself that she might be wrong about that. The work that needed to be done, the work she had usually been up at dawn to begin doing, was, as Clay had pointed out, going to still be there whenever they got around to it. There was one thing about work, he said; it was always willing to wait. Though she disagreed basically with that premise, the morning of the first day of her life as Clay's wife was not the time to stress it. Today and the rest of this week would belong to them and them alone.

However, still there was that feeling that somehow she didn't deserve this great blessing that had almost suddenly been bestowed upon her. *But why not?* she argued idly with herself as she lay there with him. Hadn't she done her best? Maybe it hadn't always been *the* best, but she had tried. She would have given almost anything to have been able to make it up to Pa for her lack of appreciation for all he had sacrificed for her. It still made her unbelievably sad that she had been too late to reach him before he died. She had wanted so much to tell him she was sorry and that she had always loved him dearly. She sighed. No point in fretting over all that now, for she knew Pa would not want her worrying about him now that she was Mrs. Clay Haynesworth! So, why the nagging worry that she was trying hard to ignore?

And then she remembered.

It was Curt and what happened to him. That was what had caused the nightmare and the black feeling that kept threatening. Even with all the wonder of having Clay, it was a feeling she could not shake. There was no way in the world that she could have left Fairdale and all her wonderful Winchester friends to go off to the North with him. With a Yankee! The idea was ridiculous, and Curt should have known that as well as she did, yet it simply broke her heart to think that she had done something that had caused real harm to a good man who she knew had truly loved her. But what could she do about it now? Nothing! Not a dratted thing.

Still, she knew that it was going to drive her nearly crazy until she knew what had happened to him. She knew too that directly or indirectly, whatever had happened to him had to have been her fault. That knowledge hurt terribly. What could have happened? Was he *dead?* When she let herself really think about it, she felt sure he must be. If not, she knew that she would have heard from him before now. She had known all the time that the silence from him was strange, but she had blocked him from her mind so completely that she simply refused to let any real thought of him enter it.

Even now, she forced herself to turn away from those

terrifying thoughts. She would think them when and if the time ever came that they would help, but wasn't it almost like some form of adultery to be lying in the arms of her husband and worrying desperately about another man? She'd have to ask Reverend Graham about... *Oh, good grief, no!* The mere thought made her twist so much that she was afraid she had awakened Clay. She knew she was just grasping at whatever straw she could find in hoping that maybe God didn't hold a thing against a person when that person really couldn't help doing it. Even as that thought came, she knew it was stupid. She didn't have to ask anyone to know the answer to that.

"I hope those are happy thoughts," she heard from over her head and felt herself almost jump again. "But from your expression they aren't," Clay went on, sounding worried himself.

"Don't be silly," she told him, embarrassed. "How could I be worrying about anything when I'm the happiest I've ever been?"

"That's what I wanted to know. I've been looking down on your face for some time now, and it's been like a map that I could not read," Clay went on. "First relaxed and happy and then looking like the weight of the world had just settled upon you. Anything wrong? Are you not feeling well?"

So, the guilt she was feeling down where she hoped it would never show was not hidden at all. She raised her own head from where it rested on Clay's chest and tried to smile brightly at him. "I'm sorry about my face, but how could my thoughts be anything but happy when thinking of you?"

It was the truth. Not the whole truth, but it still brought her a tender kiss followed by a playfully-snarled, "You'd better be. Your days of thinking about other men are over."

Oh, if only that could be true!

He kissed her again, then turned her loose to swing his feet over to the floor. "Don't go away," he told her. "I'll be right back."

"If you're going downstairs, I would suggest some clothes," she said with a grin.

"Oh, right. I'll put on that nightshirt that Brad insisted I take.

I think it was once his father's. But we're alone anyway. I told Steven and Rhody to go over and start cleaning up at Crestview today."

"You did *what?*" she cried, sitting up and staring at him. "They have work to do right here. I gave them both their instructions."

"But though you seem to have forgotten that there's a man in the house so you don't have to worry about things like that any more, they haven't. It's a man's world, honey, so they are out of the house and away. We have it all to ourselves."

She started to say, *No. Not all decisions are yours to make when it's my house and my servants.* But she swallowed the words, feeling sure that a wife should never say such things and certainly not to a husband who had been raised by Thaddeus C. Haynesworth himself. She had wanted to be exactly what she now was, and she guessed that she had better learn the family's rules. Never having lived in a home where there was a wife who could have set an example for her, she was afraid there were lots of things for her to learn.

Of course, Pris hadn't always marched to her father's tune. Why couldn't Clay be more like his sister? But criticizing her husband on their first real day together might be almost as bad as worrying about another man or keeping secrets. She simply had to get herself in hand.

Clay dug into the bag he had brought and pulled out a plaid nightshirt. He pulled it over his head and gave a little bow to his wife who was still in the bed and clutching the sheet tightly around her. 'How's this?" he asked.

Jamie giggled. "Mr. McLaurine must have been a very tall man. That thing comes nearly down to your ankles."

He looked down at himself and then over at her with kind of a puzzled grin. "What's wrong with that? It's what my father and other men always wear at night. Didn't your father wear them too?"

"I don't really know. Pa was always dressed by the time he came out of his room. He formed that habit long ago and always stuck to it." She sure wasn't going to explain that he had had to do that in the old days when her mama's father had been continuously persecuting him for taking his daughter away from him, so her pa had been unable to afford places with any decent space. She knew her pa had slept in his clothes many times, but there wasn't any need for Clay or anybody else to ever know that.

"Well, bully for him," Clay said. "And, for your information, these things are supposed to come below the knees. I guess Mr. Mac was a few inches taller that my five-eleven, but too long is better than too short in case Rhody hasn't gone from the kitchen yet. I told her to make some more of that coffee I brought and to leave it on the stove. I hope it will still be hot but not too strong by now. I'll be right back and with whatever I can find to eat."

As soon as he was gone, Jamie tossed off the sheet, grabbed up her pantaloons and chemise and put them on. She sure didn't want to show her skin and bones off in the daylight. She was hastily pulling an old calico dress over her head when Clay came back in carrying a battered-looking tray with two cups and something that must be toast.

"Aw, shucks, you're dressed," he complained. "I meant this to be breakfast in bed for our first morning together." He was obviously disappointed.

"I'm sorry," Jamie said. "I didn't know."

"Never mind. Get back in anyway." He put the tray down on the wobbly little table by the bed. "Confound that thing! I've got to steady it up some way. Here's your coffee and toast. Rhody had made it and left it in the oven warmer, so it may be as dry as an old corncob, but I want you to eat every bite of it, regardless of what it tastes like. The coffee will soften it. We've got to get some weight back on you if we ever want to have a little Haynesworth. At least, that's what Brad tells me."

"You talked to Brad about *that*?" she cried, looking stricken. "Oh, Clay, how embarrassing."

He studied her face again. "Embarrassing? Why? He's my best friend, the husband of my sister and he's gone to medical college. He may not be quite a doctor, but he's close enough to suit me. How can you possibly be embarrassed at his knowing we do things that we hope will result in a baby?"

Her face was flushed. "People don't talk about things like that." she said in a quiet voice.

Clay laughed. "You must mean that women don't talk about things like that. But I'm a man, as I hope you noticed. Men do talk."

"Well, I wish you'd stop it. Our personal life is something for nobody but us."

Holding his coffee carefully, he leaned over and kissed her on the forehead. "Honey, have you got a lot to learn."

"Maybe so, but so do you. I got dressed because I hated something awful for you to see how skinny I am. I want the figure back that I once had; but, come to think of it, you don't weigh what you once did yourself."

"Nope, that's for sure." He dunked his dry toast into his coffee and leaned over to get it into his mouth before it dripped on Mr. McLaurine's nightshirt. "Fortunately, Brad found me a pair of his father's suspenders too. If he hadn't, I'd have had trouble keeping up the trousers of my old uniform yesterday."

"You still looked awfully nice," she said, trying to make up for whatever she had said or done earlier that was wrong. "I remember the first time I ever saw you in that uniform. You looked splendid."

"Yeah," he said. Folding his pillow to raise his head, he leaned back on it, sipped his coffee and smiled as he thought about the early days of the war and how optimistic everyone had been then. "Mother had somehow gotten that fine gray wool material and had it already made for me when I came home, filthier than a hog in slop. After having been dirty for so long, getting clean and into that uniform meant a lot more to me than just something new to wear."

Jamie smiled sympathetically. "Didn't know it was to be your wedding suit, did you?" she asked.

He glanced over to the rocker where he had tossed his uniform the night before. "Sure didn't. It couldn't have been either, if Mrs.

Mac hadn't done such a fantastic job of cleaning it up for me. Brad's too. Otherwise, I'd have been married in worn-out homespun or in my drawers, if I'd had to. Ah, how I wish I had back all those nice clothes that were burned with the house."

"I know how you feel. We wouldn't even have a place to live if that one decent Yankee hadn't saved Fairdale for me," she said with real sadness. "And Mammy Rose would have been burnt up too."

"What Yankee?" he demanded angrily, turning to look at her so suddenly that he spilt coffee on himself. "That son-of-a-gun who tried his best to take you from me?"

"No, no," she assured him hastily. "It certainly was not. I had never seen the man who saved me before that day. Then, after he had talked that half-drunk captain out of gutting my house with Mammy Rose in it, I never saw him again. He just gave me a big wave with his hat as he rode away." She turned to look over at him and said, "But hasn't Brad or your sister told you about that? I'll sure never forget what Pris did that day either."

"Well, yes, I had heard about it. Mrs. Mac was the first one to tell me, and she didn't know who the Yankee was. I'm glad…well, I guess you can understand why I didn't want it to be that same Yankee fellow."

"Isn't Mrs. McLaurine a wonderful woman?" she said hastily to get away from any talk about Curt. "She called me her almost-adopted daughter yesterday. I can't tell you how touched I was."

"You don't have to tell me. I saw your reaction. But, honey, a lot of people love and admire you. I wish you could get that through your beautiful head."

"It's not beautiful any more," she lamented. "But maybe my face will look all right again when I can gain some weight."

"You want to gain weight on your head?" he teased. "I'm not sure I want you to be a 'fathead.'"

She poked him in the ribs with her elbow, causing a yelp of protest as he almost spilled the rest of his coffee.

The remainder of the day was relaxed and peaceful. Clay doted on her every wish, even walking with her out to see the areas she had picked for her apple trees. "Do you know how long it takes for an apple tree to grow and produce fruit? If you're counting on making enough money to keep us from starving, I'm afraid we'll be long-gone before that happens."

"No, I don't know how long that will take, but I plan to be here to enjoy those apples whenever they get here."

He hugged her and assured her he would be right there with her, waiting for his apple too.

The tenderloin did make a delicious supper again and, as Jamie crawled into bed that night and felt her husband's arms around her again, she thought they couldn't have had a more wonderful day.

If only....

# 10

In the days that followed, food was still barely sufficient, but Jamie and Clay's love was strong and overflowing. When Clay would be tempted to go into town and spend his remaining U.S. dollars on whatever he could find, Jamie would talk him out of it. "Let's live on the garden as much as we can for a while longer," she urged. "The corn and green beans should soon be plentiful, as well as cornfield peas, and then Steven's potatoes should be big enough to dig without feeling we're being wasteful by taking them up too soon. Some people have already done that, but I would like ours to be full-grown," she told him.

She did her best to frame her words so she didn't sound like she was trying to be bossy, for she remembered hearing Mammy Rose say that men hated having their wives be that way. Of course, Mammy Rose had never been married so how she had known that, she didn't know. She did know that she wanted to build their relationship as she felt it should be, and as she felt sure her mama's and her pa's had been. Still, there was always that nagging worry that keeping a dreadful secret from her new husband was not the way to do it. Pris had said she could not tell. Jamie was afraid her friend had been right about not telling him on their wedding day, but maybe now was different. She would open her mouth to let the secret out, but she always closed it without speaking.

Friday was a perfect June day. There was a nice breeze that kept the heat away, so Clay said he thought he'd walk into town and see what was going on. "If Mrs. Bell's kind friend over in Baltimore knows how hungry the people here have been, surely whatever government we have left in Richmond or the one in Washington City is bound to know it too," he told Jamie as they were finishing their dinner of mostly-new garden peas cooked with onions. Jamie remembered what Pris had told her long ago about onions giving some flavor when there was no other seasoning. They still had some of the salt that Clay had gotten them for their wedding supper, but both Rhody and Jamie were using it as sparingly as if it were irreplaceable gold dust.

There was also corn on the cob that was not filled out enough to be really good and some very-welcome bread that Jamie didn't know where in the world Rhody had gotten the ingredients to make. When she mentioned that to Clay, he told her to accept whatever they had and ask no questions. She did as he said.

"I'd love to have you go with me," Clay told his wife when he mentioned his walk into town, "but you need rest far more than you need a long hike. Would you mind if I leave you for a few hours?"

"Not at all," she said but then changed it quickly to, "Well, I'll miss you, but I've gotten so lazy with all this resting and sleeping late that I don't much want to walk anywhere. If you can find anything that won't take all the money you have left, it sure would be nice to have some milk and lard. I guess you heard Rhody say that Steven had gotten a big turtle from the creek and she wanted to fry it, if she could get anything to fry it in. Mammy Rose used to make turtle soup, but Rhody says that when it's fried, turtle tastes almost like chicken. Some fried chicken sure would taste good, wouldn't it?"

"Yeah, wouldn't it? Want to at least walk with me up to the pike?"

"That far I can make with no trouble," she assured him. When they reached the still-beaten-up roadway, he gave her a long goodbye kiss, a gentle pat to her skinny rear and sent her back to the house, laden with instructions to do nothing but rest while he was gone. She laughed and said, "I hear you," but she did not promise.

As soon as she got back to the house, she went looking for her two helpers. As expected, they were both in the garden Steven had dug up so laboriously and was tending with great care. Rows and rows of tomato plants stood up looking sturdy in the June sun. They'd have plenty of tomatoes to eat themselves and to share with others if only the rain would keep on coming.

"Steven," she called from the edge of the garden, "let's go stake off the area where I want the first apples to be planted. There are seeds in every apple core so that's bound to be the way to get them started."

Steven wiped his hot face, leaned on his hoe and replied, "Miss Jamie, we ain't got no apples to plant yet. I done asked ever'body I know to pass the word on dat we want all the cores of any apples, but most of 'em say dere ain't no apples to git cores from yet. And if'n dere was, folks would be eatin' dem cores too. We got to wait, Miss Jamie. Marse Frank McKay done tol' me a long time ago dat dere is some things a body can hurry and some dat dey can't. Tryin' to start a orchard is one of dem things we can't. Keepin' de weeds outta these here tomatoes and the bugs off'n them taters is things we can. Besides, Mister Clay done tol' me to make sure you ain't out here soon as he was gone, so don't you be thinkin' like I is? What I's thinkin' is dat we both best watch out for what he says."

She was astounded at his impertinence and started to tell him so in sharp words, but then she remembered that he was his own man now. She didn't own him and that, so far, he was working here for nothing but room and board. She stood there, not knowing quite what she should do with him or with herself.

Steven went back to hoeing, and she walked slowly back to the house. She wished she had one of the Waverly novels she'd always heard about, but she didn't. Even if they'd had them, they would have been trashed by those miserable Yankees. She could go to their garden that was closer to the house and pick some more green peas, but she felt sure that Rhody had already done that.

She felt useless and didn't like it a bit. There was so much that needed to be done in the house itself, and here she sat. Every piece of furniture needed heavy sanding and refinishing, but Clay had given a firm "no" when she had mentioned starting on that.

There was such a nice breeze that she sat on the side porch

steps, flipping her long hair off her neck to let the breeze cool her. She was letting her hair swing loose as Clay liked, not even tying it back with one of the few ratty ribbons she had left. Oh, would the time ever come when buying a hair ribbon was not next-to-impossible? Her beautiful hair and her eyes were the only things about her that still looked as they once had. She could still be proud of them even if her figure were gone. If only that terrible war had never come, if Pa and Mammy Rose were still here and… Then she remembered that it was old age and not the war that had taken her treasured Mammy Rose. Still, there sure were enough things that could be blamed on the war that it didn't matter if she included some that couldn't.

Finally, she grew tired of sitting there in the sun and wishing for the shade trees that had cooled her yard and porch before the Yankees had built their fires. She got up, went in and up the stairs to her room. The breeze was blowing the almost-ruined curtains that still hung there. She slumped on the bed, and in moments she was asleep.

"Hey, Jamie," she heard from somewhere below. Jamie sprang up from the bed, feeling somehow guilty. "I'm up here," she called back and headed for the stairs.

Clay was standing in the hallway with a big smile on his face. When she reached him, he grabbed her in his arms and swung her around. "Guess what?" he chortled. "We now have a carriage."

"A carriage?" she cried as soon as her feet were back on the floor. "What are we going to do with a carriage? Which of us is going to pull it?"

"Neither," he said with a big laugh. "Actually it's only half a carriage, but we also have half a horse."

"Which half?" she cut in to say. "And who owns the other half?"

"Will you please hush with the silly questions and let me tell you?" he said, laughing again and pulling her with him on into the sitting room. "Also let me get off my feet. I feel like I might have been in one of Stonewall's long marches. It's been a great day, but I'm bushed."

He sat them both down on the settee, wiggling as always to

try to find a comfortable spot on the hard seat. "The floor would be about as soft as this thing."

"If you think so," she said with a smile, "but I think I'll stay here. Maybe you've been able to put more meat on your bones than I have on mine. We could move into the parlor, if you want to. The divan there is beaten-up, but I guess it is softer."

"Nope, my backside's bones might as well get used to this. And I can't wait to tell you what happened. You're right. We don't have a horse, but Brad's got one."

"Brad's got a horse?" she cried, astounded. "Where on earth did he get it? It must have cost the world."

"No, it did not. It was the most amazing thing you ever saw and such a bargain that there was no way we could resist. That tightwad sister of mine even turned loose of enough of the twenty-five dollars Father sent her. She paid for the horse."

"Twenty-five?" she asked. "Why didn't he give her fifty like he did you?"

Clay stopped wiggling and turned to look at her as though she had said something utterly ridiculous. "She's a girl," he said, obviously thinking that explained it all.

"Oh, of course. That's right," she said. "Why in the world didn't I think of that?" Clay didn't notice her sarcasm, so she ended with, "Well, are you and your sister both now as flat-broke as I am?"

He laughed and gave her a quick kiss. "You can bet your life we're not. I only paid four dollars for the carriage, and Brad had to shell out only five for the horse. They're both great too."

"You're kidding," she said. "My pa got more than that for his mules back when he had them. I sure wish we had some of them now," she ended wistfully.

"Oh, no, you don't," Clay said definitely. Then he added, "Well, maybe you do, but if he'd tried to keep them, you know where they'd have ended up—with the Yankees—and your father wouldn't have gotten a cent for them. The horse Brad got and, as I might add, is sharing with us doesn't look like a work horse. It's a beauty."

"Sharing with us? So that's how we use the carriage? Brad's horse?"

"Of course." He jumped up and rubbed his rear. "Don't we at least have some pillows?" he grumbled, sitting back down before she had a chance to answer. "Brad and I actually own a horse and carriage together so we share them both. The way it all happened was the doggondest thing we ever saw. A fellow up a few miles north of town actually found the carriage by the side of the road a few days after the end of the war. He couldn't understand what it was doing there, for he knew if there'd been a carriage like that around when the Yankees were here, they'd have at least wrecked it. Or taken it with them."

Jamie began to get a strange feeling in the pit of her stomach, but she just looked at him and said nothing.

Clay went on enthusiastically, "The fellow—Peterson was his name—said he had the dickens of a time pulling it off the road onto his property. He figured the owner had gotten into some kind of trouble and would come back for it. He had hoped he'd get some kind of tip for taking care of it. He had no need of it himself since he no longer had a horse or even a mule, but he sure had a need for some U.S. dollars. He said he hated to sell something that didn't belong to him, but, if the fellow who owned it had wanted it, he felt sure he'd have been back for it before then. So finders, keepers!"

"How," Jamie asked in a weak voice that she hoped Clay wouldn't notice, "did you know about all that?"

"Just plain good luck," he said emphatically. "It all came from Joe Woodley, a boy who Brad had gone to medical school with. Joe's grandmother lives on the side of the mountain on further up the road. The old lady doesn't want to come into town with them, and it's a good thing she doesn't because their house is so battered it hardly stands. Also, it's been used as a stable. They can barely stand the smell themselves, but they're hoping for some government assistance sooner or later. In the meantime, Joe's mother worries about her own mother miles away and by herself, so she sends Joe up there to check on her every week.

Several weeks ago, he had come on a terrible accident." Then he hesitated and asked, "But don't you know all about that? Brad said he told you about it when he and Pris were out here a few days after the war ended."

The terrible feeling that was coming over her did not diminish. "Yes, he did and it sounded really bad. He said the injured man had been stripped of his clothes and was almost dead, but somebody had taken him in."

"Yeah, that's right. But all that happened before Joe came along. As Brad told you, some chap and his horse had apparently tried to take a short cut over a mountain trail, and the horse had slipped on some loose rocks. There was evidence of a rock fall around them where they ended up. The horse had gotten two broken legs and goodness-only-knows what else. The poor thing was screaming pitifully, which is why the fellow who had come along the pike had heard it. He set off down the little side road to investigate. Obviously, he had not been the first person to find the results of the accident, for the injured man had already been stripped of everything he'd been wearing except his drawers. Fortunately, the first finder'd had the decency to leave them on him.

"The second one who'd heard the horse's cries and came to investigate was the one who was a good Samaritan, for he had gone to a house that he could see farther on the side road to try to get some help. The old couple who lived there both came, and when they saw how terribly the man was injured, they took him home with them to try to save him. The woman said he reminded her of the grandson they had lost in the war, and they just couldn't let him lie there by himself to die. How they managed to get him to their cabin is more than I know, but somehow they did."

Jamie was feeling so much that she didn't dare speak, but her silent mind was screaming, *Curt! It was Curt!*

Clay went on in the same enthusiastic way, "After they got the man in, the good Samaritan came back to see what he could do about that poor, suffering horse. He had no gun himself so he went back out on the pike, hoping somebody would come along with one. That's when Joe found him, and fortunately he did have his gun. Said he felt like it was still wise to carry it with returning soldiers of both sides wandering around."

*Curt! Oh, dear God, it had to have been Curt.* Good, trusting Curt, who was hurrying home with his broken heart to the family he knew was waiting. She had caused his accident. She knew it as surely as if she had plotted and carried out the whole thing herself. But she couldn't have helped doing what she had done, she cried inwardly. She couldn't.

Her mind was racing now. Should she tell Clay about Dave and his search for his brother? And if she did, would she ruin everything between them? She didn't know. *She didn't know!* But she did know that it would ruin Clay's excited happiness if he knew who undoubtedly had owned the carriage and horse they were so pleased to have. Every time they used either, it would be in his mind. And in hers. Oh, yes, how it would be in hers!

She had to think.

"But what has all that to do with Brad's horse?" she managed to ask.

"That too was sheer luck that came about because of good ol' Joe." In his eagerness to tell her, he was not noticing anything unusual about Jamie. "Joe, on his weekly trip, saw a man standing out by the road with a horse. He said he stopped and called out, 'Looks like you've got a mighty good horse there. How'd you manage to keep him with our enemies running up and down the pike?' Then he wondered if he'd made a mistake. The man might have been a Union-lover and gotten preferential treatment."

"Was he a Union-lover?" she asked, as Clay stopped for a few seconds to run his tongue over his dry lips.

"No, he sure wasn't, as he let Joe know very definitely. Said he'd just found the horse. He'd seen it running loose many times but had never been able to catch it before. That day, he'd managed to grab and hold onto a torn tether that the horse had been wearing all the time. He figured somebody had been taking him along as he rode another horse, and this one had somehow managed to get away. He told Joe he was going to keep it till whoever owned it came along and would hopefully pay him for keeping it or even sell it himself if anybody came along who had some Federal money. He sure wasn't letting it go for any more useless money like he already had."

When he held up for a moment, Jamie felt she had to say something, but it wasn't easy to get the words out with the huge lump that seemed lodged in her chest. "So he told the man about Brad?"

"Well, not at that time. He didn't know Brad could buy anything any more than he could. But he had run into Brad just a few minutes before I caught up with them. He was bringing Brad up-to-date on what he had told him weeks before about the accident. Thought Brad would be interested. We both were and talked Joe into taking us up to where the carriage and then the horse would be found. Thanks to my father, we were able to buy them both. To even things up with Brad and me, I bought some feed for the horse."

Clay kept looking at her, so she was afraid her concern must be showing. Clay gave her a quick kiss and said, "I know, honey. It upsets that tender heart of yours to hear that we have gained by somebody else's loss, but how would it have helped anybody for us to refuse such bargains as we had found?"

"No, of course, it wouldn't have. It's…well, it's awfully nice for you and Brad. Is Pris excited?" What she really wanted to know was whether Pris had figured out all that she had. If so, Brad probably knew too, for she didn't think Pris would keep secrets from her husband as she herself was being forced to do. That caused another pain that she didn't know anything she could do about. "Did the folks who took in the injured man ever find out who he was? "she managed to get out. "Or did Joe know about that?"

Clay got up to rub his seat again, then sat back down and stretched his legs out before him. "Don't think so. When out of curiosity and concern for the old couple, he had gone up earlier to their house to see how they were doing with the injured fellow, they told him they had done the best they could for about a week.

They could tell that the man had a head injury because he could hardly talk at all. In falling, the horse had apparently kicked him in the head, and they had never been able to get but one word out of him. That was his name."

"They did? And what was it?" Jamie jumped in to ask with nervous haste before she could stop herself.

Clay shook his head. "Joe didn't know. He said that the old couple told him that they thought the poor guy was trying to do that, but they had no way of knowing for sure. He kept saying something that sounded like James, but he could never tell them if it were his first or last name. They thought it must have been his first since they didn't know any family by the name of James around here. Of course, he didn't have to have come from here. They told Joe that he didn't even say his name after the first few days, so they thought that meant he was getting worse. They soon knew that he was too seriously hurt for them to handle, so they got in touch with the parents of a boy who had grown up nearby. He had become a doctor and worked in a hospital in Washington City, so when he came home to see his folks, they had him check the man. The young doctor worked at some kind of a government place, I think Joe said. Anyway, he got somebody to come get the poor fellow and take him there. I guess that's where he still is, unless he's died."

The pain around Jamie's heart became intense. Curt had been calling for her. Even in his terrible condition, he had been thinking of her. And all the time, she had been deliberately blocking him from her mind.

But she had only done what she had had to do, she argued silently with herself. Somehow, she felt that she had lost the argument but didn't understand why. Nor did she know what to do now, but she did know she had to do something. If only she had Pa or somebody to tell her what to do.

Clay got up again and said, "My throat is getting dry with all the walking and the talking. Give me a minute, and I'll go get a dipper of water. Be right back." He headed for the door.

Jamie sat there on the hard settee and felt as though a load of rocks might have fallen on her too. All she could think was, *No! Please, no.*

Clay came racing back in, grabbed her up into his arms again and kissed her as passionately as if he had just returned from a long trip. "Isn't all that one lucky coincidence after another?" he asked her.

"Yes, so many breaks." She hoped her voice sounded more natural to him that it did to her.

It must have, for he let her sit back down and kept standing himself, saying, "You'll be glad to know that I did manage to get that lard you wanted and some canned milk, so we'll have fried turtle and gravy. Rhody was in the kitchen when I went down for the drink, and I told her it was up on the hall bench. I didn't worry about what that stuff cost, for I think that things may be better soon. Some Federal men have been here going over the damage and the shortage of food. Other government men have been giving out free seeds, and that's how folks have been able to plant the things they have. We should have been in line to get some of those. These Yankees sure owe our town for what they did to it. Lots of what they did was for just meanness and totally unnecessary for the war effort."

Then he added, "I hope that turtle will stretch for two more people. Brad and Pris are going to come riding up in our new carriage in less than an hour, so I asked them to supper. How about that?"

"That's great," she said, getting up again herself. "I'd better go down and see what extra vegetables we can come up with."

Clay walked with her out into the hall, then headed for the stairs. "And I've got to go wash up. It may still be June but, with all that walking we did today, I'm feeling hot and bushed. Will you see if Steven can bring me up a pan of hot water? What's on the wash stand is bound to be cold."

As they came to the staircase, he held her back and asked, "Have you heard mention of anybody missing a horse or a carriage? I'd hate like the dickens to lose our bargains, but I don't want to be riding around in something that somebody else has a claim to."

That hit her hard, but she managed to ask, "How could I know anything about that? I haven't even been to church since the war ended, and the only people I've seen except Pris, Brad and you were all those folks who came to our wedding. If anything was said about it then, I sure didn't hear it. I did hear quite a bit about something else that I want to know about, but that can wait. Pris will know about that, I'm sure."

"Just thought I'd ask." He turned back from the stairs to give her a quick kiss. "Don't fuss over supper. They will be delighted if they can have some fried turtle. See you in a few minutes." He bounded up the stairs two treads at a time, looking far less tired than he professed to be.

*Happiness cures a lot of things*, she thought, wishing so much that she could share what she knew Clay was enjoying now, although the heaviness of her heart made her know she had no chance of doing that. Curt must be in a hospital in Washington City, but how could she even let Dave know? And why hadn't he found Curt there, anyway? Maybe she was wrong and it really wasn't Curt. But that thought vanished as soon as it came. It *was* Curt. It just had to be and she had to do something. But what? She had no idea where Dave had gone when he had left here. There was nothing she could do but pray for help and also pray that, whenever it came, it would not destroy her life as a Haynesworth.

# 11

When Jamie started up the stairs that night about ten o'clock, she wasn't at all sure she could make it. The evening had been such a strain that she felt as worn-out as if giant hands had grabbed her and wrung her out like a dishrag. She had been the only one who hadn't been feeling great, so she did her best to hide that she was feeling almost as out of touch with current events as she had been before Clay had come home.

The McLaurines had come tooling out in the elegant carriage with Brad driving and Pris ensconced in the back seat. He had jumped down and opened the door for his wife with a flourish while Jamie and Clay had stood on the porch and applauded.

Steven had come running around the house to take the horse, just like in the old days when they had had a far-less-elegant conveyance themselves. By the time he reached it, Clay had brought Jamie down the steps to inspect their wonderful bargain, and the scrawny colored man had almost skidded to a stop in the dirt to look at Jamie.

"Miss Jamie," he said, looking from the carriage to her, "ain't dat the same…"

"No, Steven," she interrupted as quickly as she could. She knew she could not let him finish what he was about to say, "it's not. I'm sure Mrs. Haynesworth's carriage is still wherever she took it, unless the Yankees got it. It's certainly nowhere around here."

Clay had looked at her and asked, "How do you know that?"

"Well, isn't that right?" she had asked, a bit flustered and trying hard not to show it. "You'd recognize it if it had been one of your family's, wouldn't you? If not you, then certainly Pris would. And this one is far better than the one Pa had gotten for us."

She thought Steven caught on, for he just scratched his wooly head and said, "Sho' looks like dem fine carriages dat used to be 'round here."

"Well, it's ours now, Steven," Clay told him.

"And ours," Pris put in proudly.

Clay laughed. "Well, yes, just like that horse is ours too. But we don't have to stand here and admire them any more. Let's go on in the house. Rhody has probably gotten that turtle fried and waiting for us. My mouth is watering at just the thought of it. I hope she's right about its tasting like fried chicken. If it does, then the gravy should be good too."

"I remember we had turtle one time," Brad had chipped in as they started for the steps. "I was kind of leery about tasting it, but Mama made me. As I recall, it was pretty good." He turned back on the steps and said to the man standing at the horse's head. "Will you see to the horse, please, Steven? I expect he'd like a drink of water."

"Yes'suh. I sho' will. Course, we ain't got no real place to keep it since we ain't got no stable no more. Ain't even got a tree left that I could tie him to."

"Just give him some water and see he doesn't run off while we're eating. It won't be long."

The four of them had stopped on the porch to look back at him. "That's right," Clay said. "It will be going back with my sister and her husband. Their stall has been pretty much torn down, but there is at least the space and a hitching post. He and the carriage will stay there till we can get Crestview built again."

At that, Jamie had given him a hard look that he didn't see, but she had said nothing. Why in the world couldn't Clay see that they had to get Fairdale fixed up before giving even a thought to his old home?

"We will be wanting to take Miss Jamie for a ride after we have supper, though, so just give him some water as Mr. Brad suggested and we'll let you know when we're ready to go." The four of them turned to go in the house.

"This all seems so right, doesn't it?" Pris had said to Jamie as they went into the hall. "To ride up to someone's house in a really nice carriage and go in for supper."

"Yes, it does in a way. But I'd bet the supper you were going in to back then was never fried turtle," Jamie replied, wondering nervously if Pris could be as clueless as she appeared. "I'm so glad that Steven and Rhody don't seem to mind that we treat them as though nothing had happened."

"What are you talking about?" Pris had stopped with the men right behind her. "You're doing them a favor. Surely they know that. Where else could they go?"

Jamie hadn't answered for she had no idea where the colored people from all over the South were going. It seemed like a massive problem to her but, fortunately, not hers to solve. She already had more to worry about than she could handle. The worry about Curt was making her feel almost as sick as she had been the day she had made him leave. But saying nothing, she just led them on into the dining room.

The turtle had been delicious, they all agreed, but Jamie had to take their word for it. She was feeling so guilty and concerned that she could hardly swallow. After they had eaten every bite of the same vegetables Rhody always prepared, Jamie ran down to the kitchen to make sure there was enough turtle and gravy left for the two down there and, hopefully, a piece they could send to Mrs. Mac. There had been. It had been a big turtle.

After that, they went out for a ride with Steven driving and the four of them in the carriage. The ride had not been as pleasant as they had hoped, for the pike was nearly unusable and they had to ride a lot of the time rather far out beside it. Any repair work being done had not yet reached there.

Afterwards the McLaurines had headed for home. Jamie had dragged herself up the porch steps, relieved (at least, she had thought she was) that Pris had not figured out a thing. Of course, there was no real reason for her to recognize the carriage. She had seen what she had thought was Curt driving fast out of town but had apparently had paid no attention to what he had been driving.

All of that left Jamie dragging herself slowly up the stairs with Clay behind her, saying, "What a pleasant night!" He moved up and put his arm around her. "But you seemed awfully tired. You didn't have any trouble today while I was gone, did you? No more falls?"

"No," she assured him as she let her weary body slump against him. "You all were so excited about your good fortune that I didn't get a chance to say much." *Another truth that wasn't necessarily the* whole *truth*, she thought regretfully.

Later in bed and after Clay had fallen asleep, her mind was still twisting and turning so much that she had little hope of sleeping herself. She had hardly been able to bear the thought that Curt had somehow managed to get this fine carriage to take her away with him, and now she was riding in it as Clay's wife while Curt was lying, unknown and unloved, in some strange hospital. *Oh, Curt, Curt!* She was so sorry, but knew she could not have done anything other than what she had. Neither would she let her thoughts go to the many times she had run into his arms and thought she loved him. To even remember that now would be sinful…she knew it would…but it would be a worse sin to let him lie in that hospital and not try to help him.

Why had Dave not found him anyway when he had been in Washington City searching? Of course, he had not been looking for a nameless person and actually not for a single one either. But what could she do?

What could she do?

She had no idea where Dave had gone. Had there still been a good inn around here, she knew he wouldn't be there. He wouldn't have wanted to stay anywhere around her. So, he was gone. Should she try to write his parents? But how could she? She didn't know their address, and, even if she did, she had no money for postage. Clay did still have a little, but she sure couldn't tell him to whom she was writing…or why. That she didn't dare do.

Sometime before morning, she remembered the aunt out west of town that Curt had wanted her to meet. Maybe she could help. But how on earth could she contact her?

How could she do anything?

She didn't know, but she did know that she couldn't be lying here still awake when morning came. She finally slept.

"You don't look well," Clay told her the next morning. "Anything wrong?"

"Not really," she told him as they were drinking the last of the coffee he had brought. "I just feel worn-out. Maybe I would feel better if I started sanding some of the furniture. I noticed how bad the dining-room table looked last night. If you could get me something good to sand with, I could at least make a start."

"Yeah," he said sarcastically. "You're unusually tired, so I'd better get you something with which to work."

"Well, you could help me," she said with a little laugh.

He gave her a rather disdainful look. "Honey, forget that. If I have to work on our honeymoon, it should be something that would bring us in some money, as, for instance, my office. I plan to replace this table anyway. We need one more like the one that used to be in Crestview."

"Clay," she protested. "Our dining room couldn't begin to take a table like that. We had to have two seatings when the Yankees were all here, and there were only twelve of them. Of course, it does seat eight rather nicely and ten in a pinch, but Pris said the Crestview table sat eighteen when it was fully extended."

"Well, yes, it did. And that's what I'll have again."

"Do you mean 'you' will or do you mean 'we'?" she asked in a very small voice.

Clay laughed and reached over to give her a kiss. "Of course, I meant to say 'we.' Never again an 'I' around here. It's you and me together for always."

She wasn't going to let little things bother her, she told herself, even though his attitude did annoy her just a bit. *It's because I'm so tired,* she told herself. She'd try something else, "Well, what would you think if I went back to bed for a while? I didn't sleep well last night. Too much excitement and our first guests, even though it wasn't much of a supper."

"What are you talking about?" he said, chuckling. "We had a great supper. How many folks get to have a specialty like fried

90

turtle? And, of course, I don't mind if you go back to bed awhile. You need all the rest you can get. I'll walk into town again and make some notes about what I need to do about my office."

She sank thankfully back in bed again, but, instead of sleeping as she had hoped, her mind was still darting here and there, seeking a way she could help. But she had not found it when she finally fell into a deep sleep.

# 12

Strange as it might seem, the solution to her terrible problem seemed to be in her mind as she finally got up. She had no idea how long she had slept, but she knew she had to find a sheet of paper and an ink pen. That could be a real problem unless she could find paper in what Clay had brought with him. Surely he had brought something on which to write his parents or his grandparents. She felt guilty as she rumbled through his things but made a point of not checking anything but that which she sought. Sure enough, there was a lined paper pad. She tore off a sheet and went across the hall to look through her pa's room to see if one of his pens and the ink he always had could somehow still be there. His room had been the least-trashed by the Yankees. Praise the Lord, she found what she was looking for pushed back in the corner of the bottom drawer of his bureau. Maybe the Yankees had seen that Pa had very little for them to take and had more or less passed it up, thinking that burning would take care of whatever was there. Her thanks to that one Yankee who had saved her house filled her quivering mind again.

Now she went down to the dining room, sat down at the table and began to write. As she wrote, she was listening intently for the sound of Clay's footsteps on the porch or hall. When she had finished writing, she folded the paper and put the name of the person she was sending it to on the outside. She had no envelope to put it in but decided she wouldn't worry about that. Then she tucked what she had written into the waistband of her skirt and went down to the kitchen to ask Rhody if Mr. Clay had been in for dinner.

"No, ma'am, he sho' ain't. I had some vegetables all hot and ready for you both, but I ain't seen hide nor hair of nobody till now. You wantin' sumpthin' to eat?"

"Not right now. Do you know where Steven is?"

"Where he always is. Seems like he wants to hoe de whole county. You want me to call him?"

"No thanks. I'll go out and talk to him. Do you know where he keeps that old burlap bag of his?"

"I think dat thing be right inside his do'. He seems to think he can't git along widout it."

"Would you get it for me, please?" Jamie asked.

"Sho' I will, Miss Jamie." The woman wiped her hands, hung up the dish towel she had been using and hurried into the other part of the basement. She was back in a very few moments. "Here de dirty old thing is. I keep thinkin' we ort to wash it, but Steven, he says he ain't never heard of washin' a burlap sack."

Jamie took it with a smile and thanked her. She left by the outside door of the kitchen and went off across the weeds and dirt. In a few moments, she found Steven down on his knees with some kind of a can in his hands, knocking the potato bugs into it from the plants. She knew he would once have had some kind of oil in the can to kill the bugs, but when had they ever had a drop of oil? She wondered how he would kill them now but thought gratefully that was not her problem.

"Steven," she called, waving the sack at him, "can you come a minute, please?"

He came hustling over to her. "Wonder where all dem tater bugs come from and how dey knows a tater from a bean plant?" he said as he reached her. "Dem little critters know which of dem plants is taters, jus' like somebody tells 'em. Dere ain't no cucumber bugs or carrot bugs. Wonder why dat is."

Jamie laughed. "I don't know, Steven. I just know that potato plants always have them. Are you about finished?"

"No' ma'am, I sho' ain't, but dem bugs will still be dere after I done done what you is wantin' of ol' Steven."

She gave a sigh and wished for a place to sit. There wasn't one except the ground, and she didn't want to sit there. So she just handed him the burlap bag and said, "Would this be big enough to put a turtle in, if you should catch another one?"

He gave one of his snaggle-toothed grins. "Reckon it would.

Dat be what I just had de one we had last night in. It sho' was good, warn't it?"

"Yes, it was. I know it's not easy to find another one right away, but I was wondering if you would take this sack and follow up the creek a way. I don't know for sure, but I expect it comes out somewhere near that little road that heads west out of Winchester."

"Yes, ma'am, it do. Do you think dere be another turtle up dat way? How you know sumpin' like dat, if'n you don't mind ol' Steven askin'."

She gave another nervous little laugh. "I have no idea about that, but I want you to take this bag with you, and if anybody wants to knows what you are doing, you can be truthful and say that we liked that turtle so much, we're hoping you can find another one. Do you understand that?"

He scratched his head and thought for a moment before saying, "Waal, I guess I does. Is dat all?"

"No, it isn't all." She reached a hand into the waistband of her old skirt and pulled out the folded paper. She handed it to him and said, "While you're out looking for a turtle, you can deliver this for me."

He reached out a grubby hand and took it. "I ain't knowin' whar to take it," he said dubiously.

"I know you don't, but I'll tell you. There's a woman who lives three or four miles up that road, a woman with a big apple farm. You know where it is?"

"No, ma'am, I sho don't. What be her name?"

"I can't tell you that. Leave the creek when you think you'll come out about right on that road and head west. You can stop and ask someone along the way, if you need to."

He scratched his fuzzy head again with a dirty finger that Jamie thought shouldn't get anywhere near his hair, but she said nothing. "How I gonna ask somebody where de woman live if'n I ain't knowin' her name?" he asked after a moment.

"Just ask for the woman who has a heap of apple trees. I think they'll know who you mean. Of course, if you see a house with an unusual amount of apple trees around it, you might find it by yourself. Just go to the door, hand her this and ask if the name on it is hers."

"And if I does find her, whut I do den?"

"You give her that letter. Tell her you'll wait if there's an answer. If there isn't, just come on back home the best short cut you know. Just carry the burlap bag with you, and if you don't see anything you want to put in it, bring it on back home and forget about the whole thing."

He looked at her for a long moment, and Jamie thought she could almost see the wheels turning in his head. "You got all that?" she asked.

"Yes, ma'am. And I 'spects I'd better say nuthin' 'bout dat letter to nobody."

She gave a big sigh of relief. He understood. "Yes, that would be best. Do you want to go wash your hands before you go?"

"No, ma'am. I'll wash dem in de crick as I go. But first I got to find a rock I can smash dese bugs on. Don't want to leave dem so's dey can git back on dem tater plants."

"Yes, that's a good idea. I'll see you when you get back, hopefully, with a nice big turtle like we had last night. But if you don't, you needn't worry about it. We still have vegetables, and I expect there was enough flour for Rhody to have made some more biscuits. I sure do hope so."

"Yas'm. I does too. Dis is going to take me quite a spell of time. Dat all right?"

"Of course, it is. I'm sorry to ask you to walk so far but…"

"Dat all right. I likes walkin' in de woods. Ain't no tellin' what I might find. Lookin' fer turtles is right nice."

"I'm glad you enjoy it," she said. "If you find anything else, report that only to me." She turned and walked back to the house.

If she had ever felt worse about anything she had done, she couldn't remember when it was. Trying to conspire strange doings with a servant to do something she didn't want her husband to know about. How much lower could any woman get than that? But how else could she handle it without hurting her new husband terribly? If there could be another way, she didn't know what it was. But maybe she didn't know anything at all. She sure felt that her mind was as muddled as it had been before Curt had come and gone.

*Curt!* She had to wipe any thought of him from her mind again. Wipe him as completely as she had done before. She had done the best she could in writing his aunt. She hadn't asked him to love her in the first place and.... Again her mind went to the night she had told him about being born a woods colt. He had held her, just held her until…

*No!* she cried again to herself, lowering her head and shoulders and running as though she were escaping from something that might be after her.

Rhody was standing at the kitchen door as she burst in. "You ain't run into no nest of bees, has you?" she asked when Jamie rushed in. "You ain't got no stings, has you?"

"No," Jamie told her, "I'm fine. I think if you've got any vegetables still warm, I'd like a plate of them to take with me up to my room." She hesitated, changed "my" to "our" room and ended, "I don't seem to be feeling as well as I might, so I think I'll eat up there."

Reaching her room with the barely-warm vegetables, she sank down into the rocker and, hardly knowing what she was doing, ate the vegetables. If they had any taste at all, she didn't know it. The words she had written to Curt's aunt kept running over in her head as though they were still there for her to read:

*Dear Mrs. Darby,*

*I was Jamie Montgomery when I knew your nephew, Curt. He was wondrously kind to me during the war, and I will never forget him for that.*

*Your other nephew, David, came by my house almost a week ago, looking for Curt. At that time, I had no knowledge of his whereabouts, but I have since learned something that I feel sure explains his disappearance. It seems that he was injured on his way home. The first person to find him took all his clothes except his underpants and left him. A kind couple nearby took him in and got him to some kind of government hospital in Washington City. I don't know the name of the hospital, and I expect he is there as a nameless person. Despite that, I feel sure there is some way that he could be found.*

*I hope this will be of help to you and your family. I have since gotten married and would prefer that you not contact me about this since I want to do right by my new husband.*

It was as if the words were printed on her mind. Had she said the right things to Curt's Aunt Kate? Would she even pay any attention to a message delivered to her in the way this was? Could she trust Steven never to say anything about the letter he had delivered for her? Or could he have even been able to find Mrs. Darby with the sort of instructions she had given him?

She just didn't know.

She put the empty plate down on the floor, went to the bed and crawled back in. That was where Clay found her when he returned home after sundown.

# 13

"What on earth are you doing in bed now?" Clay demanded as he rushed into the room and saw her curled up there. "Have you been there the whole day?"

She almost laughed at the question but knew that would seem weird to him. Maybe even a little weird to her. "No," she replied, swinging her feet over to the floor and standing up, "I've been feeling a little bit like I did after the war ended, when everything seemed so bad. I guess I'm just a little down in the dumps."

"Depressed while on a honeymoon? I never heard of such a thing." He grabbed her to him and kissed her. Then, still holding her, he looked down at her and added, "And especially when you're married to the finest, best-looking fellow in the whole town, what do you have to be down in the dumps about?"

She did laugh then and said, "Yes, I am on my honeymoon and delighted to be." Then she added, "Maybe it depressed me to have my new husband leave me not long after breakfast, not come home for dinner and be late for supper. Wouldn't you be depressed about all that?"

He turned her loose but followed her as she went over and sank down in the rocker. "You really mean that, don't you? I'm sorry, honey. I would have taken you with me if I hadn't known that you need rest so much. I was obviously right about that since you've stayed in bed. I'm late because I got so involved in planning what I'm going to do to my office. The time just got away from me before I realized it. Folks kept stopping by to visit too. I'm sorry, my love. Please forgive me. Have you been worried about me?"

"Not exactly," she admitted. "I was busy for a while. I even sent Steven up the creek to see if he could find us another turtle. That one last night was pretty good, wasn't it?"

"Sure was, but I don't know that I want to go on a diet of turtle every day," he said with a chuckle, as he went to the bureau to get a fresh handkerchief. "Can't Steven rustle up a rabbit or a squirrel? They would be good. Now, would you like to go back to bed for a while?" he asked with a grin and a glance at the bed that said more than his words.

"Well, to tell the truth, if we want any supper, we'd better get ourselves down the stairs before everything is completely cold. After all the time I've spent in bed today, I can't say that bed is exactly where I want to be again right now. And I kind of doubt that you do either."

"Oh, all right. Give me a kiss and we'll go relax over some warmed-over, tasteless vegetables."

They did as she requested and left the room with their arms around each other. "Rhody!" Clay called as they stood in the hallway at the top of the stairs on down to the kitchen, "You down there?"

She came to the bottom of the steps and looked up. "Yes'suh. Me and Steven, we's just been waitin' to see if you and Miss Jamie is wantin' some supper."

"You got anything good?" he called back.

"Well, it tasted good to me and Steven. He said he ain't never had no better biscuits. And de left over turtle gravy dat I stretched wid a little more of dat canned milk ain't too bad neither. Is you wantin' me to fix plates and bring them up to y'all?"

"That would be great. We got any more coffee?"

"No'suh. Ain't you rememberin' dat you done drinked de last of dat dis mornin'?"

"Oh, that's right. Well, it's too hot for coffee anyhow. I sure wish we had ice in the ice house—that is, I would if we still had an ice house. I guess we'll have to make do with some fresh water from the spring. Has Steven brought in any lately?"

"Yas'suh, ol' Steven sho' has," came Steven's voice as he appeared beside Rhody at the bottom of the steps. "We is gonna bring up some with yo' vittles just as quick as we can make sure dey is warm."

"Sounds good to us," Clay said approvingly. "We'll be at the table waiting when you get up here." He took Jamie by the hand

and led her over to the scratched table that worried her so much and apparently him, not at all.

When they were seated, Jamie asked, "Who did you say came by your office space today?"

"I haven't said yet, but several folks I went to school with came in. Actually, almost everybody who walked down the street welcomed me back to town. Brad and Pris spent a lot of time there. They both have pretty good ideas as to how I should rebuild it. Pris leans toward making it almost like Father had it, but Brad has other ideas."

""How'd you like their suggestions?" Jamie asked.

"Well, to tell the truth, I think I prefer Brad's to Pris', but I'm going to have to be careful how I say that. Pris can be touchy. And Betsy even had some good thoughts on the secretary's space."

"Betsy?" Jamie cried and looked at him in consternation. "Do you mean she was in on your planning session?"

He moved his chair a little closer and reached over to give her a quick kiss. "Now don't worry about that. She was just trying to help."

"Help, my eye!" she scoffed and yanked herself away from him. "She just wants to be around you. She even tried to hold onto you for a while at our wedding."

"She did not," he protested with a laugh. "She's been a friend for all my life. She knows that's all she'll ever be. Well, that and maybe my secretary. She sure would like a job doing that when I open my law office."

"Your secretary?" She would have jumped up from the table, but Clay reached out and held her down. "Over my dead body!" she ended.

"I certainly hope not," he said, still chuckling. "I put her off anyway. Didn't really give her any hope of getting the job."

"I should hope not!" she exclaimed hotly, as Rhody and Steven came in carrying their warmed-over supper and glasses of water.

"Sho' wish you could have had dem biscuits when dey first

100

come outta' de oven. Dey was purty good den," the woman said, putting a cracked plate with food in front of each of them. "And I ain't used dem two new plates 'cause I didn't want dem to git cracks like dese here ones."

"That's good," Jamie started, but Clay cut in.

"Well, save them no more, Rhody. Use them. I don't like my food served on anything but decent china. We'll use these tonight, but I don't want to see these plates again."

Jamie started to protest but quickly closed her lips. She gave a quick nod and a smile to Rhody and started eating. "Hmmm, Steven is right about this biscuit," she said almost before she had tasted the first bite. "Warmed-over or not, they're delicious."

Clay gave her a look that clearly said he questioned her taste, but he ate and said nothing more.

"Anything else, Miss Jamie?" Steven asked.

"No, thank you." She was dying to know if he had found Mrs. Darby and delivered her letter, but she couldn't think of any way to ask without upsetting Clay. She went on saying, "Mr. Clay was not too happy at the prospect of another turtle quite yet, so I guess it's just as well you didn't find one today."

"No ma'am, I sho' didn't. Dey is usually awful hard to find so I warn't too surprised. But I'd say it wuz a pretty walk jest de same. I sho' do like bein' out in de woods."

Her eyes flew to his face, but she asked nothing more. She felt great relief, though. Obviously, he meant her to know that he had found the woman to whom she had written. "That's good to hear, but I expect you both are tired and want to be settling down for the night. We'll see you tomorrow."

Clay said, "Hey, wait a minute. Aren't you forgetting these plates and glasses. You'll be coming back for them, won't you? We certainly can't leave dirty dishes here on the table overnight."

"Oh, for goodness sakes, Clay," Jamie said with a laugh before they could answer him. "I'll run them down and put them in the dish water on the stove when we're finished. You two go on and get some rest."

Rhody and Steven looked at each and then at Clay When he

said nothing, they looked at Jamie. "Good night," she told them firmly. They quickly skedaddled down the steps.

"Wow!" Clay said in a disparaging sort of way as he shook his head. "Do you ever need my mother here to give you some instruction on how a mistress handles her servants."

At that sort of criticism, Jamie felt quick tears spring into her eyes. "Well," she said, blinking them away as best she could, "maybe so. But how does anybody who is no longer a real mistress treat servants who are not servants in the way they used to be?"

"Aw, honey," Clay said, reaching for her again and holding her as close as he could with them sitting at the table. "I didn't mean to hurt your feelings, and it's not important anyway. I'll run our plates down to the kitchen myself and even wash them before I'd deliberately upset you. Actually, though, I'm a mite worried about you. I'm beginning to wonder if you might need a doctor to help you get over all the bad things that happened here during the war. It certainly wouldn't be surprising if you did, and I'm afraid I've been expecting you to get over all you've been through more quickly than I should. Just finish your supper and I'll get you upstairs to bed."

"I'm all right, Clay, really I am. I'm immeasurably better than I was before you came back to me. I don't need a doctor and wouldn't want to bother one even if I did. After what they did during the war and are probably still doing with some of the injured soldiers, they certainly wouldn't want people like me taking up their time."

"We'll have to think about that. And don't forget that we've still got at least one more day of our honeymoon. Pris wanted them to come out with the carriage and take us to church in the morning, but I told her 'no.'"

"You're so thoughtful," she said gracefully. "We haven't even decided which church we'll be attending, Kent Street Presbyterian or your Christ Episcopal."

"I'd think that was pretty well-decided when you married me," he said. "You're a Haynesworth now, and the

Haynesworths have always been Episcopalians. That's where Pris and Brad go and where they'll be raising Thomas." He stopped as he saw the look on her face and quickly said, "But, as you said, we can talk about that later."

A sense of guilt swept over her. Here she was keeping a terrible secret from her husband of not quite a week. He was doing everything he could to please her, even being willing to discuss giving up his church, and she was deceiving him all the time. But she was doing it to protect him from worry, pain or disappointment, certainly doing nothing that should harm her relationship with him.

*Was that the truth?* she wondered miserably, feeling her guilt growing to such proportions that it surely would exceed the guilt a normal person would feel had he committed murder. Certainly, more than Steven had felt for killing the man in order to save her. She knew he felt that what he had done had been right and, apparently, he didn't let it worry him. What she too was doing was bound to be right and the only way she could do it, so why couldn't she feel the same?

She let herself relax onto Clay's shoulder and said, "No, Clay. You're right. I am a Haynesworth and we are Episcopalians. I'll join your church just as quickly as I can. But not tomorrow, please. Let's spend the last day of our honeymoon here at home and hopefully together."

He put a hand under her chin and raised her face so he could look down into it. "That was a mighty quick decision. Are you sure? I don't want to pressure you, and you certainly don't have to make any ironclad decision tonight."

"Yes," she said decisively, "I'm sure. I may be wrong, but I don't think any particular denomination ever kept anybody out of Heaven that another would have gotten him in. I don't think the word 'denomination' is anywhere in the Bible, is it?"

"Beats me. I've never thought about it. As far as Father was concerned, there was only the Episcopal Church and that was that. I never once questioned it. But I guess I could become a Presbyterian, if I have to."

"You don't have to," she assured him. She pulled away and reached for her water glass, noticing that it had a big chip on the top. She wondered how long it would take for Clay to decide that it had to be thrown away. Then she decided she didn't really care.

Clay jumped up from the table and picked up their plates. "I may still think that this is Rhody's job, but, after the decision you just made to please me, I'll happily carry these dishes down to the kitchen."

She laughed and waved him on down.

# 14

Jamie and Clay did all they could to make the last day of their so-called honeymoon a good one. They slept late and found that an egg had just been laid by the hen for which Steven had swapped a day's work to some woman. Clay was suspicious of the woman for even having chickens. "Reckon we ought to eat a Yankee egg? Think it will contaminate us?" Clay joked, not knowing the pang his words gave her, as she thought of all the good Yankee food she had eaten, thanks to Curt Darby.

"We absolutely should eat it and hope for more of them," she told Clay. "Food has no politics, so I say we eat any food we can get."

"Even Republican food?" Clay persisted, but still kidding.

"Well, no. I wouldn't go that far, not after what you and those men at our wedding said. I'm favoring Democratic food from now on. Got any of that?"

"Not yet, but I will have," he said confidently.

She knew she had been quoting Curt when she told Clay that food had no politics and hoped her face had revealed nothing of what she had been thinking…and remembering. Jamie had felt a bit guilty for eating the egg, but it was for an entirely different reason. She wondered how long it had been since Steven had had one for breakfast or any other time.

For dinner they took whatever they could find down to the creek and sat on the rocks to eat it. It certainly couldn't have been considered a picnic, for it had none of the foods a picnic usually had, but they decided to call it that anyway. For Jamie that day was the best they'd had all week.

She guessed that was because she hadn't been almost overcome with worry about what she could do to help Curt. Since she had sent Steven to find the Darbys' aunt, she knew she had done all she could. Now she could only wait and try not to think about what Curt's family would think of her when Dave got back and gave them his report. Thank the good Lord she didn't still feel that terrible urgency to do something. She had already done what she could.

When Monday arrived, Jamie was determined to find some chance to talk to Steven. Surely Mrs. Darby had gotten in touch with her brother-in-law in Philadelphia and they would find Curt. She had no idea how many government hospitals there were in the Union capitol, but she knew they could check them all in less time than it had taken Dave to go over every town in two states. She would not let herself think the words that kept wanting to come...*if he were still alive.* Also, when the thought would come that he wouldn't be needing help at all if it hadn't been for her, she smashed it as quickly as Steven would kill a potato bug.

It was mid-afternoon when Clay said he believed he'd walk over to Crestview. He said he wanted to poke around to see if he could find where his mother had buried their family silver. Jamie begged off from going with him, saying she would check over their own garden, then rest a bit and would come over to help him look later. He gave her a resounding goodbye kiss and went jauntily off down the avenue with Steven's hoe.

When he was gone, Jamie ran out to find Steven. He was in the potato patch again and saw her coming. He put down his can and came across the rows to meet her. "Did you find Mrs..." She cut that off quickly and changed it to, "Did you find that apple farm I sent you to a couple of days ago?"

His grin widened. "I sho' did, Miss Jamie. Warn't no trouble a-tall. When I got off de crick and out on de road, I ain't gone far befo' a man came walkin' along with his ol' hound dog. I said, 'Mister, you know a place 'round here what's got a lot of apple trees?' He said, 'Ain't dat most ever'body?' I said dat I warn't knowin' 'bout dat, but I was lookin' fer a special one dat mought have more dan most. He said, 'You must be talkin' 'bout Mrs. and he said a name.' I tol' him I 'spect so, and he said her place warn't more'n a mile and a ha'f up de road."

"And you found her?" Jamie asked impatiently, bitterly regretting that he had learned the woman's name, but knowing she couldn't do a dratted thing about it. "Was she home and did you give her the letter?" she asked quickly.

"Yes, ma'am. She sho' was and I sho' did. She was as nice a lady as you could hope to find and…"

"What did she say?" Jamie cut in again to ask.

Steven looked around. "Reckon you ort to find a place to sit down? I sho' ain't wantin' you to pass out again like you done de other day."

"Steven," she said in a voice as hard as she could make it, "if you don't tell me what I want to know, you're going to be the one needing to sit down."

He actually chuckled. "Yes, ma'am. I's coming to dat. I tol' her I had sumpin' fer her but I warn't knowin' what it was 'cause I couldn't read. She took it and started readin'. In a few minutes, she axt me if what it said be right. I said I ain't got no way of knowin' what it say, but if Miss Jamie had writ it, I'd know fer a fact dat it would be de truf."

"Then what did she do?" prompted Jamie eagerly.

"She axt me did I want some lemonade, and I said dat sho' would be nice. She said fer me to sit down on de steps and she'd be right back. So for what I thought was awful long, I sat dere waitin'. Finally, she come out carryin' de lemonade, and it sho' was good."

Jamie felt like screaming, but this time she stayed quiet and waited. "She give me some money and said it be good. Den she says does I know whar de place to send dem wireless things is. I said, 'Yes, ma'am. I know dat.' She said she done wrote down what she wanted to send and de money to pay for it. She said she knowed how much it cost, and dat she had added a little mo' fer me comin' out and all dat. She says fer me to go in dat place and give de man what she'd wrote. He'd give me what she meant me to have. So dat's what I done. I was wishin' I could tell you, but I figured dat Mr. Clay ain't wantin' no stuff goin' on 'bout de major."

"You figured right. I haven't done anything wrong…" She stopped, wondering why she had to explain anything to this servant. Then she remembered what that servant had done for her, and she went on, "You know what the major did for me all during the war. I guess you know that I wanted to repay him by going away and marrying him. But I just couldn't do it."

"Yes'm. I knows."

"I hope you do. But the major had an accident that awful morning after he left Fairdale. It hurt his head so he couldn't tell anybody who he was. You remember the man who looked a lot like the major who came the day when I was marrying Mr. Clay?"

"I sho' does."

"That man is the major's brother and had been looking for him for several weeks. I accidentally found out that the major is in a government hospital in Washington City, and I didn't know how to let his family know except by writing that woman who is his aunt. I didn't have anything except Confederate money myself, and they wouldn't let me pay for a wireless message with that. I couldn't think of any way to notify his family of his whereabouts except by having you take her the message I wrote. The major is a real fine man even if he is a Yankee, and I'm awfully glad to help him. I just don't want to hurt Mr. Clay by doing it."

"I ain't sayin' nuthin' to nobody. I ain't even tol' Rhody 'cause dat seemed like it be right to me."

"You're a good man, Steven," she told him sincerely. "You have certainly kept your word to my pa about taking care of me. I couldn't even begin to tell you how grateful I am."

"You ain't needin' to be sayin' dat, Miss Jamie. Ain't yo' pa been good to me, and ain't you givin' me and Rhody a place to live and work? We both a-thankin' you and anythin' more I can do, you jes' tell me. And look what dat lady give me. I ain't never had nothing like dat befo'. You reckon it be much?"

He dug his dirty hand into his even-dirtier loose overalls and pulled out a silver dollar. "I ain't got no idee how much it be."

Jamie looked at what Steven held in surprise and then looked at him. "It's a silver dollar. I haven't been in a place to buy anything in a long time so I don't know what it will buy. What did you have in mind?"

"I was thinkin' 'bout some fishin' stuff. Den when I had time to walk over to de river, I could catch us some fish."

She gave him a big smile. "That's a very nice and very generous thought. Why don't you see what Mr. Clay thinks about it?"

He looked at her and scratched his head. "What I gonna say when he axes me where I got dat dollar when I ain't never had one befo'?"

"I hadn't thought of that," she said, wondering why she hadn't. "But you can just tell him the truth. That you did something for another woman out in the county, and she paid you just like the other woman had paid you with the hen. You make sure you keep the dollar safe till we can find out what it will buy. I'm sure Mr. Clay will help you with that."

"Thank you, Miss Jamie. Now hadn't I better git back to dem tater bugs? They mought be missin' me."

She laughed and walked back to the house, still feeling guilty but greatly relieved. Pa had been right when he had bought Steven. He hadn't had to pay Mr. McKay much for him, but he'd sure been worth whatever Mr. McKay had wanted, plus a whole lot more. Pa had known that from the first.

She sure knew it now.

# 15

Jamie didn't know why she should still feel so worn-out unless it was the summer heat, but, whatever the reason, she sure was dragging. Sometimes she felt it had almost been easier when she had known for a fact that she had to get up at dawn and start cleaning up the mess the Yankees had left, working in the fields or whatever else there was that had to be done. Now when she had to decide each morning whether to get up or just stay in bed, it was almost more frustrating and tiring than hoeing many rows of beans had once been. She hated feeling useless, but Clay was determined that she should rest and get back to being what she had once been. And he wanted it as soon as possible.

It had been almost five weeks since the end of their stay-at-home honeymoon; and, though she had tried to keep doing some things, she hadn't been doing anything like the amount of work she had done before Clay had returned. One reason for that was his absolute refusal to allow her to do very much. The other was that he helped by doing some of the tasks himself.

But mighty doggoned few, she thought after she had asked him again to please help her start sanding and working to firm up their furniture. Every time she had mentioned it, he vetoed the idea. He had to work on his office. This she accepted as true. He also insisted that he had to look for the family silver his mother had buried. That one she questioned. She didn't doubt that they had once had all that valuable silver, much of it wedding presents her in-laws had received when they had been married in England. Neither did she doubt that it had all been buried. Who would have left all that for the Yankees to take?

What she questioned was whether any of it was still there to be found. She just couldn't see the proud, proper Caroline down on her knees in the forest in the dark of night, digging a hole big enough and deep enough for all those silver pieces and then removing all trace of the burial. No, Mrs. Haynesworth could not have done that by herself. She undoubtedly had used one or more of their people she trusted. If they had really been trustworthy, Clay would have found that silver in the spots where his mother had told him it was. If her belief was wrong and the silver was still resting in its secret grave, it could stay there safely until other more-pressing things had been done. Clay didn't see it that way. He wanted that silver found and locked up safely in the bank vault until he could establish it once more in the dining room that would again seat up to eighteen in his rebuilt Crestview.

Jamie said none of that to Clay until they were sitting on the side porch steps one unusually hot late-July night. She had tried hard to be pleasant all day, but she felt so worn and hot that she had been thinking of going down and dunking herself in their little creek to cool her off. She kept toying with the idea, but even that seemed too much to cope with right now.

"Be realistic and stop being so fanatical about Crestview," she snapped when Clay refused again to make any plans for getting Fairdale in better shape. "I know there is all sorts of talk about getting the Federal government to pay the people for all the damage, but nothing seems to be definite. The streets are being repaired and I guess some of the business establishments are being worked on, but have you gotten a penny to help you yet? I don't want to keep sitting here like a toad on a rock. I know we can't build barns and things like that, but I'm talking about inside the house itself. I want it to be back like it was when Pa and I…"

"Honey," Clay interrupted her to say rather definitely, "Fairdale has never been and can never be a Crestview. I'm grateful that we have it for the time being, but I don't want my children raised in a Fairdale. I want them raised in a Crestview."

That struck the wrong chord in her, so she snapped out a quick question. "And where are these children of yours? You never told me about having them."

Then immediately she apologized, "I'm sorry, Clay. Please forgive me for being nasty like that. I'm just so worn-out and so tired of looking at my bare still-messy backyard and my beaten-up house. I'm tired of having only one out-building and that a garden house, although goodness knows I sure am glad to have it."

Clay apparently had taken no offense at her sharp words. He just laughed and said, "We don't have a garden so how can we have a garden house? But I will admit that I too thank the Lord that we do have a privy. Steven did as good a job as possible with what he could scrounge up to work with. But where do you get that silly 'garden house' talk anyway?"

"I thought I'd told you. That's what my grandmother must have called them. That was what Mammy Rose learned when she was there taking care of my mama. She insisted that I do the same, even if there weren't a real garden within miles of where we lived."

"All right. If it came from the Haskins, I guess it makes sense. As I remember, your grandparents' plantation does have a really nice garden. At least, it did when we were kids and spent time with our grandparents on their place next to it. I doubt that even the garden is there after the Yankees got through swarming over it."

Jamie became kind of pensive. She moved her feet down two or three steps to stretch and try to get more comfortable on the hard boards. "Do you ever write your grandparents? If you do, how about asking them if my grandmother is all right. Don't bother to ask about my grandfather. I have no interest in knowing how he is. He sure has never had anything but contempt for me and my pa."

"Since that's the case, do you really want to open that kettle of fish? Could get smelly again," he reminded her, moving restlessly on the steps himself and yawning. Jamie gave a sigh as she reached up to hold her heavy hair away from her hot neck. "I thought I did, but maybe you're right. Never mind."

They had been sitting out there for probably an hour, hoping in vain for a cool breeze to come down from the mountains to cool them off before they went to bed. "We could at least be sitting in comfortable rockers if those confounded Yankees hadn't come here. Oh, how it does gall me that we couldn't give them the whipping they deserved," Clay lamented bitterly.

"Do you remember what was going on around here two years ago?" she asked.

"Yeah, how could I ever forget? But I'd rather not think about those terrible days after Gettysburg right before we go up to try to sleep. I guess it's too hot for anything else, anyway."

She gave a weak-sounding giggle. "I never thought I'd hear you say that."

He joined in the small laughter. "I never thought it would be this hot at nine-thirty at night."

"It feels as hot as any night I ever remember here, but it's really the stuffiness that makes it so miserable. Let's not keep thinking and talking about it. That makes us even more uncomfortable."

"I guess you're right. Oh, by the way, do you know where Steven got the money to buy that fishing equipment he wanted me to help him with? He actually had a silver dollar. Where did that come from?"

Jamie's heartbeat quickened, but she tried to give no hint of it. She just kept her elbows on her knees and her chin in her hands as she said mildly, "He got it the same way he got our one chicken. He did some work for somebody who had U.S. money."

"Bound to have been a Union sympathizer," Clay said, still instantly suspicious of anybody like that.

"Or maybe somebody who has a good friend or family members in the North. Having always lived here, Steven knows right many people and probably all the long-time free coloreds in town."

He looked at her sharply. "Do you know who the person is?"

She raised her head and glared back at him. "Why on earth do you want to know that? Do you want to do some work for them too?"

"If they need a lawyer, I'd sure like to."

They stayed silent for a few moments. Then Clay asked, "Do you think he could have lifted it from somewhere?"

That brought her up straight. "Absolutely not. Steve would never be a thief; and even if he would, who has Federal money he could take? You aren't missing any, are you?"

He shook his head. "Oh, no, no. Nothing like that. I was just surprised that he had any money at all. And you don't know a thing about it?"

"Sure I do," she said, forcing herself to relax again and to speak easily. "I just told you. He did something for somebody, and she paid him for doing it."

"A whole dollar?"

"Yes, that's what he said. You know, like the other lady who gave him the chicken for working for her. To me, that chicken is worth as much as the dollar. I keep thinking how good it would taste roasted, but maybe getting the eggs for a while would be best."

"And," Clay said, "he did right in bringing that chicken home to you. Don't you think he should have given that money to you too since he's…"

"No, I do not!" she said furiously. "As far as I know, that's the first money he's had in his entire life. For goodness sake, Clay! Surely you don't think I'd have taken it even if he'd offered."

"All right, all right," he said, laughing and holding his hands up as though warding off blows. "I didn't mean to start a fight. I just thought I'd ask. No harm in asking, is there?"

She wanted to say, "Yes, there was, when you were asking silly questions," but, of course, she didn't. It was so uncomfortably hot that she guessed they were both irritable. She was so tired of not being honest with her husband. She wanted so much to tell him everything and be held in his arms while he comforted her. The arms of love, Curt had… *No!* Her thoughts could not go there. So, wanting to make up for what she felt was disloyalty, she slipped over closer to him, pulled his head down and gave him a long kiss.

"That," he said, touching her cheek tenderly, "could warm me up even more than the hot air. And maybe it's not as hot upstairs as we think. We do, at least, have those tall windows to catch a breeze, if one should find its way down here. Let's go on up and find out." He got up, reached for her hand and pulled her up with him.

"We used to have a few church fans around our house," he said as they trudged up the stairs. "I sure wish we had some still."

"Well, I'd be willing to bet that there's not one of those old church fans in the whole Valley," Jamie said. "We used all we could find in the hospitals to cool the patients and to scare the flies away from the wounds. We needed a lot more than we had."

"I'm sure you did. Having fewer of those dratted flies is the one good thing about not having a barn or animal droppings to draw them."

Jamie looked at him and laughed. "That's looking on the bright side, if I ever heard it," she said.

He smiled at her. "Only way to look at things," he told her complacently. "Incidentally, Brad said today that they'd be out in the carriage to get us Sunday."

She hung onto him as they went and asked, "Don't you feel kind of funny about driving up in such a fine carriage when not many people have one any more or, if they do, it's battered and they don't have left anything to pull it, anyway?"

He stopped and stared at her. "Gosh, no! Why should I? There are people who still have money, old family money like my father. They've probably been smart like he's been and have it tucked away in safe investments. I'd be willing to bet there are many folks who didn't turn everything they had into Confederates."

Jamie shook her head. "I don't think so. I think they'd have helped when people here were actually in danger of starving, as we were last winter." Then she almost gasped. What was she saying? Clay would think she was meaning that that was what his father should have done. She did think so, but did she have to open her mouth and let any thought she had come bouncing out?

She needn't have worried about hurting Clay, though, for he didn't seem to have tied it all together. He just said, "The ones with money just haven't found bargains like Brad and I did. How could anybody blame us for accepting them?"

She didn't want to talk about that so, to change the subject in a hurry, she said, "I'm getting used to being an Episcopalian, and I'm liking it. I miss the Reverend, as I always called Dr. Graham. That's what Mammy Rose called any preacher, so I learned to do it too. He's a really good man, and when we have children, I'd like them to go to the school he holds in the church basement…that is, if he teaches all ages."

"I don't think he handles the unborn, so we'd better wait to do any signing up," he said, laughing a bit. "But if it ever cools off, I'm hoping we can change that. And I really am glad you like Christ Episcopal."

When they reached their room, he pulled her to him and kissed her. Then he got a handkerchief from the bureau drawer and wiped the perspiration from both of their faces. "Too hot," he said and started pulling off his sweaty clothes.

"It sure is," Jamie agreed and walked over to the front window. "I just saw some lightning," she said back over her shoulder to Clay. "Maybe we're about to get some rain."

"I hate to disappoint you, but sheet lightning like that doesn't really mean a thing."

"Well, shucks," she said, as she turned back into the room and started undressing too.

Lying awake beside the soon-sleeping Clay, she marveled at his ability to drop off so quickly. It must come from having to get a few winks whenever and however he could during those four years of war. Or she thought wryly, maybe from having a clean conscience. If that last thought was what made it possible, she was afraid she'd never sleep comfortably again. But how could her conscience ever be clean if she couldn't somehow find out if the Darbys had found Curt. She wanted desperately to hear, she told herself, so she could quit worrying about any man but this one who, surprisingly, was sleeping soundly beside her.

# 16

When Jamie woke up the next morning, the windows were down, there were damp spots on the floor in front of each and the air was delightfully pleasant. It was so cool, in fact, that she realized she had been clutching the sheet tightly around her. There was also a note on Clay's lined notepaper on the pillow beside her. She picked it up and read:

*My darling Jamie. There was a terrific storm early this morning and, thank God, the heat has dissipated. You were sleeping so well that I didn't want to wake you.*

*Brad is meeting me at what will be my office and help me rework the plans one more time. I hope we'll get it right this time. That may take quite a while, so I'm hoping Pris or Mrs. Mac will come up with something that will pass for dinner for both him and me. I also want to do some digging while the ground is soft over at Crestview. Today might be the day!*

*See you later this afternoon. Please be sure there is plenty of hot water, for I may end up as messy as a pig in slop.*

*All my love, Clay.*

So, Jamie thought, she was alone. Again! She had been by herself too much of almost every day since Clay had been spending so much time in town or at the remains of his beloved Crestview. She did wish, she thought as she contemplated her lonely day, that he would allow her to go with him part of the time. But, no! He insisted that she get in better shape before she did much of anything. Just yesterday when she had told him she *really* did want to join the Ladies Memorial Association, he had said, "Not yet." *Again.*

Now, as she lay there feeling useless, that restriction filled her with new annoyance, but not enough to cause her to swing her feet to the floor. Why should it when she had nowhere for them to take her and nothing to do if they got her there? She did wish, though, that she could help the ladies with their wonderful work. That would, at least, give her a feeling of worth.

She lay there, still clutching the thin sheet to herself, wishing she had something heavier and thinking about the LMA, as it was called. She had checked with Pris the first time she and Brad had come out to Fairdale after the wedding. She wanted to know what those women had meant when so many had mentioned it.

Now she remembered, with a small inward wry smile, how Pris had told her. As unusual as it was, her new sister-in-law had said almost angrily that she didn't see how Jamie had lived there and not heard about what the women of Winchester, under the leadership of Mrs. Eleanor Boyd and Mrs. Mary Williams, had been doing. Even women in Richmond, Fredericksburg and many other towns over the South had heard and followed their lead. LMAs were springing up everywhere.

Jamie now stirred uncomfortably as she remembered how hurt she had been at Pris' almost scornful attitude at her ignorance. That wasn't the Pris she had known. So, since her own nerves had not yet settled down from what had happened on her wedding day, tears had started running down her cheeks. When Pris had seen them, she had immediately become the loving, supportive Pris again.

"I'm sorry, honey," she had said. "I know you hadn't been out where you would know things, but when you mentioned your wedding, I suddenly remembered all the things I had heard from you and that Yankee boy and I got upset about them again. I have tried to forget everything said that day, for I knew that you could have had that miserable Yankee if you had wanted him, but you chose Clay. That was enough for me, but when you mentioned the wedding, I forgot that for a moment. Now let's sit down somewhere and I'll tell you all about our wonderful LMA."

So they had gone into the sitting room, Jamie remembered, and Pris had told her that the men couldn't even organize a tobacco-spitting contest without the Union military threatening indictments, but the women were non-political and not likely to start a rebellion, so they could do what they pleased. What these two outstanding women had pleased was to start an organization of women to find, identify and re-bury with honor all their innumerable Rebels in a nice memorial graveyard in Winchester to be named for General Stonewall Jackson.

"That sounds wonderful. I want to join," Jamie remembered saying.

Pris had shaken her head. "I wanted to get you involved in it, but Clay said for me to wait till you had regained your health."

"I'm no weakling," she remembered arguing. "Before Clay came home, I was working from dawn till dusk every day. So forget what your brother says and tell me more about the LMA."

"Yes, you were doing all that when he came," Pris had retorted, "and you were looking like a body someone had found but had forgotten to bury. Also you were hardly knowing which end was up." But she had gone ahead and told her about the veteran who had come home to get his farm back in shape and had dug up a decaying Rebel body. It had distressed him so much that he had run to Reverend Boyd, who with his wife Eleanor and her sister-in-law Mary Williams had been dedicated supporters of the Confederacy. Reverend Boyd could do nothing, of course, but the women could do what they pleased. What these outstanding women had pleased had been to commence their effort to honor and rebury the dead Confederate heroes lying in shallow graves. They intended to follow through with the commissioning of the Jackson Cemetery.

Jamie remembered how amazed she had been. "I guess I had heard of it," she finally admitted, "but I wasn't taking in much in those days. How in the world are they going to do all that? It will be bound to cost a fortune."

"It costs five dollars to join," Pris had told her, "and almost every woman anywhere around has found the money somewhere. And I feel sure those amazing women will have other ideas about paying for it."

"Oh, where can I possibly get five dollars?" she had wailed, but Pris had said, "Oh, don't be a goose. Clay will pay for you when you start eating right and get in decent shape."

"I eat as right as I can now," she had said. "At least, I sure try."

"Clay says you don't. He says you just push the food around on your plate but don't really eat unless you have something special."

"He's wrong. Can't you convince him that I try?" All that had irritated her back then, and it still irritated her now as she lay in bed on this damp morning, wondering what to do with herself. Well, it was certain that she couldn't do anything lying here in her room like a lost soul. She might not have anything to do, but she'd better get at it.

She had no idea what time it was and didn't really care. With everything so wet and muddy, there was no hope of spending any of this long day alone doing some more cleaning on the messy areas still all over her back yard. Steven helped when he could, but she had told him to use what time Clay didn't have him cleaning up over at Crestview to keep doing whatever the gardens needed. Clay had even noticed that Fairdale was looking a little better, but it had not occurred to him that the improved condition was because Jamie had worked every chance she got to make it that way. She did wish, though, that he would put even half the attention to her home that he did to the one he had once had.

Now she stood by the bed and wondered again if getting up alone on a wet, gloomy day like this was worth the effort. She also wondered if there really could be something still wrong with her. Surely not. How could there be since that dratted war was behind them and she was now what she had wanted to be for she long? She was a Haynesworth, wasn't she? A member of a family with a standing so high that no one would ever question her past or dare speak ill of her! She had still been a child when she had come to the conclusion that such a marriage was the only way she could be safe from whispers behind hands and ostracizing. Being married to Clay meant she was safe from all that kind of talk, so why didn't she feel any different?

Well, she couldn't stand there like a statue all day. She had to do something. She grabbed up her pantaloons, topped them with her old robe, and left the room. She was hungry. Maybe Rhody had one or two of those good biscuits left from last night. Actually, she was surprised that the woman hadn't come tiptoeing up the stairs before now to see if she were awake. And maybe she had. She was almost as bad as Mammy Rose had been about checking on her. But after she had finally dropped off last night, she had slept so heavily that the remains of the Stonewall Jackson Brigade could have come marching through her room and she doubted she would have known it.

As she went down the kitchen stairs in her bare feet, she burst into the kitchen with hardly a sound. Rhody was sitting at the table and sprang to her feet with a guilty look. Jamie laughed. "You don't have to feel guilty that I've caught you taking a rest. I want you to rest when you can. Is there anything available for breakfast? Or, since I know it's late, should I say, for *dinner*?"

"I ain't knowin' which it is since we ain't got de sun to go by, but I'm a-thinkin' it mought be closer on to dinner time. I 'spects, though, you is gonna want de same thing, whatever you calls it. I got a egg for you."

"Is there any bread for toast?"

"Yes'm, dere is, if you calls a biscuit toast."

"Oh, that's right. That's what I was hoping for, a nice warm biscuit with whatever there is to go on it. Also I'd like some more of those blackberries we had last night if we have any more. You can save that egg for Steven."

"You ain't wantin' it? Mr. Clay sho' wants to see you git on some weight," the woman said dubiously, looking back around at Jamie as she poked wood into the stove.

"Of course, I'm sure. Those warmed-over biscuits will put more weight on me than that egg. Besides, it's Steven's hen that laid it."

"If you is sho' dat be all right, I think I'll fix it fer Steven's dinner today. A egg biscuit sounds moughty good. And if I don't scramble it too hard, I can stretch dat egg enough to go in two biscuits, one for Steven and one for me. Ain't dat right?" she ended with another laugh.

Jamie joined her. "Sounds right to me," she told the woman. "Now let's have my biscuit."

"Yes, ma'am."

Jamie sat down at the table, realized she had the cracked chair and moved over to the one Rhody had been sitting in. "Has my husband been gone to town long?"

Rhody stuck the biscuits in the oven before she turned again to Jamie. "Yes, ma'am. I'd say a right smart time ago. Maybe two hours." She hesitated a moment, then said as she slid the two biscuits from the pan onto a plate and put it in front of Jamie. "Steven ain't mindin' 'bout them eggs. He knows we be owin' you fer keepin' us on like you is doin'."

"Oh, for goodness sakes! Your staying is as much a favor to me and Mr. Clay as it is to you."

"Yes'm. Now you be wantin' to have some of dat stuff Mr. Clay still drinks when we ain't got coffee?"

"No. I hope to Heaven that we'll have plenty of coffee again one of these days. Until then, I'll drink water. I'm just glad you had enough flour to make that good-sized batch of biscuits. Was that the last of it?"

"Yes, ma'am. I made it all up last night, for I was skeered it might be as hot again today. Ain't it nice dat it ain't?"

"It sure is. And since it's too wet to do much work out here, if Steven wants to go into town and see if he can pick up some work in helping clear away the houses the Yankees wrecked beyond repair, I wouldn't mind. When we took our usual carriage ride around town with the McLaurines after church last Sunday, we saw that that was being done."

As Rhody brought a bowl of berries to the table, she said, "Yes'm. Steven done told me some man done axed him 'bout doin' dat. Steven told him he had a lot to do out here for you, but he'd ax you 'bout it."

"Of course, he can do some of that. It will be good for him to have some of that precious Yankee money. Goodness knows we all need it."

"Yes'm," Rhody said as she started for the kitchen door to the outside. Then she turned back and said, "I 'spect I better see if dere be any sign of dat lady what was here and is coming back."

"What lady?" Jamie cried, jumping up and starting for the door after her. "You haven't said a word about a lady."

Rhody stopped a few feet outside the door and turned around to meet Jamie. "Ain't been no need to till now. She said in an hour or so. I'd say it ain't been dat long yet. But, since I know you ain't wantin' her to git back befo' you gits dressed, I thought I'd check to be sure she warn't early."

"Of course, I want to be dressed," Jamie said distractedly, running back inside to the table and cramming the last of the biscuit in her mouth. Who could it be? Not Pris or Mrs. McLaurine for Rhody knew them; and, besides, they would have just come on in. "Do you know who it was?" she asked Rhody, who had followed her back in.

"No'm, I sho' don't. But Steven knowed her. She's de woman what give him de money when he was out lookin' for some more turtles."

Jamie grabbed her robe and twisted it to her chest. *It was Mrs. Darby! It had to be Curt's aunt, Mrs. Darby.* She had almost given up hope of hearing anything from the letter she had written Curt's aunt, but now the woman herself had come. Not sent word but actually come! Such a nervous chill was running over her that she had to hold onto the table for support. Had Mrs. Darby come to tell her that they hadn't been able to find him? Or to lash her with accusing words like Dave Darby had done? Or…and then her heart felt that it stopped…to tell her that Curt was dead? *No, please, no! Not that.*

Rhody was staring hard at her, obviously puzzled at her reaction. "Ain't nuthin' but somebody comin' to visit," she said at last. "Ain't no call to be upset. Befo' de war, lots of folks come to visit. Miz Sally and Miss Linda, dey liked to keep cookies, cake or sumpin' to give 'em. Still ain't no big thing, Miss Jamie. Maybe she knows where another turtle is or sumpin' like dat."

"But why didn't you wake me when she was here?" Jamie

wailed, looking around distractedly.

"You was asleep and Mr. Clay tol' me not to wake you up unless de house be on fire. I ain't seen no flames so I didn't wake you. I tol' de woman dat, and she say she'd be back in a hour or a little more. Dere was another lady down de pike dat she wanted to visit too."

Jamie was now heading for the stairs, but she turned back before she had gotten up more than a couple of steps. "Oh, Rhody," she cried, "it was so hot yesterday that I need a bath, a real bath, but I don't dare take time for one. You got any warm water on the stove?"

"Dat place in dis here good cook stove where I always keep water is full. So, yes'm, you got de water you needs. You want me to bring a panfull upstairs to yo' room?"

"No, just give me the pan of water and some kind of a cloth, and I'll step into Mammy Rose's old room. I know it's yours now but whatever. I've just got to get a little fresher than I feel now."

With Rhody's help she was clean, up the stairs and into as decent a dress as she had, all in record time. She even had time to brush her long hair and tie it back with that one nice ribbon she still had. Then she raced back down and sat primly in the parlor to wait for Mrs. Darby.

# 17

*Mrs. Darby!* What was she coming to do? To tell her Curt had died and that she had killed him? The fear of that staggered her. But whatever the reason for this visit, Jamie knew she'd surely get a report on Curt. "Oh, dear God," she prayed fervently, "let him be all right. Please don't let him be dead because of me."

When she heard a knock on the side porch door, she gulped to try to swallow whatever was choking her and ran to get it on trembling legs. A very nice-looking older woman in a blue, lightweight dress and an obviously-worn but once-stylish straw hat stood there. "Are you Miss Montgomery?" she asked. Then she made a sort of dismissive motion with her hand, smiled and said, "I'm sorry. I meant to say 'Mrs. Haynesworth.'"

"Yes, ma'am, I...I am and I feel sure you're Mrs. Darby. Won't you please come in? I assume that Steven is seeing to your horse."

"Yes, he is." She went with Jamie down the hall to the parlor and allowed the obviously-nervous girl to seat her on the divan. "You have a very efficient, dependable man in your Steven. He certainly carried out your instructions and mine properly the day you sent him to find me."

"I'm glad to hear that and, yes, he is very dependable."

The woman smiled. "If you should want to get rid of him, send him to me. I have a white tenant family that lives on the place, but I'd sure like to hire him."

When Jamie heard those words of Mrs. Darby, she almost lost her breath. She had thought this woman had not come to tell her about Curt, but instead she must be here to try to hire her help. Jamie felt such a keen disappointment and so much renewed guilt that she could hardly bear it. She had hoped desperately to have helped Curt, but apparently she had not. It wasn't easy, but she did manage to say stiffly, "I'm sorry, but he has been such a dependable man here at Fairdale to both my father and to me that I would never let him go if I could help it. Have you said anything to him?"

The woman gave a little laugh. "Oh, good gracious, no! I wouldn't think of doing that. I just thought I would mention it in case such a situation should arise."

"Thank you, ma'am. I'll keep that in mind." She hesitated, then the words burst from her. "Please Mrs. Darby, tell me. Did Curt's family find him? I haven't heard a thing, and I've been so terribly worried."

The woman leaned over and reached a hand out to Jamie who was sitting in a chair angled to the right of the divan. The girl was obviously fighting tears and didn't see the outstretched hand. "Yes, I am Curt's aunt and I'm sure you have been worried, as have we all. I should have come sooner, but I had thought at first that I'd write you or suggest that my brother-in-law do so as soon as there was anything definite to report. But I was afraid that, under the present circumstances, that might not..."

"Oh, no!" Jamie broke in to plead. "Please don't write me. I never get mail and that would be..." She had started to say "noticeable" but didn't want to say noticeable to whom, so she left the words hanging.

"I thought that might be true, so I decided to come and hoped that would be all right. Is your husband here?" The woman's eyes ran over the room as though she thought he might be sitting there and she just hadn't noticed him.

"No, he's not. He in town working on his law offices."

The woman raised her eyebrows. "Oh, he's a lawyer?"

"Yes, ma'am. He's Clay Haynesworth, the son of Mr. and Mrs. Thad Haynesworth. Perhaps you know them."

The woman gave a little shrug and a smile. "Doesn't everyone? They are very—" she hesitated and then said "—well-known. I've been acquainted with them but not closely since my husband and I came to the Valley."

Jamie was sitting so close to the front of her chair there was danger that she might fall out, but she didn't make a move or say another word. She was just waiting for Mrs. Darby to tell her what she was so desperate to hear.

"Yes," the woman went on, "and it was only thanks to you that Curt was found. I don't know how he could ever have been found without your help, for the son they had sent to find him had already checked that hospital and been told that no Darby, husband or wife, was there. There were so many wounded soldiers still there that someone in a coma would have likely received too little attention until it was too late."

Jamie made a sound that was more like a groan than a word. Her visitor looked at her closely, then went on, "My brother-in-law and his wife, Curt's parents, of course, came down to Washington City immediately when they got my wire telling them what you had written. They got in touch with David, who actually was still searching here in Virginia. He joined them, and they found Curt in just two days."

"Oh, thank God! Thank God," Jamie breathed, clutching her hands together at her chest and closing her eyes.

The woman heard her and nodded. "Yes. I'm told that he is still unable to talk and sleeps a great deal of the time. It's a brain injury, you see. The horse apparently had kicked him as they tumbled down the hillside together. There were other injuries too, but the brain was what had caused the most trouble."

The tears that Jamie had been fighting sprang into her eyes and overflowed down her cheeks. "I'm so sorry, so sorry and I feel so guilty. Will...will he ever be all right?"

The woman moved her gray, well-groomed head again and Jamie hoped that it had been another affirmative nod. "Curt's parents got him out of that government hospital, rented a private coach and took him by train to New York. Their daughter and her husband..."

"Cynthia Ann," Jamie said involuntarily.

Mrs. Darby looked surprised but just said, "Yes, that's right. Curt's father had wired them as soon as they found Curt, thinking that New York might have better medical attention available than Pennsylvania. He was right. There was a specialist there who was known to be good in cases like this one. That's where Curt is now. It's a private clinic, and I'm told there is quite a bit of improvement in his condition since he's been there. He now seems to recognize his mother when she goes in; and while he still can't speak properly, he does try to say something. It…" She hesitated, then said softly, "they tell me it sounds somewhat like your name."

Ignoring Jamie's gasp, the woman went right on, "I'm told also that the doctor thinks he might very well be speaking before long. He also has great hope that he'll eventually make a full recovery."

Jamie kept her hands clasped as though in prayer and said, "I'm so glad. So glad, and thank you so much for coming to tell me. After David came and left so furious at me, I was afraid I would never know anything about what had happened to Curt and didn't see how I could endure it. He's so wonderful and he means so much, so terribly much, to me that I don't see how I could have lived if…" As she realized what she was saying, her words drained away, but her tears did not. Instead, they burst out in such a flood that Jamie turned completely away and covered her face with her hands.

Mrs. Darby jumped up, digging into her reticule for a handkerchief as she did so. She slipped the piece of lace-trimmed linen into Jamie's hand, then leaned over and put a comforting arm on her shoulder. "Here now," she crooned. "Don't cry. Curt will surely be all right one of these days. Come on over to the couch with me and let's talk."

As Jamie let her move them both, Mrs. Darby said, "We must have faith, my dear. His mother is staying there in New York with him until he is well enough to go home. She's seeing that he has wonderful care, so please don't cry anymore."

"I've been so worried," Jamie finally managed to get out between her sobs. "So terribly worried and afraid that the Darbys…would be so mad and so disappointed in me that they might not even pay attention to what I had written."

"Oh, no," Curt's aunt, again patting the girl's shoulder, said quickly, "you couldn't be more wrong than that. In fact, you could hardly believe what your message meant to them and how grateful they are for it. They'd been so worried that something had happened to both of you until they got Dave's wire after he had come here and found you still here."

"Yes, he couldn't have come at a worse time, but he didn't know…" Jamie more or less moaned when the woman stopped for a moment.

Then Mrs. Darby went on, "Curt's parents still don't have any idea why you two didn't come home as Curt had planned or why you weren't with him when the accident happened. Dave wired them some story about your marrying somebody else, but they could hardly believe that. They had been scared practically out of their minds about the whole thing, so your letter to me was like a message from above."

Jamie's tears were still coming, and she was trying to wipe them away as best she could with the borrowed handkerchief. "When Dave came," she said between sobs, "Steven thought he was Curt and told me, so I…I… The tears overtook her words again, and Mrs. Darby sat waiting for her to get herself together. Jamie felt that doing that might take forever.

"They do look a lot alike," Mrs. Darby said when it seemed that the crying might be coming to an end. "Anybody not knowing either of them well or seeing them together might make such a mistake. They're both mighty good-looking men and have hair so full and blond that any girl might envy them. Their sisters certainly do, but both boys have always hated it."

Jamie was finally managing to almost stop crying, but she was still having difficulty talking. "I…I can't talk about it, for even thinking about it upsets me terribly. But anyway, when I thought Curt had come to do murder, and…" In spite of her efforts, the tears overflowed once more. Mrs. Darby sat patiently waiting again.

"I guess…no, that's not right. I *know* I was already nervous as…as nervous as a skinned cat…about getting married, seeing all those people in my yard and everything," Jamie began again when she could, "so when I thought Curt had come to do as he'd said he would, I passed out cold and…"

"You did what?" the woman broke in so ask. "You mean you actually fainted?"

"Yes, ma'am, I did, for I was sure Curt had come to kill Clay. He had sworn more than once that he'd do that before he'd let Clay have me."

The woman's arm left Jamie's shoulder, and she was staring at her in disbelief. "Curt would never do anything like that," she said firmly. "You are bound to be mistaken."

"No, I'm not. But the war…" She gulped again before she could get the words out. "Well, it made things so different. He'd already almost killed a man who was trying… to… molest me."

"I can see Curt doing that," his aunt said, as Jamie had to stop again.

"He didn't like Clay," the girl went on when she could. "He knew I had been involved with who he called 'the Haynesworth boy' before he and I had ever seen each other." She gulped another time or two before going on, "But I had told him a long time back that I was through with all the things of the past. And it was true, really it was. I…I loved only Curt and had been waiting for him so long, but I hadn't heard anything from him for months so I couldn't even be sure he was still alive. My pa had died, my Mammy Rose had lost her reasoning and had to be cared for like a baby. Then she died too so I didn't have anybody. Then Steven had to kill…" That brought a sudden stop to her jumbled words. "No, I can't tell you or anybody about that, but I did tell Curt. I could tell him anything and he would understand.

"Oh, Mrs. Darby, you just don't know how good and loving he was. I even told him about the other thing that I thought I would die before I'd ever tell anybody, but he understood that too. But he…he hadn't been here for a long time, and I was missing him something awful. Oh, Mrs. Darby, you have no idea what he meant to me then."

She stopped again and then said more clearly than she had been speaking, "I'm awfully mortified to be acting like this, and

I'm afraid I'm embarrassing you too. I'm probably not even making sense, and I'm so sorry...so sorry about so many things, but there hasn't been anybody I could talk to about any of it. Not a single living soul."

"You can talk to me," Mrs. Darby said softly. "And you are definitely making sense. Maybe more than you mean to, but I think I am beginning to see it all."

"No, I shouldn't say any more. I'm afraid I've talked too much already. I...I'm not even sure exactly what I've said."

Neither seemed to know where to go from there, so both women sat with the only sound being Jamie's snuffling. She finally said again, "I'm awful sorry."

That brought no response from Mrs. Darby so, for what seemed to Jamie to be an interminably long time, silence reigned, and her tears eventually dried. At last, the visiting woman reached for Jamie's hand and held it tightly. "You poor little thing. I am so sorry for you that I could weep myself, if it would do any good. And when I think of what this is going to do to poor Curt when he is well enough to be told..." She shook her head sadly and said, "That really concerns me more than I can say. I'm afraid that will set back all the progress that has been made."

"Don't tell him. Please don't tell him," Jamie implored. "If I hurt him even more, I don't think I could take it."

Mrs. Darby just looked at her and said nothing for a few moments. Then she said sadly, "I hardly think that could be possible. When he recovers, I know his first thought will be coming here for you. I feel sure that would prove to have dire results."

"Oh, yes. Yes, it would. The man I married is expecting me to be faithful to him in my mind and heart, as well as in my body. And I'm trying. Trying so hard."

Mrs. Darby patted her arm and said, "Yes, I'm sure you are," but it was obvious that her mind was elsewhere. "I have been trying so hard to think of something...almost anything...but there really is nothing. Being married to one man and still loving Curt as you obviously do, it's just beyond me."

Her words shocked into oblivion any tears that Jamie might have had left. What had she done now and what could she possibly say to straighten things up? She sure hadn't meant what Mrs. Darby thought, and she had no idea how she could explain. She wanted to jump up and run from the room but knew she couldn't. She had to somehow tell the woman what she had meant.

"No. No, Mrs. Darby," she began tentatively, "you don't understand. I...I love my husband and he loves me."

Mrs. Darby looked at her, shaking her head sadly but saying nothing.

"That's true now," Jamie went on, trying hard to explain the inexplicable. "But it hadn't been true for a long time. I had had no thought of anybody but Curt, but by the time the war ended, everything was so awful, and I had been hungry for so long that I couldn't love anybody. Not even myself. I was dead. Just plain dead."

The shock on Mrs. Darby's face grew. "Dead?"

"Yes, ma'am. I was dead, really dead on the inside. So dead I couldn't feel anything for anybody. I guess that's what I was, for dead people don't feel, do they?"

"I've never been dead," Mrs. Darby admitted. Then she realized what she had said, gave a rueful little smile and added, "You know what I mean."

"Yes, I think I do. I just knew it wasn't possible for me to do anything but stay here and rebuild Fairdale in memory of my father."

Again there was a brief silence. Then Mrs. Darby asked, "Was he in the war?"

"Yes, a regular soldier. I could hardly bear to see him go, but he was a man who absolutely had to do what he felt was his duty. I think he felt it necessary to prove his worth as a man or something like that. Anyway, the war killed him."

"He actually went off to fight and left you here alone?" the woman asked wonderingly.

"Oh, no, ma'am. He thought Mammy Rose would always be

here with me, and he had Steven promise he wouldn't let anything happen to me. To Steven, his promise is like a law and he will do anything to keep it. Pa knew Steven would stick to his word, but he sure didn't know that Mammy Rose would lose her wits and then die. Also we had some mighty good helpful neighbors to keep check on me, but they got burned out and had to leave. But please don't think ill of my father. He had to do it. He really did."

Mrs. Darby patted the girl's hand, clearly intending comfort, but her face denied understanding. "Oh, you poor, poor child," she finally said. "No wonder you felt nothing. You were sick. Really sick. I can't understand Curt's leaving you in that shape."

"Oh, no. No! Don't blame Curt either. I made him go. I had to do it."

Mrs. Darby's face had worn many expressions but now seemed to show only puzzlement. "You had to?"

"Yes, ma'am," Jamie said, not sounding as rattled as she had been. "He was a Yankee. One of those people who had ruined everything good in life that Pa and I had ever had. There was no possible way I could...or would...ever go away with one of them."

"Curt wasn't..." Mrs. Darby started to say strongly but stopped and stood up. "I do think I really should be going," she said. "I have some thinking to do about all you've told me to see if there's any possible way I can help. I'm afraid not, for a marriage is, and should be, sacred for life. Still, I will somehow get word to you about Curt's progress without being obvious, even if I have to do it by coming to look for a turtle." At that, they both gave little nervous laughs.

"Steven told you about that?" Jamie asked.

"Yes, he did. I thought it was rather ingenious. As I've told you before, you have a good, dependable man in Steven."

"You're right. Pa recognized that from the first, and I certainly have for a long time." They were now starting through the hall, heading for the side porch as they talked. At the door Mrs. Darby put a hand on Jamie's arm and stopped her.

"I can't begin to tell you how concerned I am about all this. To love one man, as you obviously do my nephew, while being newly-married to another must be like hell on earth."

"Oh, no. No! You don't understand," Jamie started in again. "I'm not worried about Clay or myself. We'll be fine. It's Curt and only Curt that I'm so concerned about. It would be so much better for him if he had never met me. For him, but certainly not for me. He, and he alone, saved me during the war. I am grateful…so very grateful…but I'm afraid I haven't explained things properly."

Mrs. Darby shook her head decisively. "No, it wouldn't have been better for him. It was his destiny to meet you. I'm convinced of that. So, you see, I have no doubt your meeting Curt was meant to be. Just," she added, "not with this end, I'm afraid."

The hated tears were threatening again so Jamie turned quickly away and said, "Oh, Steven must have been watching. Here he comes with your horse and cart."

"So he does." The woman turned again to Jamie, "Well, goodbye, my dear. You have my sympathy, but I still don't understand how you let yourself get in this situation."

"Oh, no," Jamie started to say. "I love…"

"I know you do," Mrs. Darby cut in to say softly, not giving Jamie time to finish what she was trying to say. "I think we've both said enough." With that, she headed briskly down the steps to her cart.

Jamie walked down with her, said goodbye again, saw Steven hand her the reins and watched her drive away. She then went back in the house and practically collapsed into the first chair she saw. She hadn't done this right, she thought dismally. But what else could she have done? She hadn't meant to practically wash them both away with her tears, but she hadn't been able to help that either. Those tears had spoken louder to Mrs. Darby than any words she might have said. They had given Mrs. Darby the wrong impression, and she hadn't known how to change it except by trying to tell the truth. That hadn't seemed to work well either. Mrs. Darby might think she understood, but Jamie was sure she didn't.

How, Jamie thought despondently, could she have made it clearer? She had told the woman more than once that she loved her husband, but Mrs. Darby couldn't get past those tears. Of course, she had been worried, practically out of her mind, knowing that she had caused such injury to a person who had willingly risked his life again and again for her. Any girl would be. And that, added to the worry about having to be secretive with Clay, was almost enough to put her back to where she had been when the war ended. She was a Haynesworth, she whispered to herself, but somehow that did not drive away her low spirits.

The sense of guilt that troubled her so much was even heavier as she waited for Clay to come home. Would she have to bear that guilt forever? She didn't see how she could but feeling that she had somehow wronged Clay unintentionally, she waited for him in the hall, kissed him passionately and went up to their room with him eagerly after supper. She hoped she could make up in the only way she knew how for any foolish thoughts such as those she had not been able to dispel from Mrs. Darby's head.

# 18

The rest of July faded into August, and August slipped away to let September have its chance to provide pleasant temperatures. There was even a hint of the beautiful colors soon to be covering the mountains.

Jamie had finally gotten over her distress at the way she had acted when Mrs. Darby had come but was still trying to make up to Clay for the disloyalty she felt she had shown him, even though he had no way of knowing it.

She was still determined to be the kind of wife Clay wanted her to be, but she had had to take a little time out in August to get over the nettle rash that she had gotten from eating too many tomatoes, and she thought possibly also by the amount of fruit she had eaten. Those were two foods she really liked, so she had tried to eat enough of them to make up for the things that were tasteless. And she had paid for it during many hot miserable days.

They had found that the McKays' orchard had been far enough away from the Yankee fires to escape much damage, so they had helped themselves freely there, knowing that would be what the McKays would want. The itchy bumps all over her body from the acid had been a turn-off to Clay but no more so than the soda and water paste that she dabbed on the bumps to help the itching. That period of the summer had not been good. Clay had even spent a few nights in her pa's old bedroom. He had protested at first but actually seemed relieved to do it.

Now her skin was smooth again, and she was no more delighted by that than when vegetables that were not acid food came in, though it took days to counteract the rash. She tried to eat as much as she could, even though it sometimes made her feel ill. She had told him that his constant watching of her made her too nervous to eat as much as she might, but the criticism had seemed to hurt him so much that she didn't try that again. She had found that he didn't take any criticism well. But then who did?

"Maybe my stomach is like the rest of me and isn't as big as it once was," she said once at supper when he was insisting that she eat more than she wanted. "Couldn't that be the reason it takes less to fill me up?"

"I never heard of anything so silly," he told her in reply. "I don't know why, but for some reason you just don't seem to try."

"You're wrong. I do try," she said, trying the hide the hurt she felt at that. Was she just like him and didn't take criticism well either?

As the days passed, the politicians in Washington City wrangled about the best way to handle the defeated South and the thousands of freed slaves. It seemed to some that both parties were more interested in grabbing power than they were in working together to solve their massive problems.

Jamie and Clay were sitting on the side porch steps one night, as they usually did for a while before going up to bed. Clay was telling her what he had heard up around the courthouse. "The Democrats, as well as President Johnson, want to take our commonwealth and the other southern states back in with as little trouble as possible, but those confounded Republicans still won't allow it."

"But can't President Johnson do something to help since he's a Southerner himself?" she asked.

"Yeah, sure he is. But he's also a Republican. He's really just trying to follow what Abe Lincoln had set up before he was killed. They say that Abe had been working on Reconstruction plans for a long time, certainly as far back as right after Gettysburg. I guess he knew then that they were going to beat us. If our leaders had also recognized it back then, it could have saved hundreds of thousands of lives. But the South wouldn't have accepted it then."

"Some don't accept it yet," Jamie said as she straightened up and put both her hands on her back.

"Yeah, like my sister. And Mrs. Mac. But Mr. Lincoln wanted

to take our commonwealth and the other states back in if ten per cent of the voters would sign a loyalty oath to the United States. Those idiotic Republicans are insisting on fifty per cent. The Republicans couldn't get that many on a loyalty oath to God if they were the ones asking for it. There are many other requirements they are trying to force on us too. But I don't recall what they are now. They'll probably change when they come out with their next roll call. Say, is your back hurting?" Clay asked as he noticed her rubbing it with both hands.

She shook her head and quit rubbing. "Not, not really hurting. Just feeling stiff. I was trying to relax it a bit. I like to sit out here, but these hard boards don't do a thing for unpadded bones."

"Don't do a lot for even more padded ones. I'll give you a good back rub when we get upstairs."

"Sounds good," she admitted. "And now, where were we? Oh, I know. The latest requirements to get back in. Will Virginia even try to meet them?"

"Father would know more about that if he were here. I'm thinking we won't as long as those radical Republicans are concentrating on punishing the South."

Jamie gave a groan. "Hasn't the South been punished enough? If those vindictive ones could see our town, they'd realize that our part of the South certainly has. About the only thing more they could do to us would be to dig a big hole and push what's left of Winchester into it."

"Well, don't suggest that. Some of those Republicans are radical enough that they'd be here with shovels to start digging. I hate to say a kind word about Abe Lincoln, but I sure wish he could still be alive. Apparently, his idea was to get things back to where they once had been quickly and with as little fuss and feathers as possible."

They both sat silent for a while, their elbows on their knees and their chins in their hands. "Won't that urge to punish the South just keep the Confederate spirit burning in the hearts of all the people who sacrificed so much for their wonderful dream? Even those Yankees ought to know that, after going through what we have for four years, our men can't be expected to snuff out that spirit just like putting out the light on a candle."

"That's what they expect. Some fellow was in town yesterday. He'd been over in Richmond for a while. He says that whole city is like a powder keg just waiting to blow. But in spite of that sentiment, they know they can't do a dratted thing but smolder. And they have to be careful about that with the Union military swarming all over the town threatening indictments for treason."

Jamie thought that over for a few moments. "But, traitorous or not, what can they be saying or doing at this stage? The last verse of our Confederate song has been sung and all the instruments put away."

"Yes, I know. I was just telling you what the man said. Even here, I feel sure that Mrs. Williams and Mrs. Boyd would never have been allowed to start their program to find all the Confederate dead and give them a decent burial if they had been men. Women can get away with things that men can't because women are non-political."

"Huh!" Jamie said. "That's what Pris told me. Anybody who thinks women aren't political doesn't know your sister."

Clay chuckled. "Yeah. And Mrs. Mac is the same way. But I expect if anybody wants to criticize the women for what they're doing, they'd change their tune if they had been the one to find a decayed body."

"Oh," Jamie said, clinching her whole body, "that just makes me sick to think about. It scares me even now to realize that body could have been you or Brad."

"Don't think so," he said with a chuckle. "We aren't dead. And you're rubbing your back again. Time to go on up for that back rub."

The next Sunday Pris and Brad were there as usual, but Mrs. Mac was expecting them home to take over the care of Thomas so they couldn't stay for a pick-up supper. As the carriage went up the avenue, Jamie went back into the dining room to wait for Clay to wash up and join her. As she sat there, she thought back to what Brad has asked her that afternoon. When Clay was out of the room, he had asked her if she were worried about something. "Isn't everybody?" she had asked.

He said, yes, that he guessed they were, but not enough to make them really as unhappy as she sometimes seemed. She wasn't unhappy. She couldn't be. At least, she wouldn't be if she didn't have so many things to worry about, such as why Mrs. Darby hadn't let her know anything more. It wasn't that Curt was all that important to her, she assured herself. She just needed to know he had recovered from the injuries that she knew she had caused. After that, if she could get to looking more like her old self and maybe even get in a family way, everything would be great. Then she could get over the feeling that she was not doing her share in this marriage that she had wanted so much. She could then relax and be happy even if so many things she wanted were still as scarce as hens' teeth.

Clay came in rubbing his hands, gave her a quick kiss and said, "Now let's relax and eat these sweet potatoes as enthusiastically as if they were loaded with butter and spices, and the cabbage as though it's been cooked with plenty of salt and bacon drippings. Get that in your mind and you'll enjoy them as I do."

At his words, the desire for any of it left her. She knew that was foolish. Absolutely idiotic, for she loved sweet potatoes and had been delighted when Steven had started digging theirs. To cover her reluctance, she said, "I'll have the potatoes, but you know I really hate cabbage." It was hard to keep from pushing her plate away.

Clay, eating with obvious enjoyment, said, "Well, eat it anyway. It's got vitamins or something that's said to be good for you."

She tried not to let any memory of another time she had made that complaint and the different response it had received come into her mind. She really did but, in spite of her effort, it swept over her like a blast of icy wind on a winter day. Suddenly the urge to eat anything left her, and she did push her plate away. The guilt that hit her at the memory of Curt's words was keen, and it cut deep into that tender place at the core of her being that she tried hard to protect. She shouldn't even think of anything like that. It was wrong…wrong, *wrong!* She had to stop it, for what did it matter that some other man had promised she'd never have to eat cabbage again? He'd had that whole rich, undamaged North to make that possible. It wasn't Clay's fault that he couldn't make the same vow. Not his, but the Yankees! And that was what she really had to remember.

# 19

The sun was shining brightly on September twenty-fourth, but it wasn't really hot. It was Clay's twenty-sixth birthday and he announced as he and Jamie sat at the breakfast table that, though a birthday should be a holiday for the person having it, he was going to work just like a regular day. He and Brad had a lot to do on his office plans.

"Why didn't you do that when he was out here?" Jamie asked, trying to eat her cornmeal mush with dried peaches on top of it and finding it hard going.

"Work on Sunday?" Clay scoffed. "Why, shame on you! I'd have thought both you and my sister would have fought like dogs to keep us from committing a sin like that."

"You thought no such thing."

"Well, but my mother and grandmother sure would have protested if they had known. I didn't want to risk it. One simply does not work on Sunday. You know that."

"Of course, I do," Jamie said, as she resisted the urge to somehow get rid of that overflowing bowl in front of her. "I'd have thought, though, from the way you've been working on those plans, you'd have them set in stone by now. What have you been doing in town these last weeks if you haven't been working on them?"

Having finished his mush with what appeared to have been, at least, no distaste, Clay did push away his empty bowl as well as his chair from the table. He leaned back, crossed his legs and watched as she took tiny bites. At least, she was telling herself, it didn't have any acid in it. She sure didn't want that nettle rash again.

'We've also done quite a bit of tearing out of the damaged wood ourselves instead of waiting for help. And, of course, I've had to spend a lot of time over at Crestview. I'm going to find that silver that Mother buried if I have to dig up the whole eighty acres."

Jamie took another bite and swallowed hard. "Before your mother left, I thought she told you exactly how to find it," she said. "If you've dug there and didn't find it, doesn't that kind of indicate that somebody must have already found and taken it?"

Clay frowned and slapped the table with his hand as he said, "Absolutely not! She told me the number of trees from various places. The trouble is that those places and those trees were burned. I don't have nearly as much to go on, but I am going to find it. As I've told you before, that family silver will be in our dining room when we get Crestview rebuilt. I can promise you that."

"Maybe she can help you when they come back," Jamie said, hoping that day would be far, far into the future. "Do you think that will happen any time soon?"

He shook his head. "Naw. The only letter I got from Mother said that Mary Lilly was having the time of her life. She even has a very acceptable boy who is dancing attendance on her. He's the only son of an earl or a duke or one of those titled fellows, and, since Mother's father is entitled only to be called Sir Peter Cooke, that higher rank has Mother all atwitter. Of course, it's too soon for anything serious, but Mary Lilly has turned eighteen, and apparently that's the age when Englishmen check out the girls for marriage. I think Mother is kind of expecting Mary Lilly to be spoken for by Easter."

"Would you like that kind of a life?" she asked.

"Gosh, no! I like it just like it was here in America before the war. But Mother has always had a hankering to get back over there. Her family's country estate might not be as big as Rose Hill, but it's many times bigger than Crestview. She likes the country life there, and then there is London for when they want to be citified for a while. My brother, Cooke, is checking out schools so that's a pretty good indication that he's liking it. So, no, I don't think Mother and Father will be coming home any time soon. She did mention our going over to England one of these days, so we have that to look forward to. You'd like that, wouldn't you?"

"Clay, how exciting! I'd love to see England." Then her enthusiasm wavered and she asked, "Are you sure she meant me too? You know, I wasn't exactly the one she wanted for you."

He waved his hand airily. "All in the past. And surely neither of them think I'd even consider going without you. Absolutely not but, when that time comes, I want you to be once more the Jamie you were when you came to Winchester. Now eat your mush. Isn't it tasting a lot better?"

She smiled and forced down a little more.

"But," he went on, "as far as the office space is concerned, I thought I had finally gotten it planned just the way I want it, but you heard what Pris said Sunday when they were out here."

"I didn't hear a thing about anything special. What do you mean?"

"I mean that confounded medical establishment that she wants Brad to have right in with my law offices."

She took a bite of the dried peaches, then said, "But he's not a doctor yet and has no idea when he'll get to go back to school. Why does he need a medical office?"

"My thought exactly," Clay told her as he reached over and dipped up a spoonful of the mush and held it for her to take. "Eat up," he urged. "Even I have trouble eating mush when it's cold. You've heard the expression 'as thick as cold mush,' haven't you?"

Obediently she opened her mouth and tried not to gag as it went down.

Clay reached for another spoonful, but Jamie put her hand over his. "I'm not a baby. I'll eat what I can without help. Now tell me what this business is about your office."

"We talked about it Sunday. Didn't you hear?"

"You must have done that when I was outside playing with Thomas. Isn't that child a true delight?"

"He is that. But don't forget that he's not ours. We want one of our own. At least, I do."

She gave him a long look. "What's the meaning of that? I want children as much as you do. But, in case you don't remember, I wasn't in the world's best shape by the time the war ended. I guess it takes more time than I expected to regain what I lost."

He reached for her hand and kissed it. "I know, honey. And I might be in too big a hurry for everything. Maybe we should even have waited until you had gotten back some of what you'd lost before we got married."

"Oh, now you think of it!" she scoffed. "Why didn't you suggest that then instead of saying we had to get married right away so you could take care of me?"

He chuckled. "Wait around until things got settled down and that Yankee showed up here again? No, thank you. I'd had all the struggles over that I wanted. I wasn't about to risk any more."

She stared at him. "You're joshing," she finally said. "You didn't even think of that."

"Who says?'" he said, spreading his hands wide. "Let's drop it. It's in the past. I got you and that scoundrel didn't. But we're not talking about that now or ever again. We're discussing office plans. That sister of mine has decided that, no matter how they have to do it, Brad should go back to school and become the doctor he always wanted to be. And she thinks the space that Father gave me should be designed so it will work for his medical office when he's ready for it, as well as for my law business."

Jamie didn't dare say that she agreed with Pris, even though she certainly did. Instead she asked, "Would it work well for two? Since you've torn out so much of those walls damaged by the Yankees, it sure did look big as we rode by on the way to church."

"Who the heck knows? You might remember that neither Brad nor I have an architectural degree, but here we are trying to re-design what used to be a nice two-story office building as though we did." Clay shifted around in his chair and sounded disgruntled by the whole idea.

She took another tiny bite and said, "Well, no. But when the town gets rebuilt, if it ever does, that office space will still be a prime location, close to the courthouse and…"

"Yeah," Clay cut in. "That's what I need. Brad can have his medical office anywhere."

"Oh, Clay, I don't know. Pris is your sister, and you and Brad have been like brothers for years. Can't you give a little?"

He uncrossed his legs, pulled his chair back up to the table and looked at her almost-full bowl. "Well," he said, "can't you try to please me a little by eating that confounded mush? I grant you it's not great, but it does provide nourishment and that's what you need. If you just put it in your mouth and swallow, it will go down."

Clay waited a few moments, then he reached for her spoon to give her another bite. She grabbed his hand and held it. "No! I'm not going to eat it! I hate mush. I'd as soon eat…." Her face turned a vivid red and she gasped. "I…I can't believe I almost said that."

He stared at her for a moment, then burst out into a big laugh. "I can't either, but you did. I could almost hear it. But, honey, if you really would as soon eat that as mush, you've had your last bowl of it."

"Oh, thank you! Thank you so much. I do hate that mush."

"Then you can have oatmeal. Or an egg. I notice that we seem to be having right many eggs. Has some friendly neighbor been sending us some?"

She gave a little smile and said, "I do like eggs better." Then she remembered from where those extra eggs had surely come and felt like putting her head down on the table and bawling.

"But," she reached for his arm to keep him there with her until she could say carefully, "I do hope you won't let the office issue cause any trouble between you and Brad. You've been friends and brothers-in-law too long for that."

Clay gave a little chuckle. "Honey, you don't ever have to worry about that. I might have an all-out pitched battle with my sister, but I won't with my friend. She'd get over it before sundown, but he might not."

She gave a little laugh too and turned him loose. "I'm glad to hear that. Never having had a sister or a brother before, maybe I'd better take lessons from you."

"You're doing all right just as you are. They both adore you. Now do let me go or I'll get nothing done this morning." He headed for the stairs.

Jamie sat on the hall bench and waited for him to come back down. Then she kissed him goodbye and said another "Happy Birthday" but told him nothing about her day.

# 20

She was actually planning a birthday picnic in town to surprise Clay. The food wouldn't be great, but she thought she could come up with enough to make do. Rhody had made bread before the weekend, and there was one loaf left that she could use to make sandwiches. There were those eggs and some butter, as well as plenty of the tomatoes that Steven had picked green and was letting ripen in the basement. She felt sure that she had been over that miserable rash long enough that she could eat some of them without breaking out again. With that and the fruit from the McKays' orchard, they could have enough to pretend that it was a real picnic.

It had been a blessing that the McKays' fruit trees and grapevines were far enough from the house and outbuildings to escape being damaged by the Yankee fires. Jamie had been delighted when she received a letter from Mrs. McKay saying that the fruit would undoubtedly be there, but she and her sisters would not be. She wanted the Haynesworths to use it as though it were their own, as it certainly was until she let them know otherwise. She and her sisters were fine, and Malinda was keeping company with an elderly gentleman who was raising two grandchildren because their father had been killed in the war. She would let Jamie know how that progressed!

The exclamation points of Mrs. McKay amused Jamie. She sure hoped that Miss Linda wouldn't think she could have Rhody back if she found herself a step-grandmother in her late forties. Oh, well, that was not a problem for today. She felt sure that Rhody would never leave here anyway.

Jamie got her picnic ready and then began to worry about getting it there. Could she carry it all the way? As she was questioning that, Rhody came in to get some water for herself and Steven, and she saw Jamie's problem. "You ain't never gonna git all de way into town wid all dat. You wait till I tells Steven, and I'll help tote it fer you."

Jamie was so relieved she could have cried. The bright day made her feel more upbeat than she sometimes did, and she felt her heart almost sing with joy as she went to surprise her husband. Never having to argue again about eating mush was enough to lighten her heart.

That part of what she was taking for his birthday had surely come from the Darby farm put a little damper on her spirits, so she decided not to think about it. She felt sure that the two dozen eggs that had shown up at her kitchen door had come from there. She hadn't mentioned them to Clay, but she could tell that he had noticed. She felt sure he wouldn't have been so pleased if he had known where they had undoubtedly come from.

Then there had been twelve little chicks in a box, along with some feed for them. And last was a bushel basket of marvelously-delicious apples. Each gift had had a little note attached saying, "No thanks, please" so she had done as asked. Steven might have some idea about the origins of these things, but that didn't keep her from feeling even more guilt to add to what she already felt was dragging her down. Thank goodness that Rhody had taken over the care of the little biddies, so she wouldn't have to even see them until they appeared sometime later on their plates as fried chicken. She both dreaded and looked forward to that time.

"You is moughty quiet," Rhody said as they walked along toward town. "Is you all right?"

"Of course I am, but I sure am glad you're carrying most of the food. I'd never have made it by myself."

"Ain't I knowin' dat? But you reckon you could tote it all de last little way? Ain't Mr. Clay gonna' git a real surprise when he see you done it?"

"That's a great idea. His door will probably be open so don't come any closer. I'll make it somehow. Oh, Rhody, I sure do thank you. This will be a wonderful surprise."

The woman turned and hurried back down the beaten-up old street that had once been brick but was still mostly a mess, even though there were workers at various places. Jamie waited till Rhody was out of sight and then lifted the bags. She made it all right, but sure was glad she hadn't tried to do it without Rhody.

She put the bags down and tried the knob on the door, expecting to run in and yell, "Happy Birthday! I bring dinner." But she couldn't. The door was locked. *Why lock up a ruin?* she thought. She had seen the door standing wide open many times on their way to church.

Maybe Clay had gone and had something of his in there. Or maybe he was out back and hadn't heard her. She pounded hard on the door with her fists, waited and pounded again. She heard nothing, but as she picked up the sandwich and other food bags and started to walk away, the door opened. Clay, looking rather disheveled, stood there trying to smooth his hair with his hand. "Why, honey! What are you doing here?" he asked.

She held up the bags. "I've brought a birthday picnic. Scrappy but the best I could do."

"Hey, that's great," he said, glancing back over his shoulder into the room he had just left. "Since it's so nice, do you want to go to the Square and see if there's something we can sit on? Brad's not around. He stayed home to fill out some papers about going to medical school."

"That's great. I think he might as well go on and do it, no matter what it takes. Is there any place we can sit down inside to eat?"

"Too dirty and junky. Hey, why not walk over and sit on Mrs. Mac's steps? She won't mind."

"That's a good idea. I brought extra fruit for them, anyway. It's such a great day that I'd like to stay outside."

He turned back to the open door. "Let me just see that everything is shipshape in here." He left her standing there, closed the door and was gone.

Somehow, she felt strange. Why wouldn't he have left the door open or even had her come in? She did hope he wasn't working too hard and getting as muddled as she sometimes felt.

In just a moment, the door opened and he was back out. "I

wanted to put something on the plans I'd been working on," he explained as he took the bags from her and started up the street.

"Aren't you going to lock the door again?" she asked. "I thought there must be something in there you wanted to protect."

"There was," he said with a sheepish grin. "Me. I was taking a brief *siesta.*"

"A what?" she asked.

"A little rest. I guess I fell asleep."

"Oh," she said, laughing. "You lazy dog! And here I was thinking you were working away on your birthday."

"Well, I had certainly intended to and thought Brad would also. But this is great, Jamie. I'm so glad you came in to join me."

"Me too."

Just then she saw a girl's head peep out from the ruin next to his office, glance around and then step out into the street, brushing herself off and straightening her clothes as she did so. "Hey," Jamie said, "that's Betsy Gains. She looked around, but I guess she didn't see us with all the road equipment. What on earth could she be doing in that place? Is it being worked on yet?"

"Beats me," Clay said. "She ought not to be in there by herself. Or maybe the people who must have been with her are still there. Hello, Betsy," he called, "what you doing in there? Has somebody decided to fix it up, and you're hoping you can get a job?"

Betsy stayed where she was and waited till they caught up to her. "Hey, you two," she said brightly. "And, yes, Clay, that is exactly what I was doing. I was supposed to meet him and his wife there fifteen minutes ago. Since they must have forgotten, I decided to go on back home. What are you two up to?"

Jamie proceeded to commiserate with her about the discourtesy of the people who had let her down, but when she saw the other girl give a little wiggle of her well-rounded hips and step close to Clay, she hushed.

"Surprising to see you down here today," Betsy said to Clay and something about the way she said it made Jamie think the remark meant more than it said. When she saw the girl's full breasts that were stretching the low neckline of her thin cotton dress, Jamie's eyes moved unwillingly up to her husband's face. What she saw shocked her. His eyes were practically bulging at the sight. Shocked, she looked down at her still-skinny shape and wanted to hide. Or maybe she wanted to run. Anything to get away from that look.

"You're looking great," Clay said in what Jamie felt sure was intended to be just a friendly tone. Somehow, though, it sounded like more to her.

"Thanks," Betsy said with a giggle and another twist of her well-padded hips. "All of summer's bounty surely has filled us out, hasn't it? Then too Carl's grandmother lives in Baltimore. He was her only grandson, and she's still grieving for him. She seems to think that sending me a little U.S. money every week or so is doing something for him. I think it's mighty nice of her, don't you, Jamie?"

Not expecting to be called on to answer anything, Jamie gave a start. Then she said, "Carl was your husband? How sad that you had him for such a short time."

"Yes," Betsy sighed. "Just one week and then he was killed. I will be grieving for him forever."

*Not with my husband, you won't*, Jamie thought angrily.

She looked up at Clay to suggest that they go, but saw that his eyes were still on Betsy's bosom and started on for Braddock Street by herself.

"Hey," Betsy called after her, "did I say something? I sure didn't mean to. You convince her, Clay. I'll be seeing y'all around."

Jamie did not look back to see if that gleam were still in Clay's eyes as he hurried up the broken street after her. She felt sure it was not. It had surely disappeared when he lost sight of the other girl's voluptuousness and saw his wife.

When he caught up with her, she just gave him a little smile and said, "I wonder if Carl and his grandmother have any idea how lucky he was to have been killed in the war." Jamie's comment appeared to have sailed over his head, for he said nothing. She failed to give any other evidence of being upset, so they went on around to the McLaurines to share the food and their friendship.

Nevertheless, Jamie thought something was going on. She wasn't exactly sure what it was, but she could tell something was off kilter. Or maybe she didn't *know* anything, but she sure *suspected* something. Something so strong and so wrong that, in spite of her best efforts, it had planted a seed of doubt down deep within her in a spot where it's so fertile that it allows things to grow.

And grow.

# 21

Jamie made it through the rest of the birthday picnic by pure grit. Pris had looked at her right after they sat down on the McLaurines' porch and whispered, "What's wrong?" but Jamie just shook her head and smiled. She had already decided that she would not act like a jealous wife and thereby cause more trouble. Pris asked nothing more.

Clay was exuberant, moaning theatrically about becoming such an old man and seeming greatly pleased by the small gathering. Mrs. McLaurine and Thomas came out for a few moments to join in the celebration. Generally, it all appeared to be just what a small birthday party among family and special friends should be.

After they had finished what Jamie had managed to get together for their scrappy meal, she walked with Clay and Brad back to the office space, with Brad assuring her that there'd be no more naps for the birthday boy in the remainder of that day. Jamie didn't mention that it wasn't the naps that she was worried about, but she sure thought it.

"Aw, don't be too hard on him," she told Brad with a smile. "It's his birthday, and he's getting so old that he probably needs all the naps he can get."

Clay ignored her remark, but he did snort back to Brad, "Ha! You might remember that in less than half a year, you'll reach the same ripe old age that I have today."

"Yeah, but not until nearly six months have passed. Until then I'm just a boy of twenty-five. And, no matter how old I get, you'll always still be older."

Clay looked at Jamie. "Do you know if it's possible to divorce a brother-in-law?" he asked with pretended seriousness.

They all laughed and Jamie assured him that she didn't think so. Only Pris could divorce him, and she thought the world would quit turning before he could talk his sister into doing it.

"Oh, rats!" Clay griped. "Well, if I'm stuck with him for life, I might as well put him to work." He gave Jamie a warm kiss, thanked her again for coming to celebrate his birthday with him and went inside. She went off down the messy old street alone.

She had meant to go right home, eat as many apples as she could hold, along with anything else she could find, and then rest. Surely that would put a few ounces on her stubbornly-thin frame. Why, she asked herself angrily, hadn't she been able to regain at least some semblance of her former figure? Most of the people in town had practically starved, especially during this last terrible year, but, come to think of it, she hadn't noticed any of the ones she had seen at church who looked as though they had gained much weight either. *But,* she griped to herself, *maybe their husbands, if the war hadn't killed them, didn't mind cuddling with a stack of bones every night.* Well, if so, she was very much afraid Clay wasn't one of them.

Then she thought of Pris. She was tall, of course, but she was still tiny around; and if Brad ever made her feel unworthy because of that, she certainly hadn't heard him. Maybe Clay's attitude hadn't been as understandable as she had tried to tell herself it was. Of course, his sister had never been voluptuous, but she was as far from that now as a sapling was from a full-grown oak.

When she came to the first street where she could cut off and go over to Braddock again, she took it. She felt terrible doing it, but she had to talk to someone. Who better than her best friend? Since her best friend was also Clay's sister, her decision to talk to Pris did seem a little dicey but not enough to keep her from steadily marching on. She had no one else.

As she stood on the wide porch that went across the two-story house, she felt that she was as nervous as she had been on the day she had thought that Curt had come. But she knocked without hesitation and waited.

Pris came rushing to the door. "I just got Thomas down for a nap, so please let's not wake him. If he knows you're here again, he'll want to be out here crawling all over you and we won't be able to talk. That is why you're here, isn't it? To talk?"

"Well, yes, but how did you know?"

Pris finished closing the door softly and came onto the porch. "Honey, you might as well give up trying to have secrets from me. I can read your face like a book. I thought something was bothering you, but I hoped so much that this time I could be wrong. Then when I saw you at the door, I knew I hadn't been. Let's sit down again on the steps out here where we won't be heard."

They sat back down on the battered second step from the top so the upper one could provide some kind of a back rest and spread their skirts to cover them to their feet. The rocking chairs that had once graced the McLaurines' porch, as they had most of the porches along the street, had long since been gone. That was true, of course, thanks to the Yankees' brutal treatment and their desire for anything they could burn in cold weather. "All right now. What is it?"

Jamie didn't know how to start. She opened her mouth, then closed it. Opened it again and shut it once more. How could she, or any girl married for less than four months, admit that she suspected the husband who had been so eager to marry her of being unfaithful? It simply couldn't be.

Finally, Pris said, "Is it Betsy?"

Relieved, Jamie gave a deep sigh and looked at her sister-in-law with gratitude. "Well, yes. I'm an idiot to suspect anything, am I not?"

Pris started to put her elbows on the knees and prop her chin in her palms. Then she straightened up, dropped her hands into her lap and turned to look right at Jamie. "Depends on what you suspect. If you are afraid that Betsy is still after Clay in some way, I'd be an idiot if I tried to tell you that she's not. She's been crazy for him since they were young teenagers. Her two older sisters made really good marriages, and Betsy's mother expected her to do the same. Actually, I think Mrs. Gains was the one who picked out Clay for a son-in-law first. Betsy obviously liked the idea, and that was it as far as the two of them were concerned. What she thinks it will do for her now that Clay is married is beyond me…unless she wants what she must have enjoyed during her one week of married life and would like to try it now with someone she really loves."

Jamie felt a cold chill run over her and clutched both of her arms tightly around herself. "Do you think she really loves Clay?"

Pris gave a shrug. "Oh, I wouldn't know about that, but I think she feels she does. Or maybe she's just a sore loser. I might be as wrong on all of that as I would be insisting Christmas always comes in July. But, regardless of what I think, I might as well be honest and tell you that you're going to have to deal with her sooner or later. She's been dropping around at Father's old office a lot and especially when Clay is there by himself."

"How can she know that? Do you mean that she watches for him?" Jamie took her arms from around herself to rub the small of her back. She hadn't even realized that it was hurting, but knew subconsciously that it was.

"I don't know. She might have her eye out. Brad and I have been wondering if I should say something to you."

"Say something to me?" Jamie snapped. "I'm not the one doing anything so why should you speak to me? Why don't you say something to her or to your brother?"

"Well, yes, you're right." She reached a placating hand out to Jamie. "Is that splintered edge on the porch floor hurting your back? Let's move down a little bit like we had to do a while ago. Maybe we can find a spot that's smoother." They got up and moved as she had suggested. Then she went on. "Actually, Brad has warned him that it doesn't look right for single girls to stop there when he's alone. Other than that, we just haven't known what to do. Of course, I'm not saying anything happens. I don't think it does, but, if I were you, I'd try to put an end to that—for appearances sake, if nothing else."

"But how can I?" Jamie almost moaned the words and clasped her hands. "I'm never there. And I'm new at this kind of thing.

After this morning, though, I am afraid of something. I saw the way she flirted with Clay right there in front of me. I think she was trying to point out the difference between her plump body and my bones. But that didn't bother me as much as Clay's reaction. He was practically foaming at the mouth. I could have died on the spot."

Pris shook her head sadly. "I will confess that I'm surprised at my brother. I thought that the war, losing his home and almost losing you had changed him, made him more the kind of man I always wanted him to be. And the kind I think he would be if…well, never mind that."

Jamie looked at her hard, but said nothing.

"So, yes…" Pris went on, "but I'm afraid I can't tell you that you have nothing to worry about because I don't know. The one thing I can tell you is that Clay loves you as much as it's possible for him to love a woman. He certainly does not love Betsy Gains…. She has never been as straight-laced as the other girls in our crowd. As I've told you before, I would have bucked like a mule if Clay had ever wanted to bring her into our family. I feel sure that Mother would have too."

Jamie gave a sardonic sort of smile. "She sure did about me."

Pris' answering smile was also sad. "Not my parents' shining moment of good judgment, in my opinion, but that's behind us. Clay says it is and he ought to know. He went down to Rose Hill and had it out with Mother and Father before they left for England. He would never have done that if he hadn't truly loved you. But…" Her voice trailed off and she looked away.

"But what?" Jamie asked, adjusting her position so the porch edge behind her wasn't cutting into her scarcely-protected back bone. "To me, that tells it all. Either he loves me or he doesn't."

"He does."

"Then why are you looking away from me and acting funny? Believe me, I know about love. My pa loved my mama so much that he was true to her memory till his dying day."

"Your father was a fine man in every way. I think everybody here recognized that from the day y'all arrived."

"Yes," Jamie said, "everybody seemed to know that except my miserable old grandfather and me. It sure was apparent to the man who let him have Fairdale the way he did, but I don't want to think about that now. I've worried enough about my treatment of my pa to send me into a nervous decline. Now I want to know what you started to say and hushed before you got it out. Surely you don't doubt the importance of love?"

"Oh, don't be ridiculous!" Pris turned her eyes back from wherever they had wandered and looked at her squarely. "Surely you don't have to ask that after knowing Brad."

"Of course, I don't. I just want to be loved by my husband as yours loves you. You don't have to give a thought to the Betsys of this world."

"No, and I'd stake my life that I never will, but all fathers are not like Brad's or yours." She hushed again and grabbed Jamie's hand. "Can't you just know that Clay loves you and that any difference in him and some of the other men you know is not his fault? It really is not."

Jamie pulled her hand away, stood up, straightened her dress around her as carefully as if she went entering a church door and said, "Well, thanks for the talk. I shouldn't have come, but I was expecting honesty instead of excuses for your brother. Mammy Rose never had any education except what she picked up listening to Pa teach me, but she sure knew enough to straighten me out when I'd try to get out of something by saying, 'It wasn't my fault.' I'll be going now, and we'll see you as usual for church Sunday."

Pris was on her feet too. "Oh, Jamie! Please don't go. Sit back down. I was putting it off every way I could, for I can hardly bear to tell you why the fault is not Clay's. I see now that I have to, so I will."

Both girls sat back down and, from force of habit, spread their skirts to cover their ankles. Jamie was saying nothing while Pris was trying hard to speak but having trouble doing it. When she floundered a time or two getting started, Jamie didn't try to prod or help her. She just waited.

"I…I…uh…I don't want to tell you this, and I'm not even sure I should." She was looking off in the distance again as if something of vast importance were out there if she could just locate it. Then she brought her eyes back down again and watched her hands as they folded the fullness of her gray cotton skirt into pleats over her knees. "You see," she said in a low, breathless sort of way, "I have always been proud of my family. In most ways, my father is a fine man…maybe even a great one…but he has the same excuse that Clay has for something of which I am terribly ashamed. It's not easy for a girl to speak ill of a parent she loves, and I want you to know that in most ways my parents have been good ones. Oh, I know that Father has always been overbearing and blustery, but a little girl learns early how to get around her father. Some sons never learn how to do that, and Clay was one of those. But maybe that too was not his fault."

When Jamie started to speak, Pris held up her hand for silence and went right on, "He tried to buck Father when he was maybe nine or ten and got such a tanning with Father's belt that he walked and sat funny for a few days. I guess he never forgot. From that, I think he must have learned that it was better to follow Father's lead."

"You're still making excuses, Pris," Jamie said and reached for one of the hands doing the skirt pleating.

Pris looked at her and gave a weak smile. "It's hard to break a promise, even if it's one you made only to yourself. But anyway, I've given you the picture. I did not let Father terrorize me, maybe because I'd never felt his belt across my backsides and felt sure I never would. Clay has always taken most everything Father said as gospel truth, maybe because he had felt father's belt and didn't want to feel it again. Or maybe it was something more. I actually think it was, but I certainly can't say what."

"Yes, you can," Jamie put in quickly. "It's because of the kind of person he and you were put on earth to be. There's something in you that is stronger than what's in a lot of people. I thought it was in Clay too. I'm absolutely sure that some people find it much easier to resist temptation than others because they're born to be that way. Some are born to be naturally good, and some are born to be naturally bad. I would think that the ones who have to work hard to overcome their stronger tendency not to do right get special credit. I have no idea how that works, but I feel sure that God lets people be born with all sorts of differences. Think what an unworkable, dull place the world would be if we were all the same." She stopped, took a breath and said, "I sure hope He takes that inborn difference into consideration on Judgment Day."

Pris looked at her as though she had suddenly gone out of her head. She said nothing.

Jamie smiled sheepishly. "Yes, I know, I don't have any idea what I'm talking about, but in the lonely, desperate months we've had, I've done a lot of wondering. Can't you see that the world would be a mighty different place without those unusual instincts we're born with? I think that some people find it almost impossible to do wrong while some others seem born to be plain mean."

"Jamie!" Pris protested. "That is ridiculous. So you think you should overlook what Betsy does because she was born with looser morals than you and I?"

That yanked Jamie up short. Her eyes fell to the dirt in front of the steps that had once been abundant grass around a brick walk. "Well, how do I know what makes her or anybody else tick? I'm just saying that neither you nor I could do as she is doing. I'm sure she got the same training as her sisters who behaved themselves and got good husbands. I'm mixed up, I admit. Mixed up on so many things, so forget what I just said and tell me what I have to know."

"How can I tell you what I'd rather not tell you in the first place if you go off on a tangent like that?" Pris demanded.

"Sorry," Jamie mumbled. "You said you didn't know the other reason for the difference, and I was giving you one. Maybe I'm wrong anyway."

"I think you are. I remember a visiting priest saying something one Sunday that really impressed me. He said that we are all born with the same clean slate, and what we write on it in our lives is entirely up to us. If you're saying that some people are born with urges and weakness already on their slate, that kind of reinforces my statement that some things are not always the fault of the person who is faced with them. Now, can I finish what I was trying to tell…or trying not to tell…or will you just accept my word that it might not be Father's fault…or Clay's…that Betsy could be sort of a problem? Or do you just want to say that there is no hope, for that's the way we were all born?"

Jamie looked at her with a mixture of amusement, annoyance and confusion. "I'm sorry. I didn't mean to interrupt you as I have, and, of course, I won't be content until I've heard what you started to say."

Pris reached out and gave her a pat on her shoulder. "I'm sorry too. I think I was saying that Father was always very respectful and loving to Mother. It certainly never seemed possible that there could be any flaw in their relationship, and maybe there wouldn't be if things had been taught differently. I never suspected anything and I'm pretty sure Clay didn't either until he was getting to be sixteen, and Mother had Mary Lilly and Cooke with her over at Rose Hill. The female members of our family over there always came up to spend several weeks with us every winter. Mother would then take us and go down there for a month or more in the summer or fall. Of course, all that ended with the war."

"The ones from over there were here when we first came," Jamie broke in to say. "I remember thinking how nice it must be to have a family like that."

Pris smiled rather grimly. "Clay fussed about having to pay so much attention to the old great-aunts. He got awfully tired of that and would go away for a few days when he could. Still, they were family and we were always taught that families were of vital importance. We would go down there and be gone for a month or so in the summer or fall. That left Father here alone, for he couldn't leave his law practice for that long. Clay and I loved our visits there when we were young, but when we were getting older, we didn't want to leave our friends here, so we'd stay with Father while Mother, Mary Lilly and Cooke went."

She hesitated for long moments so to urge her on, Jamie said, "Yes, I understand. And I've heard others mention those long, yearly visits. I always wished I had a family to do that."

Pris, with obvious reluctance, started again, "They were still there when Clay's sixteenth birthday came around. Father said at supper that night that…that he was taking him out for his gift. I begged to go along, but Father absolutely refused. That kind of irked me, so I made up my mind I'd stay awake until they got home. I was going to see that present, one way or another. You know the table that had the front panel and sat in the upstairs hall. Well, maybe you don't. I hid myself under it and, of course, I soon fell asleep. They were coming up the stairs when I woke up. I peeped out as far as I dared, but Clay wasn't carrying a thing, so I thought his gift must have been a better horse or saddle than he already had. Whatever it was, I wasn't going to be outdone so I waited until Father had ruffled Clay's hair, given him a hug and gone to his own room. Then I sneaked into Clay's. He was lying there, still fully-clothed and wide-awake. I plunked myself down on the foot of his bed and announced that I wasn't leaving until he showed me or told me what his present had been.

"At first, he didn't say anything, but when I said again that I wasn't budging from there until I heard what he had gotten, he said I didn't really want to know. I said that I did and he might as well tell me then, for I'd keep after him till he did. So he told me. Watched his words carefully but told me and thereby changed the way I looked at my family forever."

Pris had hushed and again looked away. Far off, over the housetops to the mountains. Jamie waited impatiently for her to go on. When Pris didn't, she spoke, "Well, what was it? And, why didn't Clay want to tell you or you want to tell me? How could a birthday present do anything to your life?" Jamie's words were spoken rather calmly, but her mind was whirling wildly. What on earth had Clay gotten that had changed things for Pris, and what would it do now to *her* life?

# 22

Pris faced her again and said, "The gift was advice and experience in the family tradition. And to my way of thinking, Clay needed another horse or a second saddle a thousand times more than he needed what he got."

Jamie just stared at her, saying nothing, but her body was tingling with some kind of fearsome dread.

"Clay told me," Pris said slowly as she kept looking away to the hills, "that Father had advised him very definitely on what he needed to know as he passed from childhood into the adult world. He should be loyal to his family and friends, act in a generally honorable way, never try to force a girl to do anything she preferred not to do. He pointed out that God had obviously meant for girls to remain virtuous until marriage, for He had designed them so they could prove to their husbands that they had stayed pure. He said God did not necessarily mean for men to be that way until marriage, for He had made no such provision in the design of men."

Pris stopped speaking, and Jamie was so tense that she didn't realize she was holding her breath until she suddenly was almost choking for air. She gasped a few times, gave something like a cough and waited for her sister-in-law to speak again.

When it seemed that the other girl wasn't going to, she said, "I have to hear it all. Clay is your brother, but he is my husband. I have to know what his father taught him and if it's anything that will affect our marriage."

Pris met Jamie's eyes for a long moment. "I guess I have to so you'll know how to guard against it. But, oh, how I wish I didn't even have to remember it, much less tell it."

"Go on," Jamie said and her voice was again firm as she did so.

"All right, but remember that I do this with doubts." She

hesitated, but when Jamie just stared at her, she said, "This rule of Father's is one that Clay can easily accept. He was told that he should never consider marrying any woman he did not love with his whole heart. He was to respect and care for her in every way, never giving her reason to doubt his love. But—and listen to this, Jamie—he…he…said he wanted Clay to understand that it was possible to love a wife as he had said; and still, when the need arises, he can…" Pris hesitated, then said in a rush, "have another woman without its affecting or even touching that love."

Jamie almost laughed. The idea was so ludicrous that she thought surely Pris didn't mean it. Then she saw the look on her friend's face, and any thought of sarcastic amusement died at birth. "You actually mean that?" she asked wonderingly. "I don't see how you can, but you do."

As Jamie looked at Pris' stricken face, big tear drops started forming and then began running down her own cheeks. "Pris, if you're telling me the truth, you're practically ruining my hope for a decent future. I can't believe this. And I don't see how you can possibly know something like that."

"I do know it. I'm just telling you what Clay told me ten years ago. He was so stunned by all Father had told him that night that I know he wasn't lying. He had to believe because of where Father had taken him and what he had been encouraged to do. He, of course, told me nothing more about that except what I'm telling you, but the very thought that my father actually thinks that is possible made me sick. But I'm telling you because I think that you must stop it before it ever begins with Clay."

"Your father did that too?" Jamie whispered.

Pris shook her head so violently that the pins fell out of the bun on the back of her head, and her silvery blonde hair spread all around her shoulders. She just threw it over onto her back and let it hang. "I don't know about that. Clay didn't say that Father did a thing or ever had, except take him there. That's what I believe, maybe because that's what I want to think but anyway, I do. Certainly, at least, that night because Father did have a strong sense of decorum. Anyway, as I told you, this was to be an advice and experience lesson. Clay said Father told him that some men sneak off and do things and then have to live in fear that they'd be found out. Their tradition taught that it was better to avoid that feeling of guilt and fear by letting the wife know that if he found such action needful, it would not have the least thing to do with their love. It was nothing more than taking care of bodily needs."

Jamie was stunned into silence. Both girls sat there, staring, but not at each other. Finally, Jamie said, "I have never heard of anything that egotistical in my life. That's no tradition. That's just giving themselves a license to sin and trying not to even feel guilty about it. If Clay thinks I'll put up with that, he's got another think coming. Why any wife ever would, I can't see."

"Well, you might remember that my mother came all the way from England. She probably never heard of that stupid family tradition until she got over here, and she could hardly run home to her parents. And she does love my father. Anybody can see that. And I know he loves her."

"Then let him live like it."

"I don't know that he doesn't. And neither do you."

That hushed Jamie for a moment. "Well," she finally said, "that could be, but he's a poor excuse for a father to even tell that stuff to Clay. Or to introduce him to something that he had no business doing anyway." Then she realized she was talking about Pris' father and said, "Maybe I shouldn't have said that. But unless Cooke picks it up, that tradition is dying with my husband. And doing it long before he dies himself."

Pris actually gave a weak chuckle. "That was one reason I thought I had to tell you. I thought you'd be tough enough to get Clay back onto the right path. In trying to explain it to you, I guess I've been like a person who can't read herself trying to teach another one to write, but you do understand and will clip Betsy's wings any way you think fit?"

"You better believe I will. But why didn't you do anything? Maybe if you had told your mother what your father was teaching her son, she would have helped."

Pris gave a sort of disdainful snort. "I tried that. I had to wait for days to see how I could tell her without making it sound that Father might have been guilty of following his own advice. I did it right after Mother came home from Rose Hill. I went into her room one morning after Father had gone to the office. When I started floundering around about what Clay called a family tradition, she stopped me almost immediately. She said I had no business knowing anything about that and that I was messing into something that was none of my concern. Then she slapped me. Slapped me so hard that my head didn't feel comfortable on my shoulders for the rest of the day. That was the only time she ever slapped me, and it took me years to understand what that slap meant."

"What did it mean?" Jamie asked.

"Don't be dumb, Jamie," the other girl snapped.

"If it took you years to figure it out, why am I dumb not to know immediately?" Jamie asked.

Pris gave a sort of grim-sounding chuckle. "You're right. Now don't you think we've worn this subject down as far as it should go? From the first I wanted you to think you were coming into a great family, and you really were. Concentrate on that and don't hesitate to do what you think is best where your husband is concerned."

"Oh, I won't, but like your mother's slap, it takes some thought. I do have to think before I do or say anything. Can I tell him what you've told me?"

"Do whatever seems best, but I'm not sure I would. I do so much want for you two to have a marriage like mine and Brad's. I think you can when Clay realizes that a great figure is nothing but outer dressing. The real you is deep inside."

Jamie gave a little shrug. "Maybe. Maybe not. Thanks for talking to me. I better get on home. After Clay leaves Brad, he'll probably go on over and dig some more at your old home. I do wish he could find that silver."

Pris walked with her out the short way to the street. "Yeah, me too, but that's not nearly as important to me as to Clay."

"Maybe that's because you're no longer a Haynesworth.

You're a McLaurine now and…"

"The McLaurines had very little silver," Pris said with a laugh. "And I can't think of anything that bothers me less than that."

"I feel the same way, but it's important to your brother. And he is determined to rebuild Crestview with that silver in it. Well, I'll see you Sunday…if I'm still surviving."

"You will be," Pris told her with a fond smile. "You're a Haynesworth now, and you have to be strong."

Jamie's laugh was a sarcastic, "Yeah!" And she headed for home with a heart that felt too heavy for a weak, skinny girl to carry.

# 23

By the time Jamie got back to Fairdale, she was as exhausted as if she were back in the days of near-starvation. Her head felt as heavy on her shoulders as if it were made of lead. She could hardly wait to go upstairs, crawl back into the bed and stay there forever. But she had no intention of giving in to that temptation. She had to think and think hard about things that she certainly couldn't have even begun to mention to Pris.

"This is my punishment," she whispered to herself as she hurried to her door. "That weight that I feel on my shoulders is bound to be God's hand pushing me toward repentance. " She had hurt one man by her harsh treatment and by blaming him for a war that he could do nothing about except fight and risk his life for four years like the good soldier he was. She had wronged her husband by not being honest with him and telling him all the things that sat so heavy on her heart. She had wronged her father by her lack of understanding and appreciation for what he was and had let him die without having any idea of how much she loved him. She was a poor excuse for all the things that she wanted so much to be!

As she moved on down the avenue to her house, her eyes turned to the big oak tree down near the stream. Somehow, its heavy branches reaching out and down seemed to her to be like sheltering arms so without a thought of doing so, she bypassed the house and headed for the mound under it. That mound also spoke to her of protection and love so she went under the branches and knelt by the big rock that Steven and his friends had moved there to be a headstone. Then she cried as she had vowed she would never cry again.

"Why are you acting like this?" she asked herself with real annoyance after a time. "Clay probably hasn't done anything more than what any other young man would do if a well-built girl had insisted on throwing herself at him." She could let him know that Haynesworth tradition was over and done with—if it had ever meant anything, anyway. Pris was right. All she'd have to do was let Clay know that he could not have her and that stupid tradition too. He hadn't mentioned it to her himself, so he probably had forgotten all about it himself.

She pulled herself together, brushed off the plaid calico of her dress and headed up to the house. "I am a Haynesworth," she told herself, as she so often did. But somehow that thought was not as comforting as it had been many other times.

As she rounded the house, Steven came rushing out from the back. "Miss Jamie, dat boy who brung things before has done come again, and dis time he brung us a nice-size fryin' chicken. Said he knowed them little biddies he brung a while back warn't big enough yet to fry, but he thought we mought like some fried chicken fer supper. He also said fer you to check it carefully. Rhody ain't done nothin' to it but set it on de kitchen table to wait fer you."

Jamie reached for the handkerchief that she knew wasn't there. She sure wished it were, for she wanted to wipe her eyes and blow her nose. Instead, she just sniffled and said, "That's mighty nice. Did he give you his or his parents' name this time? I really should thank them."

"No, ma'am. He ain't said nothin' like dat. He said dey was just neighbors and liked to share what dey had."

"Well, that certainly is generous of him and his folks. If he ever comes again, be sure and tell him how much we appreciate their generosity."

"Yes, ma'am. I kinda' 'spects he'll be back," he said, then added hastily, "but I ain't knowin' nothin' 'bout who he is. I reckons he be what he says—a neighbor."

Jamie was mighty glad to see Steven turn and head back around the house. Her running nose just had to be wiped, and she had nothing but her skirt with which to do it. She wiped carefully, checking to see that she wasn't observed and went on around to the kitchen door.

"You all right, Miss Jamie?" Rhody asked when the girl went in. "I sure hope de surprise done worked out good."

"Well, maybe not as good as I expected, but it was all right. Thank you so much for your help. Steven says a neighbor brought us a chicken for supper. It sure is good that we have at least a little lard and the flour Steven got ground for us."

"Yes'm, ain't dat right! Dat's de chicken in dat bag on de table. Reckon I ort to bake it 'stead of fryin'? We ain't never had baked, and it ain't gonna take no lard."

"That's a good idea. We've got eggs so we can have dressing."

Rhody shook her head. "Ain't got no sage. Can't make dressin' widout sage."

"Oh? Well, do whatever you like. I need to change my dress, so I'll see you later."

"Yes'm. I think I'll mosey out and see what Steven can come up wid to go wid de chicken. It bein' Mr. Clay's birthday, we ort to have a cake, but I ain't got enough sugar."

"No, but we've sure got apples. But remember not to throw the cores away. We need them to go in our apple orchard."

"Yes'm. I ain't forgettin'."

As soon as the woman was out the door, Jamie was lifting the chicken out of the bag. Tucked inside of it was a folded paper. Worried, she pulled it out, unwrapped it and found a letter inside. With trembling hands and staring eyes, Jamie read, *Dear Aunt Kate.* It was from Curt!

She had never seen Curt's handwriting, but she was as sure that this letter was from him as if she had seen his hand holding the pen and forming each word. She closed her eyes for a moment, wondering if she should read it since it wasn't a letter to her. She didn't wait for an answer to that. No matter what reading someone else's mail did to her conscience, she had to know that he was all right. Maybe she was meant to read it, anyway.

*Dear Aunt Kate,*

*From the fact that I'm writing this, you must know that I am greatly improved. I will never be able to thank you and my...*

That word was marked through. The letter went on:

*...Jamie for saving me from what I am certain would have been death.*

*It was kind of rough, but that New York doctor was fantastic. I'm home, walking a lot, eating well and getting better every day.*

*I can't tell you what your letter meant to me describing your visit to Jamie's. Of course, I couldn't read it at that time, but I've read it many times since I'm myself again.*

*I will never forgive myself for what I did to her. I was so disappointed and, well, heartbroken that I hardly knew what I was doing. I knew she was sick. That was plain to see. So I thought she needed some time to get her head straight. I understood what she was feeling and wanted so much to help her, but she made it clear that was not the time I could do it. I knew the family was waiting so I discarded the carriage, and when the extra horse escaped my tether, I didn't even try to catch him. I just wanted to get home. I took a short cut I had found when I was making maps for the army, and then the horse slipped on those loose stones. That's the last I remember till I woke up in New York.*

*I had meant to be back to Winchester in a couple of weeks and get her medical aid of whatever type she needed. I knew there was something wrong, and she was accepting nothing from a Yankee right then. It never occurred to me that I would lose everything by leaving her. I'll never forgive myself, for I am very much afraid the day will come when she'll feel the same way. She needed help then, and I guess the help had to come from a Southerner, but when I think that she married to get that help, the pain is far greater than it was when I was getting kicked by old Jupiter as we slid down that mountain.*

*Please, Aunt Kate, keep an eye on her. The time will come when she will need help again, and I am determined never to fail her again. As things are now, I can do nothing but depend on you to continue as you have been doing from a distance. She's a wonderful, beautiful person, inside and out, and I will love her to my dying day. But I can hardly say that to a married woman, can I?*

*Thanks again for everything. Papa will keep sending you whatever you need, especially the U.S. money.*

*Love,*

*Curtis.*

Jamie almost clutched the letter to her breast but caught herself and held it away as if it had suddenly become hot. This was not a letter to her, and she had no right to be reading it. Mrs. Darby's mistaken romantic ideas about the situation had made her send it on. And Jamie said to herself and felt guilty at the thought, *thank the good Lord for that*!

Of course, she went on to think, still holding the letter as far away from her as she could, the real reason could only have been that Curt's aunt had known how relieved Jamie would be to know that her own guilt about his condition was less than she had once feared. But whether it was right or wrong for the woman to do it and whether she should have read it or not, Jamie was grateful to Aunt Kate. So grateful to know that Curt was not blaming her as he had every right to do. She knew that Curt's innate decency would never have let him write to a married woman, but his aunt must have felt that she should know what he had written.

The new combination of guilt, confusion and relief coming along right at this time had almost knocked her off her feet. She couldn't even think why Curt was signing himself as Curtis. Then, of course, she knew. He was probably named for his father, so he had used only the first part of his given name to keep them straight. It hadn't been meant to hide his identity.

Now she did clutch the letter to her skinny breast, realized what she was doing and pulled it away as sharply as if it had again become burning hot.

And it had.

What could she do with it? She guessed she would have to wait till Rhody built a fire in the range and sneak it in someway. She sure couldn't risk letting it stay around for Clay to ever find. She looked around to see that nobody was coming and tucked it into her stay cover. Then she snatched it out. That seemed entirely too intimate a place to hide a letter like this. She could tear it into little bits and let them fly away in the fall breeze, but somehow she didn't want to do that either. Finally, she left it where she had tucked it and headed out of the kitchen.

More guilt! More disloyalty!

Didn't she have enough to cope with now that she knew about that idiotic Haynesworth tradition? That wasn't any sort of decent tradition. It was just an egotistical announcement to a wife that she satisfy her husband always or he would find relief elsewhere. Ridiculous! If anybody thought she would live with that hanging over her head, he was completely out of his own head.

Then she thought of the letter tucked into her bosom. And felt like screaming.

She looked at the plump, already-dressed chicken. Would eating that tonight, now that she definitely knew from whom it had come, have the same effect on her as the rides every Sunday in the carriage that she, and only she, knew was really his?

She knew it would.

# 24

Jamie had changed her dress, washed herself and brushed her hair until it fell in soft waves over her shoulders. That was the way Clay liked it. She told herself that she was doing it because it was still his birthday, but underneath she knew that it was something like an attempt at atonement. She certainly hadn't done anything intentionally wrong, but still the guilt that had ridden her like a jockey on a race horse ever since her wedding day stuck even tighter. She could not be anything less than happy on the end of his birthday, and especially not when they had something really good for his birthday supper.

"If I'd known we had this chicken, I'd have blown a bit of money that I have left and gotten us some milk so we could have had gravy," Clay said as he pulled her chair up to the table.

Jamie smiled up at him and said, "That would have been nice. How can you make that money last as it has? When we have money again, I would certainly want you to handle it, for you can stretch it better than anybody I ever saw." She felt almost dishonest to be putting on this act as though nothing had happened, but she had a lot of thinking to do before she made any change in the way she had been.

He grinned as he seated himself. "You better believe that's the way it will be. And we will have money again. After all, we're Haynesworths. But as far as our present money is concerned, Father sends me a little more now and then. He knows that things are still tough here and will be until the Federal government makes amends to us. And maybe even then."

Where this reference to their being Haynesworths would have once thrilled her, it almost annoyed her now. She wanted a well-respected name, of course, but she was so all-fired tired of hearing that he and his family had to be the best in everything. Still, she had more important things than that to talk to him about, and his birthday was definitely not the time to do it.

"Where'd we get this birthday chicken?" he asked as he was enjoying his favorite piece, the breast. "It must be from some of my old friends who remembered that this was the day."

She shrugged. "Steven said that the boy who brought it said it was from a neighbor but didn't give his or his parents' names. They've done it before, you know, but I've never seen him. Steven doesn't have any idea what his name is. He just wants him to keep on sharing."

The mountain of guilt that was already almost smothering her grew even higher. There was nothing untrue about what she was saying and nothing true about it either. She hated that sort of thing. Mammy Rose had sat her in the corner enough times when she had been really small that she had learned the advantage of speaking the truth. Of course, there were times when the truth was a lie and a lie was the truth, and this was one of them.

Clay had come home late and dirty. She didn't ask if he had found the silver but knew that he hadn't. All in all, this was not the day for a serious talk about anything, so when Clay said as they were getting up from the table that he was going to wash up and hit the hay, she didn't offer any objection. When she finally fell into a restless sleep herself, he had already been sleeping for hours.

He was already up when she awoke the next morning. She pulled on her old robe and went down barefoot to join him for breakfast. He sprang to his feet at the sight of her, gave her a kiss and pointed to his bowl of oatmeal. "Since you're off of mush for life, have Rhody get you some of this. It'll put weight on those bones of yours and keep you satisfied longer than anything else."

"I know," she said, trying to sink into her chair and also attempting not to look at the deep scratches on the table that bothered her so much. "I am so glad that Steven had learned from Mr. McKay about growing oats and having them rolled for oatmeal. I don't think my father knew about that."

"Mine does. We had it a lot with raw sugar and butter. When we can get more of those things, you'll like it too."

"And get as plump as Betsy Gains? Then maybe you won't have to ogle her till your eyeballs practically fall out of your head." When she heard herself blurting out those words, she was as startled as he was. She had had no idea that she was about to say them. They had just come out as though from their own will. Clay's spoonful of oatmeal stopped halfway to his mouth. "What does that mean?" he demanded.

This certainly was not the way she had lain awake last night planning it, but she was in and she wasn't backing out now. "I saw the way you were looking at her yesterday. And I didn't like it."

His spoon dropped back into the bowl, and he stared at her for a long moment. Then he threw his head back and laughed. "You're jealous!" he almost shouted. "My wife is jealous!" And he leaned over and kissed her. "I love it."

"Don't enjoy it too much," she said, "for I don't care for it at all myself. Neither do I care for Betsy. I want you to tell her that she is not to keep coming around to your office. Either you tell her or I will," she ended in a far less defiant tone than she had intended.

His laughter died, and he looked at her strangely. "You're serious. You think I have any interest in that girl or in any part of her body?"

"By the time you had gotten your eyeballs reinstalled in your head, I was wondering. I certainly don't want other people to start wondering too. Either you tell her she is not to come there or I will." She stopped a moment and then said, "Do you want to tell her or do you want me to do it?" She knew she was probably making a mess of this whole thing. She went on, knowing that she had spoken in haste and might regret it, but not retracting a single word. Now she waited.

Clay pushed back his chair, got up and came to give her a kiss on the forehead. "I'm afraid you got up on the wrong side of the bed this morning. I'll send her packing, if that's what you want, but sometimes it's nice to have someone to talk to when I'm struggling to get old wood torn away without pulling the whole

177

wall down, or to have help in cleaning up the mess I've made."

"Then" she asked, "why have you refused every time I've offered to go in with you? I can listen or clean as well as Betsy Gains."

"I didn't want you spending your energy doing that when you need it all to put back on some weight. Your health is a lot more important to me than the office."

"My health," she asked softly, "or my figure?"

He stared at her. Then he said, "I don't believe I'll even answer a question like that."

He started from the dining room but stopped in the doorway and said, "I saw Steven carrying my pan of hot water upstairs for my shave. Come on up with me while I do that. You can eat your oatmeal so you can compete with Betsy on figures later."

Jamie didn't know if he were trying to tease or was mad, but she jumped up and joined him. He must not be mad, she decided, when he draped an arm around her as they went.

"I saw Mrs. Boyd yesterday on the street. You do know who she is, don't you?" he asked as they went.

"Of course, I do. She's the wife of the preacher who supported the Confederacy strongly. She and her sister-in-law were the ones who started the LMA. What did she want?"

They were at their room now. Jamie went in and sat down in her rocker while he was getting out his shaving equipment. He opened the long blade and drew it several times across the belt to sharpen it. Then he soaped up his face before answering her. "She wants to know why you haven't joined the Ladies Memorial Association," he told her as he screwed up his face to give himself a smoother surface to draw the razor across.

"She says Pris told her to put your name on but that you haven't paid your initiation fee. Embarrassed the daylights out of me. I told her I didn't know anything about it. You were having trouble getting your strength back after the terrible last year, so I had wanted you to take it easy for a while. She understood, but she practically reached her hand out to get what you owe. I had to explain that I didn't bring money with me but that you would pay up right away, and I felt sure you'd soon start coming to the meetings. That was all right, wasn't it?" He was carefully drawing the razor over his chin so his words were not clear.

"I told Pris to tell them that I certainly wanted to be a member and to go ahead and put my name on their list. Goodness knows, it's hard for people to have a cent of extra money. And, I might add, that's the exact reason I haven't paid. I haven't had a cent since Confederate money became worthless."

He threw his razor down and started rinsing his face before he turned to her almost angrily. "You do remember that you have a husband, don't you? Or has that little item completely escaped your memory?"

When she didn't answer, he went on, "You do know that husbands provide their wives with the money they need?"

Jamie shrugged. "Well, I guess I do. This is the first time I've lived in a house where there was a husband and a wife, so I've been kind of feeling my way. You seemed to keep your money a secret. I haven't known how much you had so I didn't want to ask for five dollars. I considered having Pris ask if I could have one of the fifty-cent memberships that she says some people have had to have, but I didn't have the fifty cents."

"And if you had done that, it would have embarrassed me right out of that year I gained yesterday." He dried his face and turned to her, saying, "You should have asked me right away for the five dollars for the LMA. I would rather go hungry than look like a cheapskate. And certainly not when we're talking about what we now are. Do you know how the LMA was started?"

Jamie was quiet for a moment, then said, "Yes, I know all about how it started and why. It's a fine organization. I first heard about it when so many women mentioned it to me at our wedding. Then I asked Pris and when she told me about it, I knew immediately that I wanted to be a member. She said you had told her not to get me involved until I regained the weight I had lost."

He gave her a hard look. "What else do you know and aren't sharing with your husband? Are there other things you aren't discussing with me?"

At those words, Jamie felt the strength seep out of her legs like water from a badly-leaking bucket. She had gotten up but now groped for the chair behind her. When she was back in it, she looked up at Clay and searched for words that were true. "I know I haven't actually mentioned the five dollars to you, but I thought I had asked you about my joining. Are you sure that I hadn't? You just haven't listened to us. You and Brad always have so much to talk about that Pris and I just kind of huddle together with Thomas."

He thought that over and grinned. "I guess you're right about that. But remember you are a Haynesworth now. You ask me for whatever you need and want. I will supply it if I can, but we do not ever appear to be cheap or refuse to do our part in worthwhile endeavors." He leaned down and gave her a kiss. "I'm taking the five dollars to Mrs. Boyd today for you. I know the whole organization has to be run by the ladies to avoid any trouble with the Union military, but I feel sure they'll accept it from me."

"Yes, I'm sure they will."

"Now you get back in there and eat a big bowl of that oatmeal," he started to say as they walked back down the stairs together, but she cut him off before he could get it out. "If you start on that again, I may find another use for your razor upstairs." And made a motion with her hand across her throat.

He chuckled and said, "I wouldn't recommend it. That old razor is so dull it would never do the job." He pulled her to him for a tight hug, kissed her and said, "Well, gotta' go. I don't want to keep Betsy waiting."

As he went down the porch steps, Jamie called out, "Josh about it, if you want, but I really meant every word I said." He laughed, made a sort of dismissive motion with his hand and headed up to the pike.

She hadn't done that right, she told herself. She had planned it so carefully and then had jumped in without a thought in her head. After that, Clay had turned the table on her by becoming an injured one himself. Still, she had told him what had to be done about Betsy, and he had agreed to do it. Maybe it hadn't been too bad, after all. Now she was going to put Betsy with the other things she was not going to think about.

But why couldn't she do that as well now as she had in the past? She had blocked Curt Darby from her mind so completely that she had given him scarcely a thought for weeks…actually, not until his brother had shown up. Now she was having trouble blocking a line of that letter she had read yesterday. She had been so afraid Clay might see it that she had slept with it under the ratty old mattress on her side of the bed last night. It could not stay there.

Curt had said she was sick. Was she and would she get worse until she lost everything?

That didn't bear thinking about.

# 25

She had dressed and done as Clay had asked, but she did not want the leftover oatmeal that she found over on the side of the kitchen stove. Still, she was so concerned about right and wrong, loyalty and disloyalty, honesty and dishonesty that she felt obliged to try to eat it. She took a bite of the too-thick, nearly-cold mixture and almost gagged. She pushed it away and reached for an apple that lay on the table. When she took a bite, at least it gave her no argument about not wanting to stay down.

She sat there and munched on it, wondering if it had come from the bushel that she knew was from the Darbys' farm. She was also wondering what she could do to get the feeling that her life would ever be as a newly-married girl's should be. She wanted to start getting her house back as it had been when she and Pa had first been here. She wanted to keep on preparing the land and planting apple seeds for the big apple orchard she had resolved to have. Clay had no real interest in her home except as a place to stay until he could get his office running and start rebuilding his old home.

She would be as true as it was possible to be to a husband, while he thought he could make love with his eyes to a girl who was not his wife. Then if he someday became stressed out, he might think he could use more than his eyes. Did his wife's shape mean that much to him? And suspecting it did, why had she found it so difficult to eat enough of anything that would put weight on her and give her back the kind of body he admired so much? Was she in some strange, mixed-up way, trying to save herself for…what?

No! Oh, no, please don't let that be it! Surely the trouble that she sensed in her marriage could not be as much for her lack of moral stability as she had thought it might be in Clay's.

She had worried terribly about another man ever since her

wedding day, but that had had nothing to do with love. It was just a terrible guilt that any decent person would have felt if she had been the cause of such damage to another person. It didn't mean love. There was no way she could have loved a Yankee. He had been good and kind, but how could she have ever spent her life among those people? Even now, she felt that she could have gone to bed with a rattlesnake as easily as with a Yankee.

The memory of Curt's saying she was sick that terrible morning when she had sent him away rang in her head like one of the bells that had tolled the death of the Confederacy. She was very much afraid that he had been right. And considering the thoughts that were still in her head, he would probably be still right if he said it again today.

But she felt sure none of those problems were exactly why she had not recovered. It was guilt that was holding her back. She would try to get rid of it, but it was always there like the mound of dirt covering a grave. She felt she deserved to feel a lessening of her guilt about Curt since she knew she had not caused his death or permanent disability. Unfortunately there was no way in the world that she could shed what she felt about keeping secrets from her husband. She felt sure that she would ruin a lot more than she cured if she confessed everything to him. The horse and carriage were an almost constant reminder of her disloyalty, and they would be the same to Clay if he ever knew.

She looked at the battered old kitchen table at which she sat. If she could have something that would sand…or whatever she would need…and could get the scratches out of this one thing, she felt that she might feel better. But Clay had refused to get anything to help get her furniture or her home in better shape. He did not want his wife doing such work and had no time for or interest in doing it himself. He said that they were going to replace all the beautiful furnishings his home had once had. She admired his determination to be a success and his faith in himself, but there was nothing about which they felt the same except the Haynesworth name itself.

When she had finished the apple, she threw the core out the

kitchen door, then went out in the yard and retrieved it. She would save it for Steven to plant. Then she wandered around, feeling like a lost soul in her own home. She didn't want to stay inside and see so many things that she wanted to start doing and know that she could not. She went through the front hall and out the generally-unused front door. Almost with no intention of doing so, she found herself following the path down to the creek. When she got there, she stepped out onto the big rock as she and Clay had done her first day here. She sat down, drew here knees up to her chest, wrapped her arms and skirt tightly around them and put her head onto her knees.

She sat there remembering all the things that had happened to her since that terrible day when she had been seven years old and knew that there was something about her and her pa that was not good. If her grandparents, who had no one but her since her mama had died, didn't want her, how could she have any worth to anybody else?

Mammy Rose had tried to cure her of that feeling, but it had stayed with her and colored almost everything in her life since then. And she thought to herself, why wouldn't it when she knew that the Pa she had once loved so much had caused her to be unacceptable to the only other family she had? Was she going to spend the rest of life feeling tainted because of being a woods colt? Hadn't becoming a Haynesworth cured her of that?

Her mind wandered on through the years, suffering again as she remembered. Then, feeling a strange, desperate need for help, she began praying. She asked God to somehow help her understand the meaning of her many troubles. To help her know how to be as happy as she had expected to be with Clay but wasn't. Had she done wrong?

All of a sudden she heard a voice saying, "You don't love that Haynesworth boy. You never did. You had a schoolgirl crush on him, but you only loved his family name." She jerked herself erect, pushing her legs straight out and feeling water up to her ankles. The rest of her followed as she slid off the rock into the stream. Standing waist deep in the water she turned and looked all around. Where had that voice come from? It had sounded so close, but there was not a soul in sight.

She went over and climbed up the bank, wiped her feet on her skirt and stood looking around almost as if she were in a trance. She had heard those words as clear as a church bell. *God?* Had those words come from God? Or had she dropped off to sleep and dreamed them? And even then, had God put them there in her dream?

Fortunately, the day was warm for late September, but she was still shivering by the time she reached the house, hoping that neither Steven nor Rhody would see her sneaking up to her room for something dry and warm to wear. She wished she still had the beautiful blue shawl that Curt had brought her that Christmas. She would wrap herself in it, but, no, that had gone with the Yankees. Some woman somewhere up in the North was probably wrapped in it now.

Then she slumped down by her bed, covered her face and wondered when she would quit foolishly digging herself deeper and deeper into the mountain of guilt that had become her home. Finally, she drew herself up, pulled on the fresh dress that had been too ugly for even the Yankees to want and slipped back down the stairs and out to the front porch. There she stood, looking around and feeling as if she were in a strange place. What did she do and where did she go now? She just crumpled down on the porch floor and wept.

When she had cried herself out, she sat up and remembered again the words the voice had spoken as clearly as if they had just been said. *Would God have called Clay "that Haynesworth boy"?* Somehow, she didn't think so. *Curt!* That was what Curt had called Clay. Had God somehow spoken to her through Curt? Or had she finally completely lost her mind? Curt had known she was sick. Somehow she felt sure that, had he known how sick, he would never have left her. And she felt sure he would have made things even worse.

However, there was nothing to be gained by thinking thoughts like that. She had to decide what to do now. Should she try to see a doctor? No! This was something she had to cure herself. She knew that the last months of the war had all but killed her, but all the Winchester people had suffered a lot of the same things and they weren't sick.

She got up and walked over to the front porch steps and sat down. She had to somehow figure out what she had done, where she had made mistakes that could be corrected. Had what she felt for Clay been nothing but grown-up "puppy love" and the desire for an outstanding respectable name? Would she have married Clay so hastily, without a thought, if he hadn't pushed her as he had? She had been so glad and relieved to feel anything for anybody that she hadn't taken the time she should have to meditate and know she was making the right decision.

Had she misread what she had been feeling? Oh, if only she had someone to talk to! And, maybe if only she could see Curt once more, she would know whether she truly loved Clay or not. Or would seeing Curt make her recapture the love for him that had once engulfed her? No, she couldn't risk that and had no way to do it, anyway. After all, she was a married woman and shouldn't even think those thoughts. Wasn't she committing the sin of unfaithfulness to Clay by wanting to see another man? She had objected to her husband's eyes showing lust for Betsy's curves, but was she doing anything less when she wanted to see Curt again? She had jumped into what she had felt would be security and love and had not had a truly comfortable day since she had said that fateful "I do."

She sat there in the late September sun and watched a few leaves come floating down from trees that had been far enough from the fires to escape damage, floating on down to the mound under the big oak tree. Mammy Rose had predicted that she would end by breaking Curt's heart. Mammy Rose had been right. That was exactly what she had done. And he, as well as she, should know there was nothing that could ever be done about it.

The day passed on. She had heard Rhody calling "Miss Jamie" a few times at what she supposed was dinner time, but she didn't answer. No one sat on the front steps—always the side ones—so no one came to look for her out here. She was going to sit here until midnight if it took that long to separate things that were true and the ones about which she had been so sadly mistaken.

At times she would pray, hoping the voice would speak again, but it did not. By the time the sun was getting low and Clay was coming dragging down the pike as though he was almost out, she had sorted out many things that she should have analyzed before she had made a move of any kind. The voice had been right. She knew now that she did not love Clay. She liked him, but she did not love him as she had loved Curt until the war's tragic end. But she also knew that it was wrong even to remember those times. She was Jamelle *Haynesworth.* She had promised to love her husband until death did them part. She could never break that vow made before God, so regardless of what she felt, she was a Haynesworth for life. If she had any feelings for another man, she must bury that love so far down into her heart that it could never surface.

One of the main things that convinced her that she had known subconsciously all the time that she did not love the man she had married was her reaction to the weight that he wanted her to regain so much. Though she had been almost starving for so long, she had found it was almost impossible to eat enough that she would be as appealing to Clay as he wanted her to be. That was the thing that had proved to her through the long hours of soul-searching that, though she hadn't known she was doing it, she was trying to draw away from the husband she should not have married.

Now that she was almost sure she had figured out what she had been doing and why, she felt confident that she could eat whatever they had. She had no choice but to accept the fact that, no matter how much she appealed or did not appeal to her husband, she was his for life. She owed him all she had promised; and, no matter what else was in her heart, she would fulfill that vow to the best of her ability. She owed Clay all that she had promised him so her mind was finally clear. Without true love, she had a duty to make the man she had married happy. She would do her best to do it. She had shed her guilt. She would not pick it up again.

She still felt that her mind was in kind of a muddle, but some things were clear. There was no pulling away, consciously or unconsciously, for she knew that was useless. She had wanted to be a Haynesworth and, though she had become one for the wrong reasons, she indisputably was one forever.

She got up, went in through the hall to the side porch and gave her husband a welcoming kiss. Then she tried to comfort him when he muttered, "I dug up a body today. He was just a boy."

# 26

After that long day of assessment and reluctant acceptance, followed by more meditation, questions and confusion, things began to seem somewhat better for Jamie. She finally came to realize she had to stop fighting against what was unchangeable. She had done what she had done, and at the time it had seemed right. For all she knew, it might turn out for the best.

If the words "I am a Haynesworth" no longer brought the thrill and satisfaction she had expected they always would, she still knew she had become a member of one of the leading families in the South, and that was still important. Whether that connection would protect her from ever being known as a woods colt, as she had convinced herself so long ago that such a marriage would, she didn't know. She did know that her children, if she ever had any, would never have to feel the shame she had felt for so much of her life.

She was finding there were many things beneath the surface of Clay that she wished she—or somebody—could change, but, after the painful period that she had been through, she had forced herself to accept that he did not now, and more likely never would, feel that any change in himself was needed. He was Clay Haynesworth, born to be pampered, selfish and egotistical. He had been raised to think a Haynesworth deserved the best of everything, and, though the war had made some changes in him, the day would no doubt come when he would be as overbearing and pompous as was the father he admired so much.

At that point in her thinking, she usually scoffed at the whole thing. What did she know about such as this? Still, no matter what she told herself, she truly felt that Clay's father really did have to share the blame for what he had passed down to Clay. But all such thinking could do for her was to make her more tolerant of what she saw as Clay's failings and hope that she might gradually change him a little. She practically blanched at the thought of someday living with another version of Thaddeus Haynesworth himself.

Even if she still couldn't figure out from where the voice that had started her on this painful self-revelation had come, she felt sure that it had spoken the truth. She might as well be honest enough to admit, but only to herself, that she did not love Clay as much as she had loved his name. But she had married him and given her word to be true to that marriage till she died. She had no choice but to do it.

But in spite of all these thoughts that kept hassling her, she did feel sure that Pris had been right when she said that Clay truly loved her. She had always known that her personal problems and worries had kept her from ever really understanding why so many were willing to give up everything for the sake of their "Lost Cause." And, whispered a part of her mind, she wasn't sure she understood even now, but she would make up for that shortage as best she could.

It had been two weeks since Clay had found that body. At that time, her mind had been in the worst of her own turmoil. Now, as she looked back, it seemed like a lifetime ago. Considering how many men on both sides had fallen in the battles in and around their town, it shouldn't have shocked him so much, but it certainly had hit him hard. "He was just a boy," he had kept saying to her when she had rushed to comfort him. "He hadn't been much older than Cooke. Just a boy."

In spite of what she had been going through herself, she had done her best to console him. She had Steven bring her tub and lots of hot water first in the yard and then later in their room to keep trying to wash away the smell that he could not forget. She had asked him then if he had advised the LMA, since she had just become a real member that day. Of course, he had. She found that he had run all the way from Crestview and could hardly talk when he had gotten to the Boyds' home. Mrs. Boyd and Mrs. Williams had both been there and Reverend Boyd too. They had assured him they would take care of the boy he had found and that the day would come when that poor lad would have his burial place marked with as much honor as the highest-ranking soldier who had given his life for the Confederacy. Jamie wondered what they could possibly have done without the LMA.

"I saw so many fallen bodies during the battles, but none of them hit me as hard as this poor boy with his filthy old uniform still clinging to his decayed body and…and…"

"Try not to think about it," she had told him, knowing that advice would be as hard to follow as telling a person not to breathe.

So even though she refused to dwell on what might have been had she waited to give her troubled mind time to get back into some semblance of order before jumping into marriage, she felt sure that she would have done the same as she had. What could she ever have done that would be better than becoming a Haynesworth and a sister-in-law of Pris and Brad? So, as one fall day after another slipped away toward Thanksgiving, she told herself resolutely that not only was she thankful, she was content.

Almost.

She had not been raised with the big Thanksgiving dinners that most people had, but she did wish there could be some way to have one this year. Turkey, dressing and all the other things like that would not only be a treat, they surely would begin to help cover some of her still painfully-obvious bones. But, of course, there was no way to do that unless Clay had gotten some more U.S. money from his father and the food was available in town. If either of those things had happened, he had not told her.

She was in the dining room on Tuesday before Thanksgiving when she heard voices in the kitchen. She went to the door leading down there and listened, wondering who it could be. Clay had already gone, and Steven was out planting all the apple cores he could find.

"Land sakes, boy," came Rhody's voice, "what you got in dat big sack?"

"It's a turkey. Ain't you never seen a turkey before?" came a boy's voice.

"Well, I sho' have, but I ain't fer so long, it ain't no wonder I'd have trouble knowin' one now. You tryin' to sell it?"

"Naw. It's a gift for Miss Jamie. Ain't you seen me when I've brought her stuff before?"

"Well, maybe I has, but you ain't had on no hat and jacket like dat. You wait right here while I git Miss Jamie. She'll be wantin' to thank you."

Jamie started down the stairs to do that but stopped when she heard the boy saying, "Naw, I ain't supposed to wait for that. You just tell her I brought it, and we hope she'll have a nice Thanksgiving."

"That moughty nice," she heard Rhody say. "Can I tell Miss Jamie who brung it?"

"I'm Eddie," he said.

"Ain't you got no other name?"

"Ain't got one I'm telling." Jamie, hanging against the stair wall, almost laughed at that.

"Waal, I 'spects Miss Jamie will be hankerin' to see you. You want to wait while I calls her?"

"I ain't got time for that. You just tell her there might be more than just the turkey in that other bag. I ain't looked so I ain't saying."

As soon as she heard the kitchen door close, Jamie raced down the stairs. "A whole turkey?" she asked Rhody, who was pulling the cloth away and peeping at the turkey.

"Yes, ma'am, and it look like a big one. And let's see what be in dis other bag." She started pulling them out. "This be a spice dat look like what Miss Sally had me put on sweet potatoes, apples and stuff like dat. Dis here sho' do looks like sage fer de dressin' and here's what bound to be at least a pound o' butter." Jamie could hardly keep herself from taking over the rest of the items in the bag, but Rhody was enjoying it so much that she let her finish.

"Dere be a bottle o' milk and dis box got what look like a dozen eggs. I sho' hope dey ain't cracked... and dere's some salt and pepper in dere. And a bowl dat's all wrapped up and I's thinkin' it full of cranberry sauce. Ain't dis won'erful?"

"It certainly is," Jamie agreed enthusiastically but with sadness. She couldn't help but remember the other time when even more welcome and more desperately-needed food had been brought to her. But this was different, she hastily told herself. This was bound to be from Mrs. Darby. Not really from anybody else, and she wasn't going to feel the least bit of guilt in accepting it all. At least, that was what she was telling herself until Rhody pulled a folded piece of paper from down beside the turkey itself. She handed it to Jamie. "Mebbe dis is finally tellin' you who sendin' you all dese here vittles."

Jamie grabbed the paper and stuffed it into the top of her stay cover. She hadn't worn her corset in so long she almost forgot what it was, but she had to wear some underclothes so she wore whatever she had. "I'll see what it says later," she said hastily. "Is there any sugar in there? I sure would like some so we can have a proper dessert to go with this feast."

"I ain't seein' none yet, but dere's sumpin' else. Yes, ma'am, I'd say dis be sugar," the woman told her.

"That's good. Now we can have pies with one of those pumpkins Steven has. And see if you can get enough cream off of that big bottle of milk to whip. I just loved whipped cream on pumpkin pie when we had it at the Taylor Hotel."

Rhody laughed as she pulled a pint bottle out. "Ain't got to do dat. De neighbor done it fer you. Dis here be cream or I ain't Rhody."

"You put all that away out in the basement where it will stay cool. I've got to go tell the McLaurines about it. They'll be as thrilled as we are. And get out those canned green beans we've been saving for Christmas. We'll have them Thursday and worry about Christmas later. And tell Steven to bring us several sweet potatoes."

"Yes, ma'am, I'll sho' do dat."

As she went on up the stairs, she heard Rhody muttering, "Mr. Clay ain't gonna be likin' her walkin' into town since she done walked in once dis week. Mister Clay ain't..."

She ignored the words and hurried on up the stairs. Clay was going to be so happy about this Thanksgiving dinner that he'd forget all about her walking in again. But now all she cared about was reading what Mrs. Darby had to say.

Then the guilt she was so relieved to no longer feel reared its ugly head and fell over her as heavily as an adult shroud over a dead child. Suddenly there didn't seem to be enough air in the room for her to breathe. She shouldn't be doing this. She should rip the message to bits and... Then she thought, why was she feeling that way? All she was doing was accepting a much-needed gift. She opened it and read, "Happy Thanksgiving to all of you." No heading and no signature and definitely the handwriting of a woman. She gulped in a deep breath and sank down in her rocker. There was no reason for guilt over a message like this. She could even save it and show it to Clay. But the relief that was mixed together with disappointment was kind of staggering.

She got up, tossed it on the bureau and did her hair up in a bun on the back of her head to get it off her neck before she raced from the room. She did hope those five hair pins would hold it, but she felt she should wear her hair as a woman, not just as a girl. She was a woman. A married woman.

# 27

When she reached the McLaurines' house on Braddock, she was worn out so she sank down on the steps for a few moments before she knocked on the door.

"Oh, no, you don't. Come here, you little rascal!" she heard Pris' laughingly cry, and then she heard running footsteps from the hall. Jamie jumped up and raced to the door. As she opened it, Pris' little boy, Thomas, almost fell through it. Jamie caught him as he looked up at her and yelled, "Aunt Jamie!" He was giggling so much that the cry was barely understandable.

Pris came almost tumbling out the door behind him. "Thomas, how in the…" Then she saw her sister-in-law holding him and said, "Oh, hey, Jamie. I didn't know you were here and thought that the little rascal had actually opened the door himself. Come on in." She reached for her boy, but he held onto Jamie and cried, "No! Want Aunt Jamie."

His mother laughed and said, "Oh, all right. Looks like you're it, Jamie. Bring him on into the kitchen. I was trying to feed him before I put him down for his nap, but he still wanted to play. It's enough to make me wish he hadn't learned to walk so soon." She waited until Jamie brought Thomas into the hall and then followed them on down to the kitchen.

"I'd like to help feed him, but I thought he liked to feed himself now," Jamie said, letting the little boy go as his mother reached for him.

"Not when we're having potato soup," Pris told her. "He'd have it all over himself. Thomas, you sit on Mama's lap and Aunt Jamie will give you some of this good soup."

He gave Jamie a big grin and willingly climbed onto his mother's lap. Jamie reached across the table for the soup, pulled it close and started dishing it up. "Umm, good," she told Thomas.

He grinned but shook his head and kept his mouth closed.

She raised the spoon in the air and zoomed it around. "Here's a big bird, and he wants to feed his friend. Open up, Thomas, so the bird can find your mouth."

Thomas giggled again and opened his mouth.

"I knew it worked when you did it," Jamie told Pris, "so I thought it might for me too. Here comes the big bird again, Thomas." Again and again, the bird landed successfully. The little boy just leaned back against his mother and ate.

"He's so tired, it'll be a wonder if he doesn't go to sleep right here on my lap. We took a long walk this morning and then played hide-and-seek when we got back. He's worn to a frazzle and, to tell the truth, so is his mama."

"Don't you go to sleep too," Jamie told her. "I've got some great news to share with you."

"What is it?" Pris asked, dropping a kiss onto the top of Thomas' head.

Thomas felt it and turned to look up at her. "Kiss, Mama," he said, wanting to return the kiss.

"Save the kiss for Mama until the big bird finishes bringing you that good soup," his mother said. "Your Aunt Jamie is letting you get soup all over you."

"I am not," Jamie protested, but she did take the spoon and scoop up some from around his mouth.

"What's the news?" Pris asked eagerly as Jamie kept on feeding Thomas and he kept opening up for her.

"You all are coming to our house for Thanksgiving dinner, and we're going to have everything from turkey to pumpkin pie."

"Pie?" Thomas said the word as eagerly as his mama had spoken.

"Yes, indeed, honey," Jamie told him. "You like pie, don't you? Now let's finish this soup, and you can get that nap before you go to sleep right here in the kitchen."

He closed his eyes and slumped back against Pris. "Thomas asleep," he said.

Jamie laughed. "I can't believe that. He's teasing us."

"He sure is," his mother said, giving him a hug. "We've got a mighty smart little boy here."

"You sure have. He must have inherited that from his Uncle Clay," Jamie joked.

"From Uncle Clay," the little boy agreed, straightening up and opening his mouth again.

Jamie and Pris both laughed, and Jamie supplied the next spoonful. "You're almost out of soup. The big bird can fly in one more time, and I think that's it."

"All gone," he agreed.

"Yes," his mama said, "but Jamie, you hold him until I can get a wet cloth to wash his face. That was a very messy bird."

Thomas laughed, but Jamie thought she'd better not argue the point. She just took him as Pris transferred him to her lap. "Aunt Jamie loves you, Thomas," she told him softly.

"Love Aunt Jamie," he said, turning and lifting his face for the kiss that he knew always followed those words.

Jamie laughed. "That bird was a little bit sloppy. I want the kiss, but let's wait until Mama wipes your face." Pris was right there with a damp cloth to clean him up. He protested but Jamie held him steady, then handed him to Pris to take to bed. When the two of them started down the hall, she followed them into the first floor bedroom where he took his naps.

When Pris laid him down, he held up his arms for a kiss from her and then did the same to Jamie. Her heart just swelled with love for the little boy. "Sweet dreams," she told him as he popped his thumb in his mouth, turned onto his side and closed his eyes.

The two girls left the room and went into the beaten-up living room across the hall. "I just adore that little boy," Jamie whispered as they went.

"Me too, but we don't have to whisper. He's so tired he's down for the count. He wore his mama out too. If you weren't here, I'd probably be right in there with him," Pris said, sinking down on the battered old couch. "Have a seat and tell me all about this Thanksgiving dinner that sounds unbelievably great."

"Yes, doesn't it?' Jamie said, sitting close by her as she re-tucked a hairpin that was sliding out of her heavy hair. "And is

Mrs. Mac here? She's invited too, of course."

"Not unless she's just come in the back door," Pris told her. "Betsy and her mother have both been feeling poorly so she took some of this potato soup over to them."

"I hadn't heard anything about that. What's wrong with them?"

"Mother Mac didn't seem to know. But whatever it is, it must be catching since they both have it. I saw Mrs. Gains on the street a couple of days ago, and she looked terrible. Mother Mac says Betsy doesn't look any better. I didn't want to bring anything home to Thomas so I haven't been over there."

"Of course not. As you know, Betsy's name is definitely not the top one on my list of favorite people, but I am sorry to hear that she and her mother are sick. Do be sure and tell Mrs. Mac that she'll be expected at our house on Thanksgiving."

"I'll tell her. But where on earth are you getting a turkey? Did Father send Clay more money?"

"If so, he hasn't told me. The things for Thanksgiving came from that unnamed neighbor who sends us things now and then. This time the boy brought us a turkey, as well as all sorts of the other things that we'll need. Isn't that almost unbelievable?"

"It sure is. Who is the boy?"

"We don't know. His first name's Eddie, but he won't tell us any more."

"Why don't you have Steven follow him and find out?" Pris asked.

Jamie knew that was a logical question so she said quickly, "And spoil the little game for whoever is playing it? We might not get anything else if we did that. I don't know about you, but I think it's great that we keep getting these surprises. Clay agrees and thinks it might be someone who had supported the North and didn't get burned out. Naturally, he wouldn't want a dedicated Confederate like Clay to know that."

"Heck no!" Pris agreed. "And again there's no name?"

"No. When we got a chicken on Clay's birthday, he said it must be some old friend of his who had remembered the day."

She cringed inwardly as she said it. The truth, but certainly not *the* truth. She was in so deep now that she had no choice but to keep on misleading. She did hope that misleading wasn't the same as lying. "Anyway," she went on, "I want you, Brad, Thomas and Mrs. Mac to join us."

"My brother said to invite us, did he? You sure he doesn't want to invite this old friend of his who has been so good to you all?"

"He doesn't have any idea who that old friend might be. And come to think of it, he doesn't know anything about the gift yet. He wasn't there when the turkey came. I was so excited that I rushed off to tell you all about it."

"Why didn't you stop at the old office and tell him on the way over here. He might have somebody else he wants to invite," his sister said.

Jamie laughed. "Now who's being silly? You know perfectly well that there's nobody he'd want as much as y'all. Who'd you have in mind? Betsy Gains and her mother?"

"Well, no." Pris said, laughing too. Then she sobered and said, "No more worries on that score, is there?"

Jamie shrugged. "I decided to mark it off my worry list completely."

"Well, thank goodness!" Pris said and let her whole body relax on the couch.

"Now, back to our Thanksgiving dinner. It's kind of a big thing to me. I've never really had one before. When there was just Pa, Mammy Rose and me, we never had big Thanksgiving dinners. As you know, I didn't have any other family to invite us to one. By the first Thanksgiving after we came here, the war was already going on, so…" She shrugged her still-thin shoulders.

"Yeah, I know," Pris cut in. "You're right, so we'll have to go all out on this one. Maybe Mother Mac can contribute a little."

"Not necessary. I think we have everything we need."

"I can see why you came right over. You were afraid Clay wouldn't want you to walk into town if he knew about it. But go by and tell him on the way home. I'm finding out myself how great it can be to have a wonderful surprise." She jerked herself up as she realized what she had said and added, "Pretend you never heard that."

"You have a surprise too?" Jamie asked, looking at her sister-in-law keenly. "Is that why you thought I might invite somebody but you all?"

Pris laughed. "Absolutely not. That was just plain silly of me."

"Yes, it was. But if you have some good news too, let's hear it. There's no possibility of an over-supply."

"I said for you to pretend you didn't hear that, and I meant it. It's not anything I can tell yet."

Jamie brought herself up on the couch, leaned close and asked eagerly, "Pris McLaurine, are you in the family way again and haven't told me?"

Pris laughed and sank back on the couch away from Jamie. "No, I am not. If we can help it, there'll be no more children for us until Brad gets that medical degree."

Jamie grinned and slumped back herself. "Only one way to be sure of that," she said, then blushed as she realized she had actually said that. Hastily she grabbed onto the first thing that came to mind. "So you have some other secret. Let's hear it."

"I didn't say I had a secret," Pris protested. "What gave you that idea?"

Jamie eyed her carefully. "Yes, you did. Or almost did. I want to know what you were talking about. I walked nearly a mile to share my good news with you. Now I want to hear yours."

"You'll hear it soon enough, for it involves you and Clay as much as it does us," Pris said.

"You're just dying to tell it," Jamie said, grinning. "I can tell."

"You can't tell anything of the sort," Pris snapped and turned away to look out the window across the room.

"Well, then I'll go ask Clay," Jamie said, getting up and starting for the door. "If Brad knows, I feel sure Clay does too. He'll tell me."

Pris jumped up, grabbed Jamie's hand and yanked her back

down by her. "You'll do no such thing! Sit there and hush, unless you want to ruin it for him."

Jamie looked at Pris for a moment, then let herself sink back on the couch. "Well, you know I wouldn't want to do that."

Pris slid a little nearer on the couch and said conspiratorially, "I give up and actually you're right. I am dying to tell it. I know Clay is going to be mad, but I guess he'll just have to be."

When she stopped, Jamie leaned even closer and urged, "Go on. I won't let him know that you've said even a word."

Pris grimaced and looked away again. "I'm so wrong in doing this."

"You are not! You know how nervous this is going to make me if he doesn't tell me right away. It's childish, Pris, to have started this and then refuse to tell me. When Clay tells me, I'll be so surprised that he'll never have any idea that I already knew."

Pris leaned close again. "You swear you'll do that?" she asked in almost a whisper.

"I've already promised. Isn't that good enough?"

Pris gave an excited laugh, "All right. A promise is good enough." She grabbed Jamie's hand and clutched it with both of hers. "We're going to England!"

Jamie stared at her. "England?"

"Yes," Pris cried. "England. That's where Mother is from."

"I know where she's from." Jamie was now sounding almost irritated herself as she tried to hold down the excitement and hope that was building in her. "What I want to know is who? Who does the trip include?"

"All of us," Pris said exultantly, letting Jamie's hand go and throwing both of hers in a wide, sweeping gesture. "I should have let Clay tell you. I know that. But, oh," and now she clasped both her own hands to her chest in a burst of ecstasy, "it's just too exciting to keep to myself." Then she let her hands fall into her lap and said sternly, "But you'd better keep it to yourself until Clay tells you, or he will probably kill me."

"He will not," Jamie cried, crowding close to her friend again. "But is it really true? And I'm invited too?"

"Of course. And why wouldn't you be?" Pris demanded. "You're as much family as Brad, and he sure is invited. And Thomas. My parents know that I wouldn't go without them."

Jamie was almost overwhelmed with excitement and wonder. Acceptance! That's what this meant. Her in-laws had seen the foolishness of their previous refusal to accept what they called her tainted blood into their blue-blooded family. They were willingly accepting her! She fell back onto the couch and clasped her hands in almost-overwhelming delight.

Then she bounced right back up and stared at Pris. "You're sure?"

"Oh, don't be such a goose!" Pris assured her with almost as much excitement as Jamie was feeling. "Of course, I'm sure. My folks know that Clay wouldn't go without you."

"Yes," Jamie agreed, "he did tell me that when he mentioned a while back that his parents would want him to come sometime."

"Of course, he did. He wouldn't go without you any more than I would go without Brad. But that's all I'm going to tell you now. I'll let Clay at least have the pleasure of telling you the rest."

Now Jamie was so eager to hear it all that she felt she couldn't wait. "There's more? Don't do this to me, Pris," she begged. "I'm feeling better than I once did, but waiting to hear how we're going to do it will make me so nervous I'll probably get back to where I once was."

"Now you're the one who's not being fair, making a threat like that! I've already told you more than I should. Let me leave something for Clay to share."

Pris was sitting up now as straight and unbending as a hitching post and staring at the mantle as though it had just said something important that she was trying to hear. Then she relaxed, muttered an almost silent 'Horseradish!' and leaned toward Jamie again. "I was vowing to myself that I wouldn't say another word, but I give up. I shouldn't have started this, but it's just too exciting to keep to myself."

Jamie gave a sigh of relief and tucked her legs under herself as she leaned forward, eager to listen.

"Clay will tell you right away anyhow, but if you let him know I've already spilled the beans, I probably won't live long enough to even try to forgive you." Then she leaned close to Jamie and said in almost a whisper, "I got a letter from Mother yesterday. She was practically out of her head with excitement about Mary Lilly. I think I've told you that the titled man who owns the country estate next to my Cooke grandparents has a son who fell for Mary Lilly as soon as he met her. Mother says Mary Lilly feels the same way about him." She gulped in a breath and rushed on, "Lord Alford and his son had just been there to ask Father for Mary Lilly's hand in marriage. The son wanted to get his offer in before somebody else could possibly get in before him or something like that. She's eighteen now and will be coming out this Season and…"

"Coming out of where?" Jamie asked. "The country?"

Pris gave a little laugh that was half-amusement and half-irritation. "No, I do not mean the country. I mean socially. Of course, they will move into Grandfather's London house during the time of the Season, and Lord Alford's family will be there in his."

"Which season?" Jamie asked eagerly. "Spring or summer? Oh, I would so like it to be fall. That would give me more time to put on more…"

"Will you please hush?" Pris snapped. "If you don't, how can I possibly explain to you that in England 'The Season' is a social period, not just a part of the year as it is here. It's when the daughters of prominent families have reached the age that they are ready for marriage. Hunting is also big in England, but the hunting period ends in the middle of February. At least, I think that's what Mother said. After that everybody who is anybody goes to their London home, and wonderful parties of every kind go on from then until Easter. The eligible bachelors can get to know the girls, see how they handle social events and that sort of thing. They can also check to find out how big a dowry the girl's father is offering and…"

"What's a dowry?" Jamie burst in to ask.

Pris looked at her again in exasperation. "Don't you know anything?"

"I sure don't know anything about a family offering to pay somebody to take their daughter. If that's what you mean, it sounds weird to me. Do you know how much your grandfather had to offer to get your father to take your mother?"

"Not one cent," Pris declared. "Mother told me that Father wouldn't accept it. I guess she did have one, for I think it's expected, but I don't think it's like—well, like you make it sound, at least not when Mother tells it. But I do urge you not to ask any questions like these when you're over there. The upper ranks in England look on their way of life as being unusually fine and successful. Mother certainly admires it greatly."

"I didn't mean to be critical," Jamie hastened to say. "I was just trying to understand what I would need to know. Will we be invited to some of those fine parties?"

"We certainly will be, since one of them will be given by my grandparents for Mary Lilly. I think each girl has to be sponsored by somebody socially acceptable. My grandparents certainly are. He is Sir Peter Cooke, and Mother says their family has been highly regarded for many generations."

"Who is offering the money for Lord Alford's son to take Mary Lilly?" Jamie asked.

Pris' exasperation grew. "If you come out with a question like that over there, I'll disown you. Clay will too. And Mother will probably borrow a dagger from anywhere she can find one and do you in on the spot."

Jamie actually paled. "I'm going to be afraid to go," she said in a meek-sounding voice. "Maybe Clay should leave me home, after all. I sure wouldn't want to be an embarrassment to you all."

Pris relaxed, reached a hand out to her and said, "We've got the rest of November, December, January and at least part of February to teach you all you'll need to know. That'll be plenty of time. Also, I feel sure Mother will be sending a protocol book of some sort to tell us all we'll need to know. And, remember, Brad will be just as much in the dark as you. But you'll have Clay, and he can handle himself in any social situation I can ever imagine."

Jamie leaned her head on the back of the couch, tucked her skirt carefully around her legs and stretched them out before her. "Just the thought of it all makes me feel almost too nauseated to stand. How I'll ever make it back home, I don't know."

"Want to ride the horse?" her sister-in-law asked. "I guess hooking up the carriage would be too much, but I can remember when you used to love to ride."

"Yeah, I did. I learned to ride when Pa had a job at a horse farm. I loved it, but I was never as good as you. Now I've got to get some fat on my backsides before I can ride and especially bareback."

"My old saddle is out there," Pris offered. "The Yankees slashed it, but it can still be used."

"No, thanks. I'll make it all right. But the first thing I have to do is to force myself to get up from this divan. This news of yours has been so exciting that it's drained me." She pushed herself up with both hands and headed for the door with Pris following right behind her. "If I didn't think you already have dibs on that spot on the bed by Thomas," she said back over her shoulder, "I'd claim it for myself."

Pris gave a little laugh. "Sorry, too late. I'm already heading for it. Remember, you're not to say a word until Clay gives you the news. Then you can get him to start teaching you all he can about English ways. Of course, if you had ever read the Waverly novels, you'd know some of this."

"Well, I didn't. Pa was awful strong on reading, figuring, spelling and penmanship, but he never once encouraged me to read novels. He did make me read history books on how our country was formed and things like that, but if he ever said the word 'dowry,' I don't remember it. If he had known about it, I doubt he would have approved."

"That doesn't matter now. At least, Mary Lilly loves everything English so Mother is floating in happiness. Let's let them enjoy it, and we'll just concentrate on Thanksgiving for the time being."

"Oh, yes, that is right," Jamie said, grateful for the reminder. "I am still thrilled about that. Don't forget to tell Mrs. Mac that she is especially invited."

She turned and started for home, still feeling a sort of nervousness at the thought of actually going to England. But over it all was the thought of *acceptance*. The family was accepting her and letting Clay and her know. How could anything ever be more wonderful than that? Maybe she had been wrong in wanting it so much, but she finally knew that she was a real Haynesworth!

Jamie walked back home with a part of her so light that she felt herself in danger of flying away as high as those mountains on both sides of her. However, there was a weight somewhere close to her heart that kept her solidly on the ground. There was so much to be decided and so much to be done before she could feel that she was actually going. Of course, the trip was not the most important thing anyway. It was the acceptance! Her joy could not be taken away, even by the painful memory of the day when her now in-laws had told her with pretended kindness how sorry they were but that the blood of a bastard could never be allowed to mix with theirs. They were now accepting her! Inviting her with the rest of their family to England! Nothing could ever match that.

If only Clay would hurry home and give her all the particulars.

# 28

Though she felt unbelievably tired, Jamie could hardly keep her feet on the ground as she raced back out to Fairdale. She hadn't gone by the office space to tell Clay about the Thanksgiving dinner, for that now seemed almost too unimportant to bother with, and besides, she was afraid she'd give something away. He would probably get his letter today and tell her this evening. Pris and Brad had already told him about the letter she had received, so even if his own hadn't come, maybe he would go on and tell her.

When she got home, she ran up the stairs, crawled up on her bed and let herself collapse in pure joy. *England!* She and Clay were actually going all the way across the ocean to visit his mother's family! It was still hard to believe. Actually, too wonderful ever to believe! *Acceptance!* Clay's parents were accepting her. They were making it clear that the words "woods colt" would never again be spoken between them.

Oh, thank you, God! Thank you!

Then she jerked herself up, slid off the bed and raced for the stairs. She had to find something to eat. She had to eat anything and everything there was that was edible. They couldn't have much more than two months before they had to sail, and she had to put on every ounce she possibly could. She wanted Clay to be proud of her. She wanted his parents and his grandparents to be proud of her. Oh, she could eat everything in sight now with no trouble.

"Miss Jamie," Rhody called as she heard Jamie racing down the steps. "I been tryin' to find you fer some dinner. Ain't you wantin' none?"

Jamie burst into the kitchen. "I certainly do want dinner and a lot of it. What do we have?"

"De same stuff we always has. Steven done brung in a fresh

batch so I tossed some of dem things in de pot with canned peas, tomatoes, corn, onions and celery, although dat is way past usin', even if it was in what Steven calls 'de late garden.' It made a purty good stew."

"Sounds like vegetable soup to me. I'd like a bowl of it right now."

"Ain't warm as it should be."

"I don't care. Just dish it up. I'll be ready as soon as I wash my hands." She dashed over to the shelf by the door where the water bucket and wash pan were. She washed her hands hurriedly, threw the water into the back yard and went back to the table.

"You all right?" Rhody asked as she put the soup bowl in front of her. "You seem kind of skittish."

"Of course, I'm all right. I'm just excited."

Rhody looked at her rather skeptically, but asked nothing further as Jamie ate every drop of the lukewarm soup. As Rhody took away the bowl, she said, "I done tol' Steven about de turkey and other stuff. He moughty glad too. He wonderin' if dere'd be enough he could ax Roscoe to join him and me dat day."

"Roscoe? Who's he?" Jamie asked.

"He de one what brung his mouth harp an played wid Steven at yo' wedding. Ain't you rememberin' dat?|"

"Rhody, I was so nearly out of my head most of that day it's a wonder I even remember Mr. Clay. But, yes, I do recall that there was music so, of course, it will be fine for Steven to invite him. If Roscoe has a wife, tell him to bring her too. The more the merrier!"

At Jamie's flippant tone, the older woman glanced over from the dish pan and gave her a piercing look. "He ain't got no wife no mo'. She died and he ain't got no young'uns here neither. Had a boy but one of them Yankees what was here done hired him and sent him to New York to work fer his family. Steven reckons he's gittin' paid, but he ain't sendin' none to his pappy. Dey was always some of dem free ones round here," she added, "so Roscoe ain't got to go to none of dem places where dem as ain't got no place to stay."

Jamie had heard all she wanted to hear about that so she changed the subject. "If we have any apples here, I'd sure like one."

"Yes'm. Knowin' we'd be wantin' some fer Thanksgivin', Steven brung a batch in a while ago. Dey's pretty good too. Dey ain't as good as what has come from de neighbor, but Steven says yo' trees is needin' some care dat he ain't had time to do yet."

"I'm sure he's right, but it can wait. We've got to find out a lot more than we know now about how to build an orchard."

"Yes'm." Then she grinned and said, "Dat soupy must be good."

"It was not only good, it was delicious," Jamie declared. "It even tasted almost like it's got salt."

Rhody laughed. "Dat ain't no surprise. I done added some of dem seasonin's de neighbor done sent us. Reckon we soon be gittin' all we want o' stuff like dat?"

"I surely hope so. Is there enough for me to have some more? I seem to be awful hungry."

"I reckons dere is if'n you ain't wantin' to save enough fer supper."

'No, I'll eat it now. Then I'll eat whatever you can scrounge up for supper. I've got to put on some weight fast."

Again the woman looked at her keenly. "Dat so?"

"Yes, it is. I'll eat it and then go rest till Mr. Clay comes home."

But when she got back upstairs, she couldn't rest. She was too keyed up to do anything but sit in the rocker, jump up and pace, crawl up on the bed, get off again and pace some more.

By the time Clay got home, Jamie felt that she had undoubtedly walked off every ounce of any weight she had managed to put on by the heavy eating. As she paced, she kept munching on apples, but felt pretty sure they were doing no good. Her mind was a whirling dervish of thoughts about the multitude of things she would need, especially the clothes she did *not* have and wondering how she could get them. But hadn't Pris said her father was sending money for her to get something to wear on the boat and they'd get the other clothes there? Surely he would know that their daughter-in-law needed even more than their daughter, since Pris had some things that had been at the McLaurines' house and had not been burned. She wasn't at all sure that would help. All those things would be over four years old and certainly wouldn't do to be worn at fancy English parties where even royalty might be in attendance.

Oh, thank the Lord that they had more than two months to get ready. But would even that be enough? Just thinking about it gave her the heebie-jeebies so much that she felt that she was almost jumping out of her skin with every step she took.

Rhody had already come up to say supper would be ready in a few minutes before Jamie saw Clay coming down by the pike. It was all she could do to keep from running out to meet him, but she held herself back. She didn't want to do anything that would let him know she was expecting anything out of the ordinary. It was hard, so hard, to wait while he went out back to wash himself before coming in to find her.

When she heard his step in the hall, she rushed out of the sitting room. "Hey, honey," she called. "I heard you going out back to wash up so I guess you've been digging today." She tried to speak as casually as possible.

"No, I have not." He almost spit the words out. Then he came and gave her a quick kiss. "I'm almost afraid to disturb the ground any more. I'm not sure I could handle another find like that other one. Mostly, what I'm doing now is drawing a map of every tree still anywhere where the house was to take to—" he stopped as though he had just caught himself in time, gave a little shrug and finished, "—anybody I can think of who might help me find the right spot. It's got to be there."

"And who," she asked innocently, "would that be? I would think it would be impossible to find anybody but your mother or the ones who helped her." As she said that, he put his arm around her shoulders and led her with him up the stairs. Was he going to tell her now, she wondered. He had almost slipped but cut off his words in time. He probably wanted a more relaxed moment to tell her the wonderful news. Of course, she was thrilled about the trip itself, but the proof of acceptance was far more important. She almost had to pinch herself hard to keep from blurting out something.

He changed clothes, and then they came down for supper. As they were eating the grits, gravy, sweet potatoes and dried peas, she suddenly remembered the Thanksgiving dinner. If it hadn't been for the other news, she would have been bursting with excitement to tell him, but waiting for him to speak had driven any thought of it from her.

As she scooped bite after bite of the grits into her mouth, she told him about the gift that had arrived. When she told him that the boy who had brought it had been named Eddie, he became very thoughtful.

"Eddie?" he said, mulling over the name. "Who do I know who might have a boy named Eddie?" Finally, he shook his head. "Can't think of a soul. How about you?"

"No, I can't either. Pris said we should have Steven follow him…"

"Good idea," he cut in and reached for the bowl containing the sweet potatoes. "Let's do it."

She hoped the shaking of her head wasn't strong enough to cause suspicion. "No, I told her that would ruin the game for whoever was playing it and that we might not get anything more."

He gave her a quick look. "You saw Pris today?"

"Yes, I went in to invite them to our Thanksgiving dinner. I was so thrilled that we could have a real one that I couldn't wait."

He went back to his potato, "They're coming? Mrs. Mac too?"

"I didn't see her, but I told Pris to invite her for me. She was delighted at the prospect."

"I'm sure she was. Did she have any news about folks in town?"

"Well, yes. She did have one thing of interest that I was sorry to hear about. She said Mrs. Gains and Betsy have picked up some kind of a germ. They are both sick."

"Yes, I heard about that yesterday, but I hadn't thought to tell you. I didn't really think you'd be interested, anyway." His voice sounded so hard that she looked at him in surprise.

"Don't be ridiculous. Of course, I am concerned. Have you heard what they have?" she asked.

"No, and I don't care to hear," he said. "You told me to cut my acquaintance with her, and I obeyed the order."

"It was a request, not an order," she started but hushed. Maybe it had been pretty much an order, but she didn't like the sound of it when he put it as he had. "Well, anyway, I sure wouldn't wish her ill, so if you want to show a friendly interest in her and her mother, I certainly wouldn't be upset about that. I just didn't want her flaunting what she still has and what I have lost."

"You would have regained a lot of it if you had eaten as I wanted you to do. I'm glad to see that you've finally decided the same thing. I've noticed that you're eating much better."

"Yes, I am. I guess I've been kind of sick since those last months of the war, but I do think I'm getting over it. I guess lots of people were the same way. But I expect what Betsy and her mama have is something different."

"I don't care to hear anything more about it," he said more sharply than she thought the occasion warranted. To get off of that subject, she said, "I was hoping we could have had some meat for supper this evening. Steven was trying to capture us a squirrel, but I guess he had no luck. When we can, let's get him some bullets so he can hunt instead of having to set traps."

"I'm a far better hunter than Steven," Clay said, still sounding out of sorts. "If there's any hunting to be done, I'll do it."

She again looked at him in surprise and something akin to distress. Was he going to tell her that he wanted to go to England for hunting instead of for The Season. If so, that would leave her out, wouldn't it? Surely he wasn't looking for a way to go without her.

"Are you in a bad mood?" she asked rather hesitantly.

The relaxation of his body was obvious and, she was afraid, forced. But he looked over with a smile and said, "No, of course not. Why?"

"Oh, I don't know. You just seem to be awfully tense and a little out of sorts."

"Well, I'm not. Did you and Rhody come up with anything for dessert?"

"Not much. She has been hoping the frosts we've had would get the persimmons on the tree over on the McKays' land right for a pudding. Of course, since she's been helping Steven plant all those apple cores, they couldn't find any time to go see. Maybe tomorrow. As I guess you know, persimmons have to have a good frost before they make good pudding."

"No, I didn't know that. Persimmon pudding has never been a favorite of mine."

"You liked it once when you had it the way Mammy Rose made it. I remember when you asked for a second serving."

He gave her another smile. "You remember the strangest little things," he said and leaned over to give her a real kiss.

*Now*, Jamie thought, *he's going to tell me now*. Waiting until the right moment was the reason he had seemed so tense. She sat there, almost holding her breath, but he just finished eating without another word.

He's waiting until we get relaxed after supper. *I can wait that long,* she told herself, but wasn't sure it was the truth. The nervous tension was literally driving her up the wall.

He finally said, "I guess we can't do any more damage here. I'll grab the lamp and let's go into the sitting room for a while." He got up with the lamp in one hand and the other arm around her waist, moving with what appeared to be great weariness.

She turned back at the door. "Wait till I get our supper dishes downstairs. I know Rhody is bound to be more tired than I am. She has helped Steven plant apple cores with every spare moment she's had."

"Absolutely not." he said, putting the lamp down on the sideboard and beginning to stack the dishes himself. "I'll do it, although I do think those two owe us decent service for our keeping them from having to go to one of those campgrounds or whatever the Union government is providing for the ones who were hell-bent on leaving where they'd been but had no other place to go."

Jamie grabbed up the serving bowls and added them to the tray. "You are not going to come home from working and do what should be my job. I grant you that I've had some problems, but I'm getting better every day. Surely you can see that."

"I can and I'm grateful for it. I just…"

The door to the kitchen stairs opened, and Rhody peered in. "Y'all through?" she asked.

Jamie and Clay looked at each other and grinned. "We are," he said, "and the dishes are all yours."

"Yes'suh. Dat dey is." She took the tray, added everything that was left on the table and headed down the stairs with it.

Clay picked up the lamp again and said, "Come on, honey. Let's go in the sitting room and see if we can get comfortable."

Her heart swelled. He was getting ready to tell her. She felt it in her bones.

But obviously her bones were mistaken. He just slumped down on the horsehair settee that she knew he hated and said, "On practically the top of my list of things to do around here is the tossing of this thing."

It was not what she wanted to hear, but she knew she couldn't do anything but wait.

"As soon as we get the money, we need to do something about the furniture here," he went on.

She started to remind him that that was exactly what she'd been saying but caught herself. She didn't want to utter a word that would delay his telling her what she desperately wanted to hear. He was sprawled on the settee, trying to find a comfortable spot. Finding that as difficult as usual, he said, "Let's toss this miserable thing and get ourselves a more comfortable sofa in here. Wouldn't you like that?"

"Of course, I would, but don't we need a lot of things more than that? I will admit that I'll never know why Pa selected it."

"Your father didn't select it," he said, giving up the hope for relaxation and moving to one of the chairs by her. "It was one of the things left by the Chases. I remember it well from our childhood."

Jamie eyed him carefully. "Are you sure of that? I thought Pa said Mr. Chase had burned most of their things to be sure he wouldn't be leaving typhoid germs for somebody else to get."

"Maybe he thought that thing was too uncomfortable for even germs to stay on it," he grumbled.

"Whatever you think," she said. But, her mind was screaming, *Come on. Tell me. Please tell me! Why aren't you telling me?*

She finally gave up, accepting that his letter must not have come today. She wanted desperately to ask but knew Pris would never forgive her if she did. There wasn't a thing she could do but sit there like a bump on a log, hearing nothing she wanted to hear and saying nothing she wanted to say. Finally, she asked, "Is anything wrong, Clay? You aren't feeling down about anything, are you?" *Surely,* she thought, *it wouldn't hurt to ask that.*

He sprang up as straight in his chair as if she had stuck him with a pin. "Not a thing," he assured her. "What makes you ask?"

"Oh, I don't know. You just seem not quite yourself."

"You're wrong. I was just kind of remembering other Thanksgiving dinners at Crestview. Mother, being English, never saw quite the need of its being a big holiday, but Father always insisted. Our dining room would be full of friends or relatives. I guess I kind of miss things like that."

"Well, maybe those days will come again," she said, wanting to encourage him every way she could. Obviously his letter hadn't come today, and maybe he was as eager for it to arrive as she was, although, she told herself with an inwardly wry smile, that was doubtful. But if he could wait another day, then so could she.

Finally, they went up to bed where each of them stretched out as straight and stiff as if they were two porch posts lying there. Jamie didn't know how long it took him to relax and go to sleep, but she thought the sun was surely peeping up over the Blue Ridge before she did.

# 29

The place beside her in bed was empty when Jamie woke up the next day, but there was a note on Clay's pillow. She snatched it up and read, "I've gone into town and will see you sometime this afternoon. Love, Clay." Her heart sank. She could hear nothing until then. Then immediately she perked up. Of course, he had gone to town. He wanted to see if his letter had come. Then, remembering that Thanksgiving was the next day, she bounced out quickly. Oh, she did hope that letter would be there waiting for him. Surely he would tell her as soon as he got it.

As she hastily pulled on her clothes, she felt new excitement. Soon she could forget these limp, faded things and be dressed again as she had been when Pa had brought her to Winchester. But no, she assured herself. Even better than that for, though Pa had tried, he certainly hadn't made any effort to dress her to mingle with English aristocracy.

Her feet hardly seemed to hit the steps as she raced downstairs; then they almost skidded to a stop when she saw Clay sitting slumped over the table with his chin in his hands. She hesitated only a moment, then rushed on in, crying, "Clay, what's wrong? Are you ill?"

He straightened up immediately and got up to give her a kiss. "Absolutely not. You were still sleeping, and I didn't want to wake you so I wrote you that note. Then I thought maybe I should stay around here today and see if there were anything I could do to help get ready for tomorrow. It won't be like the old days, but a Thanksgiving dinner is still a lot of trouble."

She did the best she could to hide her consternation and sank into the chair he had pulled out for her. "That was thoughtful of you, but you'll probably be like I always am. I don't know whether either of us will be a help or a hindrance to Rhody." She wanted to scream, *Why aren't you there to get that dratted letter?*

*Are you trying to drive me crazy*? But she couldn't. She couldn't do a thing but wait.

"Absolutely not," he told her as he sat back down in his chair, pushed it back and crossed his legs. "I've already gotten my assignment."

Jamie gave him a quick but searching look.

"I'm to decorate the table," he went on, "and the sideboard with the prettiest greens I can find. I'm also to go to Mrs. Mac's and see if she doesn't have some plates better than the ones we have. Of course, we do have those two good ones, but our others are a disgrace. Somehow, it doesn't seem right to be giving thanks for cracked and chipped dishes."

She felt a slight uplift at that. He was still going to town. For that, she could feel grateful. But if something didn't happen soon, she felt that she might not even make it to the next day. For the moment, at least, she swallowed her disappointment as best she could and said, "Maybe not, but I'm thankful to have any dishes at all. I once felt that I wouldn't have a single one. Now, what's for breakfast?"

"I had cornmeal mush, but you don't even have to look at it. Rhody's keeping some oatmeal warm on the back side of the stove for you. She said for me to tell you not to use any of the milk we have because she'll need that for tomorrow. But there is butter and raw sugar, which is what you want on it, anyway. Sit down and I'll call her to bring it up. No," he amended, "I'll run down and get it. She's moving around down there as fast as if she were being chased by an irate bull."

He headed down the kitchen stairs, and Jamie sat there feeling a strong urge to scream. *Why wasn't Clay already in town to see if his letter had come?* Or if it came yesterday, why didn't he want to tell her yet? Then an exciting thought hit her. He must be waiting to tell her at dinner tomorrow so they'd really have something for which to be thankful. Yes, that was bound to be it. But how she could make it until then, she didn't know. Then she remembered how Clay had looked when she had come into the room, and she fell back into a slump. What had that all been about?

Her next thought brought her almost to the breaking point again. Had he gotten the letter, and his parents had told him not to bring her? That possibility grabbed her so hard that she could hardly sit there and wait for whatever happened next. Should that be it, it was no wonder that he looked depressed. That would mean that he wouldn't go either, for he had sworn that he would never go without her.

When he came back in with her big bowl of oatmeal, she wondered if she could possibly force it down until she knew. But by the first bite, she was berating herself for being an idiot. There was no reason in the world for her to fear a disaster like that. That couldn't be it. He was just trying to be theatrical about how he told her. She had waited four years for that miserable war to end. Surely she had developed enough strength to wait twenty-four hours.

She ate her oatmeal with real enjoyment. She might have messed her life up in ways that she still wasn't sure about, but she didn't know what else she could have done. It was a time to be thankful that she had a husband who loved her and a family who was finally welcoming her. So, in spite of everything, there would be no one at their table tomorrow who would be more thankful that she would be. If, she added to herself with a somewhat bitter inner smile, she could last that long.

Clay did head for town as soon as he saw her obviously enjoying her breakfast. He said he wasn't going to do any work, even though the lumber store that was back doing business in town was getting in what he would need, and the town itself was beginning to look as though it might actually live again. Damages would be bound to be paid, and progress was already being made on some of the business establishments that had been ruined.

Jamie did whatever Rhody gave her to do and tried not to get in the way as the woman did things that she had to do herself. Clay came home and did what he had been assigned to do. He seemed a bit glum, but Jamie told herself that might be because he was making himself wait until the next day to tell her the wonderful news. If they could just get through this day, she felt sure that the next one would truly be one about which they could all give sincere thanks. At times she couldn't help but wonder if she were singing in the dark to keep from being afraid, but she pushed that fear down deep and tried to tell herself that fear wasn't even there.

On Thanksgiving morning Jamie got out of bed early. She wanted to enjoy every moment of her first real Thanksgiving Day. There was very little she was allowed to do, since the woman in the kitchen was in her element, finally having food that justified her cooking skill. That was good, for Jamie was about as nervous as she had been on the morning of her wedding. Her legs were weak, and she felt a trembling on the inside of herself that she was trying hard to ignore. *It's just a Thanksgiving Day dinner,* she told herself, but she knew that wasn't so. Having Clay tell her that his parents and grandparents wanted her there with them for this important family time in England would mean the removal of the final dregs of her lifelong feeling of unworthiness. She would finally know that she was as much a Haynesworth as any of them. But how she could wait, she didn't know.

"What's wrong, honey?" Clay asked as he put his arm around her and felt her trembling. "It's just a family dinner. No reason to be nervous."

"It is my first real Thanksgiving dinner," she told him, trying to hold herself steady as she pulled away. "I wish the McLaurines would come on."

"I think I hear them right now," he said, after listening for a moment. "Want to go out on the porch to greet them?" But his question was unnecessary, for Jamie was already heading out the door.

The McLaurines, of course, arrived in the carriage with Thomas sitting on Brad's lap as he drove. Clay rushed down the steps to get the little boy who was yelling excitedly, "Me drove, Uncle Clay. Me drove."

"I saw you," Clay assured him as he put the little boy on the steps and turned to assist the older Mrs. McLaurine. Brad handed the reins over to the waiting Steven and then lifted his wife down.

It was almost as it would have been in the past.

Thomas met Jamie on the steps, yelling, "Aunt Jamie, Papa let me drive." In his hurry he caught his foot on one of the steps and would have fallen if Jamie hadn't caught him.

"Watch it, Thomas," his mother called. "Get him, Brad."

"Uncle Clay's got him," Clay said, taking him from Jamie and whirling him around before putting him down on the porch. The little boy ran back to Jamie to give her a kiss, then back to Clay to do the same. As his parents and grandmother laughed fondly, he ran from one to the other of them, giving out kisses and hugs.

"Come on in," Clay invited, holding the door open for them all to get into the warmth of the house.

"Oh, this is great!" Mrs. McLaurine said, giving Jamie a pat on the cheek. "I wish I could tell your benefactor how much we all appreciate his generosity."

"We'll try to pass that on to Eddie the next time he comes," Clay told her, closing the door behind them.

"Oh, you know who he is?" Brad asked, as he and his family were all taking off coats, hats and gloves.

"Haven't the slightest idea," Clay said as he took their outer garments and tossed then across the stair banister before ushering them into the parlor. "All the boy who brought it would tell Rhody was that his name was Eddie. I hate to think what Father would say if he knew that we were enjoying a big dinner courtesy of someone other than ourselves. But come on in and get seated. Steven has a fire going here in the parlor, the sitting room and the dining room. We're leaving the door down to the kitchen open too, so the heat from the stove will add to our comfort. We'll not only eat well, but we won't be shivering while we do it."

"Beats last year," Brad said as they found seats in the parlor with Thomas still in Jamie's arms.

"Not in every way," Pris said, being loyal as always to her memory of the Confederacy. "Last year, we still had a chance at victory."

"Let's not think about that today," her mother-in-law said. "I'm too happy about this wonderful treat to worry about anything else today."

"Me too," the men said together, then looked at each other and gave rather sad-sounding chuckles.

"At least, we're warm," Brad added, moving closer to the fire to hold out his hands to the warmth.

Thomas was now running from one to the other in his excitement at being there. "T'ank you," he said to each of them. They all accepted his thanks with hugs, kisses and laughter.

"We've tried to explain Thanksgiving to him," his mother said. "He sure seems to have gotten some idea of it." She grabbed him up and hugged him. "Your mama is sure grateful for you. That means I'm thankful."

Thomas laughed happily and scrambled to get down. Pris let him go and turned to Jamie. "I remember from the days of working at the convalescent hospital here how good Rhody is at cooking, but shouldn't we, at least, see if she could use some help?"

"We certainly should," Jamie said, eager to get alone with her. "Come on." She led the way out into the hall and headed for the kitchen stairs. They were hardly on the top step before the two girls grabbed onto each other. "Has he told you yet?" Pris asked as Jamie was saying, "Has his letter come?"

They giggled and moved on down a few steps. "Now let's have it," Pris said. "I asked him yesterday and he said 'no.' Hasn't he said anything yet?"

"Not a word. And it's driving me *cra-a-zy*. Do you think he is going to tell me at dinner?"

Pris stared at her. "At dinner?" She thought for a moment and said, "Well, maybe. I don't know. He's been kind of funny for the last few days."

"You've noticed it too?" Jamie asked, getting a strange feeling as she did. "He's been almost grumpy at times. I think it started even before you told me about the trip."

"Well, yes, maybe so. I've felt that he's been a little depressed. You know he has wanted to get his office set up early and hasn't been able to get the materials or the money to do it as he wanted."

Jamie stood leaning against the stairwell a few steps below Pris. "Maybe," she said dubiously," but surely the trip will get him out of whatever he's worrying about. He said something about wanting to go hunting. That scared the daylights out of me, for if he goes to your grandfather Cooke's to hunt with them, I feel sure that leaves me out."

"Don't even think it!" Pris snapped. "And stop biting on your nails too. You don't want to go over there with your nails a mess."

Jamie snatched her hand away and said, "Yes, ma'am" with a grin and headed on down the stairs. Pris followed her.

"We have two pairs of hands that are willing to help if you need them," Jamie told the woman bending over the open oven door.

"I need to git dis here turkey out and de dressin' in," Rhody said, straightening up and turning around. "You reckon dis thing be done?"

The girls turned questioning looks to each other. "Looks nice and brown," Jamie ventured.

"And it smells awfully good," Pris added, "although I've never heard that's the way to tell. What do you think?" she asked the woman. "You've cooked them before, haven't you?"

"Yes, ma'am. I sho' have, but I ain't too sure how many hours we let dem cook over dere at Miss Sally's. Since we ain't got no clock, I can't say how long it been cookin', but I sayin' it be done."

"Then I'm saying take it out," Jamie told her decisively. "You got the dressing ready to go in?"

"Right dere in dat pan. But I got to poke de fire up and git de oven hotter. Dressin' cooks hotter dan turkeys."

"If you say so. Is it too early for us to be taking the cold things up?"

"No, ma'am, it ain't," Rhody said as she strained to move the heavy turkey from the oven to the table where she had put two or three pieces of stove wood to provide protection for the old table that had long since lost its ability to benefit from such protection.

She added a few more sticks to the stove to chunk up the fire, slid the dressing into the oven and then turned to look at the girls. "All dem things on de table by de turkey is ready to go up. De cranberry sauce what Eddie brung is in dat bowl, and de spiced peaches Mr. Brad's mama sent is next to it. Dere's cole slaw since we got cabbages, and you ain't likin' it cooked, Miss Jamie. But don't take de pies yet fer dere ain't room on de sideboard. I needs de table space fer de other things."

"I am so thankful," Pris said in an almost reverent tone, "that we don't have to drink any more of that Essence mess. If I didn't despise the Yankees for any other reason, I'd hate them for those blockades that made us have to drink that stuff."

Jamie whirled and looked at her. "Don't you include..." she began, but bit off the words as fast as she could. She had been about to say, "Don't you include in that accusation the one who is furnishing this dinner for us all?" Where was her mind? Was she losing it, after all?

"What were you saying?" Pris asked as she picked up some of the dishes and prepared to carry them up.

"Oh, nothing. I wasn't wanting us to even think about those folks today. We might not have our own country, but we, at least, don't have any of them underfoot."

"That is a blessing," Pris agreed, heading on up the stairs. "I didn't mean to say anything otherwise. I just wish that brother of mine would go ahead and tell you so we could all be making plans."

"Me too. But we're going to have to make more than one trip for all this. You go on with what you've got, and I'll be right behind you with the slaw and those spiced peaches Mrs. Mac sent out by Clay yesterday. I was sorely tempted to have one already, but I thought that would be kind of tacky."

"It sure would have been," Pris said back over her shoulder, "since she only sent one apiece for us and another two for Rhody and Steven."

"Actually, they need three," Jamie told her as they got to the top and turned from the landing into the dining room. "Steven invited a friend of his to join them. He's Roscoe. He was the one who helped Steven provide music for our wedding."

Pris put what she had brought down on the sideboard and turned to look at her. "Roscoe? Sure, we all know him. He's always been one of the free ones here. Mother Mac mentioned at your wedding that he's the one her husband always tried to hire whenever he had a need for help. So, yes, Roscoe gets my spiced peach," Pris declared.

"Ain't no need fer dat, Miss Pris," Rhody spoke loudly from the bottom of the steps. "Steven ain't never liked peaches all spiced up that way. He'll be glad for Roscoe to have his."

The girls chuckled as they went back down to get another load. However, their laughter had a nervous quality. They were both more than a little jittery about Clay.

It was not more than an hour later when they came back from another trip to the kitchen and reported that the Thanksgiving dinner was on the table. Thomas was practically beside himself with excitement as they all crossed the hall and headed for the dining room.

"Eeeee," Thomas squealed as he saw the decorated table and the turkey on its battered platter sitting at the end of the table.

Clay was busy placing Jamie at the head, as Brad seated his mother and his wife on either side of him. Steven was busy bringing in every loose cushion he could find to make Thomas high enough to reach the table.

"Want chicken," the little boy announced, as soon as Steven lifted him into position by his grandmother.

"Shhh," whispered his mother from across the table. "We want to say 'thank you' before we eat."

"I already said it," he whispered back and they all laughed. They bowed their heads so he bowed his too, but he kept peeping around as Jamie said, "Will you give thanks for us all, please, Clay?"

He started off in a strong voice, "God, our Father, we give thanks for all You have brought to us these last months. For peace, such as it is, and for the aspirations for success we all feel that the future will bring to us again someday. Thank You for these much-loved people who are with us today and for the generous friend who has shared his food. Please forgive our sins and any hurts we might have caused, voluntarily or otherwise, and grant that…" Suddenly, his voice broke. He said a hasty "Amen" and coughed into his napkin to try to mask the emotion he obviously felt.

"Amen!" shouted Thomas. That brought chuckles from around the table and relief to Jamie. She had felt an urge to rush around the table to Clay, but her common sense held her in her place.

"He's used to doing that at home," Thomas' grandmother said. "No matter who says the blessing, he wants to get his 'amen' in."

"I know," Jamie said and threw him a kiss. He threw one right back, then said again, "Want chicken."

As his grandmother tried to explain about the turkey not being just a big chicken, Clay was carving as his father had always done. For some reason Jamie felt like bursting into tears herself but wasn't sure why. Instead, she started passing the mashed potatoes, green beans, sweet potato soufflé and the baked apples. Steven offered the cold items from the side board, filled the coffee cups and generally made himself useful.

"This is the first real Thanksgiving dinner I've ever had," Jamie volunteered as the turkey slices were being passed, followed by the dressing and gravy. "When it was just Pa, Mammy Rose and me, we were like Thomas and only expected chicken."

Thomas pointed at what looked far more chicken-sized than it had before Clay had done his expert carving and said, "Now chicken." That brought more laughs from all around again.

"No, still a turkey. But," his mother added, turning to her brother, "you're as good at that as Father ever was. Did he actually teach you, or did you just watch him and learn?"

Clay grinned, seeming to have gotten himself back under control, "A little of both. Or maybe I should say, a lot of both.

Father knew I would need to know how to carve meat at some time, and he wasn't one to leave a lesson half-learned."

"I'm proud of you," Jamie said sincerely.

He gave her a warm smile and mouthed a "Thank you." If she hadn't known better, she would have thought his eyes glistened like there might be tears there, but she knew that was pure foolishness.

"Last Thanksgiving none of us could even imagine a meal like this in our future," Mrs. McLaurine said. "Though I'm like others around this table, I do wish the suffering we went through could have resulted in a different ending, but I too am grateful for what no one could take from us. That's our family's love and our ability to give thanks to the One who makes all things possible."

"I'll say 'amen' to that," her son said, and there were other soft amens from around the table. Thomas bowed his head again and added his in a loud voice.

That brought more smiles and chuckles, and then they all turned their attention to enjoying the best food they had had for such a long, long time.

"If we ate like this all the time, I sure couldn't keep on wearing these pants of Mr. Mac's," Clay said.

"And he would quit insisting that I eat more than I want and would probably be urging me to go on a diet," Jamie added.

"I would not. I like a woman with curves…" Then he apparently remembered how that *liking* had gotten him in trouble. Clay decided to let his words drain away.

"If," Jamie said hesitantly, "no one will have any more of this, Steven and Rhody can clear it away and bring out the pumpkin pies. We have Steven to thank for the pumpkin that made them possible, so we should all say a quiet word of thanks to him as well and to our unknown friend."

"We certainly are grateful to him and also to you and Clay," Mrs. McLaurine said. "You have really made this holiday one to remember forever."

"Indeed, you have, old friend," Brad said, reaching out a hand to clasp Clay's.

Again Jamie saw emotion on Clay's face and felt a flood of anticipation run all over her as she waited for him to start telling something for which she certainly would be forever thankful. But nothing happened. Steven and Rhody performed just as they would have before any proclamations had been handed down to change their lives. Jamie had to keep thinking of something like that, for otherwise she would have burst out in tears of disappointment. Clay was not going to tell her anything special.

Everyone but Jamie seemed to be enjoying the pie. She was eating hers but having to force it down when Steven stepped behind her chair and said, "Miss Jamie, could Rhody and me say sumpin'?"

She turned around in her chair and looked back at him. "Of course, you can. Is something wrong?"

"No, ma'am. Ain't nothin' wrong. We heerd all de talk 'bout givin' thanks, and we wanted to say dat we be thankful too. To Miss Jamie, fer keepin' us from havin' to go to dem places where folks what ain't got no home has to go. We jest was a-wantin' to say our thanks to Miss Jamie. And," he added, "to Mr. Clay fer lettin' us stay at what has always felt like home to us."

Jamie felt tears come into her own eyes and wished she could have jumped up and given both of them a hug. She knew, of course, that would definitely be out of order, so she just said, "Steven and Rhody, you are no more grateful to me and Mr. Clay than we are to you. We will always be thankful that you were willing to stay here with us instead of looking for greener pastures as so many have done. But we thank you for those words, don't we?" And she turned to her husband.

He, to her great surprise, came around the table and held out his hand to Steven. "Thank you, Steven. My wife and I greatly appreciate your words and look forward to having you here or with us at our new Crestview. Should I ever have to be away, I know I can depend on you and Rhody to keep Miss Jamie safe again."

As he turned around and went back to his place at the table, Jamie felt that she had never been more surprised at, or prouder of, the man she had married than she was then.

Then came another thought, *Why had he even mentioned being away?*

# 30

Later Jamie and Clay went up the stairs with their arms around each other. For some reason she felt that she wasn't sure which one needed the support of the other more. She had finally accepted that there would be no announcement that day from Clay about the trip, and that made her feel terribly sad.

Pris had even prodded him a bit as they had a pick-up supper, asking if he had anything to say that would be of interest to all of them, but he had shaken his head and said nothing.

As the two of them now moved slowly up the stairs, she was sure that something was wrong, and she was frantic to know what it was. She and Pris had whispered in the hall about it as Brad carried out the sleeping Thomas and Clay was helping Mrs. McLaurine into the carriage for the trip back into town. Pris held herself back just inside the door as Jamie had asked softly, "Do you think your parents told him not to bring me, and he doesn't know how to tell me?"

"I can't believe they'd do a thing like that," Pris had protested. "You're their daughter-in-law as much as Brad is their son-in-law. Of course, if they did, that surely would have upset Clay, but I can't believe they'd be that cruel."

*I can*, Jamie thought as she remembered a time when they had been just as cruel but knew nothing would be gained by telling their daughter that now. Instead, she said, "Well, there's something bothering him. Would you mind terribly if I tell him that I know about the letter you got and ask him what his said?"

"Please don't do it yet," Pris begged. "I'll talk to him tomorrow and try to get him to level with you before we both have nervous breakdowns. In the meantime, I have sent out word to everybody who might know what happened to the seamstress Mother always used when we had special needs. If I can find her, we'll get some fabric if we have to go all the way to Baltimore."

"Did she sew for anybody other than your mother?" Jamie asked.

"Yes, of course, she did. I remember that Mother recommended her to Mrs. Gains when those two older Gains daughters were getting married in that double ceremony and Mrs. Gains was practically climbing the wall about clothes for all of them."

"Betsy's sisters?" Jamie had asked.

"Yes, of course. They were several years older than Betsy. Really nice girls, but having them both get married at the same time practically made Mrs. Gains a basket case. But she did manage to get it all together, and the girls moved away with their husbands. That gave Mrs. Gains all the time she needed to spoil Betsy rotten, and she sure did it."

"Can't you ask Mrs. Gains if she knows where the seamstress went?" Jamie had urged. "If we can't find somebody to sew and get some decent fabric, we may have to go someplace where there are ready-made clothes. I would think Brad and Clay would have to go somewhere too, so surely we can go with them."

"Maybe so, but I don't think I'll ask Mrs. Gains about it, anyway. I went over yesterday afternoon to see how she and Betsy were feeling, and she didn't even invite me in. She looked terrible and said Betsy didn't feel like having company. Made me feel like about two cents."

Jamie had stared at her friend. "That does seem odd. I always thought that Betsy wanted to think of you as her best friend."

Pris shrugged. "I guess she more or less was until you came. She and Serena. But there were things about Betsy that always rubbed me the wrong way. So, if she doesn't want to be friendly with me now, that's…"

"Pris!" came Brad's loud call from outside. "If you don't get yourself out here, we're all going to be icicles. Thomas is even so cold that he's waking up."

"Gotta go," she said hurriedly to Jamie and rushed on out the door and down the porch steps. Clay was there to give her a hand up into the carriage. Then he slapped the horse on the rump, and the carriage moved on out.

So now, after everything was in order in the house and the fires were dying down, Jamie and Clay were on their way up to bed. Though she knew that, thanks to Rhody and Steven, she had done very little and Clay even less, here they were dragging themselves up the stairs as if they were both worn out. "I'm as tired as I used to be when I'd worked hard all day," she admitted as they rounded the landing and went on up the final steps to their room.

"Me too," Clay admitted. "I feel about like I did when I'd been on one of Stonewall's long marches. Yet I hardly turned my hand all day. Steven even kept the fires going for us."

"I wish he could have kept doing it," she said. "A day like this with fires heating up most of the first floor makes the thought of cold bedrooms seem foreboding."

"Yeah, I know what you mean. I long for the days when we had all the people we needed to keep fires all over Crestview. Mother said she had been so cold growing up in her folks' big old country home that it took her years at Crestview to thaw out properly. Father did what he could to see that she kept reasonably warm."

Jamie suddenly pulled herself to a stop and went as stiff as the icicles hanging outside on the roof. *He was about to tell her. She could feel it.*

"Wait till I can get where I can sit down," she almost gasped and hurried on into their room.

"What's wrong? Did you suddenly get a pain or something?" he asked as she almost fell into the rocker.

She gasped in several breaths as she waited. He stood over her, looking concerned but saying nothing more. "Weren't you going to say something?" she finally got out.

He looked confused. "Was I? I don't remember what... Oh, yes, I do. I was telling you how much my mother hated the cold in that big old country estate of theirs." He gave a little shrug and moved over to the bureau where Steven had left a lamp burning very low. He turned up the wick to brighten the room. "Nothing special but we did enjoy all the many fireplaces at Crestview. When we get it rebuilt, we'll have them again. I'm hoping we can have gas lights too. You know there were lights like that in the courthouse in town before the Yankees ruined it." He started unbuttoning his shirt. "I wonder if Winchester can ever again be the very special little town it was before the war."

She leaned her head on the back of the rocker and felt like she might be about to break out into hysterical laughter. Or maybe tears. Whatever, she simply could not live much longer with this tension.

"Shall I go back down and get water so we can wash up and brush our teeth? I see the pitcher and wash basin there on the wash stand, but they're both empty. I guess Steven forgot that."

She opened her mouth, fully expecting to hear her voice giving an answer to his question. Instead, she heard herself say, "Pris said she got a letter from your mother inviting all of us over there to some special affairs for your younger sister. She also said that you were expecting a letter from your father. Hasn't it come yet?" She was so surprised at her words that she couldn't have gotten up if fire had suddenly broken out in the room.

Clay stood looking down at her for what seemed to be eons. She said no more. She just sat there, waiting.

Finally, he slumped back against the foot of the bed only a few feet from her chair and said, "I told her not to tell you. I wanted to think about it before I said anything."

She just stared up at him with her big black eyes glistening brightly with fear.

"I did get a letter from Father. It said more or less the same as Mother's to Pris. They are all so excited about Mary Lilly's secret engagement that they feel the whole family must be there to celebrate." Then he hushed, obviously waiting for her to say something.

She didn't.

He began again, "Father knows that this trip will be very expensive so he sent money. He has made the reservations on the best ship he could find that would be sailing from Boston to

England about the first of next February. I'm to pay for them over here. The first-class cost is just a few dollars under a hundred each for adults. He says that it was considerably less when they went over about six months ago. Wartime prices had still been in effect, but now prices have risen."

Clay continued, "Then there is the matter of clothes. He knows that the war had left us all destitute, but he is insisting that we all be dressed well enough on the ship and upon arrival. We don't want to cause any embarrassment to ourselves or to our Cooke family. Whether the money he sent will be enough to accomplish that, I do not yet know."

Jamie finally spoke, "How much did he allow for each of us?" she asked in a weak-sounding voice.

"That's the problem," Clay said. "I haven't figured a way to do all he says with the amount of money he sent. I haven't even told Pris yet, but I know they aren't expecting her to come without Brad and Thomas."

'So," she said jerkily, "that means me."

Clay turned around, tried to prop an elbow on the bed but found that awkward and straightened himself again. "I wrote the steamship company to see how many adults' reservations he made, but I'm afraid it was only three." Then he started speaking as rapidly as if he found what he was saying so distasteful that he couldn't wait to get it out of his mouth. "Father certainly didn't say for you not to come. He did point out that the trip over could take as long as three weeks and might be very rough at that time of the year. He was trying to be considerate of you since he knew that you had not regained your health or your..." He caught himself before he said "looks," but she knew that was what he had almost said.

He went on, "They know the terrible ordeals you went through and are afraid you wouldn't be able to stand the trip...and the festivities." The words had rushed out so fast that he was breathless when he stopped speaking.

"So, there was no reservation made or money included for me," she said in such a low voice that Clay had to lean over her to understand. Suddenly, she felt that she might have swallowed the whole remaining carcass of the turkey. Pains were shooting up from places she did even know she had, and swallowing seemed out of the question. "Did they..." she started, but could not finish the question.

"Did they what?" he asked, clearly also greatly agitated.

She couldn't speak so she just pointed at herself.

Clay pulled away from the bed and whirled around so his back was to her.

"Clay?" she began again but could get out no more.

He gave a deep, drawn-out sigh or groan and turned back to look at her again. "I don't know," he said, the words just bursting from him. "He must know that I won't come without you, but I guess he also knows that I wouldn't want to subject you to something that would make you sick again. He's thinking of what is best for you, Jamie."

Finally, she tried to get up, struggled and sank back down. He sprang to help her. "I just want to go to bed," she murmured. "Why don't you do the same?" So silently they undressed. He blew out the lamp and joined her in the cold bed, where they lay beneath the layers of quilts as far apart as if they were strangers. When he finally tried to reach for her, she didn't relax a muscle. She held herself as stiff as if she were a walking cane lying on the far edge of the bed.

"They mean for you not to bring me, but they think that doing it this way will be easier for you. They aren't thinking of me at all," she said after a time.

"Oh, no, you're wrong. You know Father well enough to know that he would say that straight out if that was what he meant."

She turned her head toward him, and her big black eyes were luminous in the faint moonlight and starlight coming in through the two tall windows.

"He would," Clay insisted.

She looked away from him, tugged the quilts closer around her and said, "Goodnight, Clay."

"No, wait," he said urgently, raising himself on one elbow and trying to look into her face. "Please don't shut me out. Can't you see their point? You and Mary Lilly have never been close. She came of age in terribly difficult times. Now that she has really come into her own, they want to give her all the support they can. They don't want her to go into her future looking like a poor relative of Sir Peter..."

Her voice was so low that he could hardly hear her as she said, "Sir Peter?"

"Yes, Grandfather Cooke. All of this is terribly important to him and to his wife, who is our grandmother. Try to see if from their side."

Again her head turned to him but only her head. "I'm afraid I do. That's the thing I can see through the mountain of hurt that is still telling me that I'm unacceptable."

"*You are not!*" He almost shouted the words. "Yes, I would want you to regain your figure and your beauty by the time we went, but even if you were still just a sack of attached bones, I would want you there with me. If I had the money, I'd buy the whole dang ship before I'd leave you behind. But," he ended sadly, "I haven't."

Though his words added to the hurt, she didn't tell him. She had married him for selfish reasons, and this was her punishment. He had probably lamented to his parents that she was gaining very little weight, looking scrawny and gaunt. Of course, they wouldn't want her there to put a blight on their younger daughter's social success. "Don't worry about it, Clay. I wouldn't want to go where I'd be an embarrassment to your family."

"It's not that way, Jamie," he said, putting all the strength he had into the words. "They're just thinking of what is best for you."

She thought of Pris' word and almost yelled, "Horseradish!" but it wasn't worth the effort it would take. Instead, she whispered a soft, "Goodnight, Clay," and closed her eyes.

"I am a Haynesworth," she whispered to herself as she had so many times but knew that she had been mistaken. She was still just a woods colt. And it was partly her own fault.

So she said nothing more and neither did he. But the silence was so heavy that, added to the weight of the quilts over them, she felt that she was covered with layers of lead.

# 31

When Jamie got up the next day, Clay still lay there looking dead to the world under the quilts. She felt pretty much the same, she thought, as she pulled on her old ratty silk robe that she had once been so proud of having. For the last few days, she had hoped she could put it away till next spring and would soon have a nice new woolen one. *False hope*, she told herself bitterly. But, she added mentally, surely she was used to handling false hopes by now. She turned to the wardrobe and considered putting her old green cloak over herself but gave herself a shake and made a dash to the hall. Surely Rhody or Steven would have a good fire in the cook stove and the kitchen would be warm. She could shiver until she got there.

She felt the warmth as soon as she opened the door that led to the kitchen stairs, so she knew that the lower area would be toasty warm. It was, but it was also empty. "Rhody," she called, peeping into the adjoining room that had once belonged to Mammy Rose. No one was there either, so she went back and pulled the better one of her two kitchen chairs up close to the stove. Though she knew now that she wasn't going anywhere, she still was determined to get her looks back, so she told herself she would eat oatmeal until it came out her ears if it took that long. There was coffee in the pot so she poured herself a cup and sipped it, feeling terribly lonely and unwanted.

In just a few moments, Rhody came bursting in from the outside, wrapped in an old coat and hugging herself tightly. "Brrrr," she was saying. Then she saw Jamie. "I warn't expectin' to see you, Miss Jamie. Ain't you up kinda' early?"

"Maybe. I didn't check Mr. Clay's pocket watch for I was ready to get up anyway. What's Steven doing out there on a cold, misty morning like this? I would think he might as well be in here where it's warm."

"No, ma'am. Not Steven." Rhody took off the coat, tossed it into her room and came back to hover close to the stove. "It'done took a turn to be awful cold, so I took him a extra old sweater and two bricks I had heated so he could warm his hands. He ain't doin' nothin' pressin' no how, but he's done set his mind on findin' sumpin' dat he thinks ort to be done." She pulled the saucepan that was on the back of the stove over to her, stirred the contents and looked at Jamie. "This here be yo' oatmeal. Is you ready for it?"

"In a little while…"

Rhody reached up on the shelf by the stove and got a bowl. "Don't you reckon you better eat 'fore it cools? Steven and me is like Mr. Clay. We sho' is glad to see you tryin' to eat like you ort to."

Jamie didn't meet the woman's eyes as she got up and said, "The last year of the war nearly finished me. I guess I wasn't thinking quite right when I couldn't eat as I should."

"Ain't we been knowin' dat?" the woman said fervently. "But we is thinkin' you is gonna be all right now. You is, ain't you?"

Jamie didn't know whether to laugh or be annoyed.

She decided on neither, so she just said, "I haven't even washed my face and hands yet. Give me just a minute."

"Yes, ma'am," the woman said as eagerly as Mammy Rose once would have done. "I'll git de butter and sugar."

Jamie went over to the wash pan that sat on the shelf by the door, dipped some water into it and washed her face and hands. Then she shivered as she dried them on the towel hanging over the shelf and said, "That water from the spring sure is cold."

"I shoulda' gotten you some of de warm water from de stove. I just warn't thinkin'." She put the oatmeal down on the table and said, "I's thinkin' you be wantin' coffee too."

"You're thinking right," Jamie told her as she sat back down at the table. In spite of everything she could do, the word "unwanted" was flashing in her mind. She shook her head and started eating furiously, trying to blank all of that out again.

Suddenly, there was a loud knocking on the side porch door.

"Will you see who that is, please, Rhody? I'll get my coffee."

"Yes, ma'am." She started for the stairs but stopped and turned back. "I done heerd him goin' down de porch steps. He must be comin' back here."

She was right and by the time she hushed, Pris burst into the room. "Where's Clay?" she demanded, so breathless she could hardly speak.

"He's still in bed," Jamie said. "Sit down and have a cup of coffee while you get your breath. What's wrong?"

"Oh, Jamie!" Pris cried, sinking into the other chair. It was the unsteady one, and she almost toppled over. Rhody grabbed her and Jamie quickly changed chairs with her and sat back down herself.

Pris grabbed the cup of coffee that Rhody was putting before her almost before it hit the table.

"This is terrible, Jamie," she said distractedly. "I refuse to accept it."

"Yes, I know. I feel the same way, but I don't know anything else we can do."

"You know?" Pris cried and put the cup down so hard that some of it spilled across the beaten-up old table. "How can you possibly know?" she demanded.

"Clay told me last night."

Pris grabbed her head with both of her hands. "That idiot!" she cried. "Why did he do that?"

"I asked him," Jamie said. "I hated to do it, but I couldn't help myself."

"And what did he say?" his sister asked in a terrified-sounding whisper. "Did he deny it?"

"How could he?" Jamie asked. "Here, Pris, drink your coffee and try to calm yourself. It's not the end of the world. I can accept it."

Pris stared at her, open-mouthed. Then she turned to the woman who was standing there obviously taking in every word.

"Can you excuse us for a few minutes, please, Rhody?"

The woman looked at Jamie. "Please," Jamie added. "I'll call you if I need you." Rhody gave her another look, then hurried into the room next to the kitchen.

"Now," Pris went on, picking up her cup again with trembling hands. "What do you mean 'you can take it'? If it's true, it will be the ruin of our family. I am so worried for you both than I'm practically out of my head."

"I can see that but, Pris, calm down. I'll admit that I'm terribly hurt, but I've been hurt before. But I am determined it will not ruin our whole family." She was trying hard to hold onto some semblance of confidence in an attempt to steady Pris, but whatever control she was holding onto was eroding fast.

Pris stared at Jamie as though she thought the other girl had surely lost her mind. "But there's never been anything like this in our family. Actually, not in any decent family. It's going to just kill my parents."

"What do you mean, 'it will kill your parents.' They're the cause of the whole thing."

"*They are not!* Has it caused you to absolutely lose your mind?" Then a strange, twisted look came over her usually-smooth face. She looked at Jamie and said slowly, "Exactly what did Clay tell you? And how in the world did you know to ask him anything?"

Jamie was now terribly scared and confused. "I didn't mean to do it, Pris. I know I had promised you I wouldn't, but the words just came out on their own. I'm sorry I broke my word, but…"

Pris slammed the coffee cup down again. It broke and the remaining coffee flew all around, but neither girl noticed it. Pris reached for Jamie's hand. "Forget about that. Who cares about that now? What else did Clay tell you?"

"I don't know what you mean by 'what else.' He told me your parents hadn't sent money for me to go on the trip because…"

"The trip?" Pris cried, turning away and looking as if she might get up and run. "Who cares about that now?"

"Then what are we talking about?" Jamie almost yelled the words. The door to Rhody's room opened but was hastily shut again as the two girls sat there as though frozen. "Your parents don't want me there in England, and I'm doing everything I can to keep from letting it just about kill me."

Pris' eyes filled with tears. "Oh, Jamie, Jamie," she moaned, "I didn't even know that and I'm so sorry. It's no wonder that Clay has been feeling depressed." Then she gave a gasp and said, "I can't tell you anything more. I have to talk to Clay. Where is he?"

"He's still in bed. And, you *can* tell me. No matter what it is, if it concerns Clay, it concerns me too. I *have* to know."

Pris took a few deep breaths before she tried to speak again. "You thought I was having a nervous breakdown. I haven't yet, but I felt like it when Mrs…" She cut her words off and jumped up to run for the stairs. "What is Clay doing in bed at this time? I've got to talk to him first." She headed up the steps with Jamie right behind her, trying to grab her skirt and hold her back.

As they crossed the hall to the steps going on up, Pris turned back to Jamie with both hands held up. "You stay down here. I've got to talk to my brother."

"No," Jamie cried in reply, "I will not. He's my husband so, like I said, if whatever this is affects him, it affects me too."

They stood there with Pris a few steps above Jamie, staring at each other. Finally, Pris gave in, said a weak, "All right" and went on up. When they got to the top hall, Pris looked at Jamie strangely and said, "It can't be true."

"*What can't be true?*" Jamie screamed. "I have no idea what we've been talking about."

Pris reached back for Jamie's hand and held it tightly. "But will Clay?" she said almost under her breath and opened the door.

Clay was sitting up in bed, rubbing his eyes and asking, "What's all the hollering about? And what are you doing here at the crack of dawn, Pris?"

Pris went to the bed and said, "It's not the crack of dawn, Clay. We've got something really serious to talk about."

"I know," he said, swinging his feet over to the floor and adjusting Mr. Mac's old nightshirt. "But, can't it wait until I can get dressed?"

"No, it can't. Mrs. Gains was over at our house at the real crack of dawn this morning. It took Brad's mother and me what seemed like forever to calm her down. Not completely, but we did get her to stop screaming."

Clay slid off the bed and was suddenly as straight as a soldier on guard duty. He stared at his sister and said, "And what was she screaming about? I hope it had nothing to do with me."

"Unfortunately, it did. She said…" she began, then hushed and looked at Jamie, then back at him again. "Maybe you want me to go out in the hall and let you tell your wife yourself. As she has said, this is going to affect her as much as you."

"Me?" Jamie cried. "What have I done now?"

"You haven't done anything, honey," Clay said, reaching an arm out and drawing her close to him.

"Then what's the problem?" she asked, looking first at one and then the other.

Pris stood shaking her head sadly. "I know you didn't get Betsy in a family way, but how can we prove it?" she said in a voice less strident than it had been since her arrival.

"I can tell you and you can accept my word," he said. "That should be all the proof you need."

"It is but Betsy told her mother she had been with no one but you."

"She has not been *with* me. I reminded her of that several days ago when she came out to Crestview where I was working. She was crying all over herself, saying that she knew she was in trouble and that it was my fault. I told her then that it certainly was not, that if she were in trouble, she had gotten herself that way. I had nothing to do with it."

Pris and Jamie stood staring at him. "How," Jamie asked, "could she get herself in that condition? I'll admit I don't know much, but that…"

"Don't be an idiot!" Pris snapped. "Even Thomas knows that's impossible." Then she caught herself and said, "Well, I guess not but you certainly do." Pris turned to her brother again. "If not you—and I can't believe it is you—then who can it be?

Has she been seeing anybody?"

"How do I know?" Clay demanded. "I haven't even seen her except once on the street since you— " he turned to look at Jamie's stricken face "—told me you didn't want her coming around any more. I told her and that was that."

Jamie sighed. "I wish I had told you that sooner."

"Why?" he demanded, taking his arm from around her. "Are you doubting me just like my sister? Does no one have any faith in me?"

"Yes," Jamie said with all the assurance she could manage, "I do believe you."

"And so do I," Pris said staunchly. "But Mrs. Gains was so sure. She said that she and her daughter couldn't face the humiliation of a…"

"Wood's colt," Jamie supplied sadly.

"Don't say that!" The words were almost like explosions from Clay. "I don't want to ever hear that expression again."

They were all three silent for a few moments as the girls stood with drawn faces, and Clay stood by the bed as though still at attention.

Finally, Pris reached for Jamie. "Let's go back down to the kitchen and let Clay get out of that ridiculous nightshirt."

Jamie looked at her husband to see if the suggestion suited him. He nodded and she followed the other girl out into the hall and down both sets of steps. When they got to the kitchen, they both sank down in the chairs. Jamie's tilted dangerously, but she didn't even notice. "What can we do?" she asked finally.

"I don't know," Pris admitted. "There's no way in the world that proof could be found either way. I wish so much that Father could be here. He'd straighten this out in a hurry."

"Well, he isn't," Jamie said sharply. "So what can we do?"

"Nothing that I know of. What had Mrs. Gains so worried this morning was that Betsy was vowing she'd go to that free colored woman at the edge of town who is said to be able to end things like this. She says that Betsy really means that unless Clay divorces you right away and marries her before the…" She let the words fade away and then added, "she will go to that woman."

"Isn't that terribly dangerous?' Jamie asked, appalled at the thought.

"Yes, of course, it is. I've certainly never known anybody who did it, but you know how girls whisper in school."

"No, I don't know,' Jamie said sadly. "I had very few days in any school. Pa was always my teacher."

"Really?" Pris asked, surprised. "He sure did a good job."

Jamie gave a weak smile. "With the things he was good at. I wouldn't say that I had a well-rounded education."

"Who does? There are things Brad doesn't know even after being smart enough to go to medical school."

There were loud steps clattering down the kitchen stairs, and Clay came into the room wearing a pair of checkered pants that had also belonged to Mr. Mac and buttoning the blue shirt that had been Jamie's father's. In spite of her seriously-troubled mind, she couldn't help but think how good it would be to soon see him again as he had been in that other life. They had seen each other then as the epitome of what they wanted as a life companion, and now she was wondering if… Then she hastily cut off the thought. She was not going to admit to any doubts.

"Now," he said, "before the inquisition begins again, may I have something to eat and some coffee?" He addressed his words to his sister.

Jamie jumped up and said, "Here, have my chair. I know you like to eat in the dining room, but it's too cold in there today. There's oatmeal, if you want that. We ran Rhody out so you'll have to do with my help."

"Keep your seat. I don't need any help." He went to the wall shelves that held the old dishes and carefully selected a bowl and a cup without comment. He dished up the remains of the oatmeal and poured himself some coffee. He wolfed the oatmeal down standing up, then said to his sister, "What do you propose?"

She moved nervously in her chair, clasped and unclasped her hands and said, "I don't propose anything. What are you going to do?"

He took a big swallow of coffee before he answered, "Not a dratted thing. Sometimes the more you stir things, the worse they smell. We aren't going to stir this at all."

Jamie looked from one to the other, stark terror showing on her face. Pris was not looking much better. "But Mrs. Gains said…" his sister began.

He cut in, "Who gives a tinker's damn about what Mrs. Gains says? We're going to England for Mary Lilly's big events. By the time we come back, Betsy will have found some way to end her problem, one way or another. She isn't the first girl to get in this situation, and she won't be the last. And it is her problem. It is not ours."

Jamie felt a surge of hope, but it sank right away. "You won't be going for at least two months. A lot of things can happen in two months." Neither of the other two said a word.

"Have you eaten?" Clay asked his wife solicitously after a few moments.

She nodded. "I think so."

"I want you to keep on doing as you have been these last several weeks. I can see the difference in you already. In two months you might have regained at lot of what you lost." His smile to her was warm, but somehow it did nothing for her. No matter what she could do about her looks in two months, she would still be left here alone.

"Won't you at least go and talk to Mrs. Gains? Or maybe Betsy herself?" Pris asked.

He finished his coffee before saying firmly, "Absolutely not. That would be the same as admitting I had something to do with it, and *that* I am not doing. We all know that Betsy has always had trouble behaving as she should. If she let herself be caught up in a real disgrace, she is not going to take me and my wife down with her."

His words filled the room as completely as a loud pound on a drum and left them waiting for another pound that did not come.

Clay replenished his coffee while the two girls sat quietly. Then Pris got up and said, "Maybe I shouldn't have bothered you."

"That's right," he said to her shortly. Then he turned to Jamie. "What are you going to do today?"

She felt at a complete loss for words. "I…I hadn't made any plans, though there is work at the LMA headquarters that I need to do. I let Thanksgiving get me a little behind on recording some of the graves that have been found and need to be matched up with the proper veterans. We don't want to ever make the slightest mistake."

"No, of course not. I'm proud of you for what you're doing."

As Pris pulled herself to her feet, she said, "If you both are heading into town, I guess I'll walk in with you and see what Mother Mac might need before I decide on doing anything. I left her to see to Thomas and to nurse her sympathy for Mrs. Gains. Either of them could be wearing on her."

"Has she already declared me guilty?" Clay asked as all three of them headed for the stairs.

"No, she hasn't. As you well know, she is very fond of you. I hope when I tell her what you have said, she will feel better. But, I will admit, she was awfully worried by the time she got Mrs. Gains calmed down."

"As we all should be when a friend is in trouble," Clay said. Then standing on the bottom tread with Pris a few steps ahead of him, he turned back and called to Jamie, "Coming, honey?"

"I'll be right there, but I've got to get myself dressed in something warm before I go anywhere. Then I'll have to find Rhody and tell her I'll be going into town."

The door of the room next to the kitchen popped open. "I's right here, Miss Jamie. Should I be fixin' dinner for you and Mr. Clay 'fore long?"

"No, we're all going into town. You and Steven can do whatever you want." And she wanted to add, "Don't you dare tell a soul about what I know you have just heard." But she could say nothing that would allay the fear she felt.

The three of them went slowly up the stairs and out across the hall. Jamie knew that at least two of them were still terribly upset with questions unresolved. If the third one had a worry in the world, it wasn't showing on his face.

Friday continued to be a day like Jamie hoped never to have again. She went through all the regular motions, but she couldn't keep her mind from being terribly torn. Of course, she accepted Clay's word that he had not been responsible for getting Betsy in a family way, but she felt that everybody she saw was looking at her with unusual kindness and sympathy. She knew it was bound to be her imagination for surely no one but the McLaurines knew about Mrs. Gains' accusation of Clay. At least, she sure hoped that were true.

When she had finished her work for the LMA, she didn't know what to do with herself. She didn't want to go by Pris' again. The other girls she had once felt close to were either married or still away wherever they had gone during the war. As she walked slowly toward Fairdale, she felt as lonely and bereft as a lost kitten. She wanted her pa or Mammy Rose, but they were both far beyond her reach. She knew that Clay was the one to whom she should be able to go for comfort, but somehow she felt that he had none to spare for anyone. He was too much in need of comfort himself.

She knew she was wrong in feeling that way and felt sure that it was more because she was not invited to the family gathering in England than because of any doubt of her husband. She was glad that she had taken a firm hand in getting Betsy away from him as she had right after his birthday. Otherwise, she would be frantic with fear. How could any girl married only about six months think such a thing of her husband?

The world that she had thought would level off when the terrible war had finally ended was still so tilted that she felt she must grab onto something to keep herself in place. She still remembered Clay's birthday over two months ago when Betsy had upset her so much. Surely Clay was grateful to her now for forcing him to stop allowing Betsy's visits to him while he worked.

Maybe, she told herself as she trudged along by the pike with its desperately-needed repair work in full swing now, the war years hadn't been as bad as she had thought. What could be worse than not being wanted at the most important event ever to happen in the family that she had wanted to be her own and, in addition, having your husband of only about six months accused of being unfaithful?

She felt that Clay had probably written his father protesting about her exclusion from their trip, but with that all-important English Season starting in two and a half months, she knew that nothing could be done. Or maybe Clay hadn't even done that. But even if he had and his father sent money for her to join them, she couldn't go. She wouldn't even want to go under those circumstances. She would feel like an unwelcome woods colt again.

And, in addition to everything else, she had been having a weird feeling that she was being watched every time she went into town. She knew that was foolish, but it still gave her the creeps. Even now, close to home, she looked back to see if there were anyone watching her. There were workers on the pike, but if they had even noticed her, they gave no sign of it. That, in itself, added to her depression. There had been a time when men and boys noticed her, no matter where she was. Now, still thin with no real light in her eyes, she felt old and drab. And she knew it showed. No wonder that Clay hadn't made it clear to his parents that his wife could not be left out. He too must be ashamed of her.

Then she gave a sardonic smile at that, for those thoughts were ones she had never expected to have again. Why had she allowed everything to keep herself torn-up since her marriage? Had she been able to eat everything in sight, as she guessed people who had been hungry for a long time did, she wouldn't have had Clay pushing her to eat until she simply couldn't do it. Also she probably wouldn't have had that queasy feeling that had bothered her so much.

If Betsy did have a baby, she for one was going to show it every consideration. She would even love it, for no one should have to bear what she had borne for being born out of wedlock.

Betsy's baby would too, no matter what she did. It was just the way things were.

She turned in at Fairdale and sank down on the side porch steps. So much had been seen from these steps. She usually refused to let herself think about the handsome Yankee who had sat there with her one bright night. Now she let the thought of him swamp her. She remembered the nights she had waited so eagerly for his steps coming up from the basement. How she had run into his arms. Of course, she still knew that she could never have accepted a Yankee into Fairdale and her life, but she felt sure that, if she could have, the time would never have come when she had to be frightened that another woman had been in the position to give her husband what, so far, she had not.

Partly her own fault, she said again. Everything was partly her own fault except her own birth. She had had nothing to do with that, but she had punished her father for it for years when it really wasn't his fault either. *So where did the blame fall?* Had all this terrible scenario been written by her grandfather who loved his daughter so much that he could not share her with an ordinary man like Pa? But Pa hadn't really been ordinary, and she should have seen him as most other people did. Too late. Too late for almost everything.

She dragged herself up from the steps and went into the house without having resolved any of the troubling things in her mind.

Saturday was no better. She moved around the house as though she were recovering from a severe illness. And maybe she was. She didn't know. She did know that Clay was being very caring and supportive, even though she felt that he was the one who needed support. He was almost exuberant except at those times when he thought no one was looking. Then he looked as despairing as she felt. They were both acting. She wondered if he knew it as definitely as she did.

Sunday came and the McLaurines were there in the carriage to pick them up for the trip to Christ Episcopal Church. Jamie felt a reluctance to go but said nothing about it. Since she and Clay were so faithful about going, she knew that this was not the day either of them could miss. Of course, she hoped no one knew about the predicament Betsy was in and her mother's accusation of Clay, but things like that were hard to hide in a small town.

Mrs. McLaurine touched Clay's cheek when he helped Jamie in and then sat down beside his wife. Brad got down and handed the reins to Steven, who would drive them to church as he had in the days when Pa had been there. Not many families still had the advantage of having a carriage and a driver, so the traffic around the church was far less than it had once been.

As they pulled up in front of the church and the men jumped down to help the ladies and Thomas out, Jamie couldn't help but look at each person they saw to see if their expressions were any different than they usually were. She saw nothing that concerned her, but then Betsy and her mother attended Kent Street Presbyterian. Their closest friends were probably over there in the church Jamie and her father had formerly attended—as had Stonewall Jackson, she reminded herself, knowing that fact had nothing to do with anything on this cold last November Sunday.

She presumed the priest's sermon was good, but she was hardly able to take in a word of it. Thomas must have sensed the tension in his family for he was so restless that his mother had to slip out with him a short time before the final song and benediction.

As Steven pulled the carriage up before the church to get them, Jamie headed for it with a feeling of deep relief. "Put your feet on those hot bricks Steven put in while we were in church," Pris said. "They do feel so good."

"Where to, Mr. Clay?" Steven called to him. "Home?"

"I reckon so, Steven," Clay called back. Then he turned to the McLaurines. "That's all right with you all, isn't it? We won't have anything like we had Thursday, but Rhody said she could come up with enough of something for us all."

"Take me by home," Mrs. McLaurine said. "I want to hear from Betsy. I do hope that things are better there today."

*How can they be?* Jamie thought but didn't ask.

Clay directed Steven to take Mrs. Mac home first.

"Maybe we should get out too," Pris said. "Thomas was so restless in church that I know he needs a nap."

"He's taken plenty of Sunday naps at our house," Clay reminded her.

"Want to go to Aunt Jamie's," the little boy said.

"No, honey," his mother told him. "Not today. We're going on the big choo-choo train tomorrow afternoon. We've got to get ready for that, so we'd better stay home today. You'll want to be rested for that ride on the big train."

Jamie shot a questioning look at Clay. He gave a little nod.

"Me going on the choo-choo?" the little boy said wonderingly. Then he turned to look up a Jamie. "You go, Aunt Jamie?"

"No, honey, not this time, but you have a wonderful time." By now they were pulling up at Mrs. Mac's house.

"I'm terribly disappointed that you aren't going on the big trip, Jamie," Brad told her as he reached across her to open the door for Clay to help his mama down. "We're both in-laws so if you stay home, I should too."

"Oh, no!" she protested. "I wouldn't have you even think of that. And I partly brought this on myself. For some reason I just couldn't eat enough to keep me going and put on weight too. I'm getting to be fine now when it's too late to do any good. But who can blame them for not wanting an unattractive bundle of bones putting a blight on all the wonderful doings?"

"With eyes like yours and that beautiful hair, you could never be unattractive," Brad said as he followed his mama and reached back for his wife's hand to help her down.

"And besides, you're family. When will the family ever have a more exciting time than this?" Pris put in as she reached the ground and turned back to say goodbye to her sister-in-law and brother. They called goodbye to Mrs. Mac and Thomas and moved on off for home.

"How long have you been planning to go to...I guess...Baltimore?" she asked.

"Just a couple of days. I didn't tell you for I didn't want you to have time to think of reasons you couldn't go. You will go with us, won't you?"

She shook her head. "No, I can't. I appreciate the invitation, but I really couldn't stand to see you all buying all the things you have to have and…well, you know."

"I know I want you there with us. Please change your mind and come."

"I can't, Clay. Please don't ask me. To insist just makes a bad situation worse. There is nothing you could say that would make me change and go. I can't. I just can't. Now let's get on home and start making a list of things you'll need. The suits, top coats and waistcoats you won't forget, but it's the little things we need to list. And don't forget to buy some tan trousers and a dark green jacket. That's what you had on the first day I met you. You looked good enough to make me fall in love with you. Let's see if they still work."

He shook his head sadly, then pulled her into his arms and whispered, "Do you have any idea how much I love you?" She snuggled close but made no answer.

# 32

The temperature was better the next day. Clay had a few things pending about his office that he needed to see about before heading for the train station so he had Steven go in early for the carriage. By the time it was there, he had eaten an early dinner and was ready to go. As Jamie rode with him to see them off, she had a strange feeling about the whole thing. Since the Tuesday before, her life had been in turmoil, so it was almost with a feeling of relief that she viewed the few days she would have alone.

She waited in the carriage as Clay took care of what he had to do. She wondered why she didn't want to go in and see the progress that might have been made, but feeling that it had nothing to do with her, she had no desire to do so. She had forced herself to accept with all the grace she could manage that she was not included in the invitation to England, and somehow she felt out of everything.

After Clay had completed what he had to do, they went over to pick up the McLaurines. "Aren't we a motley-looking crew?" Pris asked as they climbed in the carriage. "It will be a wonder if the hotel will even let us in. Since I'm a little better than the men, they're sending me in to explain our situation. We don't want them to think we'll be looking this bad the whole time we're there."

Jamie said nothing.

"I'm still hoping that when we get to the train, she'll get on with us," Clay told them.

"Oh, I do hope so," Pris said. "I'd almost rather not go than to leave her at home alone."

Thomas tugged on her skirt and said, "Aunt Jamie go."

She hugged him and whispered, "I can't."

When they got to the station, she reminded Clay of what she

had told him the night before. "Don't forget the tan pants and dark green jacket. That's what you had on when we met. You looked so good that I fell in love with you. Now I want to see if they still work."

"Get on with us and you can see for yourself," he told her. "Please come."

"Don't be silly," Jamie said, biting back the tears as best she could. "Surely you don't think I'd want to be seen in those fine Baltimore stores with a bunch of folks dressed like you all are."

Pris laughed and looked down at her old black dress and her mother-in-law's woolen coat in disgust. "I can see your point, but we'll hope to come home looking somewhat better."

Jamie could make no answer to that, for the tears were too close to the surface.

Clay could obviously tell her problem and said, "I wish I could let Brad buy things for me," he told her just before he gave her a final kiss and climbed on the train. Thomas was so excited and yelling so shrilly that she could hardly understand Clay's words.

"Have a good trip," she said hastily and turned back to their carriage before he could see her tears. The last thing she heard was Thomas screaming, "Aunt Jamie. Come too."

"Let's go," she told Steven and they headed for Fairdale as the train pulled from the station. She cried all the way home and dashed up the stairs to climb up on her bed and cry some more.

Steven had said nothing to her the whole time, but she had known he was worried for he kept leaning down to look in at her. As she now lay on the bed, she had trouble keeping from screaming. She knew that would scare both of them down in the kitchen and bring them running. She didn't want to worry anybody.

Rhody came tiptoeing in after what seemed like a decade, but without Clay's pocket watch, Jamie had no idea how long it had been. "You all right, Miss Jamie?" she said in what was little more than a whisper.

Jamie moved to the side of the bed and let herself slide off to the floor. "I'm fine," she said in a voice that made a lie of the words.

"Steven went out to a trap he set and found dat he had a nice big rabbit. I fixed it and you got fried rabbit, gravy and biscuits for supper wid some dried black-eyed peas. He also got a fire in de dining room. Ain't you ready to come down and eat?"

"I reckon I am. That sounds mighty good. Thank you. Do you know if I have any water on the wash stand? I need to wash my face."

"Yes, ma'am. And I 'spects it still warm. If it ain't, I'll git some mo'."

"No, that's fine. I'll wash up and be down in a minute or two. And tell Steven thanks from me."

"He ain't needin' no thanks, but I'll tell him." She went back out as quietly as she had come in. Jamie dragged herself over to the washstand and actually did feel better after she had washed her face and brushed her hair. The rabbit even sounded good, so she went on downstairs to eat her lonely meal. She almost wished she had been allowed to eat down in the kitchen, but she wasn't about to mention that. At least, there were two people who still cared for her. Then she was ashamed of herself for feeling self-pity, so she straightened herself and marched into the dining room as staunchly as if she were going in to be awarded some kind of honor. And maybe she really was.

The four days until her family returned seemed almost as long as it had taken for the war to end. But when Steven went to get the horse and carriage and then came to get her to meet the train, she felt almost as much worry as relief. When she saw them coming off with all their purchases, she was afraid she might burst into tears again. She forced herself not to do that for she didn't want them—especially Clay—to know what the exclusion had done to her.

"You wanna wait in de carriage, Miss Jamie?" Steven asked. "I can go and git 'em."

"No," she told him, "I'll be there to meet them."

*It feels like that day when the church bells all rang to announce our loss,* she thought to herself, feeling as defeated as General Lee must have felt. Then Clay was down the steps and grabbing her in his arms. The others were right behind him with Thomas screaming, "Aunt Jamie! Aunt Jamie!" and she felt for a moment as though she hadn't really lost a thing. But as she saw all the packages being lifted out by the porter, she knew she had. Nevertheless, she was determined not to add to the sorrow by making a scene.

She looked at Clay in his tan trousers and dark green jacket and laughed. Then she threw her arms around him. "You look almost the same," she cried. "I'm so glad to see you like this again." She then looked at Pris in her blue traveling suit with a heavy cloak thrown around her shoulders, "And look at you! Aren't you the smartest-looking girl I've seen in years! You too, Brad." Then she looked down at the little boy tugging at her skirt and saying, "Look at me, Aunt Jamie. I got new clothes."

"You certainly have and aren't you the best-looking little boy in the world?" she said, scooping him up in her arms. He laughed delightedly and said, "Aunt Jamie got new clothes too."

"No, honey, I didn't but that's all right. You're going on a big boat and you'll need new clothes."

"Aunt Jamie go too," he declared. She kissed him and put him down. The men started gathering up the packages and carrying them to the carriage. "We brought as much as we could. The rest will be sent," Brad told her.

When they and their packages were all in, with Thomas sitting proudly up by Steven, Pris turned to Jamie, "You won't believe all the clothes in the ready-made stores in Baltimore. Mother was right. We'll be fine on the boat."

"Ship," her husband reminded her. "You've got to quit calling it a *boat.*"

"Oh, all right. On the *ship* then. I can't believe all the things I bought. I just hope we didn't buy so much that we don't have the money for the tickets. Clay's got to send that to the office in Boston."

"There'll be enough," Clay said shortly, tightening his arm around Jamie.

"Only not enough…" The words slipped out before she knew they were coming, but she managed to cut them off before she completed the sentence.

Clay held her even tighter. "That makes me so mad. I'm still tempted not to go," he muttered into her ear while Pris and Brad exchanged worried looks.

"And not get to impress all of Mary Lilly's new friends with those trousers and that jacket?" Jamie teased and was proud that she could do that instead of shrieking like she felt like doing. "Absolutely not!"

"Have you heard anything more about…?" Pris asked but did not finish the question.

Jamie knew exactly what she meant without the complete sentence. "Not a word from anybody about anything. But actually, I haven't been into town. Not even to the LMA."

"You didn't want anybody asking why you weren't on the shopping trip with us," Clay said, sounding bitter. "I don't blame you."

She reached up and touched his cheek. "Don't feel so bad. Maybe it's my own fault for not somehow getting my shape back. I can see why your parents would be embarrassed to have someone looking like death warmed over with all those fine folks over there. I've adjusted to the fact that I'm not going. Really, I have. I wasn't going anywhere before. I'm not going anywhere now. I haven't lost a thing that I had."

"Like heck you haven't," Clay muttered. "And if you haven't, I have."

Jamie turned to Brad. "Did you get some fabulous clothes too?"

He grinned. "I got whatever Pris told me to get. I don't think any of us will be an embarrassment on board or when we land. Beyond that, I have no idea. But I'm like the others. I sure wish you were going with us."

"Me too, but I don't want to hear another word about it. Listen to Thomas squealing delightedly up there with Steven. He's had a great time, I guess."

"You better believe it! He was as proud as punch when trying on clothes. Never made the least complaint," his mother said, "except about his Aunt Jamie not being there. I don't know how many times he asked, 'Where's Aunt Jamie?'"

In spite of herself, Jamie felt tears running down her cheeks. To hide them, she hid her face in Clay's dark green shoulder.

By then, they were at the McLaurines' house. Steven pulled up in front and lifted Thomas down to run into the house calling, "Grandma! Grandma!"

"No, not that one," Clay said as Steven started to pick up one in a rather fancy box.

"You sure?" Jamie asked.

He just took the box and laid it to the side while he helped sort out what belonged to whom. By now, Mrs. Mac had come out to welcome them home with Thomas running right along by her.

When finally everything was straight, the McLaurines said goodbye, and Steven took the Haynesworths on out to Fairdale. When they pulled up by the side porch, he and Clay loaded up the remaining packages and carried them up the steps. Then Clay reached for a small package and handed it to Steven. "Here's a few plugs of chewing tobacco for you and some candy for Rhody. I started to get snuff for her, but I didn't know if she dipped or not."

"Thank you, Mr. Clay and I thank you for Rhody too. She done tried dat snuff once, but I tol' her it was a nasty habit so she ain't done it agin. She sho' will be happy to git this candy."

Clay laughed. "And she doesn't consider chewing tobacco a nasty habit too?"

Steven grinned. "She ain't never said and I ain't axed," he said and picked up another package. When they were all in the hall, Clay said, "You can go ahead and take the carriage back to the McLaurines'. I wish we had some way to keep them out here, but since we don't, I don't reckon that would be a good idea. What did you do about the horse while we were gone?"

"I done like Miss Jamie said and went up ever day to feed and water de horse."

"I should have thought of it," he said, then added to Jamie, "I'm sure glad you did."

The two of them carried the packages upstairs and put all but the one in the fancy box into Jamie's pa's old room. Then he handed that one to Jamie. "I didn't care how short on money I ended up, I wasn't coming home without something for you too. Open it and see how I did."

"Oh, Clay," she cried softly. She was almost as moved as she would have been if he had suddenly announced that she was going with them. She tore the box open and found a tan suit that almost matched his pants and a dark green shirtwaist that was almost the same shade of green as his jacket. "The saleslady said the suit would be great for church or even for parties. Of course, I knew it would. She also said that she thought hoops were gradually going out. So I didn't worry about them in the other dress that I thought you'd like. I did get a good petticoat to go with the dress. The rose color reminded me of the dress you wore the night the war started. You were so beautiful in it."

The tears were pouring so much that she could hardly get out the words to say, "Oh, yes, Clay, I remember that dress and I love this one." She hastily wiped her eyes and grabbed it to hold it up to her. "You shouldn't have, but I'm so glad you did. I haven't had anything but what the Yankees didn't want for their women in what seems like forever. Thank you, thank you, thank you!" She was so thrilled by the gifts and by his thoughtfulness that she almost forgot about the trip on which she would not be going.

But she sure remembered it before the night was over. And cried herself to sleep as usual.

# 33

Jamie went in the next day to see all the purchases the McLaurines had made, exclaimed over them excitedly and did not run screaming from the house as she felt like doing. Mrs. Mac came in to give her a warm welcome, and Jamie could feel the sympathy in the older woman. She wanted to ask if there had been any further word about Betsy's female problems but didn't dare.

When she left for the walk back to Fairdale, she was feeling about as lonely and defeated as she had ever been in her life. Added to that was the curious feeling that there were eyes on her from somewhere. She kept glancing around to see if anyone had her in his sights but saw no one who seemed to be interested in her. Was it someone from the Gains' house farther up on Braddock? And, if so, why watch her? She decided it was bound to be no one and that her nerves must be acting up.

Sunday came so she and Clay dressed up in their new outfits for church. She was wearing the rose-colored wool since the day was not terribly cold. She liked it so much that she was willing to shiver to get to wear it.

"You did awfully well on your shopping," she told Clay as the light-weight wool fell in fullness from the waist down and over her hips…hips that, incidentally, were not quite as boney as they had been.

"Still a little large," Clay decided as he looked her over. "Pris said it would be but that you're finally gaining and would be filling it out soon. I sure wish I had known you would do that before…" He broke off and Jamie had a funny feeling that he had been about to say something like "before I told my parents that you were looking terrible." She gave him a quick look but nothing more. If he had done that, it was her fault as much as his, and nothing could be gained by further talk.

"You both are looking mighty handsome today," Brad said with a big smile as they came down the porch steps to join him and his family.

"I'm going to be shivering something awful, but I simply couldn't put that old green cloak of mine over this dress. I've worn it as a robe, I've slept in it and worked in it," Jamie said as she seated herself on the back seat by Pris, Mrs. Mac and Thomas."

"Look, Aunt Jamie," Thomas was tugging on her arm and saying urgently. "I got new clothes too."

She gave him a hug and said, "Yes, you have and you look wonderful. You won't even be cold like your Aunt Jamie because you've got a nice wool coat." Then she looked on to Pris. "Your mama looks great too in that nice suit. You really do, Pris."

"Well, why didn't you wear the suit Clay got you? That dress sure is pretty, but you're going to be just a big icicle by the time you get home."

"Oh, no," Thomas cried and grabbed onto her. "I don't want you to be an icicle. They break and they melt. I don't want you to melt, Aunt Jamie."

Everybody laughed, but Jamie held him tightly and whispered, "I'm not going to turn into an icicle, honey. Your mama just meant that I'd be cold. And I expect I will be, but I won't ever melt."

"Promise?" he whispered back.

"I promise," she assured him. Then she said to the others, "I know I'll be chilly and I don't care. I just feel so good to have something new and pretty that I wanted everybody to know it."

"Those who still haven't had anything new in years might not be as impressed with all of us as you think," her brother-in-law put in dryly.

"Yes, I know. But how a person feels is largely up to the person herself. I have decided that I'm going to feel good, no matter what."

"Hear, hear!" Brad said, but his mother reached a sympathetic hand over to Jamie's arm and murmured, "Keep it up, dear."

They did look good as they marched in to sit in the pew that had always been the Haynesworths. They joined in on the hymns and listened intently to the sermon. Thomas was asleep with his head in his grandmother's lap long before the benediction was said. Brad took his son from his mother, and they all trooped out to get back in the carriage.

"I didn't see Mrs…" began Clay as they went off down the street.

"Of course, you didn't," snapped his sister. "You know perfectly well that they've always been Presbyterians."

"You getting to be a mind reader?" Clay asked from across the carriage, sounding annoyed.

"No, but I knew what you were thinking."

*And so did I*, Jamie said, but she spoke only to herself. The specter of Betsy was hanging over them all, but nobody dared mention her name.

Mrs. Mac wanted to be let out at home, and she took Thomas with her, thinking that he might get his new clothes messy if he wore them through dinner. The others headed out to Fairdale as they usually did on Sunday.

"The folks who no longer have help in their kitchens or someone to pick them up after church have a lot more reason to be jealous than they might be over our new clothes," Jamie said as they were jostling along toward home.

"Yeah," came the quick agreement from Pris.

"I was surprised that Thomas didn't cut a rusty about not going on out to Aunt Jamie's and Uncle Clay's," his father observed.

"He's still tired from the trip," Pris said. "Oh, by the way, Jamie, did you know that Mother Mac has rented her two downstairs bedrooms to some of those government men who are in town?"

"No, I didn't!" exclaimed Jamie. "Why, one of those bedrooms was her own. What's she going to do?"

"She moved upstairs across the hall from us. I know it'll be annoying to have Yankees in her house again, but these won't be like those others. Also, she can kick them out if she wants to. And having a few more Union dollars will be nice."

"What will she do when you all go on your trip?" Jamie asked. "Won't she mind having strange men in the house when she's there alone?"

"Could be. She said she might leave the house to them and go stay with her sister over in Fredericksburg. Y'all met that aunt of Brad's at our wedding." Then she changed and said, "Oh, that's right, Jamie. That's when you came down with the typhoid, and neither of you met anybody. Anyway, Brad's aunt is suffering from rheumatism so bad that Mother Mac has been feeling she ought to go help her for a while."

"That's kind of Mrs. Mac, but then she's one of the kindest people I've ever known," Jamie said sincerely. Brad smiled and reached across from the front seat to touch her hand in gratitude for her appreciation of his mama.

"She is that. I'll miss her when we're gone," her daughter-in-law said just as sincerely, "but not as much as I'll miss having you with us."

Jamie tried to smile at both of them but could do nothing more. She would hold back the tears if it killed her.

In the next few days, their lives settled back down into the usual pattern. Clay was working with the Union men on rebuilding Loudoun Street and was excited about the success he was having with them.

"They should get started on my office before we go to England," he told her enthusiastically one day toward the middle of the second week in December. "Of course, Christmas may hold us up some."

"That's great," she agreed, although she did wish he was saying that her outbuildings were going to be rebuilt. She didn't even mention that. Neither was she objecting any more to his spending so much time at Crestview digging whenever he could get a pick or a shovel in the ground. She realized that she was becoming more and more placid in her reactions to everything in her life. She knew she might as well.

Then one December morning in the week before Christmas, Pris came in almost a run out to Fairdale. "Betsy's dead," she gasped, as she fell onto the hall bench. Jamie was coming up from the kitchen and stopped momentarily to stare at her friend. Pris was still trying to get her breath and having a hard time doing it.

"Dead?" Jamie then cried, falling onto the bench by her. "Oh, no! No! She just can't be! Does Clay know?"

"I... I don't guess so. I... didn't try to find him. I just came...out here so you'd be prepared if...if Mrs. Gains tries to cause trouble." With her gasping, it was hard for Jamie to understand her.

She did get enough to shock her so that she almost slid off the bench. She grabbed onto the seat with both hands to steady herself and cried, "Make trouble? How could she do that? And why would she want to? Neither Clay nor I have done anything to Betsy." She was feeling almost as weak and breathless as her sister-in-law.

"She...says that...that Clay has."

"Who says that?" Jamie demanded. "Betsy?"

"No, you...goose! I told you...that she's dead. She...she went to that...woman she's been threatening...to go to. You know, the one who claims...she can fix troubles like...Betsy had."

"But that's crazy," Jamie cried. "And I don't know anything about such a woman."

"I know, I know," moaned Pris, beginning to breathe a little better but now holding her head with both hands and still bending almost double. "But Betsy had a friend...in Lexington...where her mother took her to get away from what was happening here.... That friend must have been a lot like Betsy. Her grandmother...had made blackberry wine for her grandson who was coming home on leave. The friend invited Betsy to join her in getting into it. They got really tipsy and the friend...foolishly told Betsy a closely-guarded family secret."

"I can hardly understand you," Jamie told her. "Can I get you something? I think there's still coffee and fresh..."

"Yes, hot coffee. I'm freezing."

"Go into the sitting room. There's a fire or come down to the kitchen. It's really warm."

"No time. Just get the coffee."

Jamie ran for the stairs. In a moment she was back with a cup. "It's still hot, but it might be awfully strong."

"I do hope so. My head feels like it's splitting." She straightened up, took the coffee and sipped. "Oh, it is hot." She put it down at her feet, clutched her coat tightly around herself and went on. "What made the friend think of telling her was the connection to Winchester. Several years ago the friend's family had a woman from one of the islands working for them. The woman's son is one of the many free ones who've always lived here.

"Betsy's friend's family was in terrible turmoil once back then when her sister got in trouble. They thought they were ruined. The island woman heard and said she could help if they wouldn't let her son know about it. They all promised…so the woman went out in the woods at midnight, built a fire and concocted something. She gave it to the sister to drink and it worked. Nobody ever knew. Later the sister married a nice man.

"Everybody in the friend's family swore they hadn't told, but somehow the woman's son knew. He came to Lexington, got his mother and made her come to live with him and his family here where he could keep an eye on her."

Pris stopped to gasp in a few breaths and to try the coffee again. It must have been better, for she gulped it down and went on. "The friend was appalled when she realized what she had done, so she made Betsy swear never to tell it. It was witchcraft, and he had told her if she started doing it in Winchester, he would send her back to the island."

"Oh, my goodness!" Jamie cried. "No wonder Betsy's mother was beside herself."

"Yes, but listen to the rest. Betsy wrote the friend for the son's name here. When she got it and realized that he was someone her mother had had do some work for them, she confessed everything to her and asked her to go with her to see him. Mrs. Gains said she saw it as a ray of hope too, so she and Betsy went to the son's house. The woman wasn't there, but the son talked to them. He was furious that they knew anything about it, and he absolutely refused to let his mother help them. He said the whole thing was evil, and he wasn't letting his mother get involved in that 'black magic' or witchcraft again. He scared Mrs. Gains so much that she forbade Betsy to have anything to do with it, but he must not have scared Betsy. She somehow contacted the woman and had it done. And it killed her."

"Oh, how awful! But Betsy didn't tell her mother who had gotten her that way?"

"I've already told you! She said it was Clay and that he forced her."

At that, Jamie practically fell off the bench again. "No! He did not! He wouldn't ever do that! He told me he didn't touch her, and I believe him. Who is the woman and her son? Do you know them?"

"Not personally. He's a carpenter and apparently a good one."

"How do you know all this?" Jamie asked, absolutely appalled at what she was hearing.

"I've told you that! Mrs. Gains talks to Mother Mac. She needs somebody to whom she can vent. Also because of our connection to Clay, she feels that we won't tell. She thought she could get us to pressure Clay to do something to get free to marry her daughter. She's been desperate to avoid a scandal."

"And she thinks it's not scandalous for a man to leave his wife to marry someone else who is already in a family way? What does it take to make a scandal for her?"

"I know, but the woman is practically out of her head with worry. But Clay would never leave you. He loves you, but he sure doesn't love Betsy."

"Well, somebody has got to tell Mrs. Gains to hush about Clay. He hasn't even been around her daughter. Brad can testify for him, can't he?"

"Yes. Mother Mac told her, but Mrs. Gains doesn't believe it.

Oh, I do wish my father were here."

"We don't need him. We'll just go to Mrs. Gains and tell her how we know Clay is innocent. He hasn't even been around her since his birthday."

"That's right," Pris said. "And that's been four months. That does clear him."

"No, not four months. From September twenty-fourth to December twenty-second is three, but that was long before any of this mess with Mrs. Gains started. He's…"

"Oh, no! No!" shrieked Pris. "I've got to go!" She jumped up and headed for the door. "You stay here in case Clay comes home. I'd keep the door locked too," she yelled as she ran.

"What's the matter?" Jamie cried frantically. "I didn't say anything. Don't go. Not yet, for maybe we'd better find Clay and tell him."

"That's exactly what I'm going to do," she called back over her shoulder. "You stay here in case he comes home before I find him."

"But, Pris," Jamie yelled, following her down the porch steps. "I don't understand…"

Pris turned back for a second. "Stay here," she said again. "Don't you dare leave this place." Then she was off again, running like she was in an important race and was determined to win, even if it killed her.

Jamie hurried back up the steps, shivering and almost as breathless as Pris had been. What was wrong with her? And what had she said that had added so much to her panic?

# 34

Clay came home at the time she would normally be expecting him. By that time, she wouldn't have been surprised if she had looked into a mirror and found that her hair had turned completely white. 'Where have you been?" she cried, running down the stairs when she heard his step in the hall.

"Just where I told you I'd be," he replied imperturbably. "Where have you been?"

"Right here, trying not to lose my mind. Did Pris find you?"

"She did. Came running over to Crestview as though her skirt tail was on fire and she wanted me to put it out."

Jamie sank down on the hall bench as he pulled off the old jacket that had once belonged to her pa. "What is wrong with you?" she demanded. "This is no laughing matter. Betsy Gains is dead, and there is something about it that has scared your sister half to death."

He leaned on the door facing into the parlor and looked at her. "Who's laughing? Certainly not me. And I didn't have anything to do with her death, as both you and my sister seem to think I did."

"*We* don't. It's Betsy's mother who does. And that worries me terribly. I don't want her making false accusations against my husband. It reflects poorly not only on you, but also on the whole family."

"Well, that's too bad, but I don't know what I can do about it. When Betsy came running out to Crestview a few days ago, wanting me to take her out to some colored woman who pretends she knows how to end problems like Betsy had, I refused, of course. I wasn't about to have any part in it."

"She did that?" Jamie asked, astounded.

"Yes, she certainly did. Hadn't I told you that before? Or maybe it was Pris who I told."

Jamie just looked at him. He stood there looking back at her for what seemed to her like forever. She finally took several deep breaths and asked as casually as she could manage, "Do you want to wash up before supper?"

He stood up straighter and looked down at himself. "What do you think? Would you want to eat supper across from all this dirt? I have renewed my efforts to find the silver. If I can do it before the ground is as hard as a chunk of ice, I intend to sell a few pieces and take you to England with us."

She had started away, but she whirled back around. "Oh, no, Clay."

"Oh, yes, Jamie," he said, coming to her. "I've seen your face every time anybody mentions the trip. I'd even sell a few acres of Crestview land to some of those Yankee carpetbaggers who keep sniffing around if I could do it without Father's signature. When he learns what I've been hearing about what the taxes are now going to be, he might even agree to selling more. But there's no time. I'm trying every way I can to get the money to take you to England with us."

"No, Clay, don't you dare do that," she begged, sinking wearily back down onto the bench. "There is no way I could go."

"And why not? Crestview has eighty acres. We could get along fine with less. Fairdale has over two hundred, and I'd say I could get enough for, say, twenty-five of them with road frontage and…"

"And," she put in quickly, "I want to fill every one of them with apple trees. I've told you, Clay. Apples are what will someday make us rich."

He gave a derisive snort and a gesture with his hand before turning back to her. "We'll be rich long before then. But getting rich is not our problem right now. The problem is how I can get enough money to dress you properly and pay your fare on that dratted ship."

She reached a trembling hand out that he didn't take. "But, Clay, you don't understand. Your parents don't want me there. They might have if I looked like the Jamelle Montgomery they once knew, but I feel sure they know I don't. This is an important time in their life, and they don't want anybody who would put a blight on it. There's no doubt that's exactly what they think my presence there would be."

He sat down beside her and pulled her close. "You have at least two months to regain most of what you lost. I thought at one time that you weren't even trying, that you might even be trying to punish me for something I hadn't even known I'd done. Or whatever. I've been wanting that Jamie more than I could ever tell you. Now you are trying. I'm going to get her back, and I want all those English folks to know it."

"Oh, Clay," she murmured sadly into his shoulder, "we don't have time. And there's no way I could possibly do it. I wouldn't even want to go. Don't you realize that ever since my own grandfather rejected me when I was seven years old, I've spent most of my life feeling unwanted? Why would I want to go thousands of miles across that ocean to feel that way again?"

He just held her tighter and said nothing. When he felt her trying to pull away, he did speak, "If that's the way you feel, I guess I'll have to forget what I've been trying to do."

"You do, Clay, you really do. I can't tell you how much I appreciate your wanting me to go, but I can't go now. Surely you can see that."

He finally nodded.

At supper when she was calmer and he was cleaner, she returned to the subject of Betsy. "Are we sure we can ignore Mrs. Gains' accusations?" She spoke hesitantly but felt she had to ask.

"I can," he said emphatically. "I hope you can too."

She shook her head sadly. "I don't know when the funeral will be. Since it's cool, I don't guess there'll be quite the hurry there would be in hot weather, but whenever it is, we'll have to go to that. Also, Rhody and I will have to fix food to take for the wake. I expect Steven will have to kill some more of those chickens we raised from biddies."

Clay finished buttering his baked potato before he looked over at her and said, "I thought we'd eaten all of those."

"No. We have three or four left, but they're getting to be almost too big for fryers. I was planning to use them for Christmas, but I guess I'll have to take two of those to the Gains' house. It will be expected."

"You know, don't you, Jamie, that practically every woman in Winchester is trying to think what she can take over there. They won't need our chickens. Besides, I've never really cared for Mrs. Gains. She's always been so pushy."

"That doesn't matter right now," she told him. "And, yes, I do know that many people are looking around for something to take over there. That doesn't matter either. I have to take something."

"Oh, all right. But don't you do it. Let Rhody take it. I don't want you anywhere near the Gains' house."

Somehow that order annoyed Jamie. "And," she snapped, "do you want me to pin a note onto what I send saying that I couldn't come myself because my husband feels guilty?"

Clay's fork fell and so did his jaw. He jumped up and started for the door.

Jamie was right behind him, reaching for him. "I'm sorry, Clay," she said before he could reach it. "I shouldn't have said that, but I just have to take something over there myself. It's expected and you know it."

He turned back and grabbed her tightly in his arms. "I'm sorry too," he murmured into her dark curls, sounding almost distracted. "But being accused of something like this has hit me hard."

"Of course, it has. Come on back and finish your supper. I think Rhody has a couple of baked apples for us."

"Don't tell me we're eating up what's going to make us rich," he said, obviously wanting things on an easier basis.

She gave a weak grin and they sat back down. "I was not expecting that of these two particular ones. They're off the old trees that were here when we came." Then with great trepidation, but being sure that it would have a lot of influence in helping him know she was right, she said, "I'm sure your mother would want us to take some food. She and Mrs. Gains have been friends for years."

Clay was shaking his head. "Not really. Mother was always very nice and polite, even to people she feels are beneath her."

Jamie's big eyes flew open wide. "Mrs. Gains was one of those?"

"Of course, she was," he said matter-of-factly. "The Gains own nothing but that house over there on Braddock."

"But isn't that true of the McLaurines too? I've never heard of their having anything but their once very nice house, also on Braddock. Does your mother look down on them?"

"Of course not. Mr. Mac had a successful surveying business, and his father and grandfather had big farms out in the county. They've been prominent around here ever since George Washington had his surveying office here in town. Mrs. Mac sold her husband's farm after Mr. Mac died. Brad said she got a really good price and..."

He hesitated for a moment so Jamie broke in to hazard a guess, "And Mrs. Mac invested all of that into the Confederates."

Clay gave sort of a chuckle. "Well, yes, but the whole thing is different. Both of my parents always had a lot of respect for the McLaurines. You don't think they would have let Pris marry Brad if they hadn't, do you?"

"I don't think," Jamie said with assurance, "that there is a person on the earth who could have kept Pris from marrying Brad or anyone else she loves."

Clay chuckled and accepted the baked apple that Rhody was putting before him. "I guess you're right. But my parents would have tried had they thought he didn't meet their lofty standards. And they certainly would have let their feelings be known if I had exhibited any interest in marrying Betsy. I have always liked the girl, but I have never loved her for a single second." He ate his apple slowly, then pushed his chair back from the table and said, "Now, if you'll excuse me, I'd like to go on up and start getting ready for bed. I've had a very wearing day and I'm tired."

"I'll go up with you. This hasn't exactly been a day of relaxation for me either."

As they went up the stairs together, she asked, "Do you have any idea what day will be the earliest they can set for the funeral? I want to get the food over to Mrs. Gains."

"I'd think probably the day after tomorrow. Betsy's sisters and their husbands will have to have time to get here, but they don't live all that far away. I don't know whether there is more family somewhere else or not."

"What about her husband's grandmother? I think she lives in Baltimore, and Betsy indicated that they were close. His grandmother kept sending her a little money."

Clay looked down at her with surprise. "You don't actually think that her family will want that poor cluck's folks to know anything about the situation here now, do you?"

She gave a little shrug. "Well, maybe not."

*Another sleepless, miserable night,* she told herself sadly as she pulled the quilts over her, but she was partly wrong. It wasn't long before Clay's deep, regular breathing told her he was already asleep. Surely there was nothing really worrisome on his mind or his conscience if he could sleep like that.

But there sure was on hers.

## 35

Steven was out killing two of their four remaining chickens by the time Clay had gone off to do whatever he was going to do that day. Jamie didn't ask what his plans were. She was feeling so torn-up inside that she really didn't care what he did, as long as it was done someplace where no accusing eyes could fall on him.

Of course, she was sorry about Betsy, but she had never really like or trusted the girl, so she couldn't see why she was so upset about her death. Clay *was* telling the truth. He had to be. Oh, if only there could be some way that he could prove his innocence to Mrs. Gains and shut her up, but there was no way in the world that could be done. But what was it that had upset Pris even more yesterday morning? If she didn't stop all this, she was afraid she would be wearing away all the weight that she was trying so hard to put on. Was her life never going to smooth out and let her live in peace?

"Those two chickens will be enough to take, don't you think?" she asked Rhody later in the morning. "I've never done this before, but you took food to wakes when you were with Mrs. McKay, didn't you?"

"Yes'm, I sho' did. I ain't rememberin' 'zackly what she done, but I'd say dem chickens be maybe more'n enough."

"That's what I thought, so would you please let me know when they're ready? I've got to go up and do something about my hair." She started up the kitchen steps.

"Mr. Clay tol' me I was to tote de stuff up dere widout you, if you'd say I could," the woman called after her. "Is you sayin' dat?|"

Jamie turned back and spoke rather sharply, "I certainly am not. I want you to go with me. With the two of us, one can carry them while the other rests her arms."

"I ain't thinkin' my arms would git dat tired," Rhody replied, "but 'course I do what you wants."

Jamie went on upstairs, feeling a little more worried and annoyed but not knowing exactly why. *Thank goodness that's decided*, she told herself as she went on up to brush her hair a hundred strokes, as Mammy Rose had taught her. "Of course," she muttered to herself, "in those days I had a decent brush that the Yankees hadn't tried to break."

After stopping the brushing at no more than twenty, she parted her hair in the middle and did it up in a bun on the back of her head. She didn't like it that way, and neither did Clay, but she was as determined to look as much like a proper lady as she possibly could, and that was the way most of the women wore their hair. Thank the good Lord, the makeshift stores in town were now coming back to something like life, she thought, as she took a final look in the broken mirror before heading on back downstairs. She did hope that Clay would get her some personal items like a good brush and some combs for Christmas.

As she sat waiting for Rhody to say she was ready to go, she began to wonder what on earth she thought she was doing. Was she putting what Mrs. Gains might think ahead of what her husband thought? That woman was trying to ruin Clay, and here she was thinking she had to march about a mile to pay her respects. Respects, heck! She raced back upstairs, took out the five pins and let her hair fall all around her shoulders. Then she raced down to the kitchen. Rhody was just taking up the chicken.

"No, Rhody. I've changed my mind. Just put one chicken on the platter to go. We're going to have the other one for our dinner. And if you're sure you can carry it by yourself, I want you to do that too."

"Yes, ma'am, I sho can and I be glad to. Me and Steven was seein' dat Mr. Clay warn't lookin' good dis mornin', and we was wonderin' if it was because he not wantin' you to walk in agin. So Steven, he tol' me I should tote it in by myself 'cause he knows I is strong."

"Thank you so much," Jamie told her sincerely. "And I'm

275

awfully glad you are strong."

When Clay came in for dinner, he gave her a kiss and sniffed the air. "I at least get to smell the chicken. And it does smell good."

"You'll like the chicken itself ever more. And the gravy to go over some potatoes Rhody was baking."

"You're joshing."

"No, I'm not. I got my common sense back and thought, *why should I be taking two chickens to a woman who's accusing my husband of something I know he didn't do?* And I wasn't going myself either. Wash your hands and come on in to dinner. I started a fire in the dining room myself. It's not burning too well, but with the door open to the kitchen stairs, we won't freeze in there."

He grabbed her in a fierce hug, picked her up off the floor and swung her around before releasing her. "Your doing all that means a lot more to me than that chicken I'm going to eat."

She smiled in pleasure. She was so glad that she had gotten her gumption back.

"I've been at the lumber company trying to find the paneling I want for the office," Clay volunteered as they pulled up to the dining room table. "What they had was wrong by a country mile. We'll have to wait until they get in more. I want my office to have an old, classic look, not new and shiny. Christmas will be here in two days so no point in doing anything until after that. I really should stay home from Mary Lilly's big to-do, but my folks would never forgive me if I did that."

"And," she reminded him, "don't forget that there'll be Betsy's funeral before any of that."

He gave her a sharp look. "I hope you aren't still thinking I'm going to that."

She put her fork down and looked at him seriously. "Clay, you have to. I won't even suggest that we go to the wake, but I truly believe that the funeral is necessary. Think how it will look with Pris, Brad and me there and you absent."

"You could stay home too. You and Betsy were never really friends."

"Well, I don't care to advertise that to everybody in town. Mrs. Gains won't want anybody to know the real cause of Betsy's death. She tried to make it look as if both of them had the same thing. But if some of Betsy's oldest friends don't even attend her funeral, don't you know that will look odd to people?"

"No, I certainly do not. Besides, I've got to meet somebody in a few minutes so as soon as we finish eating, I'll have to be off. Until then, let's turn our chairs to the fire and relax. He did as he said, and they stretched their feet out to the fire. "I don't know when I've enjoyed a dinner more," he said as he finished up on a drumstick. "How I could have been so lucky as to have gotten you as my wife, I don't know. But I want you to know how much you're appreciated."

"Clay, I did no more than I should have. I was wrong before. I just wanted you to know how important you are to me too. It made me madder and madder when I thought about your being accused of something you'd never even think of doing, and here I was feeling I had to show proper respect to your accuser. I'll show my respect where it's due right here at home. But now if you want anything more to eat, you'd better have it and then get going. I don't want to make you late for your appointment."

When he was gone, she sat there before the dying fire and took pleasure in having done as she had. Maybe if he really didn't want to go to the funeral tomorrow, she ought to stay home with him. He was right in that she and Betsy had never been real friends, so again maybe she should put what he wanted her to do above what other people expected of her. She'd tell him after supper tonight that, as far as she was concerned, they could both stay home.

But before she could do that, he told her that he had run into Pris and Brad on the street this afternoon. They had told him it would look mighty odd if he didn't go to Betsy's funeral. "If you want to look guilty, stay home, but if you want to show that you have nothing to hide or be ashamed of, go." So he told her he didn't really want to, but he would go. She said nothing about what she had decided.

He didn't go into town the next morning. They slept late, had a leisurely dinner of really good vegetable soup and cleaned up to get dressed. Brad and Pris were coming out in the carriage to get them. "I told them I did not want to get there a second before two o'clock. Let's sit at the back of the church where we can get out in a hurry. I don't want any visitation time."

"Neither do I," Jamie assured him. She was wearing her new suit that she loved, but she did wish she had something darker. Most people wore black, if they had it. Fortunately Brad and Clay were going to look elegant in their new clothes. As she saw Clay putting on his dark-gray striped trousers, black double-breasted waistcoat and frock coat, she thought she had never seen a more stylish-looking or handsomer man. She also thought they might be rubbing in their affluence at this sad time and might attract more attention than they wanted, but she was afraid to offer any complaint.

"You look wonderful," she told him as they waited for the carriage.

"So do you," he replied. "I'm beginning to see the look of the girl I once knew and loved."

"Loved?" she questioned. "Past tense?"

"No, you know what I mean," he said and gave her a light kiss.

"I should have on black too, but I don't have a black dress to my name. I couldn't resist wearing my new suit anyway. Dark enough not to stand out, isn't it?"

"Sure is." He told her with what she felt sure was an admiring look.

The church was nearly full when they got there. The stove was good and hot, and the church was not terribly cold. "Let's sit as close to the back as possible, and I want to sit on the aisle so we can get out right away," he murmured to Brad as they headed for the church door. Brad nodded.

The open casket was in the front of the church; and soon after they were seated, the family came down the aisle and were seated on the front row. The service, and even the songs, could have been in some alien tongue as far as Jamie was concerned. When it finally ended and the undertaker was guiding the people row by row to go by and view Betsy for the last time, Clay whispered to Jamie, "No." She understood what his refusal meant so when the usher came to their row, she didn't protest when Pris and Brad climbed over them to walk to the front of the church in line with the other people. Then they climbed over them again to return to their seats.

When the benediction had been said and the coffin lid closed to shut the once-lively girl away forever, the minister led the pallbearers who carried the casket. Pris whispered to Jamie, "I would have thought Brad would have been one of them."

"So would I...and Clay too," Jamie whispered back. Pris gave her a strange look.

Mrs. Gains was right behind the casket, being more or less held up by a daughter on each side of her. Her two sons-in-law and other assorted family members were close behind. The congregation was falling in behind them row by row as they came. When the entourage came on down, Mrs. Gains raised her head just as they came to the pew where Clay was sitting on the aisle. If she had been suddenly struck by lightning, she could not have reacted more. She pulled her daughters to a stop and screamed, "You! What are you doing here? You're the one who ruined my baby girl! You killed my precious little Betsy!"

Clay turned his back to the woman and grabbed Jamie to him as though to close her ears. "Shhh. Be quiet, Mama," one of Betsy's sisters said as she tried to quiet her. They then pulled her on out the door. But Jamie heard the accusation, as had everybody else in the church. She felt Pris' hand on her, pulling her back to let Brad slip around them so he could take the place by the aisle. He pulled Clay back to shield him as much as he could.

Jamie held onto Pris, and they both were now crying so hard they could see or hear nothing more. When the time came for them to fall into line behind the other members of the congregation, the four of them rushed out like a bunch of scalded cats and ran for their carriage. Jamie felt a hand reach out to her as they passed a bunch of people standing outside the church and could tell it belonged to an older woman, but she had no time to see whose hand it might be.

Nobody tried to speak to them as they ran. Everyone was still clustering around Betsy's family as Clay yelled up to Steven, "Get us out of here as fast as you can!"

"Yes'suh."

Jamie put her hand on Clay's arm and whispered, "I'm sorry."

He looked at her angrily. "I told you I didn't want to go, but, no, you had to insist."

"No more than I did, Clay," Pris spoke up. "Leave her alone."

Steven leaned down to ask, "Is we heading for Fairdale?"

"Yes, as fast as you can, but first go by the McLaurines' house!" Clay yelled back.

When they got there, Brad helped the stricken Pris down as quickly as he could and gave a sympathetic look to his friend before the carriage raced on. When they reached Fairdale, Clay jumped out almost before Steven had pulled the horse to a stop. He yelled to him to help Miss Jamie down and to keep the carriage there. He tore off his new frock coat as he raced up the steps.

With great trepidation, Jamie followed him up the stairs to their room. She had no idea what to say, except another sad, "I'm sorry, Clay." Sorry for far more things than that terrible confrontation for she knew, as definitely as she knew the South had lost the war, that she had lost her husband.

Clay was tearing his clothes off as though he didn't care what he did to them. "The nerve of that woman!" he muttered. "How did she dare do that to me? *To me? A Haynesworth?*"

*Because you're the one who is guilty,* Jamie knew she could say…but didn't dare. She just stood there, having no idea of what to do with herself.

"Get that new suitcase I bought in Baltimore!" Clay yelled. "It's in your father's old room. And bring all the new things that I have in there." He had his bureau drawer open and was throwing things helter-skelter onto the bed.

"What are you doing?" she turned back from the door to ask.

"I'm getting out of here. You surely don't think I would stay around here after what that woman did to me. I'm a Haynesworth, and we don't take insults like that lying down."

"But…" she began again, but when he yelled, "Get that blasted suitcase!" she turned and ran as fast as her trembling legs would carry her. When she lugged it back in, he began grabbing things up and throwing them in.

"Here, let me help," she said, smoothing and folding everything as best she could. "You don't want to get wherever you're going with your clothes…"

She didn't get to finish the statement, for he broke in to say, "I'm going to England for the hunting season. Surely you know that."

"But…but Christmas is almost here. I'll be…"

"I know, but you're the one who insisted I go to that blasted funeral. I have to get away from here now. Maybe I can come back someday, but…"

"But is it true?" she asked, hoping with all her heart that he could somehow convince her that it wasn't. "If it isn't true, running away isn't the way to combat it. I'll help you, Clay. I'll do anything you say."

He gave her a despairing look as he kept grabbing things from the bureau. "I can't prove anything. Surely you know that."

"But…" she began but got no farther. He whirled around and grabbed her fiercely, looking right down in to her white face with an anger that scared her.

"I didn't mean to. I swear I didn't, even though my father said that there might be times when it would be all right. It was just that Betsy remembered that it was my birthday and came in to spread the present she was offering before me. I'd swear on a stack of Bibles as high as the Blue Ridge that neither of us meant to complete it. She teased me too far and, then when I heard the pounding on the door, I jumped forward and suddenly it was too late to stop. Somehow I knew it was you at the door, and I could have died. I jumped away from her so hard that the stock of old lumber that we were on fell all over the floor. I could do nothing but button my trousers as fast as I could and send her out the back way. I've died a thousand deaths since then. I love you, Jamie," he cried despairingly. "Only you wouldn't let yourself come back to the old Jamie. If you had, I'd never…"

She was crying so hard that she couldn't have heard more, even if he had kept on speaking. She grabbed him tightly and tried to say, "I'm sorry" again but couldn't make the words come.

Clay yanked off his new drawers and undershirt, tossing them across the room and yelling, "And you get out of that suit, if you don't want it torn from you. You caused all of this. If it hadn't been for you…" She tried not to listen, as she fearfully tore her new clothes off and let them fall on the floor around her.

"No!" she was crying. "No, not like this. Please, Clay." But as he threw her on the bed, she knew he wasn't listening. At first, she tried to fight him but found that hopeless, so she lay there feeling a devastation that nearly knocked the life from her.

When he was finished, he pulled on his clothes while she lay on the bed crying. She had pulled a quilt over herself to hide from him, from herself, from the whole world. Once he was dressed, he put a hand on the part of the quilt that covered her head and whispered, "I'm sorry. So sorry about everything. I will be back. And please, honey, be my old Jamie when I return."

And with that, he was gone.

# 36

Jamie never knew how long she lay there, sobbing and mourning. Their whole life was ruined, and it was her fault as much as Clay's. She had held the real person who she was away from him, and she didn't know why. Hadn't she always wanted to be a Haynesworth? Well, now she was one, and she had to live with it.

There was darkness outside her windows when she heard footsteps racing up the stair. Pris burst in the door and threw herself on her knees by Jamie. "Oh, Jamie! I'm so sorry. So sorry for you and so distressed for my poor, idiot brother. But what on earth are you doing huddling there under those quilts? You can't be naked, are you?"

Jamie clutched the quilts tight around her. "It's cold in here."

"Of course, it is." Pris snapped. Then she looked around the room. "Is that your new suit on the floor? For goodness sakes, Jamie! Are you as dumb as my poor brother? Get yourself out of there and into something warm." She slid off the bed herself, picked up the suit and smoothed it over the rocking chair.

Still trying to hold the quilts up to her chin, Jamie raised herself on her elbow and said, "He's guilty, Pris. He's the cause of Betsy's death."

"Horseradish!" Pris exclaimed. "Those Yankees and their terrible war did this to all of us. Was the war your fault too? Now get yourself out of that bed. I'm going back downstairs to that good fire Steven has going in the sitting room. But if you aren't there in five minutes, I'm coming back again to drag you out."

Jamie knew she had no choice, for Pris would do what she had said. Besides, she wanted to be up and away from this bed. She wasn't sure she'd ever want to get in it again. She pulled on an old, dark gray wool dress that Mammy Rose had cut down from one Pa had bought years ago at a sale. She had never liked it, and the Yankees must not have either for they hadn't taken it for any of the fancy women who followed them. Mammy Rose had made her keep it, saying it might be good if she ever had to go to a funeral and didn't have anything black. Well, she sure had been to one, and it had ruined everything forever.

When she went into the sitting room, clutching the old dress around her, she saw Pris sitting in a chair drawn up close to the fire with another one by it. She sank into that one and said, "He's guilty, Pris. Your brother…my husband…caused Betsy's death."

"Horseradish!" Pris snapped. "He sure didn't hold her down and attack her. She was as guilty as he was. Actually, far more so because she came looking for him. He wasn't out looking for her."

Jamie held her shaky hands out to the fire. "That's right. But how did you know?"

"I knew it as definitely as if he had confessed when you told me that it had been three months since his birthday. When Mrs. Gains came tearing down to our house for Brad, she was screaming something about three months. When I was thinking it had been four months since Clay's birthday, I thought that let him off. Brad and I had been keeping check, and we felt sure she had not been alone with him since the day you had told him her visits had to stop."

"Even after Mrs. Gains had first accused him, I kept on believing in his innocence," Jamie said, watching the flames in the fireplace and not looking at her sister-in-law.

"I know you did. I guess we shouldn't have insisted that he go to the funeral, but I thought his being there would make him look less guilty."

"It would have come out sooner or later," Jamie said sadly. "Mrs. Gains wouldn't have given up."

"I'm afraid you're right about that. I wish so much that she could know how Betsy kept throwing herself at him, even after she knew he was married. Since you were so slow in getting your health back, I think Betsy actually thought you wouldn't make it and she wanted to stake out her claim early."

Jamie looked at the other girl. "How did you know to come out here?"

"Steven told me. He had stayed at the station with Clay until he caught the train somewhere. Then he came by the house and told me he thought Miss Jamie might be needing me. When I asked where Clay was and he told me, I put two and two together in a hurry and knew pretty much what had happened. I knew that Clay was not a person who could stay here and accept what had just happened."

"How could anyone? But fortunately, no one in England will know anything about it."

"England?" Pris asked in surprise. "Is that where he's gone?"

"Yes. He said he was going for the hunting."

"But that doesn't start until February. Actually, I think he was running to Father, thinking Father would tell him that what he had done wasn't as bad as he already knew it was," Pris said and then added, "but, come to think of it, it would take him nearly until February to get there. I wonder what he did with the money for our trip."

Jamie shook her head. "I don't know. He didn't mention it."

Pris gave a shrug. "Doesn't matter. Brad and I have been talking this afternoon about not going. He hasn't been keen on having to rush like this anyway. And though my Mother thinks that Mary Lilly's marrying into the upper ranks of English society rivals the second coming of Christ in importance, Brad doesn't see it that way. And actually, I don't either."

The two of them were thoughtful for a few moments and said nothing. Then there was a tap on the door, and Steven came in carrying more wood for the fire. He added a couple of logs and put the rest on the hearth to be handy when needed. He stepped back and asked, "Is you wantin' me to start a fire in de dinin' room, Miss Jamie? It don't take long to knock de chill off in dere. And Rhody say she got plenty of soup left fer Miss Pris too."

Jamie looked at the other girl. "Can you stay? We had some of that soup last night, and it's really good."

Pris got up and turned her back to the fire to warm that side too before leaving. "No, I've got to get home. Steven's got the carriage out there, and I'll go back home when he takes it back. He won't want to be walking back too late."

"I ain't mindin' the wait," he said.

"Well, since everything seems to be all right here, I guess we'd best be going," She turned to give her front side another warm touch before heading out. "Why don't you come with me?" she then asked Jamie. "We've got the two spare rooms ready for the new boarders, but you could sleep in with Thomas. He'd love to have his Aunt Jamie with him."

Jamie was already shaking her head. "No, I'll stay here but thanks for the invitation."

"Whatever you say," Pris said as she pulled on her cloak.

Then turning, Jamie said, "And, Steven, you can forget about the fire in the dining room too. I'll go down and have my soup in the kitchen."

"So, Steven," Pris said, "I'll see you outside in just a minute."

When he was gone, Pris said to Jamie, "Don't you worry about anything you don't have to. That means the trip. I don't see why even my parents couldn't see that our going at this time would put too much pressure on all of us, but that's how our mother is where all this English aristocracy and rank are concerned. And now with Clay gone…"

"He said he'd be back," Jamie interrupted her sister-in-law to say. "Do you think he will?"

"Oh, land sakes, Jamie! I don't know," she said as she sank back down in her chair. Then, remembering the time, she jumped up again and started inching toward the door. "If he doesn't, what would you do?"

"What could I do?" Jamie was up too. "Clay and I are married, Pris. You know that marriage is forever. I know he did a terrible thing, but he says he truly didn't mean to."

"And Betsy didn't mean to die," Pris retorted. "That's stupid, Jamie. But I know he loves you. If he wants you to come to England and live there, would you do it?"

That question knocked what strength Jamie had left right out of her. She grabbed for the chair back and held on. "Is that what he means for me to do?" she asked.

Pris didn't seem to notice her distress and just said, "How do I know? I didn't see him before he left, but, knowing my brother, I'd say that's what he'll end up doing."

Jamie just stood there shaking her head, "Leave Fairdale? And, Winchester? I couldn't do that, Pris."

"Well," the other girl said as she opened the door and was about to leave, "I've got to get out of here, and you can't decide anything until you know what he wants. Goodness knows that he is class-conscious so maybe when he gets over there, he'll feel as Mother obviously does and think that Mary Lilly's marrying into one of the most prominent families raises all the family in stature. My grandfather Cooke is already well-accepted, and my parents may think that Clay's disgrace might ruin them around here. That could even be true, for I'm afraid that the only way to shut Mrs. Gains up would be to shoot her. Since none of us feel inclined to do that, we can do nothing but wait to hear from Clay. Now I've got to go, but you stay in here by the fire. I'll be back to see you real soon."

With that, Pris dashed out, leaving Jamie standing alone before the fire but still feeling cold chills running all over her. Would Clay actually insist that she join him in England? And could she possibly make herself do it if he did? Wishing with all her heart that Mammy Rose could be downstairs waiting for her, but knowing her mammy couldn't ever be there again, she went on down to the kitchen.

Rhody gave her a tentative smile as she got off the bottom step, so Jamie felt sure that she too knew that something odd was afoot. "We got a apple pie dat still warm and some fried apples too," she told Jamie. "Dat boy Eddie what just brung dem to de kitchen door run right off widout sayin' nothin'."

Jamie almost fell into the one good chair at the table. "I wonder how she knew," she mused out loud. Then she wondered no more, for now she realized that the sympathetic hand she had felt must surely have belonged to Kate Darby. Was she a friend of Mrs. Gains? Oh, goodness, she surely hoped not but knew that was a foolish hope. Who went to the funerals of strangers? Now Mrs. Darby would be bound to tell Curt, and that would mean one more thing to worry about. It was all so overwhelming that she put her arms on the table and rested her head on them.

"A funeral ain't no secret. Don't matter who knows," Rhody said, obviously having heard Jamie's question to herself and trying to be helpful. "And I got yo' soup nice and hot. I'm thinkin' it be even better today dan when I made it. I'll git it just as fast as I can dip it up."

Jamie wouldn't have felt like eating the best supper that Mr. Taylor could have ever served in his once-fine hotel, but she wasn't about to say that to Rhody. So she ate and told the woman how good it was. She also ate some apple pie and wished she could tell Mrs. Darby how much it meant to have a show of kindness at this heart-sickening time.

Finally, trying to ignore her aversion to the sight of it, she turned back the quilts and got into her bed.

# 37

Jamie didn't even go in to the next meeting of the LMA. After what had happened at the funeral, she didn't feel she could face anyone. Not today and maybe not ever. Steven brought the carriage out to pick her up for church, but she refused to go. She still didn't feel as at home at Christ Episcopal as she had in her own Kent Street Presbyterian. Actually, she longed to go there and maybe talk to the man she had always called "the Reverend," but she didn't dare. He was bound to have heard Mrs. Gains' accusation of Clay, and besides, Kent Street Presbyterian had been the Gain's family church far longer than it had been hers and Pa's.

On Christmas Eve the McLaurines came on out after church, insisting that she go in and have dinner with them, but Jamie refused even that. With Christmas being the next day, they wanted her to join them. She refused to leave the house.

"Then we're bringing Christmas to you," Pris said.

"You can't do that," she had protested, but on Christmas morning there they were. They came bustling in, bringing food and presents. Steven had slipped out on Christmas Eve and brought in enough greenery and berries to decorate the main level, but Jamie wished he had not. She felt no more festive than she had the last Christmas during the war.

Mrs. Mac had managed to get some ham and enough ingredients to make something approaching a fruit cake. "It's not as good as it should be," she explained as she carried it in. "Things are getting to be more available but not everything, so my cake is heavy on raisins, hickory nuts and walnuts but light on citron and some other dried fruits. Everybody knows you can't make a decent fruit cake without citron."

"I'm sure it's delicious, but even if it weren't, it's Christmas. Mammy Rose always made one if we were where she could."

Thomas was as excited as any almost three-year-old boy

could be about the small presents his parents had managed to get him in Baltimore and had hidden until he got up this morning. His grandmother had given him a cap, mittens and scarf she had knit, and Jamie had two children's picture books for him that she had had Clay buy for her. Every once in a while, the little boy would look around and say, "Where Uncle Clay?" Jamie left it to his parents to explain his uncle's absence.

When the dinner had been eaten and the gifts opened, they sat before the parlor fire and thought about Christmases past. Pris and Brad had many good ones to remember, including the first after their wedding. Mrs. Mac told about the time that she had married Mr. Mac on the day before Christmas Eve in 1815. Jamie told about the Christmas Pa had come home and the wonderful time she had spent with him before he had trudged back over the mountain never to return again. She didn't mention the Yankee who had brought her such wonderful gifts and then had to slip away without a bite of Christmas food to keep her pa from being upset by his presence. Tears came into her eyes as she remembered that day, and everyone was sympathetic because they thought she was thinking of Clay. And maybe she was.

As the women were packing up the food containers the McLaurines had brought, Brad told Jamie that they had about decided not to go to England after all. "Oh, no!" she cried. "Just because of Clay?"

"Well, yes, but also because it somehow seems wrong for us to leave you here alone."

When she started to protest, Brad said, "You're not the only reason. We've already written him in care of the Cookes to see if he doesn't think it might be best if we stay home. Of course, we'd probably already have one foot on the ship by the time we could hear from him, so we've decided definitely not to go. At least, Mary Lilly will have someone from here, and, depending on when her wedding is, it might be better for us to wait until then. Pris and Clay are supposed to be in the wedding, and we certainly couldn't go back again. So we're staying home now. You know what folks say, 'If given time, things usually work out for the best.'"

"Do they, Brad?" she asked. "Do you see any way they can for Clay?"

"He's not the first man to break his wedding vows." Then he almost smiled as he added, "But I'll admit that he's probably the first to have a transgression like his announced at a funeral."

Jamie wanted to point out there was nothing the least bit amusing about it, but she knew that Brad too was suffering from Clay's failure to live up to the standards they both believed in and to which he, at least, still adhered.

"I have kept hoping I'd get a wireless from him," he said when she said nothing.

"And you haven't?"

"Not a word...and that's worrying the dickens out of me. As you know, I never had a brother. Well, I did have one but he died before I was born. But for as long as I can remember, Clay has been a brother to me. I'll admit he's always been a bit more free-wheeling than I have, but I've always felt that was because of the difference in our fathers. Clay has always felt that he could do whatever he wanted to because he was a Haynesworth. I've felt that I had to watch what I did because I was a McLaurine. But we've always gotten along great. I think I'm feeling sorrier for him and even more..."

"What are you two plotting?" Pris asked as she came out of the door to the kitchen steps. "You look like you might be planning to open up a war again."

They both chuckled. "Could be," Brad said. "You'd better watch your step."

"Don't I know it? Well, Jamie, thank you for a wonderful Christmas, but Mother Mac says we'd better be getting home."

"You all provided it far more than I did. I was going to skip the whole thing. So I'm the one who ought to be saying 'thanks.'"

"We knew you were," Pris said. "That's why we're here. Mother Mac has left you all enough food for supper, including some of the cake."

"It was really delicious," Jamie said. "It was as good as any fruit cake to me."

"Thank you, my dear," Mrs. McLaurine said as she joined them in the hall. "I thought it turned out surprisingly well too. Now, son," she said to Brad, "if you'll round up Thomas, I'd say that we're ready to go." Then she put a hand to Jamie's cheek and said softly, "May this be the last bad Christmas you'll ever have."

That brought tears to Jamie's eyes. "Thank you, Mother Mac," she said, calling her that for the first time.

"None of that," Pris said as she noticed the tears. "Things may not be as bad as they seem."

*How could that be?* Jamie wanted to ask, but didn't.

As Brad came out carrying a sleepy Thomas in his arms, he said, "Oh, by the way, I meant to ask if you've gotten anything else from that neighbor who's been so generous to you and Clay. I kept hoping his boy would come in bringing some goodies for today."

"Not a peep from him," Jamie said. "Maybe he's gone to have Christmas at his grandmother's," she said, feeling guilty but knowing that she could say nothing more. As they were going down the side porch steps, Pris called back, "Had Clay already given you the present he got for you in Baltimore when we were there?"

"Present? I thought we had all decided not to give each other presents this year."

"We did, but he got you something anyway. I was about to forget it. Look around. It's bound to be here."

"I'll do that. Bye, Thomas. Aunt Jamie loves you," she called as she caught the kiss he leaned out to throw her as the carriage began to move on.

When they were gone, she climbed the stairs and went into Pa's old room. Somehow, it seemed odd to be looking for a gift from someone who had gone as Clay had. It was almost like looking for one from a person who had died.

There were two neatly-wrapped packages in the bottom drawer of Pa's bureau. She carried them back downstairs to the parlor that was still warm. The bigger one had a beautiful white silk shirtwaist with long sleeves and a high collar. "I love it," she said to Clay, wherever he might be, "and it will be so nice with my new suit."

The other one was flat, and she knew it was a book. It was actually a Waverly novel. There was a note attached to it that said,

*I remember that time over four years ago when Pris and I were inviting you to your first Tournament here and which, thanks to the war, turned out to be our last. We explained that it was something like out of a Waverly novel. I could tell that you didn't know those popular books so when I found this one in a book store in Baltimore, I had to buy it for you.*

*Merry Christmas, my love, Clay.*

Then the tears came in torrents.

# 38

When New Year's Day arrived, Jamie refused to go in to the McLaurines' home or to have them at Fairdale. She had not been out of the house since Betsy's funeral and had no intention of going anytime soon, not even to the LMA meetings that she hated so much to neglect. Pris would come out every few days to report that the program in retrieving the bodies of Confederate heroes was moving along wonderfully well. There were reports of there being groups in many other towns who had followed the lead of the women in Winchester and doing the same for the men who had died in or near their areas. The Union Burial Corps was doing the same for their dead, but nobody really cared what the Union was doing.

Virginia had still not been accepted back into that dratted Union; and while many of them didn't give a gnat's eye about that, it was still annoying to Winchester's leading men who were eager to see their town become what it once had been. Jamie still had no word from Clay, but during the first week in February, Pris came out with a letter she had gotten from Boston. She came into the kitchen where Jamie was sitting by the hot cook stove and handed the letter to Jamie without a word.

"From Clay?" Jamie asked, not knowing whether to be happy about it or not.

Pris shook her head and said, "Read it."

Jamie opened it and read:

*Dear Priscilla,*

*I don't know whether you remember me or not, but I was a good friend of your brother Clay when we were both at that wonderful university of Thomas Jefferson's there in Virginia. I met you when you and your family came for Clay's graduation. I was invited to visit Clay at his home and had intended to do that, but the war separated us.*

*Clay must have remembered me as fondly as I do him, for he showed up at my home nearly three weeks ago. I was pleased to see him and invited him to stay for as long as his time would allow. That has been quite a time and would be quite all right with my wife and my parents, but I am sorry to report that he has not been truly sober a single day since his arrival. I remember his father as being—if you will forgive me for saying it—rather forceful, and I was afraid I would cause real trouble for my old friend if I tried to contact your father. I finally thought of you and hope that if you are now married (as I feel sure you are) someone there in your town will remember you by your maiden name and get this to you.*

*I am terribly worried about Clay. I could tell that something was bothering him when he arrived. Since then, I am distressed to say, I think he has been drinking excessively every single day. He will tell me nothing of his problem but mostly stays in his room and drinks. My wife and my parents welcomed him gladly when he arrived for, in spite of our differences during the war, we still have fond memories of the South and of Clay.*

*I don't want to ask my old friend to leave, but the problem is getting to be acute. He says that he is waiting for a ship to England where his parents are, but he has, as yet, made no effort to leave.*

*My address is on this, and I do hope I will hear from you soon to help me solve this problem that, I am sorry to say, is becoming intolerable.*

*With friendly memories and hopes for help,*
*Deaton Smitherman*

When Jamie finished reading the letter, she handed it back to Pris without a word.

"Isn't that the most distressing thing you've ever read?" Pris said sadly.

"Oh, yes, Pris, it is."

"I am so heartsick for my brother that I can hardly stand it."

"I have to help him some way, but what can I do?"

"Brad is already doing it. He left as soon as he could pack a few things and catch the next train to the north. He'll get to Boston as soon as he can. When he gets there, he'll take Clay out of the Smithermans' house and straighten him up. I think it will probably take my father to put some sense back in Clay's head, but he has to get to the ship in decent shape. Brad will be able to do more with him than you or I ever could."

"Oh, Pris, what have I done to your brother?" Jamie said mournfully.

"You haven't done anything but love him and marry him. I thought the war had made a real man of him, given him the strength to lessen Father's hold on him and his onto Father. I guess I was wrong, but don't blame yourself for what he has done. If Betsy weren't already dead, I could almost kill her for she did to my brother."

*But don't you know,* Jamie said mournfully…but only to herself, *if I had loved him as I thought I did, and as he thought I still did, I would have forced myself to be the girl he wanted me to be again so badly. Why couldn't I do that? Why was I holding back? I knew I was married for life.* But all the sad questions she was asking herself did not answer what she needed so desperately to know.

"Have you all cancelled all the reservations you had to England?" she asked. "Did he have a reservation anymore?"

"Yes, he did. When you gave Brad the envelope that you had found where Clay had left it, Brad took care of cancelling our tickets, but he left the one for Clay in place. That date will be coming up soon. I just hope that Brad can get there in time to get him into shape and on the ship."

"Oh, so do I! So do I! Should I have gone with Brad?"

Pris looked as her as though Jamie might have suggested something as ridiculous as swimming alongside the ship to England. "Are you as crazy as a loon?" she demanded. "What could you do that Brad can't do better? And why would I want my husband travelling around with any woman but me?"

"Then why didn't you go?"

"Jamie, honey, come back from wherever you are. Surely you

know I couldn't go, that I'd be a problem instead of a help if I were there. Just give thanks that Brad was willing to go and that he's the right one to do it."

Jamie gave a deep trembling sigh and said, "You're right, of course. And I am practically out of my head. I am so grief-stricken about the whole thing that I feel I could run shrieking somewhere, but there isn't anywhere I could go."

"You could come home with me," Pris suggested. "Just please skip the shrieking part. Maybe Mother Mac and I could get your feet back on the ground."

"No," Jamie said firmly. "I couldn't leave Fairdale before, and I can't leave now. I'm staying right here."

"Before what? Do you mean Clay asked you to go with him?"

Jamie gave a start. She did have to get her mind working before she gave something away that would make everything even worse. "No," she finally said. "I don't think he had a thought about anything but getting away."

Pris asked nothing more. She just looked around the kitchen and asked, "Where's Rhody? Do you have any decent food?"

"I don't know where she is, and I have no idea about what food we have. I haven't felt like eating, anyway."

"No!" Pris almost yelled. "We aren't going through that again. You *are* going to keep eating. I know you have food here, so you are *not* going to lose the weight you're finally putting on." She chewed on a knuckle as she thought before going on. "I will confess that the lack of your old figure might have made Betsy's voluptuousness more appealing to Clay. That doesn't excuse him in the least, but wherever you two live in the future, surely you aren't going to risk that again."

"Do you think I will live with him again?" Jamie asked. "Would you if it had been Brad instead of Clay?"

"After I'd killed him so he'd know he couldn't ever do anything like that again, yes. I love him so much I couldn't live without him. I hope you feel the same way about my brother."

"Of course, I could never break my wedding vow, but Clay might not want me. He blamed me for what happened."

Pris jumped up. "I never said he wasn't an idiot. But he is my brother and he is your husband. Neither of us can do anything about that. Give me that letter and I'll be heading home. I know it's too soon for Brad to be sending me a report on the wireless, but I'll let you know as soon as I hear."

Jamie walked up the steps with her. "Yes, do that and keep praying that Brad can get Clay sobered up in time to get on the ship. I think you spoke the truth. Right now he needs your father."

"He does indeed. I'll see you," Pris said as she clutched her cloak tight around her and ran out into the bleak coldness of the day.

The next hours were sheer agony for Jamie and, she felt sure, for her sister-in-law. She wondered when Brad would get to Boston, what he would find when he got there and what any of them could do if Clay missed his reservation to England. She knew that she had promised herself to him for life so she could never desert him, but how could either of them ever feel right again? And had it ever felt right, anyway?

With all the trouble Clay's hasty departure had caused, Jamie had forgotten the exact date that had been set for the trip. She was thinking it had been February first. If she were correct, that date was fast approaching. If Brad had not gotten there in time to get Clay on board and had to bring him home again, what could they possibly do? No, she told herself, that wouldn't happen. Clay could not come back here now…and perhaps never.

It was nearly a week later when Pris came running to tell Jamie about the message she had just received. "Brad says all is well, and he'll get back home as soon as he can," she panted.

Jamie sank onto the hall bench with Pris right beside her. "That's bound to mean that he got Clay sobered up and onto the ship, doesn't it?" she quavered, trying to ignore the sick feeling in her stomach.

"Oh, I do hope so," Pris said, clutching both hands to her breast, "I'm too old to run like that. That brother of mine is going to kill me yet."

"Me too," Jamie said, "This has upset my stomach so much

that I've thrown up the last two mornings. Maybe when Brad gets back and tells us everything, I can stop that."

Pris gave her a strange look. "Do you think…?" she began.

"No, I surely do not," Jamie almost yelled.

"You do," Pris insisted, "or you wouldn't be acting like that."

Jamie jumped up. "Rhody has coffee on downstairs. You need a cup to warm you up. Come on down."

But Pris wasn't moving. "Is there any possibility?" she persisted hopefully. "If so, that might change everything."

Jamie turned away with an almost angry gesture. "How do I know?" she asked. "It's only been six weeks since…" And then she remembered Clay on that day and stopped. She couldn't bear to remember it now and certainly didn't want anything that might be a lifetime reminder of it. "No!" she cried. "Not like that."

"Like what?" Pris demanded, jumping up and trying to turn Jamie to face her. "Oh, this is wonderful, Jamie. This is what Clay has been wanting so much." She pulled her cloak around her and started for the door.

Jamie grabbed her back. "Where are you going? You can't leave like this."

"I've got to send a telegraph to Brad. Oh, if only there is still a chance for him to tell Clay before the ship sails. This will give my brother the boost he desperately needs. I've got to go." She pulled herself free and dashed out.

Jamie stood in the doorway and watched Pris race down the steps. She wanted to stop her. She didn't want Clay to know anything about what she was beginning to feel sure he had left behind. She had been telling herself that two mornings of sickness didn't mean a thing. Nevertheless, she had been afraid. She had wanted a family but not one started as this one had been. She told herself there had been enough other upsets to cause her sick stomach. It didn't mean... But in her heart she was afraid it did. She moved back to the bench and sat there until she had to run again for the porch and vomit again over the railing.

Later, as she sat on her bed, she thought that she ought to be writing to Clay at his grandparents' home. He did deserve to know. Then she remembered that he had left in such a hurry that he didn't even leave her an address or any money. Maybe he didn't deserve to know anything, after all.

It was late on the third day after that when Pris and Brad came walking out to Fairdale. Jamie was huddled by the cook stove in the kitchen and feeling miserably sick.

"Where are you?" she heard Pris calling.

"I'm down here where it's really warm. Come on down."

Jamie heard their footsteps on the stairs and got up to greet them. "Oh, Brad," she cried to her brother-in-law, "did he get off all right?"

"Yes, he did," Brad assured her with a sympathetic hand on her shoulder. 'I've never felt so sorry for anybody in my life as I was for him when I got there. But by the time I took him to the ship, he was sober and looking like the Clay we've always known."

Jamie turned away, hoping to hide the tears that were running down her cheeks. "I ruined him," she moaned. "He should never have married me."

Pris pulled her back down onto the chair where she had been sitting, then looked for two others that she should have known were not there. She did find the unsteady one and seated herself while Brad stood with his back to the hot stove, watching Jamie. "You're wrong about that," Brad assured her. "He wanted you more than anything in life."

"He wanted the old Jamie," she managed to say as she tried to dry her tears. She had already cried more than enough. "I just couldn't be that person again."

"Horseradish!" Pris snorted. "You are as much the old Jamie as any of us are the persons we were before the war. It killed more than those poor soldiers whose corpses littered the land."

Pris' comment caused Jamie to think of the LMA meetings that she had missed. Pris recognized that so she hastened to assure her. "I've told them that you aren't feeling well but that you'd be back as soon as you could."

"As soon as I can face anybody," Jamie said bitterly. Then

she looked up at Brad." Tell me everything," she begged.

"Well," he began, "things were pretty bad when I got there. The Smithermans were trying to be decent, but they had had it up to their eyeballs. If I hadn't shown up when I did, I don't know what they would have done. Maybe Clay would have remembered the date and tried to get to the ship."

"Could he have been in shape to do that?"

"Heck, no! Certainly not when I got there, but he had told his friend not to let him forget the date. Those folks may be Yankees, but they are mighty good people in spite of that. If a drunk Yankee had come to spend weeks at my house, my mama would have made him sober up, or she'd have gotten him out of there faster than ice can melt in July."

"She would not," Pris said with a chuckle. "Your mother has one of the biggest hearts I've ever known."

"Not when it comes to drunks. She was always as hard as a hickory nut shell on that."

"I've never known Clay to drink," Jamie said. "Of course, there never seemed to be a time for it except at our wedding supper. And even then, we only had wine and he didn't overdo."

"I'll bet he didn't. You remember, Brad, the time you boys found that bottle of homemade whiskey somewhere, drank it all and came stumbling in home drunk as coots, don't you?"

"I sure do. That was when I found out that I wasn't about to do that again. Papa made me work hard and pay that man far more than his lousy whiskey was worth. I think Clay found the same thing at your home."

"He sure did," Pris said. "Father didn't make him pay, but he took his horse away and made him stay in his room for a week. I can still remember Father storming around, saying that if Clay came in drunk again, he'd lose his horse forever and he'd stay in his room for the same length of time.

"Yeah," Brad added. "Clay said his own grandfather drank way too much and probably still does, so Mr. Haynesworth and his brothers had learned early to duck fast and to never drink to excess."

"I'm surprised Clay would take to drink like that," Jamie said. "I sure hope he won't do anything like that over in England."

"He said it helped him forget what a terrible mess he had made of things. I got him out into a rooming house that his friend knew about and poured so much strong coffee into him, he almost sloshed as he walked. He was as meek as a lamb by the time I got him dressed and down to the ship. Fortunately, he hadn't missed the date. I feel pretty sure, though, that the Smithermans would have gotten him there if they had had to pour him on board themselves."

"Would the ship have taken on anybody who was drunk?" Jamie asked just as Rhody came bustling in from outside. The woman stopped and looked at Jamie in surprise.

"Is you wantin' me out agin?" she asked.

"No, we'll move up to the dining room. I made sure the door to the steps was open and have kept the fire going so the heat would knock the chill off in there. You two warm enough?" she asked, turning to the McLaurines.

"Sure," Brad said. "It's not that cold anyway. Pris stepped in some mush ice on the way out here, but she's okay now, aren't you, Hon?" Pris nodded that she was.

As the three of them headed up the stairs, Brad said, "I talked to one of the officers on the ship, and he said they were expecting a rough trip. He also said that, if Clay had had a reservation on one of the steamships that are getting to be popular, he could have gotten there in at least half the time they would take. But he felt that their ship was more opulent and dependable. Some people are kind of scared of those new steamships. Mr. Haynesworth must have been one of them."

"Well, I wouldn't be," Pris declared. "When we do finally go, let's make sure we get on a steamer. I'm surprised that Father didn't tell Clay about the possibility."

"Clay was too concerned about too many things at that time to check into that," Brad said. Then he added a soft sad, "Poor guy."

"Did you get Clay plenty of things to read or puzzles to work on?" Pris asked. "If he has nothing to do, he might…"

"I thought of that," her husband said. "I told the first-class officer that Clay had suffered a family loss and to please keep an eye on him, to see that he met people and things like that. Then I gave him a pretty good tip out of Clay's money, and I hope he'll do as I asked."

"I'm sure he will," Pris decided definitely for all of them. "Now, Jamie, we can relax and stop worrying about him. He's on his way and, once he arrives at Cookeshire, Father will straighten him out in a hurry. It's partly his fault anyway. He never should have told Clay about that stupid 'tradition.' By the time Father has him back under his thumb, he'll have Clay feeling that he has done nothing wrong. Or he would, if only Betsy hadn't died. But I can't bear to think of that."

Brad broke in to say, "I sure wish the telegraph cable that they tried to lay on the floor of the ocean had worked. If we could just wire your folks, it sure would make things easier for them."

"A wire all the way across the ocean?" Jamie asked, surprised. "I've never even heard of that."

"I bet your father did. Some fellow by the name of Cyrus Westfield or something like that thought he had accomplished it several years ago. Our President and the Queen met out there and made a big thing out of it. The only trouble was that the dratted thing didn't keep working. It's not working yet, but I'd be willing to bet that before long, it will be. The cost might be sky-high, but think how wonderful it would be if we had it now."

"Oh, would it ever!" Pris exclaimed as she moved her chair over close to the open door in order to feel the heat coming up from the kitchen. "And if we can get our letters on one of those steamships instead of on a sailing vessel, think about what a help that would be. Times are changing at amazing speed. If only our Confederacy could be here to grow with them."

"Can't have everything," Brad said philosophically. "What I'm worrying about mostly is when those confounded Radical Republicans are going to get their heads on right and take all the rest of the Southern states back in."

"I don't care if we never get back in," Pris said strongly.

"Yes, you do," her husband replied. "You just don't know it, so quit talking foolishness, and be glad that we could do what we did for your brother. I felt so sorry for him that I would have stayed on and sailed to England with him, if I could have."

Pris glared at him. "And risked your own life?"

"Those ships are safe," he protested.

"I was not referring to death by the ships," she said pointedly.

Brad and Jamie both laughed and Pris said, "Now that that danger is over, Jamie, do you mind if I tell…" She let her words trail away as she saw Jamie violently shaking her head. "No change?" she finally ended.

Jamie shook her head again. She wasn't about to go into any talk about her condition in front of a man, even her brother-in-law.

When Pris and Brad left, she wandered back down to the kitchen. She might not be able to eat in the mornings, but she was feeling ravenous again now. It would probably come back up, but she was going to eat. Rhody was just turning back from the door with a big pan in her hands. She set it carefully down on the table before shutting the door.

"What's that?" Jamie asked.

"It somepin' dat boy, Eddie, just brung. Said it a chicken pie, already cooked. Didn't need nothin' but a few minutes in de oven to be sure it be warm enough."

"That's amazing," Jamie said. "I've been wondering what had happened to…to…the neighbor who used to be so generous to us. We haven't heard from…him since Mr. Clay left."

"Dat's's right. But Eddie said not to tell nobody he ain't brung nothin' 'cept dat apple pie just befo' Christmas. Said he mought get in trouble if his ma knowed they been 'posed to send you some stuff fer Christmas. He said he ain't forgot, but his mama had felt so bad when Christmas come, he knowed she warn't feelin' like doin' all dat extra cookin', so he never said nothin' to her 'bout it. I told him there warn't no need fer him to be worryin', 'cause I knowed you wouldn't tell on him. Ain't that right?"

"Well, of course, it is. Did he say if his mama was all right now?"

"Yes'm, he said she was, but that she had been moughty sick. I told him to tell her dat I could cook too, and if I could help her, I sho' would be glad to do it. You wouldn't be mindin' dat, would you?"

"That was good of you, and no, I wouldn't mind at all. Now let's get that chicken pie in the oven. I'm starving."

Rhody gave her a sympathetic look that Jamie chose to ignore. She opened the door to the cook stove and stuck a few pieces of wood in. She then shoved the chicken pie in the oven. Jamie did hope that it would be as good as it looked and that it would stay down. Surely she would get back to feeling normal if she heard that Clay had gotten to England and that he was all right.

So the days of waiting began again. Pris and Brad kept insisting she go with them to church, but she refused. She would have gone gladly if she could have gone to her own church. She even felt the need of it, but that was also the church that Mrs. Gains had always attended, and Jamie never wanted to face that woman again. She felt sure God knew the situation and would understand.

It soon was evident that she had diagnosed her morning sickness correctly. Knowing as little as she did about such things, she had thought the sickness would last for only a few days, but it went on and on. Pris would come and do what she could, but actually that wasn't much. Brad had finally remembered that Clay had given him some money for her, so they kept enough food on hand to keep things going. Even in her distressingly poor condition, she wanted food when she wasn't actually sick. "I wish that Mrs…" she caught herself in time and ended with, "the neighbor would send us another apple pie. Somehow I seem to be craving that."

"Ain't no cause to wait fer dat," Rhody said. "We still got apples down dere in de basement, and I can make a apple pie as good as Eddie's mama. Why ain't you said you is wantin' one?"

"Oh, I don't know. I guess I thought by the time you got one made, I'd be sick again and couldn't eat it."

Rhody gave her another quick look. "I been wishin' Miss Sally was right down dere next to here, like they used to be. I been thinkin' she could tell you some things that I ain't knowin' nuthin' 'bout."

Now it was Jamie who was giving the surprised look. Then she gave a deep sigh, pulled up a little closer to the stove and said nothing. Of course, Rhody had seen her throwing up every morning and her listlessness or actually being sick the rest of the day. She couldn't expect Rhody to be blind and deaf, but somehow she just couldn't bring herself to admit that she was going to have a baby.

Pris, in spite of Jamie's request that she not do it, had told Brad about her condition. He had said nothing except to suggest that anybody in need of a doctor ought to consult one. His mother had gone on to help her sister as she had promised, when she had thought Brad and Pris were going to be in England. Jamie was thankful for that, because if that caring woman were here, she would have been telling Jamie any number of things she ought to be doing. "Mother Mac made me drink all the milk I could get," Pris said. "You get Steven to find you a quart a day."

Jamie promised she would drink the milk, but she felt sure there was nothing else she needed to do. She had heard that some women worked in the fields right up to the time of the birth, so why should she be different? Somehow, though, she felt that it would be like telling how her condition had originated. There was once a time when both she and Clay would have been delighted at the thought of having a little Haynesworth, but now she could hardly bear to remember the terrible time when her baby-to-be had been created. At that time Clay had not been the man she wanted to father any child of hers.

Pris kept insisting that Jamie write to Clay in England, but she refused and begged Pris not to tell him yet. She didn't know if Pris had complied with her request or not. If she were being honest about it, she was not sure she had been right in asking that of her best friend.

So the dreary winter days moved on. Pris came as regularly

as she could, sometimes riding the horse with Thomas on before her, sometimes walking and on Sundays coming in the carriage. She kept wondering if Jamie's body was responding properly. "I didn't feel like you do," she told Jamie.

"You had your husband with you," Jamie said.

"I did not. He was off fighting a war, and I didn't know if he would live to see his child. At least you know that Clay is alive and well. Actually, he has probably had a wonderful time on that luxury liner." The look on Jamie's face would have told anybody that those words were not the ones Jamie wanted to hear right then, but Pris was not looking.

"I'll be doing as you did and soon be feeling fine," she assured her sister-in-law.

But she wasn't.

# 39

February was over and they were into March when Jamie realized that the ship carrying Clay should have reached Liverpool in England. She lay in bed wondering if her in-laws would be there eagerly waiting for the rest of their family. Well, they'd have Clay, at least, and he was their pride and joy anyway. She certainly wasn't on their list of anything but an unwanted wood's colt. The letter that Pris had written, telling of their change in plans, was probably in the mail on the same ship Clay had taken. What would she do if they kept Clay there with them? Would she...? Then she was scrambling up and frantically reaching again for the chamber pot under her bed. This was too much to go through to have a baby she didn't even want. That was the way she felt and was ashamed to admit...even to herself.

Pris and Brad came out later in the day to see if she were feeling any better and to ponder with her the same things about Clay's arrival in England alone. "What if he got to drinking again?" Pris said worriedly, as they sat in the sitting room by the fire. "If he should be drinking when he got off the boat, Mother will be furious that I didn't 'come along to watch out for him and..."

"We don't need a litany of the problems there," Brad reminded her. "And you're being silly," he went on, more sharply than he usually spoke to her. "You've always felt that you had to keep an eye on him, but he's a grown man. He doesn't need his sister to be taking care of him. Or his best friend either. I gave him the straightest talking-to that I've ever given anybody. I told him I'd never claim him as my anything again, neither best friend nor brother-in-law, if he made another idiot of himself."

"Oh, Brad...." mourned Pris.

"Well, what did you send me to Boston to do?" he demanded.

"To pat him on the shoulder and tell him it was all right for him to make an even bigger fool of himself than he had already done? Well, I didn't do it. I was as tough as I thought Mr. Haynesworth himself would have been. I was so sorry for him that I almost wept, but pity wasn't what he needed. He needed strength, and I did everything I could to instill it into him before that ship sailed."

"I'm so glad you did and I'm sure Pris is too," Jamie said, fighting the inevitable tears again. "When he left, he wasn't the Clay he had always been. I'm hoping so much that he became that man again before he met his father."

"He did," Pris insisted. 'He'd have to be to endure what I know my folks will put him through."

"He's not enduring it yet," Brad told them. "I stressed that he not tell them what happened at Betsy's funeral until he was alone with his father… and to tell him how Betsy was offering herself. Of course, she was teasing, and knowing that Clay wouldn't really accept what she was appearing to offer."

"Hush, Brad," Pris snapped. "We don't need to hear that."

"He said," Jamie couldn't help saying, "that my knocking on the door startled him and was what made him jump forward…"

"Jamie! Hush" Pris cried.

"I…I think he…he blamed me," Jamie managed to get out before she had to run out to the porch and throw up over the back rail once more. She came back in, weak and wobbly, to fall into a chair.

Brad came rushing from downstairs with a pan and a glass of water. Jamie took the water gratefully, washed out her mouth and leaned her head back again. "It's not morning," she said. Pris and Brad looked at each other, confused. "I thought it was supposed to be just in the morning," Jamie explained. "Nobody told me about afternoon and night sickness."

The others chuckled in sympathy, and Pris said, "That kid just hasn't learned how to keep time."

After they had given her time to feel a little better, Brad said he had some news for her. He had asked the government men who were now living in his mother's house if they could divert any money that had been allotted for the rebuilding of his and Clay's office to some kind of outbuilding for their horse and carriage out at Fairdale. They couldn't do that, he explained, for the downtown area was of prime importance, but they would try to find other funds for Fairdale.

"And they'll do it?' Jamie asked with more enthusiasm than she had shown for weeks.

"They think they can. They have seen how inconvenient and cramped it is to be keeping the horse and carriage at Mama's house. Also, one of them has his own horse and would like to keep it there instead of at the livery stable. Keeping ours out here would give him the space he needs. If it could be a benefit to him, I feel sure he'd try to do it. They may be Yankees, but actually they seem to be pretty good chaps, don't they, Pris?"

"For Yankees," she said shortly. Then she added, "I'm practically a nervous wreck just thinking about what must be happening over there in England. I bet even Mother and my grandparents went along to greet us at the ship. Or maybe they stayed home in London to see that there's a big welcome party for us. I don't remember my grandmother too well, but I do seem to recall that she was a lot like Mother. They'll all be sick when they realize we aren't there."

"Don't think about it, honey," Brad advised. "Just remember that we'll try to be there for Mary Lilly's wedding. I'd think that would be more important, anyway. You and Clay are supposed to be in the wedding. If we had gone now, we sure couldn't go back for the wedding."

"Well, once we got there, they were going to try to keep us until then," Pris admitted. "I had thought it best not to mention that. But I guess they'll tell Clay." She gave Jamie a sheepish look. "I didn't say anything to you about that, for I didn't want you to be here alone all that time."

Jamie didn't know whether to shriek with frustration or ignore the whole thing. Ignoring it seemed to be the better choice, so she just shrugged and said nothing. But Brad spoke up sharply again,

"Confound it, Pris. You didn't even tell me that. And you'd be willing to go off and leave your sister-in-law here by herself for months?"

"I did not say that," Pris answered hotly. "I just don't believe in fighting battles in a war that hasn't even started."

"It doesn't matter," Jamie broke in to say. "Everything is different now from what it was when your mother was making those plans. I can see why she'd want you all there."

Pris had edged over to Brad where he sat on the settee and put her arms around him. "Don't be mad at me," Jamie heard her whisper. "I never said we'd do it."

He laughed and pulled her around into his arms. "I'm not mad at you. I might be a little irritated at your mother, but I'll get over it."

Jamie watched them with an envy she didn't want to admit. She had always wanted a husband who would love her as Brad loved Pris. Instead, she had one who couldn't make it through the first six months without…

Brad stood up with Pris and said, "Since there's nothing we can do here but wonder and hope, I guess we might as well go home and do our wondering and hoping there. But, Jamie," he added as he came over to put a hand on her shoulder, "whatever happens over there will not affect the true love Clay feels for you. He told me that just before he sailed off. I can't excuse him for doing what he did, but I guess it was a character flaw, not a lack of love for you."

She felt that same urge to scream, but again she restrained herself. "I wish that could make me feel better, but, under the circumstances, it may take years for me to ever feel that way. Even though Clay may have fallen short in the husband department, you certainly have never done that as a brother-in-law. Thank you so much. I really mean that."

He leaned over and gave her a kiss on the forehead. "I know you do."

As she got up and started walking with them to the door, she said, "Well, I can at least look forward to the possibility of new outbuildings. Steven hasn't been able to do any more on the ice house, and though that would be great to have, I don't know whether we should continue on it or not. I had been waiting for Clay to decide. But one thing I sure hope we can get is a new garden house. Every time a stiff breeze develops, I am afraid that thing Steven built with scrap lumber might be blown away. If we ever get in another war, I do hope the other side doesn't consider destruction of our outhouses as one of their big weapons."

"Me too," Pris said, as she slipped her arms into the coat that she had been holding out to the fire to warm before putting on. "If the loss of them hadn't been so terrible, it would be kind of funny."

"Funny as a coffin," Brad said. Both girls winced.

As they stood at the door, Jamie said, "I'm going to be losing my mind before we hear anything from over there. Maybe they'll get their mail on one of those fast steamships, and we could hear something in not much more than a week. Otherwise, it will be closer to a month. I'm afraid by that time, I'll be crazy as a loon."

"You will not," Pris said staunchly. "Look what you've had to endure, especially in the last two years of the war. You didn't come apart then and you won't now."

"And look how close I came to being nothing but a stack of bones without a workable brain on top of them," Jamie reminded her.

"Well, yes, you were that," Pris acknowledged with a laugh.

"Pris!" Brad remonstrated. "She was not."

"She was too," his wife insisted. "If Clay hadn't come back when he did, I don't know what she would have done. The only thing I know for sure is that she'd have had one of the biggest gardens in the Commonwealth of Virginia. She was out every day working like a field hand with Rhody and Steven."

Jamie gave a little embarrassed laugh. "I was trying to bring Fairdale to life again in honor of my father. Also, I'd been hungry for so long that I couldn't bear the thought of anybody ever being without food again."

"And then you couldn't eat the stuff from it!" Pris said, still amazed at the thought. "I'll never understand that. Everybody else was wolfing down everything they could find that was edible and maybe some things that weren't, and your stomach refused to let you eat properly. Well, I'd say that is over or it sure will be when you get over this all-day sickness."

"Pris," her husband reminded her. "We've got to get home and get Thomas from over at Willy's. Also, Jamie is freezing standing here in the door."

"Oh, sorry. We'll see you again soon."

As Jamie shut the door and hurried back to the fire, she gave thanks for Pris and Brad. Without them, she felt she would surely die. And, right now, she didn't much care if she did.

The morning sickness that seemed determined to last all day continued. Jamie wondered at times if it were more because she was so torn-up inside from worry than from anything else.

She still refused to leave her house, saying she was too sick to do it but knowing that even if she were feeling the best she ever had, there was no way she could show her face in town. She had felt shame for much of her life, but it not been because of anything she had done herself. Now she felt an even deeper shame, and again it wasn't because of anything she had done.

Or was it?

# 40

Every day was like a lifetime as she waited for some word from England. What it would be, she didn't know and that haunted her too. She worried constantly about whether she should have written to Clay and told him about the coming of the little Haynesworth who he had seemed so eager to have, but somehow she could not bring herself to sit down and put the words on a page. In a way she felt he deserved to know and, in another, it seemed that sharing it with him would make it be more true. Then she would berate herself again. No mother-to-be should ever feel that way. Was she any less guilty because she couldn't seem to help herself? How could she need any more proof of the situation than the sickness that persisted no matter how much milk she forced herself to drink? This child seemed to be telling her in every way he could that he was no more pleased about the situation than she was. Would she feel different when he arrived? She didn't know, but she sure hoped she would. It could even be a little girl who would be like Pris, but she felt sure that was wrong. It was a boy, and he would be as proud and pompous as Clay and his father.

Then she would remember the Clay who was actually loving and kind. That was the Clay she had known and loved before the war had changed everything. He still loved her. That much she did not doubt, but she wanted a husband with the strength to be true to her, in spite of the women of the world like Betsy. Then the memory of how her worry about the Yankee had absorbed so much of the time that she should have spent in cementing her new relationship as a wife, and guilt would swamp her again. Without the true love that she knew she had not felt for her husband, she had felt enough affection that their marriage should have endured, since there was no other choice. If there had been no Betsy...

What was she doing to the child by worrying about everything the way she was? In a different way, hadn't she been as unfaithful to Clay as he had been to her? Neither had intended to do as they had. But then she would draw herself in with a loud, but silent *NO!* Clay had put himself in a position that she would never have done. He *did* carry far more guilt than she did.

*But how did that help anything*? she would ask herself as she sought the chamber pot again...and again.

No one had come to visit in the first few weeks, and Jamie didn't know whether everyone knew of Clay's departure or not. After Pris had told the women at the LMA meeting that Jamie was sick and could not be there until she was better, a few hardy souls did come, bringing whatever they could. Jamie saw none of them. She told Rhody to thank them kindly for coming, but she did not feel well enough to receive guests.

Until the day Mrs. Darby came. Jamie was lying on the settee in the sitting room with a quilt over her. When she heard the knock on the door, she drew herself in tightly and waited for Rhody to send whoever it was away. Then there came a tapping on the sitting-room door. Rhody came in hesitantly, saying, "Dere a lady at de door and she ain't wantin' to go away."

"Oh, no," Jamie could hardly get the words out. "Who...who is it? Can't you make her go? I don't want to see..."

"No, ma'am," the woman said firmly. "She say she ain't goin' nowhere till she sees how you is."

"How did she get here?" Jamie asked. "Did she walk?"

"No, ma'am. She come in a horse cart. Steven was in de yard when she come, and he seem to know her. He takin' care of the horse fer her now."

*Mrs. Darby!* It had to be. But how could she possibly let that woman see her as she was? Her hair was a mess, her...

But the door was opening, and Mrs. Darby was standing in the doorway. Rhody gave Jamie a scared look and hastily skedaddled. Mrs. Darby stepped aside to let her out the door, then closed it and came with an outstretched hand to where Jamie was tossing off the quilt and trying to right herself.

"I'm sorry," she began to apologize, but Mrs. Darby waved the words away.

"You poor child," she said. "I've thought of you so much since that day in the church. I would have come sooner, but I had a reservation on the train heading for Philadelphia later that afternoon. I had already left word with Eddie to see that his mama sent you a surprise now and then. I hope they did."

"Well," she said, remembering that Rhody had said Eddie had asked that his mama not be told on for not being able to do as her employer had asked. "He has been here and you have been awfully kind. I have wanted so much to thank you." And, then she stopped trying to fold the quilt that had been over her, held it up close to her chin and blurted out "But how is Curt? I do hope he is still doing all right."

"Oh, yes, he's fine," Mrs. Darby said, taking a corner of the quilt that Jamie held and helping her fold it. Jamie then tossed it on a nearby chair.

"Do have a seat," she invited, then added, "or do you prefer to keep standing close to the fire a while. I expect it's pretty cold out there."

"Yes, it is, but I'm used to it and always dress for it. I'm fine in here," she said, seating herself on the settee by Jamie. "So how are you? I hear that you have been sick."

"Well, yes, a little," she admitted. "Things have been…well, you know. Not so good."

Mrs. Darby reached for her hand again. "I know. I could have wept for you that day at the funeral."

"Thank you. Are you friends with Mrs. Gains?"

"Yes, in a way. We had seen each other at the LMA meetings, and she has seemed to be a nice woman. I felt terribly sorry when I heard that her daughter had died and felt that I just had to make time to go to the funeral before I left."

"You've been away?"

"Yes, my brother and sister live in Philadelphia, as well as my brother-in-law and his family. I went for Christmas and stayed for several weeks. I hadn't been there since the war had started.

To be honest, I needed to get over being mad about what their army had done to Winchester and so much of the South before I wanted to go."

"You…you told Curt about what happened that day." It was not a question. Jamie knew she had.

"Yes, I did. Maybe I shouldn't have but I did."

"And I guess he said it was no more than he'd expected," Jamie said bitterly as she fought the urge to break out into tears. She would not do that again.

"What he said was extremely dumb," his aunt said with another smile. "He actually jumped up and headed for the door. When his mother asked where he was going in such a rush, he said he had to come to you, that you needed him and he was never going to let you down again."

"Oh, no!" Jamie gasped. "Doesn't he know that I'm married?"

"Of course, he does. You know that. His brother Dave was here the day…"

"I remember," Jamie broke in to say. "I'll never forget that."

"Nor will either of my nephews."

Jamie gulped down the tears she would not shed. "I would like to see him, but that would be unacceptable now."

"Of course, it would," Mrs. Darby agreed. "And you can be sure that his mother pointed that out firmly. She said your husband had apparently ruined his reputation here, and that his running here to you would ruin yours."

"I think mine is gone too," Jamie murmured. "When did you get home from Philadelphia?"

"Last night. I had a wonderful time up there with all those Yankees," she said with a little laugh. "They aren't nearly as bad as we thought they were during the war."

"Many of the ones here were," Jamie said, bitter again.

"I certainly hope that doesn't include Curt?"

Jamie managed a little smile. "No, not Curt. Although I first thought it did when he took over this house as his quarters."

"He did that to get to know you and, hopefully, to let you know him."

"And it worked. Too well, I guess."

"If the South had won, as we both wanted them to do, are you still sure that would have been best for the country?"

Jamie thought that over for a few moments before she attempted to answer. Then she said, "Oh, goodness, I don't know. I was so young and, I guess, so self-centered that I don't think I ever really understood what everybody was so worked up over. I just knew I didn't want a war, no matter who was right or who was wrong."

Mrs. Darby gave a thoughtful, "Hmmmm," but said nothing more.

Jamie went on, feeling a little foolish for doing it, but not wanting an uncomfortable silence after what she had been saying. "Pa revered Thomas Jefferson and always thought the South would have followed Mr. Jefferson's example and freed the slaves someday themselves without tearing the nation apart. But I know that slavery was not the reason for the war anyway. I myself saw innumerable men who had never had the first thing to do with slavery going off willingly to risk their lives for the Confederacy. My pa was one of them. My mama's father was one of the biggest slaveholders in the commonwealth. But why did you ask?"

"Oh, I don't know. Maybe I just want to know you better. And I might mention, the North did not get away scot-free themselves. They lost hundreds of thousands of men too," the woman reminded her softly. "My sister lost both of her sons. She still resents my allegiance to the South during the war. I tried to set her straight on some things while I was there. We're friends again now. At least, I think we are."

Jamie looked at her in surprise. "So you've reinstated yourself as a Yankee?"

"I didn't have to reinstate myself. I was always one. I just forgot it for a time. And, to tell the truth, if I had it to do over again, I'd do the same. But I think that Curtis, my brother-in-law, was probably right when he said that the United States was designed by God to be exactly that. Had the South won, the

Confederacy would have lasted for a while and probably done well. But, sooner or later, the states would have come together again."

"In a way, I think my pa would have agreed with that, but he sure did disagree with the sledgehammer way Abraham Lincoln went about it. And, to try to correct that, he gave his life for the Confederacy."

"I'm so sorry," the woman murmured. "I too feel that Lincoln should have at least tried diplomacy at first. He had at least four years to try. But let's forget the Confederacy and think about you. I've been terribly worried since that day in the church, but I haven't known what to do except send a few things that we have on the farm. I thought you'd have regained a lot of the weight you had lost during the war, but you haven't added much, have you? Are you truly ill?"

"Sort of," she admitted. "If I didn't have Steven and his wife, I don't know what I'd have done. Then too there are Pris and Brad McLaurine. They're my in-laws as well as my dear friends."

"Yes, I know. I've gotten to know Pris the same way I met and became, at least, casual friends with Adeline Gains. Your Pris is a dear girl. But I never saw you at those meetings. Have you not been a member?"

"Of the LMA? Oh, yes, but not at first. Clay was doing everything he could to force me to eat anything and everything that didn't eat me first. He didn't want me to be walking into town and wearing off anything I might be putting on."

There was a light knocking sound on the door, and at Jamie's "Come in," Steven stuck his head in. "Is you needin' more wood on de fire in here? I got some right here, if you is."

"Yes, bring it on in. I wouldn't want Mrs. Darby to get cold before she goes out again."

He came in, stirred up the fire and added the logs. Then he tipped his head at Mrs. Darby and gave her a smile. "That ort to fix it fer a while, Miss Jamie."

"Yes, thank you, Steven." He went out and closed the door behind him.

Mrs. Darby said with a smile, "You aren't meaning for me to go, are you, Jamie?"

Jamie felt color flooding in her face. "Oh, no ma'am. No, I didn't mean that. I just wanted you to be good and warm whenever you felt you had to leave."

Mrs. Darby chuckled. "I knew what you meant. I was just teasing you. But where were we? Oh, yes, I know. You were telling me why I hadn't seen you at the LMA meetings."

"After Clay thought it was all right for me to join, I guess I was busy with the record-keeping at the time of the meetings when you were there. Or maybe there were just so many women that we didn't notice each other. I don't know how we could have gotten along without the LMA, do you?"

"I agree and have tried to do what I could by helping pay for some who needed it. Somehow, it seemed kind of nice to be giving those Yankee dollars for a good Southern cause."

"Yes, ma'am, it was. Clay was one of the people who dug up a body. It upset him terribly."

"Yes, I know. I was there when he came panting in to report it."

Jamie was surprised. "You knew who he was?" she asked.

"Of course, I did. How many young Haynesworth men were there in town? I looked him over carefully while he was talking to Mrs. Williams. I wanted to see the man you had married."

"And?"

The woman smiled. "I could see that he was a young man that girls would like. I also sensed something in him that made me greatly surprised later at his being the man whom Adeline Gains accused him of being in church. When I came today, I already knew that he was no longer in town."

"Oh, no! Do even people as far away as Philadelphia know?" Jamie asked in a scared voice.

Mrs. Darby gave a little laugh. "Goodness, no. It's just that a lot of people in the South seem to be kin to nearly everybody else. The tenant who lives on my land is the cousin of the boy who married the oldest one of the Gains' girls. Since he knew that his boy, Eddie, brought things once in a while to you all, he couldn't wait to tell me about it when he met me at the station."

"And what did he tell you?"

"He said that the Haynesworth chap couldn't get out of town fast enough after the funeral."

"I'm sure he said more than that," Jamie persisted, wanting but still not wanting to hear. "What else did he tell you?"

Mrs. Darby hesitated, looked at the fire for a moment while Jamie stared at her, then said, "Well, he said he sure felt sorry for your husband because humiliation like that would be hard to take, especially for a Haynesworth. He also said that, if it had been he who was being accused like that, he would have denied it right there on the spot. That is, he would have if he hadn't been as guilty as sin. He added that everybody seemed to think the same as he did. Running away was the same as a confession. I'm sorry, honey, but you did ask."

"Yes, ma'am, I did," Jamie said around a lump in her throat that felt as big as a pumpkin, "You don't need to apologize. I vowed that if I ever saw you again, I wouldn't drown you in a flood of tears…and I'm not. But I'm the one who should be apologizing. It's been hard. I haven't stepped a foot outside this house since that funeral, and I'm not going to until…"

When she stopped, Mrs. Darby inquired softly, "Until what, dear?"

"I…I don't know," Jamie said, biting her lip until it hurt. "Maybe forever."

"Oh, Jamie, Jamie!" Mrs. Darby cried, reaching out to put a hand on her arm. "You don't mean that. I know you don't."

"Yes, I do," Jamie cried. "How can I do otherwise? Everybody is saying the same thing. I haven't heard them, but I know they are. I can never hold my head up in this town again. And how can my child?"

"Your child?" Mrs. Darby echoed. "I didn't know you had a…" And as her words faded away, her hand tightened on Jamie's arm and she stared at the girl. "You're in a family way?" she asked in a whisper.

The tears that Jamie had vowed she would not shed gushed out. She buried her face in her hands and turned completely away from her visitor. "There. I've…gone and…and done it again," she moaned when she could speak, still looking away. "I'm sorry, Mrs. Darby."

"Good grief, Jamie. Don't worry about it. But you don't look…"

"It's too soon," Jamie whispered, still not looking at the woman. "It just happened when…" And she hushed again.

Mrs. Darby sat in stunned silence, but her mind must have been flying. Oh, why couldn't she keep her mouth shut? Jamie moaned to herself. Now everybody would know that too.

As though she could read Jamie's mind, Mrs. Darby said, "You needn't worry that I will tell anybody…and I do mean, *anybody*…about that. I've never had a child myself, but I have heard about morning sickness. If that's troubling you, it should soon be over."

"Pris says I should already be over it, but, if anything, it's getting worse. I'm sick nearly all day." Then she clamped her mouth again. What on earth was wrong with her? This woman was practically a stranger, and here she was telling her things she didn't want anybody to know.

"Have you seen a doctor?" the woman asked.

"No, I know that having a child is a natural procedure. A woman doesn't need a doctor to handle it."

"A person who's sick needs a doctor, whatever the situation."

Jamie shook her head adamantly, but she said nothing.

"Are you eating right?" inquired Mrs. Darby. "I know that's important."

"I'm not very hungry, but I am drinking all the milk that Steven can find. Some people are getting cows again."

"I have several. I'm sending you one so you'll have milk every day."

"I can't accept that, Mrs. Darby. I've felt guilty enough about accepting the other things you have sent and not being able to admit where they've come from. You don't have to do anything more, but I sure do appreciate all you've done. You're…you're a lot like your nephew."

Mrs. Darby chuckled. "Honey, I'm a lot like most people, be they Southern or Northern. I will confess that I let myself feel that the Yankees were pretty terrible during the war. And they were, but that's the way it is with wars. Now that I'm looking at things as I should, I know that we're all the same. The Mason-Dixon Line should separate only the land but never the people. I still love the South, especially this Shenandoah Valley, but I can appreciate my family and friends up in Philadelphia too. I hope you can see things that same way one of these days."

"It's too late. Too late for me."

"In some ways, yes, but not in others," Mrs. Darby said sadly but sensibly.

When she finally left, Jamie felt that she had been wrung out like a washcloth and not even hung up to dry. "Don't let any other visitors in the house," she told Rhody as she was trying to eat a bowl of potato soup down by the cook stove and feeling sure it would be up again before long. "I don't want to see anybody except the McLaurines."

"Yes, ma'am, but ain't you needin'…?"

"No, I'm not needing anything."

That went on more or less the same until one rainy day in early March when Pris, crying so hard that her husband had to be holding her up, appeared at Jamie's door.

# 41

"He's dead," Pris gasped between sobs. "Dead. I'll never see my brother again. Never see his smile or…"

At the same time, Brad was saying, "Shhh, Pris. Not like that. Don't tell her like that."

Jamie had been lying on the settee before the fire, trying to get over her last bout of vomiting. When she saw them, she had started to get up, but at Pris' words, she fell back again. She was amazed but somehow what Pris was saying didn't really sink in. Clay couldn't be dead. He was safe in England. There was no possible way he could be dead. She looked at Brad with her big somber black eyes asking what her lips could not seem to be able to say.

He carefully sat Pris down by Jamie and knelt beside her so he could still hold her.

"I…I got a letter from Father," Pris finally got out. "I just got it a few minutes ago. And, oh, Jamie, he's gone! Gone forever and in such a terrible way!"

Jamie put her hand on Pris' arm, but it was to Brad that she looked. "Tell me," she whispered. "Tell me this isn't true."

"I'm afraid it is,' he said, and his voice broke as he said the words.

"But…but…there must be some mistake. Clay can't be dead. I'd have heard. I'm his wife, but I haven't heard anything. Besides…"

"Dead!" Pris screamed. "Oh, Jamie, I'll never see my brother again. I won't even get to say good…bye..e..e. " The word seemed to stretch out forever.

Tears were beginning to run down Jamie's face. There was some mistake. She knew there was, but she couldn't bear to see the strong, always-steady Pris acting like this. She watched Brad hug Pris as he was again trying to quiet his wife.

"Tell me," Jamie begged. "Why does she think Clay is dead? He just can't be, but…"

He took one arm off of Pris and reached into a pocket for a long white envelope. He handed it to Jamie and said, "I'm sorry. I feel like a part of me died too. That poor, poor sad fellow…."

Jamie felt like screaming too, but she took the envelope and opened it, her tears falling almost as copiously as Pris'. She couldn't make out a word. "I…I can't read it. Tell me, Brad. What does it say?"

He swallowed visibly a few times before saying, "When his father and Grandfather Cooke went to the ship to meet him, they met the captain instead. He said that Clay had been drinking for most of the trip and was actually drunk part of the time. Then when they were going by Ireland, a terrible storm came up. The…the ship was rocking terribly…." He turned to Pris and covered his face with both hands. "I can't go on, Jamie. I just can't. Dry your eyes and read it. Please read it."

She looked down at the words again, but not one of them stood out. "I can't do it. I can't. Oh, Clay! Clay! You can't be dead. You just can't be."

Pris was getting herself in a little better shape so she said, "Yes, Jamie. He is. He went out on the deck just as a terrible blow came and he… he—" her words ended in a scream "—he went *over*!"

"No!" screamed Jamie. The door opened and a scared Rhody and Steven peeped in, but nobody saw them. They quickly withdrew and left the three of them to tend to their grief. Jamie was now being held in the arms of the other two, and they cried until even the heavy horsehair covering on the settee was damp. Finally, Jamie extracted herself from their arms and righted herself.

"Was there no hope? No chance that he could be found?"

"No, the storm was so rough that he wasn't even missed until several hours later when the storm had died down and his drinking buddy went to find him to share another drink. They searched the ship from top to bottom but had no idea what had happened until some lady said she had heard a young man saying, 'I've got to see this.'

"She said she had told him that he didn't want to go out there, but he ignored her and went on out."

A terrible thought hit Jamie. "Do you…?"

"Definitely not. He did not go out to kill himself. My brother did not do that. He may have had too much to drink and wasn't thinking right, but he went out to see the storm, not to die!" Her voice ended again in a wail.

"He never knew, did he, about the baby?" Jamie whispered. "I should have written him, but I have been too upset to do it. I should have told him. He wanted a son so much." And her words too ended in a wail.

"Don't chastise yourself about it," Brad said. "He wouldn't have been there to get the letter if you had written."

That caused fresh bursts of tears from both the girls. When she could speak again, Jamie asked, "How is your father taking it? Is it ruining everything for them?"

"Yes, pretty much. The Season was already in full swing by the time he would have arrived, so they were all in London. Mary Lilly was making a great hit with everyone. They were just sick that Brad and I had decided not to come, but they could understand and were too devastated about Clay to care. When he and Grandfather learned the awful news at the ship, that knocked all their plans out of kilter. They cancelled the big party to introduce Mary Lilly, and they all went back out to Cookeshire. Apparently, Mother is actually ill from grief. My father was so upset that he could hardly write. And," Pris wailed as the tears flowed again, "I'm too sick to do anything."

"I wish I could get my hands on that porter or whatever he's called. I gave him that tip to keep an eye on Clay and especially on his drinking," Brad snarled in a non-Brad-sounding voice.

"What could he have done?" Pris asked. "He could hardly stand watch over him." Jamie, feeling too sick to say anything, dashed for the porch.

When she came back in, holding a wet bath cloth to her face, she said in a shaky voice, "Even his little son-to-be is grieving for him." Pris burst out into tears again.

"He'll never even know he left a son behind him," she moaned. "Oh, I do wish you had told him."

"I didn't know," Jamie cried, sinking back down on the settee. "I never saw him again after that. I think, though, that was exactly what he was trying to do. But I didn't know. I was too upset to know anything." And she began to cry bitterly again.

"What can I do?" she finally asked Brad. "Or do I do anything? Am I expected to have a memorial service or something? I just couldn't now. I couldn't."

Pris gave her a reassuring touch on the shoulder. "Father said he would be coming over to straighten up everything here when things were better over there. I think that would be the time for a service or whatever. Of course, Father knows nothing about what happened here that drove Clay to leave. I can't even begin to think about what that will do to them when they know."

By the time Brad and Pris got back up on the horse they had ridden rather than getting out the carriage, all three of them were wracked and worn. Jamie felt like giving up on everything. She was as low as she had been at the worst time in the war and felt that she had lost everything. Then she had, at least, had the hope of Curt. She had given that up and was training herself not to think of it.

Now she felt she had nothing to look forward to except somehow getting over feeling sick. She felt guiltier than she would ever admit that the thought of the baby she would have did not give her any real pleasure. Though she could never let Pris or Brad know, she felt that it would be a constant reminder of what she had withheld from his father without really knowing why. Actually, she still didn't but felt that it was punishment for…for something. Or…maybe for everything. She seemed destined to destroy every man she touched.

By the cook stove in the kitchen, she told Rhody that Mr. Clay would not be coming back. The woman just turned to face the stove and said nothing for so long that Jamie thought she had not understood. "I'm sorry to tell you that he died at sea."

Now Rhody turned back around to look at her. "Steven and me, we wuz skeered sumpin' bad had happened when we heerd all the screamin' up dere. We is both awful sorry. Is you gonna stay here?"

"Of course, I'm going to stay here. I have nowhere else to go. I'll stay here, with your help, and we'll keep planting apple seeds all over the place. We have no one but ourselves anymore." And, in spite of herself, she burst into tears again. "I...I guess I'm not hungry, after all."

She still refused to see anyone who came to express their sympathy for her loss when word spread about Clay's death. She knew that was wrong, but she just couldn't see people. Eddie brought over many food gifts that Jamie tried to eat, even though she knew it might not be with her long. She began to lose her resentment of the baby she would have in the summer and felt the first stirrings of her love for it. It was not the poor baby's fault that his father had been weak and his mother an idiot. She even began to think of it as a little Clay, to whom she could make up for the wrong she had unwittingly done his father. "I'm naming the baby Clay Montgomery Haynesworth," she told Pris on one of her friend's regular visits out to Fairdale.

"If she's a girl, she's going to hate you for giving her a name like that," Pris said with a sad smile.

Jamie gave a weak laugh. "You might be right," she said. "But it's not going to be a girl. He's a little Clay. I know he is. And I'm going to give him all the love and care that I never got to give his father."

Pris had been sitting in a chair drawn up close to the fire, but she now turned around to stare at the other girl. "What *are* you talking about? You were a wonderful, loving wife to my brother. If he were here, he'd tell you the same thing. He loved you, Jamie."

The familiar feeling of tears came over Jamie. "I know he did. I never had to wonder about that."

"Then," Pris said in her old firm way, "stop that crying and start making plans for the little fellow. We've shed enough tears to add a few extra feet to the Shenandoah River had we been closer to it. Clay wouldn't want you to grieve any longer, so buck up and become Jamie again."

At those words, the tears became a flood. "That's what he told me so many times that he wanted."

"What are you talking about?" Pris cried. "And whatever it is, I don't want to hear any more about it."

"He wanted me to be Jamie again," Jamie said, picking up her skirt and wiping her eyes.

"You've always been the same Jamie," Pris told her staunchly. "Now I think I'd better be bringing out the clothes I wore before Thomas was born. That dress is getting tight around your middle."

Jamie gave a look down at herself. "I do think you're right."

"I'll bring them the next time I come. The cow that woman out in the county sent you was a wonderful gift. You see, Jamie, you're hiding out here like you've done something wrong. You haven't and people love you. Accept that love and enjoy it."

"It's pity," Jamie said. "I don't mean to be ungrateful, but I just can't accept it yet. Maybe when the baby comes…"

"Yes," Pris agreed as she stood and let her back side warm well before going out. "Now I'd better be getting home, but before I go, let me change the subject. Frankly, we've pretty much exhausted this one. So, aren't you enjoying that new barn out there in your backyard?"

"I sure am. Once they got to it, they put it up in a hurry. And Steven talked them out of enough lumber for Roscoe and him to build us a real, steady outhouse again. A nice two-holer."

Pris giggled. "I never have seen why outhouses are ever built with more than one hole—or seat, we should say, but I knew one that was a five-holer. Three large ones and two small ones for the children. They obviously believed in the family plan."

Jamie smiled. She knew what her friend and sister-in-law was doing. She was saying anything and everything she could to take

Jamie's mind off of her troubles.

Now as Pris was holding her cloak out to the fire to warm it before putting it on for the trip back home, she asked, "You read the letter from Mother, yes?"

Jamie shook her head. "I hope you did as I said and wrote her that I would be writing her later. I just haven't felt like facing that yet. I'm afraid she is blaming me somehow for what happened."

"My mother has not always followed the paths that I would have chosen for her, but I can't believe she'd ever do anything as dumb as blame you for Clay's stupidity."

"I hope you're right. We'll see one of these days."

"We will indeed." And Pris went out into the brisk spring air, having no idea of the changes that would be made before she came again.

# 42

The scream that Rhody gave when she found Jamie lying on the steps with blood streaming around her was loud enough to be heard clear over in Loudoun County. She had made it up to the landing before looking up and seeing her. Jamie was stretched out over the first three steps from the upper hall with her head on the third step down and her feet reaching up to the hall above. She had obviously fallen as she had started down the steps and landed face-down. Blood was streaming around her, reaching even as far down as the long hair that was falling down over the steps below her.

"Is you dead?" Rhody whispered. She moved up cautiously, looking at her from one side, then turning to the other. She was wanting to touch her to, at least, turn her so her head was back up where it should be, but she didn't dare.

Instead, she practically fell down the stairs as she ran screaming for Steven.

He was out far beyond the new barn, checking to see if the ground was ready for him to start planting those apple seeds like Miss Jamie wanted. When he heard Rhody screaming for him, he dropped everything and raced to her. "What's wrong? Is de house on fire?"

"No," she cried, panting so hard she could hardly speak. "It Miss Jamie. I…I's thinkin' she be dead."

He asked nothing more, just took off for the house with his wife panting behind him. He raced through the kitchen, up the first stairs and heading for the staircase going on up.

When he saw her, he came to a dead stop. "Miss Jamie," he called softly. "Can you hear me, Miss Jamie?"

When she didn't answer, he moved on up and tried to tuck her hair back around her. It fell again by the time Rhody came struggling in. "Does you know how to do dat stuff when dey puts

331

deir fingers on a hurt person's wrist?"

"I sho' do. Ain't I done dat plenty of times when Marse Frank was so sick?"

"Den he'p me turn her 'round and do dat."

The woman came cautiously, asking, "How we gonna' do it. I ain't wantin' to hurt her no mo'."

"I ain't neither. I reckons we ort to git her head so it ain't down below her feet. When we gits her turned right, we'll git her back up dere in de hall and make sure she ain't died."

"How we gonna' do dat? We can't jest drag her up by her feet, can we? And first, I got to git' up above her and see dat her dress be done right. She won't be likin' it if we let dem pantaloons of hers show."

"Well, go ahead and check. Then you take her feet and I'll take her hands, and we'll lift her up."

The woman stepped carefully around Jamie, making sure she missed the blood, and did as he said. Then the two of them lifted her up as gently as possible and laid her down on the hall floor. "I ain't thinkin' she be dead," the woman said. "She just done sumpin' like a groan. I ain't thinkin' dead folks groan."

"Well, thank de Lawd fer dat," Steven said fervently. "Now you do dat wrist-touchin' thing and see what you thinks."

In a moment she looked at her husband and said, "She sho' ain't dead. Her wrist is a-poundin' to beat anythin' I ever heard. Ain't you best be headin' to town to git Miss Pris and a doctor?"

"Reckon so but I ain't likin' to leave her out here on de floor. Let's put her up on de bed."

Rhody hesitated. "Miss Pris and me done dat once, and it like to have killed her."

"I ain't no Miss Pris. I can lift her up by myself, if I has to. Now is you he'pin' or not?"

"Course I's he'pin'. Just let me git a few breafs and I be ready."

They lifted her up on the bed without too much struggle. Then he said, "I be back as soon as I can. Don't you be lettin' her do nuthin' like dyin' while I's gone."

She gave him a disgusted look and said, "You git. But I sho' ain't likin' to see dat blood runnin' out all over her bed. I'd try to git a quilt under her, but I skeered to move her again."

He was gone before she finished speaking and was running for the town as fast as his short legs had ever carried him, forgetting that the horse was now in the barn there at Fairdale. In what seemed like a decade to the woman watching the unconscious girl, he brought Miss Pris and Mr. Brad and panted out that the doctor would be there soon.

Brad felt her pulse, looked at his wife and said, "It's too fast. Way too fast to count," he said sadly.

"Isn't there anything you can do?" Pris asked frantically. "We can't let her die. We just can't."

"Come out in the hall." When he got there, he said, "Sometimes when a woman is having a baby, something happens to their blood pressure. Our professor said he had seen a case like that."

"And what happened to the woman?"

He hesitated a moment before he pulled her into his arms and whispered, "She died. If we had any way to check blood pressure, maybe we could do something. I don't know what, but we don't have anything like that. And if we did, the doctor might still be unable to do anything. It's God's will and we have to accept it."

"You do the accepting. I'll do the praying," Pris snapped. She went into Jamie's room and knelt down by her high bed. Her head didn't reach up to Jamie, but she didn't care. God would hear her wherever her head was. Soon she felt Brad come and fall to his knees beside her. That was where they were when the doctor came.

Steven and Rhody, filled with worry, huddled together in the hall waiting; and if Jamie had known enough to know anything, she would have been sure they were praying for her too. When the doctor had checked her as best he could, he turned to Pris and Brad, who were now on their feet. "We've got to get the bleeding stopped, or she'll surely die. Then she'll need a blood transfusion, but there's no way to know whether that will help or hurt. I'll just have to chance it with any blood we have available and hope that it matches hers well enough. It might not work, but it's the only chance she has. She's lost way too much blood to make it without the addition of some." He put a hand on Pris' shoulder and said sadly, "I know how fond you are of her, but I'm afraid I have to tell you that, well, that her chances are not good."

Out in the hall, Steven and Rhody heard the grim prognosis. Rhody gasped but Steven said, "I got to go somewhere, and I gonna go on dat horse out dere in de barn. I be back as soon as I can."

"Where you goin'?" she called as he raced down the stairs, almost tripping as he skirted the blood and having to grab the banister to keep from falling. He was out the door before his wife heard anything more.

No one in the house knew where he had gone, but he was riding as fast as he could to the house where Miss Jamie had sent him many months ago. When he got there, he tore around to the back and pounded on the door.

A short while later he was back on the horse heading for the wireless office, and the woman he had come to find was rounding up her own horse and cart and heading for Fairdale. When she reached there, she didn't even knock on the door but just hurried in and up the stairs to the upper hall where Rhody still hovered. "How is she?" she asked.

"I ain't knowin' nuthin' 'cept dat de doctor been wantin' a lot of boilin' water, and someone from his office done been bringin' him some stuff. I thinkin' Mr. Brad been givin' her some blood someway, but I ain't sure. I heerd him insistin' dat he was de one to do it, when Miss Pris sayin' she wanted to. Has you seen Steven?"

"Yes, I sent him to send a wireless, but he should be back here soon."

"Is you wantin' to go in?"

"I'd better wait. I suppose she lost the baby?"

"Reckon so. Dere sho' be a mess in her pantaloons dat I he'p Miss Pris clean up 'fore de doctor got here. He ain't said nothin', but I thinkin' there ain't no baby no mo'.'"

"I expect you're right. And I expect that, all things considered, it might be for the best."

Rhody gave her a strange look but said nothing.

After what seemed like forever to the two women waiting in the hall, the doctor came out with Pris who was saying, "I usually would object to my husband lying in bed with any woman other than myself, but there wasn't any way we could have gotten him up, was there? He is almost as out as Jamie. She does have a chance, doesn't she, Doctor?"

He didn't answer immediately. He was looking at the visitor in the hall and saying, "Why, Mrs. Darby, I didn't know you were here."

"Yes, Jamie is a friend of mine. How is she? Can you tell us anything?"

As he was pulling his shirtsleeves down and buttoning them, he shook his head sadly. "She lost a lot of blood, and I have no way of knowing whether Brad's will work with hers or not. Still, it had to be risked, for without it I feel sure she would be gone by now."

"Then," Mrs. Darby persisted, "she does, at least, have a chance."

He nodded and took his satchel that Pris handed him. "She might have, but don't be too hopeful. I've done the best I could, but sometimes when a lady is in the shape that Mrs. Haynesworth is in, something happens that sends the blood pressure sky high and it's terribly difficult to treat. I've only seen one other case like that in my practice and heard about one other but... well, the end was not good in either."

"She's going to make it," Pris put in determinedly. "She's just got to."

"I'll do my best to see that she does, but I did want you to know the situation," the doctor said. Then as he started down the steps, he said, "I'll be back later tonight. Good afternoon, ladies."

When he was gone, Pris looked at Mrs. Darby with what she hoped was a smile. "I appreciate your coming and I'm sure Jamie will too if—" she hesitated, wiped her eyes and ended with "—*when* she's better. I didn't know that you two were friends. Did you meet at the LMA?"

"Not really, but I'm very fond of Jamie. I pray that she'll be all right, but I know the doctor was speaking the truth. If she has what he thinks she does, I'm terribly worried for her."

'Oh, no," Pris moaned, turning away from the visitor but then turning back and saying, "First, my brother and now his child and his wife. I…I don't think I can take it."

Mrs. Darby reached out a comforting hand to her. "Yes, you can, Priscilla. You're an amazingly strong girl."

Sniffing and wiping her eyes with the already-damp handkerchief she pulled from her pocket, she said, "I hope that's true, but I hope even more than I don't have to prove it once again. But I don't want to keep you standing out here in the hall. Would you like to go down to the parlor, or could I have Rhody get you a chair up here?"

Rhody started for the stairs, but Mrs. Darby stopped her. "I'll go downstairs. Then when Jamie is conscious, I would like to see her." As they walked down the stairs together, she said, "I've had friends in Winchester for years, but my closest ties are out in the country near our home. We've always gone to a small Baptist church out there, but I haven't been there since I came back after the war. So many of the people have left and haven't come back yet that I'm thinking of joining a church in town. Are you a Baptist?"

"No, ma'am. Episcopalian. We'd certainly like to have you come visit there. You might like it."

"I may do that. And Mrs. Gains has insisted for some time that I try her Presbyterian church too. I'll decide later."

By that time, they were seated in the parlor and Pris asked, "Can I get you something to drink? I would think you might be thirsty."

"No thanks. Nothing to drink. I'll just wait here until I can slip in and see Jamie. You will let me know when that time comes, won't you?"

"Yes, ma'am. And if you'll excuse me now, I'm going to run back up and see if my husband is coming around. I do hope the doctor didn't take too much of his blood for Jamie. But if he did, at least it was for a good cause. The doctor said it would take a while to know if her body would accept or reject it. I should have asked him how long 'a while' is, but I didn't."

"I expect it will be hours or maybe even days, but I shouldn't say that. I know nothing about transfusions. As soon as he's awake, I'd give him some fluids, if I were you."

"Fortunately, my husband does know something about transfusions. He had two years in the medical school here before the war. He hopes to get in over at the University next year. He has always wanted to be a doctor."

"And I once wanted to be a nurse, but not nearly as much as I wanted to be the wife of Mr. Darby," the woman ended with a smile.

Pris had started for the door, but she turned back. "Darby? Somehow that name sounds so familiar, but, for the life of me, I can't remember where I've heard it. Have you always lived around here?"

"For many years," the woman answered, adding nothing more. "Now you run along and see about your husband. I'll be fine here by myself."

So the afternoon passed. Jamie was lying on her bed as though she had died, but her shallow breathing proved that she had not. Pris found Brad sound asleep when she checked, and she felt that was exactly what he needed.

Mrs. Darby still sat in the parlor where Steven had built a fire to knock off the chill after the sun had sunk down behind the mountains. When Pris came in to check on her again, she asked her, "Could I slip in and see Jamie before I leave? I hate to go without knowing anything, but I do want to get home before dark."

"Of course, you can," Pris assured her. "The last time I was in there my husband was still asleep. Let me go in first to see that he's ready to come down or, at least, move across the hall." As the two of them got up and headed for the stairs, she added, "I've never known anybody who gave blood for a transfusion before, so I don't know what to expect. My husband insisted it would do him no real harm. Still, he wouldn't let me do it."

When they reached Jamie's door, she told Mrs. Darby, "Just wait out here while I check. I do wish I'd asked Rhody to put a chair out here, but I'll be right back."

And she was. She came out holding Brad as though she felt he had become fragile, but he was assuring her that he was fine. "But, Jamie, poor Jamie isn't," he added sadly. "I'm so afraid for her."

"Hush!" Pris chided him gently. "The angels guarding her might be listening, and I don't want you putting any idea like that into their minds. She's going to make it. She just has to."

"I'm awfully afraid not, so try to brace yourself. I don't want you going to pieces, no matter what happens." Then they turned to Mrs. Darby and he said, "She won't know you're there, but feel free to speak to her, if you like. And a prayer might help too. She sure needs all of them she can get."

"I won't be but a moment," Mrs. Darby said. She slipped into the room, went to the bed and said softly, "It's me, Jamie. Curt's Aunt Kate. Hold on, honey. He's coming, I know he is. Hold on with everything you've got until he gets here." Then she touched Jamie's cheek softly and left the room.

# 43

The doctor came just as darkness fell. He rushed up to Jamie's room with Brad right behind him. When they came out to where Pris was waiting in the hall, they were both shaking their heads. "Isn't she better?" Pris asked, almost desperate to hear she was, but was very much afraid she wasn't.

The doctor shook his head sadly. "Her pulse isn't as fast as it was, but there is no other change that we can see." He turned to Brad as though he were already a doctor too. "Don't you agree?"

"I'm afraid so, but I've had no experience or study of what you're pretty sure she has. I'll stay the night if Pris can ride back with you in your buggy. Thomas is over at a friend's house up the street from us, so she'll have to go get him."

"I'll be happy to do that. In fact, I came in the buggy for that reason. There's nothing we can do anyway, but none of us would want that poor girl to die alone."

Pris burst out into tears. "I'll stay, Brad. I have to. You go and get Thomas. I...I can't leave her."

"I know," Brad whispered and held her close for a long time while the doctor stepped outside. Then he and the doctor left.

Pris sat by the sickbed all night, at first in the little rocker and then in a more comfortable chair that Steven brought up from the parlor. She would drop off to sleep once in a while, then awake to jump up guiltily to make sure the girl on the bed was still breathing. *There should have been something the doctor could have done,* she thought angrily to herself. *Were they going to just let Jamie die without doing a thing?* But she knew she was wrong. The doctor had already done what he could. Jamie was now out of his hands and only in God's. So she would kneel and pray fervently for a time and then drop off again.

When the early rays of daylight were coming in the window, Brad and the doctor came again. One of the women from Jamie's old church was with them. Brad explained that another one of them was at their house to take care of Thomas when he woke. Somehow the word must have spread that Jamie was sick, and the women of Winchester were responding as they always did in times of need.

The rocker was now out in the hall, so Pris sat there while awaiting word from the doctor. "I'm sorry," he said as he came back out. "There's no change. But, to be honest, I didn't really expect any. From what I've known about what I believe Jamie has, there is nothing that can be done. Something happens to cause the blood pressure to rise to dangerous levels, but we have no way to check it. And if we did, I don't think there's anything I could do about it."

"You're giving up?" Pris cried furiously. "You're going to just let her die without doing anything?"

Brad heard her and came rushing up the stairs. "No, Pris, no! He's doing everything he can. It's just that Jamie has a condition that no doctor can do anything about."

She fell against him, weeping copiously. "We can't lose her. We just can't. My brother is gone, his child is gone and now my best friend is leaving. I can't take it, Brad. I just can't take any more."

He did everything he could to quiet her, but nothing worked until he said, "You don't want Jamie's last conscious moment to be the sound of your tears, do you?"

"Is she conscious?" she gulped and tried to dry her eyes with her hands.

"No, not really, but I read somewhere that unconscious people have actually heard things."

So Pris did the best she could to be upbeat when she went in to wash Jamie's face and try to get some kind of reaction from her. There was none. Brad kept insisting that she go back into town with the doctor, but she refused. "I'll just go into Mr. Montgomery's old room and rest a bit. You go on back to relieve the woman who is with Thomas. I'll be all right here alone with Jamie."

"Well, all right, if you insist. But you won't be here alone. You'll have Steven and his wife plus that nice Mrs. McAllister who is keeping watch downstairs. If the word is really out, there'll be others who'll want to come and do what they can."

"Jamie wouldn't want them. I know she wouldn't. She has been refusing to see anyone, and she'll feel the same way now. Please tell Mrs. McAllister to thank anyone who comes, but to send them away."

"I'll do that if you'll go into Mr. Montgomery's room and sleep for a while. You can't be of any good to Jamie if you're practically out on your feet."

"I'll go for a little while, but tell Rhody to wake me in an hour and for her to come sit here with the door open so she can hear if Jamie makes a sound."

"All right," he agreed and went down to pass on her requests. He knew that Rhody would have no way of knowing when an hour was up, so he ignored that part of the instructions. It was probably more than an hour when someone came bursting in the side door and started to race by the woman sitting in the hall. "Stop right here, young man!" the woman cried, jumping up and trying to grab his arm. "There's a girl dying up there! You cannot go up."

The tall man with hair as yellow as the sun on a hot August day hesitated only briefly. "No, ma'am. You're wrong on both counts. That girl is *not* going to die, and I *am* going up." He took the steps two at a time and at breakneck speed.

"Well, I never!" Mrs. McAllister said as she sank back down.

When Curt reached the top floor, Rhody jumped up from the rocker but made no effort to stop him as he dashed on into Jamie's room. When he got there, he stopped for a moment to look down on her. He then took her into his arms as gently as he would have a newborn baby. "You are *not* going to die, Jamie, my love. You can't. You and I have a life to live together. God meant that to be. We got derailed for a time, but He has brought us together again. He is not going to take you away now. I know it deep in my heart, but He may need some help from you.

341

Breathe, my love, and fight whatever is wrong with you. *You can do it.* I know you can."

Downstairs Mrs. McAllister was almost beside herself in wondering who that man could be and what she should do about him. What on earth was he doing up there? She got up and tiptoed up to the landing. Hearing nothing, she went on up to see Rhody standing in the hall, frantically wringing her hands.

"I ain't knowin' what to do," Rhody whispered when she saw the woman. "Miss Pris ain't awake, but ..."

"Then wake her," Mrs. McAllister snapped. Then she changed her mind and said, "No, I'll do it" and headed for the door across the hall. At Rhody's added whisper, "I think it must be de Major," she whirled around and asked, "What major?"

"De Yankee one," Rhody said in a frightened voice. "But I ain't never see'd him, so I ain't knowin'."

"What on earth is he doing here?" Mrs. McAllister asked foolishly, surely knowing that the woman knew no more than she did.

"Steven used to know him."

"Then you get Steven right now, and I'll wake up Miss Pris." The two women dashed off in their separate ways, and in a moment Mrs. McAllister was back in the hall with a still-drowsy Pris. "What do you mean there's a Yankee in there? There are no..."

"He's tall, good-looking and seemed to know exactly what room was Jamie's," the woman began, but Priscilla cut her short.

"Don't you dare imply what I think you are. If he is a Yankee, he's bound to be the one who was headquartered here. Of course, he knew which room was Jamie's. He once drove her out of it. Maybe he's now a doctor," she added, more for Mrs. McAllister's benefit than her own. Then she fell into the rocker, grabbed her arms around herself and moaned, "Oh, dear God, what do I do? *What can I do?*"

Steven came running up the stairs with his wife behind him. "Is it de Major?" he asked.

"I certainly don't know," Mrs. McAllister said, sounding

highly irritated. "I've never seen such doings in my life."

"If it de Major, he sho' ain't come to hurt her," Steven told Pris. "It like to have killed him when she made him go away. I know 'cause I was here."

"That doesn't matter now," Pris said distractedly. "What matters is what's going on in there." She looked at Mrs. McAllister for help, but the woman just shook her head and said nothing. "I'm going to get him out of there," Pris said, suddenly sounding firm and heading for the door.

When she opened it, she saw a tall, blond man in tan trousers and shirt that looked as though they'd been slept in, holding Jamie in his arms. She heard him urging her to keep breathing, to let nothing take her away. And she also heard him confessing undying love that would follow her wherever she went. After a moment, she shut the door softy and said to the others, "I guess it's all right. You all go on back down. I'll wait here." But inside she was practically breathing fire. The nerve of that man! Who did he think he was! That was Clay's wife he was holding, and he had no right to do it. No right at all. But somehow she couldn't make herself do anything about it. She wanted to but she couldn't.

"You surely don't..." began Mrs. McAllister, but Pris interrupted her.

"Excuse me, but I expect Rhody can get you a cup of coffee in a little while, if there's not some already made. I also expect that you need it, and I sure know I do."

"Yes, ma'am. It be ready and I'll git it," Rhody said and hurried away, followed by a greatly-flustered Mrs. McAllister. Steven still stood there and in a moment he said, "I hope I ain't sayin' nothin' wrong, but I ain't never thought he gone for good."

Pris gave him such a hard look that he scuttled away as fast as his short legs could carry him. She sat and waited. At times, she could hear the Yankee's voice talking to Jamie, but she couldn't, and didn't even try to, hear what he was saying. She was too busy deciding whether to go yank him out of there or wait to lambast him when he came out. A Yankee right here in

Clay's house! And in there with Clay's wife! If Mrs. McAllister told this over town, what little reputation Clay and Jamie had would be ruined forever. Clay wouldn't know, but Jamie would and, oh, what it would do to her in her present condition. It was unthinkable, abhorrent, almost unbelievable, but still…

If she could have heard, she would have known that the Yankee was still entreating Jamie to hold on and begging God to help her. He was telling her not to give in to anything that would take her away. That he loved her, that he always had and always would and without her, his life was nothing. She could not let herself die.

After what seemed an interminable time, Jamie finally moaned and said faintly, "Curt…" in nothing more than an escaping breath. He almost yelled in relief and joy. She was going to live! He knew it as definitely as if God had written it in the sky above.

Pris felt that it surely must have been several decades later when the door opened and he came out. When he saw her sitting there, he said, "Hey! You're the Haynesworth girl, aren't you?"

"I was, but I've been a McLaurine for several years," she said stiffly, getting up but apparently not knowing what else to do. Finally, she said rather unpleasantly, "You're her Yankee, aren't you?"

He gave her a smile that relaxed the tension that had been drawing her face into a worried frown. "That's what I've tried to be since the first time I saw her years ago. I'm surprised, though, that you know it. I didn't think she had ever talked to you about me."

"She didn't," snapped Pris. "She knew better. But everybody knew about your almost killing a man over her. I never knew your name or, if I did, I made myself forget it. I didn't want to know and didn't want anybody else to either."

"Because of your brother?"

"Of course, because of my brother, and because you were a despicable Yankee." She walked over to the banister and looked down into the hall below as though looking for help, then came back and asked, "Why are you here today? Why did you come and what makes you think you have the right to come in and take over? It's positively indecent for you to be in the bedroom of a sick woman. You have ruined what's left of her name. Was that what you were trying to do? To disgrace her so no decent Southerner would want her?"

"You know I'm not. My aunt knew that Jamie was in a dangerous situation. She knows how I feel about her so she wired me. Of course, I came. I was so afraid that she had lost the will to live and wouldn't fight. I couldn't let that happen, for her sake as much as for mine. I wish that you too could be thankful."

"You think your coming made her better?" Pris asked scornfully.

"I do. I not only think it—I know it."

Pris glared at him. "If my brother were here, there would be a glove slapped across your face."

"He'd challenge me to a duel?" Curt said, holding in a chuckle. "I don't think so. And, isn't that sort of thing out of vogue? But forget that I mentioned him. I know the situation here is mighty strange. If what my aunt told me is true, allow me to offer my sympathy to you and your family. Had I not known of your brother's death, my hands would have been tied. My aunt would never have wired me to come, not even to Jamie, while she belonged to another man. And again, I do offer you my condolences on your loss of your brother, Clay."

"Keep your condolences to yourself. I don't want to hear them from a miserable Yankee. Don't you ever dare to mention his name," she said angrily, but she did let her stiff body relax a little. A very little. "Even though I know you don't mean it, I guess I should say thank you for your expression of sympathy before I say goodbye."

He looked surprised. "You're going? Leaving her before you eve…?"

"No," she snapped. "*You* are. There's already enough talk going on about…" She hesitated, looked around as though seeking a path or escape, then faced him square on again and said,

"Well, about things. We do not need any more of that and certainly not from or about a disreputable Yankee. For you to show up so soon after my brother's death is…well, absolutely unacceptable. You have to go and please do not come back."

He stared at her, saying nothing, but his effort to do what she said was no more evident than it would have been if she had told him he had to make the sky fall.

Finally, Pris looked away, sat down, covered her face with her hands and moaned, "Oh, I don't know. I don't know. I'm so confused that I don't know what to do." She was searching again for the handkerchief she no longer had. Then she admitted, "I've known more about you than I've said, more than I wanted anybody to know. I resented any thought of you and let her know but now…now…" Her words were lost, and her shoulders shook with the sudden burst of sobs.

Curt moved swiftly to stoop down by her. He put a hand on her shoulder and said gently, "Hush, Pris. Don't cry. I know you've been under terrible stress yourself, but crying won't help."

"I know. I don't usually cry, but…"

"There now. Wipe your eyes on this clean handkerchief of mine and give thanks that Jamie is going to make it."

"You don't know that. She might…"

"She will not. So wipe your eyes and go in and see for yourself. Surely you know that the will to live can sometimes be the difference in a person living or dying. I had to get through to her and make her want to stay alive. We've all had a rough time these last years. All of us. But I truly believe that better days are ahead."

"For you maybe, but you're not dead and…" she started to say, but Curt interrupted her with a chuckle.

"Well, yes, and I can't apologize for that. But I might not be on my feet much longer if I don't get something to eat or drink pretty soon. I can't even remember the last time I had any food, but I do know it wasn't last night or today. Now let me get you up. While you slip in to see Jamie, I'm going to run downstairs and see if Rhody can't scramble some eggs or something of the sort. After that, maybe you can fill me in on what's been happening around here."

Her wealth of long, blonde hair had come undone and was flowing all around her. Annoyed, she tossed it back over her shoulder, started to accept his hand, then drew hers back and got up without help. "I expect my husband, Brad, will be coming out with the doctor soon. He'll fill you in on whatever he thinks it's your business to know. I certainly can't." As she spoke, she was trying to do her hair up again in its usual bun. Then she faced him and added, still in an angry voice, "But how do you know all that? And what made you come today? If my husband had been here when you showed up, he'd…"

"No, he would not," Curt cut in to say firmly while such an intense light burned in his blue eyes that she felt it might even burn her. "Had the whole Confederate army been arrayed out there in the yard, they couldn't have kept me from Jamie today." Then his lean body relaxed noticeably and he added, "But the war's over. Let's not keep our armor on or our weapons cocked any more. I've heard from Jamie what a wonderful person you are, and I'm sure she's right. Now, let me assure you that, had Jamie still been married to your brother, I would never have contacted her in any way. My aunt knows of Jamie's and my past, and she has kept an eye on her for me. I just wanted to know that she was all right; and though you might not want to hear this, I always felt that God had meant for us to be together. If that upsets you, I'm sorry, but some things are true and have to be accepted."

Pris just stared, saying nothing, but she did seat herself again.

"Incidentally," he went on, "my name is Curt Darby. I guess you too were there that day at the Tournament, but I could see no one but Jamie. I loved her from that moment, and I might as well admit that I not only did what I could to protect her and keep her from starving, but I also did what I could to let her know me and to make her love me as I loved her. That she was a Rebel made not a whit of difference to me, and sometimes my being a Yankee made no difference to her," he added in a softer tone and with a smile. Then the smile faded as he said, "I was injured and unconscious myself when she married your brother. I knew I had failed her by leaving her here, alone and sick as I knew she was. I felt that my heart had been actually yanked out by the roots when I heard a few months later that she had married your brother, but I loved her enough to be glad that she had someone to take care of her when I could not. I didn't know then what would happen to either of us, but, no matter what you think of me for saying it, I somehow have always known the day would come when we would be together." Then he gave a shrug and the smile returned, "Now that I've bared my soul to you, do you still want your husband to try to run me out of here?"

Pris stared at him for a long time. He just stood there waiting for her to lambast him or whatever, obviously thinking he had told her what she had to know and hoping she would understand.

Finally, she said, "Darby? I knew Jamie was involved with a Yankee that some said…"

"And they were wrong, dead wrong," he broke in to say with great firmness and some anger. "Jamie was as pure the day she married your brother as she was the day she was born."

"I know that," Pris said, sounding annoyed too. "I was just going to say that there was a Darby woman here yesterday who works in the LMA. If you're a Yankee and she's your mother, why isn't she one too?"

He laughed. "I thought I had told you that she's my aunt, not my mother. Even you yourself were no more a Rebel than my Aunt Kate. Why, by the time bells rang all over the South to announce the end of the war, probably half the Rebel army was wearing socks knit by her."

Pris looked at him for a while longer, obviously sizing him up every way she could. "I do not like Yankees," she finally said. "In addition to your terrible war, you broke up the romance between my brother and Jamie for a time. Had you never come along, my brother and Jamie would have been married years ago and…"

"Would they?" he asked pointedly as he raised his eyebrows at her.

She gave an annoyed shrug, jumped up and said, "I'm going in to see her. Since you seem so familiar with the house, you might want to go down to the kitchen and have Rhody give you a cup of coffee and something to eat."

"Hold up a minute," he said, reaching out a hand to stop her. "Does your willingness to feed me mean that I'm forgiven for being a Yankee or for whatever other sins you feel that I've committed? I'll be going back to Philadelphia soon, and you won't even see me again until Jamie sends for me. She will have her proper mourning time for your brother. And she will mourn for him. I'm sure of that."

"Of course she will. She loved him. If you want proof of that, just remember that when she had the chance to choose, she chose my brother instead of you. No matter what happens some day, I'll always have that," Pris said. "And so will you," she added scornfully.

He didn't argue that point. He just said, "Yes, you're right. She did turn me down and accept him. I can't blame her for that or him for wanting her."

Pris gave him a grudging sort of look that could have been a faint smile and said, "The jury is out on what can ever be forgiven when it comes to Yankees and probably will be for many years yet to come, but if you've been of help to Jamie today..." Then she clinched her whole body as she opened Jamie's door, stepped in and closed it behind her.

At Jamie's bed, she stopped and listened. Jamie *was* better. Even she could tell that she was breathing more easily, so she leaned over and said, "Oh, Jamie, thank God, you *are* better. Oh, I wish the doctor would come and tell us that it's really true."

Curt was soon back and sitting by Jamie, holding her hand and talking to her in a low tone. Pris sat with her eyes closed and listened. She was grateful for what he was doing to instill the will to live in Jamie. Nevertheless, she still resented the fact that he was the one doing it.

He was reminding Jamie of the times they had shared in the past, such as the night he had brought a wonderful load of fine food, including some champagne, that was all supposed to go to a Union general. And, oh, how beautiful she had been in the Christmas present he had brought her. And then there was the night when she had told him what she could never admit to another person about her birth.

Pris was practically seething with anger at the things she was hearing that she had never known a thing about. Without knowing it, Curt was giving her an insight into the two of them that annoyed her greatly at first.

Then she surprised herself by realizing that Jamie had chosen her brother instead of this man who obviously loved her so much. Would Clay have risked his neck and his life for a few hours with Jamie? Had Clay ever loved her as this man did? Somehow she doubted it, but she felt terribly disloyal to even have that thought. Clay had loved Jamie, loved her as much as he was capable of loving anyone. But her brother was gone, and Jamie had just escaped death by a hair.

She began to feel like an eavesdropper and knew it wasn't fair of her to listen to any more. When she got up and started for the door, Curt jumped up and said, "Oh, I thought you were asleep. You haven't made a sound."

"I rarely ever do when I'm asleep," she said and was almost ashamed at how nasty she sounded. Then she reminded herself that he was a Yankee and that Jamie had chosen her brother over him and had loved and supported him even after... Her tears were flowing by the time she got to the door.

"I expect the doctor will be here soon. If I were you, I'd go into that room across the hall when he comes. It might look strange to see an unknown Yankee watching over her. Her reputation here means a lot to us, and it sure doesn't need anything you can do for it. Oh, I think I hear the hoofbeats of a horse."

Curt hurried by her and said, "Thanks for the warning and you're right. We don't want to give Winchester anything more to talk about where Jamie is concerned." He was across the hall and the door was shut before Brad and the doctor came up the stairs.

When Jamie had been checked, the doctor said to Pris, who was standing at the window with her back to him, "Mrs. McLaurine, I am glad to report that your sister-in-law is certainly no worse and actually is breathing much better than she was when I left here this morning. If she has what I was sure yesterday she was bound to have, the fact that she is still here means she is showing amazing improvement."

Pris whirled around when she heard his assessment. "Oh, doctor, that's wonderful. I thought she might be, but I don't know anything about such illnesses. I just knew she was breathing better, and her pulse felt slower."

"I'm afraid you underestimate yourself, Miss Pris," he said with a smile at her as he fastened his satchel and prepared to leave the room. "I'm sure you learned a lot when you were helping us treat all those veterans during the war."

Pris gave a little self-deprecating laugh and said, "Yes, sir, I did, but if a single one of those veterans had what Jamie has, I never heard of it." Then she almost gasped at what a risqué thing she had said and buried her face in her husband's shoulder. He held her close as he and the doctor both laughed.

"I think that all these recent troubles may have unnerved your wife a bit. Goodness knows, she has had enough reason to be that way. I remember when they were children. If we saw Clay, Priscilla was always close by, but," he added in almost a whisper, "we don't want to say too much in here. Clay's death is probably what started his wife's troubles. That's awfully hard for a young wife to take."

Neither Pris nor Brad said anything. They just waited for him to leave. Before he got to the door, a faint murmur came from the bed, "I want... want C..."

All three of them turned to stare, Pris scared to death, Brad concerned and the doctor leaning over her to say. "Yes, Jamie? Can you answer me? You know me. I'm the doctor. Can you speak to me?"

Nothing more came from the bed, so the doctor turned to the others. "Isn't that enough to break a person's heart? Here she is not yet conscious, and she's calling for her husband."

"I'll stay with her for a few minutes," Pris said. "You all go on down. If she says anything more, I'll call you."

"You want me to stay with you?" Brad asked.

"No. I'll be fine."

"Good idea," the doctor said. "If she's regaining consciousness, as she is obviously getting ready to do, I want to talk to the colored woman who is still here. I presume she cooks, so I want her to have some broth ready to give Jamie as soon as she can take it. I'll go on downstairs and you listen to see if she says anything more."

She didn't, for which Pris knew she'd be eternally grateful. What on earth could they have done if Clay's wife had been heard whispering for a man who was definitely not her husband? "Oh, Jamie," she whispered to the girl, "He's here, but don't speak his name yet. Please, not yet."

Then she slipped across the hall and told Curt, "Don't dare show yourself yet. The doctor is still downstairs. Jamie actually was calling for you, but the doctor thought she was wanting my brother."

A big smile lightened the strain on Curt's face. "Did she really? Oh, how wonderful."

"Wonderful, my eye! You let the doctor or anybody else know anything that's going on here, and Jamie's reputation will be ruined beyond repair."

"I'm just so happy that she's better. She really is, isn't she?"

"Of course, she is, you numbskull," she said angrily. "But don't you dare go in there until Brad or I tell you." She went out, wringing her hands and wondering what on earth she could be doing trying to protect a Yankee. She ought to do something about getting rid of him, but she knew that anything she did would hurt Jamie maybe even more than it would the lousy Yankee.

When Pris went downstairs, she explained that there were no further words from Jamie. "That's no reason for worry," the doctor told her. Then he looked at Brad and said, "You going to ride back into town with me?"

"No, sir, but my wife is." When Pris started to protest, he said, "That's not going to work tonight. I promised Thomas that you would be there to read him a story and put him to bed. Don't make a liar out of me."

"All right, but let me run upstairs for just a minute. I'll be right back." And she was halfway up to the landing before she finished talking. She went into Jamie's room and whispered urgently that the doctor said she was better and for her to keep on doing what she had been doing.

Then she rushed across the hall, tapped on the door and went in to whisper, "She's better. She really is, and I wanted you to know before I left. Brad will stay the night, but he knows you're here."

Curt raised his eyebrows at that and gave a big smile. "Thanks, Pris. That's wonderful. I felt sure she was, but I appreciate your giving me the doctor's report. I'll be going soon myself. I'll be back in the morning but not until the doctor has come and gone."

She was back downstairs in time to hear the doctor saying to Brad, "I may be jumping the gun, but I want some nourishment in her as soon as possible. She'll need liquid and don't forget that you do too. Lots of it. I'm not expecting her temperature to go up, but if it should, put cold cloths on her."

"I've been looking forward to being a doctor," Brad said with a chuckle, "and here you are trying to make a nurse out of me."

"A little of both," the doctor said as he helped Pris into the buggy that Steven had ready for them. "We're over a big hurdle since her body doesn't seem to be rejecting your blood. We'll see you in the morning."

The whole of the next week was devoted to getting Jamie better. Curt had spent time with her every day with Pris, his aunt or Brad sitting outside in the hall with the door partially open. "It was amazing," Pris later told Brad. "His coming did help her immeasurably. I would have felt like killing her if she had run off with him after the war ended, but things have changed so much that…" And her words were lost in the flood of tears that were becoming as common with her as they had been for so long with Jamie.

# 44

When Curt was taking the train back to Philadelphia later that afternoon, he came to see her without his aunt. Pris stayed in the hall with the door almost shut, still feeling disloyal to her brother but knowing she really had no choice.

"You saved me again," Jamie told him.

"It was my turn," he said, smiling.

"Well, it's now more than two to one in your favor. Please don't do anything that might make me have to try to even the score."

"I'll be careful," he assured her. "No short cuts over mountains this time. A safe train ride all the way home."

"I wish you didn't have to go," she said, reaching a hand up to his cheek.

He grabbed it and pulled it to his lips. "Not nearly as much as I wish I could take you with me, but Aunt Kate says we've skirted around enough with your reputation. I know how important that is to you since you want this to be home to us in the future. I guess I have no choice but to allow you a proper period of mourning for the Haynesworth boy."

She gave a sad smile. "It was his twenty-sixth birthday before he proved you were right about him. How did you know?"

"I had to know my competition," he said. "So I made it my business to learn everything I could about him. He'd always been pampered, was egotistical, selfish, conceited about his looks, long on education but short on common sense. He thought that being a Haynesworth entitled him to the best of everything so, of course, he wanted you. The most worthwhile thing he had going for him was his friendship with the McLaurine boy who has always been as straight as a rifle barrel."

She pulled herself up in the bed and looked at him in amazement. "Being a Yankee, how in the world did you learn all of that?"

He gave a little shrug. "Easy. I got the tenant on Aunt Kate's place to do the investigation for me. He already knew most of it. He was quite a few years older than Clay, but his younger sister had known him in school and had once had a terrible crush on him. Clay, of course, never gave her the time of day. The tenant's father had owned a nice farm at one time, but there was trouble about a debt he owed. Clay's father had been the lawyer who had sued the tenant's father. He won and caused the tenant's father to lose their farm. He didn't tell me any particulars about that, but he said he had kind of kept his eye on the Haynesworths."

"Maybe he was already prejudiced against Clay," suggested Jamie.

"Heck no!" he said emphatically. "Didn't Clay prove him right on everything he told me?"

"I guess he did, but I still think he loved me and had meant to be true to me," Jamie said. It was the only thing she could think of to defend Clay a bit. She felt she owed him that much.

"Of course, he loved you. How could he not? But that's not the kind of love I've always felt for you."

"I know. I always knew, but I had deliberately blocked you from my mind because…. But you know that."

"I do. Because I was a Yankee, the only one you knew that you could lay the blame on for the war. So I got it all."

"Yes, you did, but I wasn't thinking right. I felt then that I'd rather die than admit I loved a Yankee. Now I'd rather die than *not* be loved by one, as long as he's you."

He laughed and grabbed her in as much of a hug as he could manage with her in bed. "You're going to have a long, long life if that's what it takes to get you," he assured her, "for you've got me and my love forever. This isn't even a real goodbye, for I'm leaving you surrounded by my love. I'll be back before long, but not so soon that it causes talk. I also want you to come up and meet my folks when you're feeling a lot better. They already love you and when you know them, you'll love them too."

"If you'll promise to tie down your brother, Dave. He was ready to throttle me when I last saw him, and he might not have gotten over it. He even accused me of killing you. Upset me so much that I had a horrible nightmare that same night."

"Are you making that up?" Curt asked with a smile and a twinkle in his bright blue eyes.

"No. It's the gospel truth. Scared me nearly to death. Clay too. He was afraid I might have those things regularly and was anticipating a heart attack. I could only tell him I'd never had one before, but I couldn't tell him why I'd had that one. Pris said I'd ruin everything if I told him anything about Dave and why he had come."

"Let's not think any more about that now. We have some important things to discuss. I still want Aunt Kate to bring you up, but we'll talk about that later too. She says that we have messed around enough for your reputation, and it's time to make amends. She went right away to see the woman who was here the morning I came. She told her more than she wanted to, but the woman understood and promised not to say a word to anybody about my being here."

"Who was the woman?"

"I don't know, but my aunt does. She says that's under control. But she reminded me that there's a well-established rule that a woman does not remarry until till she has been a widow for a year. I knew that too, but I was going to ignore it and take you with me as soon as you were able to travel."

"I knew that rule too, but I hadn't been thinking about it either."

"She says that if we expect this to be our home base in the future, we can't do anything that would make it look as if we've had something going on while you were married to Clay. People would wonder how we could marry so soon after Clay's death if we hadn't."

"She's right, Curt. I know she's right."

"I finally had to accept that she was. So will you marry me one year and one day from the time you got the notice of Clay's death?"

"Surely you know now that I will," she said, blinking away

the tears that came into her eyes.

"Can I take that as a yes? I want to hear you say it."

"Yes," she cried. "I'll gladly marry you a year and a day from that date. And I can hardly wait."

He grabbed her in his arms again and held her as close as he could. He kissed her hungrily and then put her back down. "I guess you know that I am again Aunt Kate's heir. She's always kind of looked on me as the son she and my uncle never had. She and I are glad you have Steven and Rhody planting apple seeds. Someday we'll put her farm and your land together under one name, and we'll ship our apples all over the country. Are we on the same page so far?"

"Sounds great to me."

"Good. Now that we have that settled, we'll move on. For the time being, Papa needs me. His business has always been good, but since the end of the war, he's been swamped with orders for his luxury carriages. Several of his old workers have returned from the army and are back on the job, but he's still short of supervisory help. I'm training Dave to take my place as assistant manager, but right now I'm needed."

"Of course, you should stay there as long as you're needed. I'm no longer afraid of Philadelphia as I once was. It all sounds wonderful. And Steven and I do need your aunt's help. We aren't sure we're starting our orchard right. She already seems to thinks a lot of Steven."

"Indeed she does and so do I. If it hadn't been for him, I wouldn't have known to come and you might have died."

"I would have."

"I think we should do something to show our appreciation. You may not own him and Rhody anymore, but ..."

"I never owned Rhody."

"No matter. You've got her now. What do you think of cutting off about a half acre or maybe a whole acre on the back of your land and deeding it to him? We could build a little house on it for when they need to retire."

"Oh, Curt! What a wonderful idea. Let's do it."

"I thought you'd want to do it. And he is one appreciative fellow. I can tell you that."

"You've already told him?"

"Last night. I didn't think you'd mind."

"Of course, I don't. I owe him so much. You remember....."

"Yes, I do. Well, that takes care of him. Now on to other things. I know you want this to be our home base, and that certainly suits me, but I feel that we maybe ought to wait a while before we set your Yankee down in the midst of those who suffered so much because of us. Helping Papa for a while will give some time for the hatred of Yankees to lessen ..."

"Oh, Curt," she broke in to say. "Surely we don't have to wait that long. That will take several generations. The people who have lived through it will never forget, and neither will their children. Then they'll tell the grandchildren, and it will go on and on. No one can treat people as some of the Yankees treated us and expect us to forgive and forget in a few weeks, months or years. No, we can't wait for that, for it's going to take a long, long time."

"You're wrong," he said just as assuredly. "You're talking about the Southern view of the whole North. You may be right about that, but not when they know us personally as individuals. Then they'll find that we're really pretty much like them. Take that firebrand Pris, for instance. When I got here, she would have gladly run me off with a club, if she'd had one. Now in a week's time, she almost accepts me as a friend. A little more time and she'll feel the same about me as if I had been Southern-born."

Jamie thought that over before saying rather dubiously, "You could be right. I don't think I've heard her say an insulting or really unpleasant thing to or about you for the last day or so. But, if you're wrong, I love you enough to make up for anybody who doesn't."

He pulled her as close as he could again and said softly, "Hearing that is worth all these years I've waited. My love for you filled my heart that first day as surely as if I'd known you all my life. I've never doubted it for a moment since."

"And I'll never again doubt mine for you," she whispered back. "I can't explain it, but everything feels in its place now. I can't even remember when I last had that feeling."

He kissed her gently. "We're both going to have a lifetime to feel that way. And it's not a whole year we have to wait, anyway. Can't be more than nine or ten months. Be sure to check that and let me know. During the time you can heal yourself in every way."

"And regain my weight and my looks," she said with a sad smile, remembering how vital that had been to Clay.

"Yes, that's important for your health…but not for our love."

She reached up and pulled him down to her to say softly, "Oh, Curt. I love you so much. I just wish I hadn't taken so many people down with me before I was able to admit it."

"You did not! Clay Haynesworth caused his own downfall. He and that girl herself caused her death. You had nothing to do with it." He kissed her and straightened up again. "I've got another thing to discuss with you before I leave. If you don't like it, just say so, but I figure it will be quite a while before your friends, Brad and Pris, can get in shape to build a nice house for themselves, so I was wondering if you would want to turn Fairdale over as their home too, until that time comes."

Jamie's big black eyes were shining like the brightest moonlight, as she exclaimed, "That's a wonderful idea! They love this place almost as much as I do. I hadn't even thought of it, but that would let Mrs. Mac rent more of her house and take in more of the Yankee dollars to pay those taxes that she's so worried about. Her house is practically a wreck now, but she can get good rent when it's back in shape again. I'm so glad you thought of it and can't wait to tell them."

He smiled at her enthusiasm, but cautioned her, "You realize, don't you, that they might not be interested."

"Free rent till he gets set? Are you joshing? They'll love it! And it will be nice to have the house running and waiting whenever we come."

"Which we'll do as often as you want or think wise, but I want

360

us to do some traveling, maybe even to foreign countries. Would you like that?"

"Oh, I would. That would be wonderful. Curt, how can I ever thank you for all you've done for me over the years and especially this time. Thank you for so many things that I can't list them. But I will have a lifetime to be thanking you, won't I? It would take that long, anyway."

"You don't need to thank me. My coming was an even bigger favor to myself than it was to you." He held her gently and kissed her. "Just knowing you love me almost as much as I love you is all the thanks I'll ever want."

"Then you're already thanked more than you know, for I not only love you as much, but even more than you love me," she said, reaching both arms up to hug him again

"Impossible!" he said, holding her as close as he could. Then he reached down and pulled his watch out of his pocket to check the time.

"You aren't missing your train, are you?" she asked.

"No, but I do need to go or I might. I wish you could be out of that bed so I could kiss you goodbye as I want to, but I know the doctor said for you to stay flat on your back for another week."

As he was talking, Jamie was busy throwing off the cover, straightening her night dress and trying to stand.

He grabbed her in his arms, lifting her clear off the floor. Then he was kissing her so long and so deeply that had he turned her loose, she would have collapsed.

"There," he said huskily. "That will have to hold me till I see you again. But, oh, how I do wish I didn't have to leave you." He picked her up again and put her gently back in bed. As he pulled the sheet over her, he whispered, "I do have to go now, but my love will be right here with you every moment of every day." He kissed his fingers, laid them on her lips and rushed from the room.

Jamie lay in bed, still trembling, partly from weakness but more from the emotion of the last few moments. She was also giving fervent thanks to God that Curt had come back into her life, just as he had always been in her thoughts. She felt absolutely sure that he was right when he said that they had been created for each other and that their lives would fit together forever.

Sometime later, she heard the always-mournful sound of a train's whistle. She knew it was taking him away, but she didn't feel bereft as she once would have. She was not really alone, for he had left her his love. It was so strong that she could almost feel it physically engulfing her, and she knew that it would be there for her as long as she lived.

It still hurt to think about poor Clay and to a far, far lesser extent, even Betsy, but she had not been able to do anything to keep them safe from each other when they were alive. She sure couldn't do anything now that they were both dead. But there would always be a tiny place in her heart for the boy she had met that first day she and Pa had come to Winchester. That spot would never harm her love for Curt, for the boy who had put it there had never really existed.

So, she thought, she had nearly ten months to be tied to the name she had once wanted so much and that she was now so eager to give up. Still, during the time she was a Haynesworth, she would do all she could to uphold the honor and dignity of that name. She would no longer hide herself in her house as though she had done something shameful herself. She would not by act or word do or say anything to indicate that she was anything but proud to have been Clay's wife.

She would meet with the priest and have a small but proper memorial service at his church. And she would once more welcome the friendship that the people of Winchester were always so willing to offer. She would work diligently for the LMA while keeping Steven busy planting their apple orchard...with Aunt Kate's guidance.

She would open the letter that she had gotten from Clay's mother. Regardless of what it said, she would write her a kind, respectful, even loving letter in return. She would tell her how sorry she was about Clay and how much she had grieved about the loss of their grandchild that she had been so sure would be a boy that she had already named him Clayburn for his father.

She would never tell them why Clay had had been drinking or about that horrible moment at the funeral. They might hear it from Pris or someone else, but they would never hear any criticism of their son from her. And if she should be invited to Mary Lily's wedding in England, she might even go.

She knew that once she could have done none of these things, but the love she shared with Curt seemed to make all things possible. So until next February she would enjoy being one of the Haynesworths. After that, she would gladly give up the name and welcome her new one.

As she lay there feeling a mixture of gladness and sadness, she made another resolution. Someday she would go to whatever remained of Bayberry Plantation, the home that had been her mother's. Regardless of what her grandfather said, she would see the grandmother who had been nice to her for maybe fifteen minutes when she had been seven years old. She wanted that grandmother to know that her kindness had never been forgotten and that she still had a granddaughter. And who knew? Maybe someday there would be great-grandchildren she could know and love.

Curt had not only brought her his love. He had also brought her hope for the future. As long as she had love and hope, the world was open to her.

# The End